Nora Roberts is the number one *New York Times* bestselling author of more than one hundred novels. She is also the author of the bestselling futuristic suspense series written under the pen name J.D. Robb. With more than 200 million copies of her books in print, and eighty-six *New York Times* bestsellers to date, Nora Roberts is indisputably the most celebrated and beloved women's fiction writer today.

Judgement in Death

Nora Roberts

writing as

J.D. Robb

PIATKUS

Visit the Piatkus website!

Piatkus publishes a wide range of bestselling fiction and non-fiction, including books on health, mind, body & spirit, sex, self-help, cookery, biography and the paranormal.

If you want to:

- read descriptions of our popular titles
- buy our books over the internet
- take advantage of our special offers
- enter our monthly competition
- learn more about your favourite Piatkus authors

VISIT OUR WEBSITE AT: www.piatkus.co.uk

Copyright © 2000 by Nora Roberts
Material excerpted from *Betrayal in Death* by Nora Roberts writing as J.D. Robb copyright © 2001 by Nora Roberts

This edition published in Great Britain in 2004 by
Piatkus Books Ltd of
5 Windmill Street, London W1T 2JA
email: info@piatkus.co.uk

Reprinted 2004, 2006 (twice), 2007

First published in the United States in 2000 by Berkley Publishing Group, a division of Penguin Putnam Inc., New York.

The moral right of the author has been asserted

A catalogue record for this book is available from the British Library

ISBN 978 0 7499 3437 8

Typeset in Times by
Palimpsest Book Production Limited,
Polmont, Stirlingshire
Printed and bound in Great Britain by
Mackays of Chatham Ltd, Chatham, Kent

The vices of authority are chiefly four:
delays, corruption, roughness and facility.

FRANCIS BACON

More things belong to marriage
than four bare legs in a bed.

JOHN HEYWOOD

Chapter One

She stood in Purgatory and studied death. The blood and the gore of it, the ferocity of its glee. It had come to this place with the willful temper of a child, full of heat and passion and careless brutality.

Murder was rarely a tidy business. Whether it was craftily calculated or wildly impulsive, it tended to leave a mess for others to clean up.

It was her job to wade through the debris of murder, to pick up the pieces, see where they fit, and put together a picture of the life that had been stolen. And through that picture to find the image of a killer.

Now, in the early hours of morning, in the hesitant spring of 2059, her boots crunched over a jagged sea of broken glass. Her eyes, brown and cool, scanned the scene: shattered mirrors, broken bottles, splintered wood. Wall screens were smashed, privacy booths scarred and dented. Pricey leather and cloth that had covered stools or the plusher seating areas had been ripped to colorful shreds.

What had once been an upscale strip club was now a jumbled pile of expensive garbage.

What had once been a man lay behind the wide curve of the bar. Now a victim, sprawled in his own blood.

Lieutenant Eve Dallas crouched beside him. She was a cop, and that made him hers.

'Male. Black. Late thirties. Massive trauma, head and body.

Multiple broken bones.' She took a gauge from her field kit to take the body and ambient temperatures. 'Looks like the fractured skull would have done the job, but it didn't stop there.'

'He was beaten to pieces.'

Eve acknowledged her aide's comment with a grunt. She was looking at what was left of a well-built man in his prime, a good six-two and two hundred and thirty pounds of what had been toned muscle.

'What do you see, Peabody?'

Automatically, Peabody shifted her stance, focused her vision. 'The victim . . . well, it appears the victim was struck from behind. The first blow probably took him down, or at least dazed him. The killer followed through, with repeated strikes. From the pattern of the blood splatter, and brain matter, he was taken out with head shots, then beaten while down, likely unconscious. Some of the injuries were certainly delivered postmortem. The metal bat is the probable murder weapon and was used by someone of considerable strength, possibly chemically induced, as the scene indicates excessive violence often demonstrated by users of Zeus.'

'Time of death, oh four hundred,' Eve stated, then turned her head to look up at Peabody.

Her aide was starched and pressed and as official as they came, with her uniform cap set precisely on her dark chin-length hair. She had good eyes, Eve thought, clear and dark. And though the sheer vileness of the scene had leached some of the color from her cheeks, she was holding.

'Motive?' Eve asked.

'It appears to be robbery, Lieutenant.'

'Why?'

'The cash drawer's open and empty. The credit machine's broken.'

'Mmm-hmm. Snazzy place like this would be heavier in credits, but they'd do some cash business.'

2

'Zeus addicts kill for spare change.'

'True enough. But what would our victim have been doing alone, in a closed club, with an addict? Why would he let anyone hopped on Zeus behind the bar? And . . .' With her sealed fingers she picked up a small silver credit chip from the river of blood. 'Why would our addict leave these behind? A number of them are scattered here around the body.'

'He could have dropped them.' But Peabody began to think she wasn't seeing something Eve did.

'Could have.'

She counted the coins as she picked them up, thirty in all, sealed them in an evidence bag, and handed it to Peabody. Then she picked up the bat. It was fouled with blood and brain. About two feet in length, she judged, and weighted to mean business.

Mean business.

'It's good, solid metal, not something an addict would pick up in some abandoned building. We're going to find this belonged here, behind the bar. We're going to find, Peabody, that our victim knew his killer. Maybe they were having an after-hours drink.'

Her eyes narrowed as she pictured it. 'Maybe they had words, and the words escalated. More likely, our killer already had an edge on. He knew where the bat was. Came behind the bar. Something he'd done before, so our friend here doesn't think anything of it. He's not concerned, doesn't worry about turning his back.'

She did so herself, measuring the position of the body, of the splatter. 'The first blow rams him face first into the glass on the back wall. Look at the cuts on his face. Those aren't nicks from flying glass. They're too long, too deep. He manages to turn, and that's where the killer takes the next swing here, across the jaw. That spins him around again. He grabs the shelves there, brings them down. Bottles crashing.

3

That's when he took the killing blow. This one that cracked his skull like an egg.'

She crouched again, sat back on her heels. 'After that, the killer just beat the hell out of him, then wrecked the place. Maybe in temper, maybe as cover. But he had enough control to come back here, to look at his handiwork before he left. He dropped the bat here when he was done.'

'He wanted it to look like a robbery? Like an illegals overkill?'

'Yeah. Or our victim was a moron and I'm giving him too much credit. You got the body and immediate scene recorded? All angles?'

'Yes, sir.'

'Let's turn him over.'

The shattered bones shifted like a sack of broken crockery as Eve turned the body. 'Goddamn it. Oh, goddamn it.'

She reached down to lift the smeared ID from the cool, congealing pool of blood. With her sealed thumb, she wiped at the photo and the shield. 'He was on the job.'

'He was a cop?' Peabody stepped forward. She heard the sudden silence. The crime scene team and the sweepers working on the other side of the bar stopped talking. Stopped moving.

A half dozen faces turned. Waited.

'Kohli, Detective Taj.' Eve's face was grim as she got to her feet. 'He was one of us.'

Peabody crossed the littered floor to where Eve stood watching the remains of Detective Taj Kohli being bagged for transferal to the morgue. 'I got his basics, Dallas. He's out of the One twenty-eight, assigned to Illegals. Been on the job for eight years. Came out of the military. He was thirty-seven. Married. Two kids.'

'Anything pop on his record?'

'No, sir. It's clean.'

4

'Let's find out if he was working undercover here or just moonlighting. Elliott? I want those security discs.'

'There aren't any.' One of the crime scene team hurried over. His face was folded into angry lines. 'Cleaned out. Every one of them. The place had full scope, and this son of a bitch snagged every one. We got nothing.'

'Covered his tracks.' With her hands on her hips, Eve turned a circle. The club was triple-leveled, with a stage on the main, dance floors on one and two. Privacy rooms ringed the top. For full scope, she estimated it would need a dozen cameras, probably more. To snag all the record discs would have taken time and care.

'He knew the place,' she decided. 'Or he's a fucking security whiz. Window dressing,' she muttered. 'All this destruction's just window dressing. He knew what he was doing. He had control. Peabody, find out who owns the place, who runs it. I want to know everybody who works here. I want to know the setup.'

'Lieutenant?' A harassed-looking sweeper trudged through the chaos. 'There's a civilian outside.'

'There are a lot of civilians outside. Let's keep them there.'

'Yes, sir, but this one insists on speaking to you. He says this is his place. And, ah . . .'

'"And, ah" what?'

'And that you're his wife.'

'Roarke Entertainment,' Peabody announced as she read off the data from her palm PC. She sent Eve a cautious smile. 'Guess who owns Purgatory?'

'I should've figured it.' Resigned, Eve strode to the entrance door.

He looked very much as he'd looked two hours before when they'd parted ways to go about their individual business. Sleek and gorgeous. The light topcoat he wore over his dark suit fluttered a bit in the breeze. The same breeze that tugged at the mane of black hair that framed his poetically sinful face. The dark glasses he wore against the glare of the sun only added to the look of slick elegance.

And when he slipped them off as she stepped out, the brilliant blue of his eyes met hers. He tucked the glasses in his pocket, lifted an eyebrow.

'Good morning, Lieutenant.'

'I had a bad feeling when I walked in here. It's just your kind of place, isn't it? Why do you have to own every damn thing?'

'It was a boyhood dream.' His voice cruised over Ireland, picked up the music of it. He glanced past her to the police seal. 'It appears we've both been inconvenienced.'

'Did you have to tell the sweeper I was your wife?'

'You are my wife,' he said easily and shifted his gaze back to her face. 'A fact which pleases me daily.' He took her hand, rubbing his thumb over her wedding ring before she could tug it free again.

'No touching,' she hissed at him, which made him smile.

'That's not what you said a few hours ago. In fact—'

'Shut up, Roarke.' She glanced around, though none of the cops working the scene was outside or close enough to hear. 'This is a police investigation.'

'So I'm told.'

'And who told you?'

'The head of the maintenance team who found the body. He did call the police first,' he pointed out. 'But it's natural he'd report the incident to me. What happened?'

There was no point in griping because his business had tangled around hers. Again. She tried to console herself that he could and would help her cut through some of the muck of paperwork.

'Do you have a bartender by the name of Kohli? Taj Kohli?'

6

'I have no idea. But I can find out.' He took a slim memo book out of his breast pocket, keyed in a request for data. 'Is he dead?'

'As dead gets.'

'Yes, he was mine,' Roarke confirmed, and the Irish in his voice had taken on a cold note. 'For the past three months. Part time. Four nights a week. He had a family.'

'Yes, I know.' Such things mattered to him, and it always touched her heart. 'He was a cop,' Eve said. This time his brows lifted. 'Didn't have that data in your little scan, did you?'

'No. It seems my personnel director was careless. That will be fixed. Am I allowed inside?'

'Yeah, in a minute. How long have you owned the place?'

'Four years, more or less.'

'How many employees, full- and part-time?'

'I'll get you all the data, Lieutenant, and answer all pertinent questions.' Annoyance gleamed in his eyes as he reached for the door himself. 'But now, I'd like to see my place.'

He pushed inside, scanned the destruction, then focused in on the thick black bag being loaded on what the death attendants called a stroller.

'How was he killed?'

'Thoroughly,' Eve said, then sighed when Roarke simply turned and stared at her. 'It was ugly, okay? Metal bat.' She watched Roarke look toward the bar and the spray of blood sparkling on glass like an incomprehensible painting. 'After the first few hits, he wouldn't have felt anything.'

'Ever had a bat laid into you? I have,' he said before she could answer. 'It's not pleasant. It seems far-fetched to think it's robbery, even one that got well out of hand.'

'Why?'

'There'd have been enough prime liquor, easily fenced, to keep anyone cozily fixed for some time. Why break the bottles when you could sell them? If you hit a place like this, it's not

7

for the bit of cash that might be copped, but for the inventory and perhaps some of the equipment.'

'Is that the voice of experience?'

She teased a grin out of him. 'Naturally. My experience, that is, as a property owner and a law-abiding citizen.'

'Right.'

'Security discs?'

'Gone. He got all of them.'

'Then it follows he'd cased the place carefully before-hand.'

'How many cameras?'

Once again, Roarke took out his pad, checked data. 'Eighteen. Nine on this floor, six on two, and the other two on the top level for full scope. Before you ask, closing is at three, which would have staff out by half past. The last show, and we've live ones here, ends at two. The musicians and the entertainers—'

'Strippers.'

'As you like,' he said mildly. 'They clock off at that time. I'll have names and schedules for you within the hour.'

'Appreciate it. Why Purgatory?'

'The name?' The ghost of a smile flirted with his mouth. 'I liked it. The priests will tell you Purgatory's a place for atonement, rehabilitation perhaps. A bit like prison. I've always seen it as a last chance to be human,' he decided. 'Before you strap on your wings and halo or face the fire.'

'Which would you rather?' she wondered. 'The wings or the fire?'

'That's the point, you see. I prefer being human.' As the stroller wheeled by, he ran a hand over her short brown hair. 'I'm sorry for this.'

'So am I. Any reason a New York City detective would have been working undercover in Purgatory?'

'I couldn't say. It's certainly likely that some of the clientele might dabble in areas not strictly approved by the NYPSD, but

8

I've not been informed of anything overt. Some illegals might change hands in privacy rooms or under tables, but there's been no large transactions here. I would have known. The strippers don't turn tricks unless they're licensed, which some are. No one under age is allowed through the doors – as client or staff. I have my own standards, Lieutenant, such as they are.'

'I'm not coming down on you. I need a picture.'

'You're pissed that I'm here at all.'

She waited a minute, her short, choppy hair disordered from its dance outside in the early breeze. As the morgue techs opened the door to transfer Kohli, the sounds of the day punched into the club.

Traffic was already thickening. Cars crammed irritably on the street, air commuters swarmed the skies. She heard the call of an early-bird glide-cart operator call to the techs and ask: 'What da fuck?'

'Okay, I'm pissed that you're here at all. I'll get over it. When's the last time you were in here?'

'Months. It ran well and didn't need my direct attention.'

'Who manages it for you?'

'Rue MacLean. I'll get her information to you as well.'

'Sooner than later. Do you want to go through the place now?'

'No point in it until I've refreshed myself on how it was. I'll want to be let back in once I've done that.'

'I'll take care of it. Yes, Peabody?' she said, turning as her aide inched forward and cleared her throat.

'Sorry, sir, but I thought you'd want to know I reached the victim's squad captain. They're sending a member of his unit and a counselor to inform next of kin. They need to know if they should wait for you or see the wife alone.'

'Tell them to wait. We'll head over now and meet them. I have to go,' she said to Roarke.

'I don't envy you your job, Lieutenant.' Because he needed it, he took her hand, linked their fingers firmly. 'But I'll let you get back to it. I'll have the information you wanted to you as soon as I can.'

'Roarke?' she called as he started for the door. 'I'm sorry about your place.'

'Wood and glass. There's plenty more,' he replied as he looked at her over his shoulder.

'He doesn't mean it,' Eve murmured when he'd shut the door behind him.

'Sir?'

'They messed with him. He won't let it go.' Eve heaved out a breath. 'Come on, Peabody, let's go see the wife and get this particular hell over with.'

The Kohlis lived in a decent, midlevel building on the East Side. The kind of place, Eve mused, where you found young families and older retired couples. Not hip enough for the single crowd, not cheap enough for the struggling.

It was a simple multiunit, pleasantly if not elegantly rehabbed post-Urban Wars.

Door security was a basic code entry.

Eve spotted the cops before she'd double-parked and flipped her On Duty light to active.

The woman was well turned out, with gilt-edged hair that curved up to her cheeks in two stiletto points. She wore sun shades and an inexpensive business suit in navy. The shoes with their thin, two-inch heels told Eve she worked a desk.

Brass. Eve was sure of it.

The man had good shoulders and a bit of pudge at the middle. He'd let his hair go gray, and there was a lot of it. Currently, it was dancing in the breeze around his quiet, composed face. He wore cop shoes – hard-soled and buffed to a gleam. His suit jacket was a little small in the body and starting to fray at the cuffs.

A long-timer, Eve judged, who'd moved from beat to street to desk.

'Lieutenant Dallas.' The woman stepped forward but didn't offer her hand for a polite shake. 'I recognized you. You get a lot of play in the media.' It wasn't said with rebuke, but there was a hint of it in the air, nonetheless. 'I'm Captain Roth, from the One twenty-eight. This is Sergeant Clooney out of my house. He's here as grief counselor.'

'Thanks for waiting. Officer Peabody, my aide.'

'What is the status of your investigation, Lieutenant?'

'Detective Kohli's body is with the ME and will have priority. My report will be written and filed subsequent to notification of next of kin.'

She paused to avoid shouting over the sudden blast of a maxibus that pulled to the curb half a block down.

'At this point, Captain Roth, I have a dead police officer who was the apparent victim of a particularly brutal beating in the early hours of this morning while he was in a club, after hours. A club where he was employed as a part-time bartender.'

'Robbery?'

'Unlikely.'

'Then what is the motive, in your opinion?'

A little seed of resentment planted itself in Eve's gut. It would, she knew, fester there if she wasn't careful. 'I've formed no opinion as to motive at this stage of my investigation. Captain Roth, do you want to stand on the street and question me, or would you prefer to read my report when it's filed?'

Roth opened her mouth, then sucked in a breath. 'Point taken, Lieutenant. Detective Kohli worked under me for five years. I'll be straight with you. I want this investigation handled out of my house.'

'I appreciate your feelings in this matter, Captain Roth. I can only assure you that as long as I'm primary, the investigation into the death of Detective Kohli will receive my complete focus.'

Take off the damn shades, Eve thought. *I want to see your eyes*. 'You can request the transfer of authority,' Eve continued. 'But I'll be straight with your. I won't give it up easy. I stood over him this morning. I saw what was done to him. You couldn't want his killer any more than I do.'

'Captain.' Clooney stepped forward, laying a hand lightly on Roth's arm at the elbow. There were lines fanning out from his pale blue eyes. They made him look tired and somehow trustworthy. 'Lieutenant. Emotions are running pretty high right now. For all of us. But we've got a job to do here and now.'

He glanced up, homing in on a window four stories above. 'Whatever we're feeling doesn't come close to what's going to be felt upstairs.'

'You're right. You're right, Art. Let's get this done.'

Roth turned to the entrance, bypassed the code with her master.

'Lieutenant?' Clooney hung back. 'I know you'll want to question Patsy, Taj's wife. I have to ask if you could go a little easy just now. I know what she's about to go through. I lost a son in the line of duty a few months back. It rips a hole in you.'

'I'm not going to kick her while she's down, Clooney.' Eve shoved through the doors, caught herself, turned back. 'I didn't know him,' she said more calmly, 'but he was murdered, and he was a cop. That's enough for me. Okay?'

'Yeah. Yeah, okay.'

'Christ, I hate this.' She followed Roth to the elevator. 'How do you do it?' she asked Clooney. 'The counseling thing. How do you stand it?'

'To tell you the truth, they tapped me for it because I have a way with keeping the peace. Mediation,' he added with a quick smile. 'I agreed to survivor counseling, to give it a try, and found I could do some good. You know what they feel – every stage of it.'

12

He pressed his lips together as they stepped onto the elevator. The smile was long gone. 'You stand it because maybe you can help . . . just a little. It makes a difference if the counselor's a cop. And I've discovered in the last few months it makes a bigger one if the counselor's a cop who experienced a loss. You ever lose a family member, Lieutenant?'

Eve flashed on a dingy room, the bloody husk of a man, and the child she'd been, huddled broken in a corner. 'I don't have any family.'

'Well . . .' was all Clooney said as they stepped off on the fourth floor.

She would know, and they were all aware of it. A cop's spouse would know the minute she opened the door. How the words were spoken varied little, and it didn't matter a damn. The minute the door opened, lives were irrevocably changed.

They didn't have the chance to knock before it began.

Patsy Kohli was a pretty woman with smooth, ebony skin and a closely cropped thatch of black curls. She was dressed to go out, a baby sling strapped across her breasts. The small boy at her side had his hand clasped in hers as he danced frantically in place.

'Let's go swing! Let's go swing!'

But his mother had frozen in place, the laughter that had been in her eyes dying away. She lifted one hand, pressing it to the baby, and the baby to her heart.

'Taj.'

Roth had taken off her sunshades. Her eyes were coldly blue, rigidly blank. 'Patsy. We need to come in.'

'Taj.' Patsy stood where she was, slowly shaking her head. 'Taj.'

'Here now, Patsy.' Clooney moved in, sliding an arm around her shoulders. 'Why don't we sit down?'

'No. No. No.'

The little boy began to cry, wailing yelps as he tugged on his mother's unresponsive hand. Both Roth and Eve looked down at him with stares of sheer, hot panic.

Peabody eased inside, crouched down to his level.

'Hi, pal.'

'Going swing,' he said pitifully, while great tears spilled down his chubby cheeks.

'Yeah. Lieutenant, why don't I take the boy out?'

'Good idea. Good thinking.' Her stomach was busily tying itself into knots at the rising sobs. 'Mrs Kohli, with your permission, my officer will take your son outside for awhile. I think that would be best.'

'Chad.' Patsy stared down as if coming out of a dream. 'We're going to the park. Two blocks over. The swings.'

'I'll take him, Mrs Kohli. We'll be fine.' With an ease that had Eve frowning, Peabody lifted the boy, set him on her hip. 'Hey, Chad, you like soy dogs?'

'Patsy, why don't you give me your little girl there.' Gently, Clooney unhooked the sling, slipped the baby free. Then, to Eve's shock, he passed the bundle to her.

'Oh listen, I can't—'

But Clooney was already guiding Pasty to the sofa, and Eve was left holding the bag. Or so she thought of it. Wincing, she looked down, and when big, black eyes stared curiously up at her, her palms went damp.

And when the baby said, 'Coo,' she lost all the spit in her mouth.

She searched the room for help. Clooney and Roth were already flanking Pasty, and Clooney's voice was a quiet murmur. The room was small and lived-in, with a scatter of toys on the rug and a scent – one she didn't recognize – that was talc and crayons and sugar. The scent of children.

But she spotted a basket of neatly folded laundry on the floor by a chair. Perfect, she decided and, with the care of a woman handling a homemade boomer, laid the baby on top.

'Stay,' she whispered, awkwardly patting the dark, downy head.

And started to breathe again.

She tuned back into the room, saw the woman on the sofa gathered into herself, rocking, rocking, with her hands gripped in Clooney's. She made no sound, and her tears fell like rain.

Eve stayed out of the way, watched Clooney work, watched the unity of support stand on either side of the widow. *This*, she thought, *was family. For what it was worth. And in times like this, it was all there could be.*

Grief settled into the room like fog. It would, she knew, be a long time before it burned away again.

'It's my fault. It's my fault.' They were the first words Patsy spoke since she'd sat on the sofa.

'No.' Clooney squeezed her hands until she lifted her head. They needed to look in your eyes, he knew. To believe you, to take comfort, they needed to see it all in your eyes. 'Of course it's not.'

'He'd never have been working there if not for me. I didn't want to go back to work after Jilly was born. I wanted to stay home. The money, the professional mother's salary was so much less than—'

'Patsy, Taj was happy you were content to stay home with the children. He was so proud of them and of you.'

'I can't – Chad.' She pulled her hands free, pressed them to her face. 'How can I tell him? How can we live without Taj? Where is he?' She dropped her hands, looked around blindly. 'I have to go see him. Maybe there's a mistake.'

It was, Eve knew, her time. 'I'm sorry, Mrs Kohli, there's no mistake. I'm Lieutenant Dallas. I'm in charge of the investigation.'

'You saw Taj.' Patsy got shakily to her feet.

'Yes. I'm sorry, very sorry for your loss. Can you talk to me, Mrs Kohli? Help me find the person who did this?'

'Lieutenant Dallas,' Roth began, but Patsy shook her head.

'No, no. I want to talk. Taj would want me to. He'd want . . . Where's Jilly? Where's my baby?'

'I, ah . . .' Feeling sticky again, Eve gestured to the hamper.

'Oh.' Patsy wiped tears from her face, smiled. 'She's so good. Such a love. She hardly ever cries. I should put her in her crib.'

'I'll do that for you, Patsy.' Clooney rose. 'You talk to the lieutenant.' He gave Eve a quiet look, full of sorrow and understanding. 'That's what Taj would want. Do you want us to call someone for you? Your sister?'

'Yes.' Patsy drew in a breath. 'Yes, please. If you'd call Carla for me.'

'Captain Roth will do that for you, won't you, Captain? While I put the baby down.'

Roth struggled, set her teeth. It didn't surprise Eve to see the annoyance. Clooney had essentially taken over, gently. And this wasn't a woman who liked taking orders from her sergeant.

'Yes, of course.' With a final warning look at Eve, she walked into the next room.

'Are you with Taj's squad?'

'No, I'm not.'

'No, no, of course.' Patsy rubbed her temple. 'You'd be with Homicide.' She started to break, the sound coming through her lips like a whimper. And Eve watched with admiration as she toughened up. 'What do you want to know?'

'Your husband didn't come home this morning. You weren't concerned?'

'No.' She reached back, braced a hand on the arm of the couch, and lowered herself down. 'He'd told me he'd probably go into the station from the club. He sometimes did that. And he said he was meeting someone after closing.'

'Who?'

'He didn't say, just that he had someone to see after closing.'

'Do you know of anyone who wished him harm, Mrs Kohli?'

'He was a cop,' she said simply. 'Do you know anyone who wishes you harm, Lieutenant?'

Fair enough, Eve thought and nodded. 'Anyone specific? Someone he mentioned to you.'

'No. Taj didn't bring work home. It was a point of honor for him, I think. He didn't want anything to touch his family. I don't even know what cases he was working on. He didn't like to talk about it. But he was worried.'

She folded her hands tightly in her lap, stared down at them. Stared, Eve noted, at the gold band on her finger. 'I could tell he was worried about something. I asked him about it, but he brushed it off. That was Taj,' she managed with a trembling smile. 'He had, well some people would say it was a male dominant thing, but it was just Taj. He was old-fashioned about some things. He was a good man. A wonderful father. He loved his job.'

She pressed her lips together. 'He would have been proud to die in the line of duty. But not like this. Not like this. Whoever did this to him took that away from him. Took him away from me and from his babies. How can that be? Lieutenant, how can that be?'

And as there was no answer to it; all Eve could do was ask more questions.

Chapter Two

'That was a rough one.'

'Yeah.' Eve pulled away from the curb and tried to shake the weight she'd carried out of the Kohli apartment with her. 'She'll hold it together for the kids. She's got spine.'

'Great kids. The little boy's a real piece of work. Conned me into a soy dog, three chocolate sticks, and a fudgy cone.'

'Bet he really had to twist your arm.'

Peabody's smile was sweet. 'I've got a nephew about his age.'

'You have nephews every possible age.'

'More or less.'

'Tell me something, through your vast experience with family. You got a husband and wife, seem pretty tight, good, solid marriage, kids. Why would the wife, who appears to have a backbone and a brain, know next to nothing about her husband's job? His business, his day-to-day routine?'

'Maybe he likes to check work at the door.'

'Doesn't play for me,' Eve muttered. 'You live with someone day after day, you have to know what they do, what they think, what they're into. She said he was worried about something but doesn't know what. Didn't press it.'

She shook her head, frowning as she wove through crosstown traffic. 'I don't get that.'

'You and Roarke have a different couple dynamic.'

'What the hell does that mean?'

'Well.' Peabody slid her eyes over to Eve's profile. 'That was a nice way of saying neither one of you would let the other get away with holding back. Something's going on with one of you, the other sniffs it out and hammers away until it's all out there. You're both nosy, and just mean enough not to let the other one slide by. Now, you take my aunt Miriam.'

'Do I have to?'

'What I'm saying is, she and Uncle Jim have been married for over forty years. He goes to work every day, comes home every night. They have four kids, eight, no, nine grand-kids, and a very happy life. She doesn't even know how much he makes a year. He just gives her an allowance—'

Eve nearly back-ended a Rapid Cab. 'A what?'

'Yeah, well, I said you have a different dynamic. Anyway, he gives her the house money and stuff. She'll ask how his day was, he'll say it was fine, and that's the end of the topic of work.' She shrugged. 'That's how it goes for them. Now, my cousin Freida—'

'I get the point, Peabody.' Eve engaged the car-link and called the ME.

She was transferred directly to Morse, in autopsy.

'I'm still working on him, Dallas.' Morse's face was uncharacteristically sober. 'He's a goddamn mess.'

'I know it. You got the tox reports yet?'

'I tagged them first. No illegals in his system. He'd had a couple ounces of beer, some pretzels just prior to death. It appears he was having the beer when he was hit. Last meal, some six hours before, was a chicken sandwich on whole wheat, pasta salad. Coffee. At this point, I can tell you the victim was in excellent health and good physical condition before some son of a bitch pounded him to pieces.'

'Okay. The skull fracture the killing blow?'

'Didn't I say I was still working on him?' Morse's voice sliced out, laser sharp. Before Eve could respond, he held up a hand, protectively sealed and bloody to the wrist. 'Sorry.

Sorry. I can piece this much together. The assailant came at him from behind. First blow to the back of the head. Facial lacerations indicate the victim hit glass, face first. The second blow, jaw strike, took him down. Then the bastard opened his head like a goddamn peanut. He'd have been dead before he felt it. The other injuries are postmortem. I don't have a final count of those injuries.'

'You gave me what I needed. Sorry for the push.'

'No, it's on me.' Morse puffed out his cheeks. 'I knew him, so it's a little too personal. He was a decent guy, liked to show off holo-shots of his kids. We don't get many happy faces around here.' His eyes narrowed on hers. 'I'm glad he's yours, Dallas. It helps knowing he's yours. You'll have my report by end of shift.'

He broke transmission and left her staring at a blank screen.

'Popular guy,' Eve commented. 'Who had it so in for a decent guy, proud daddy, loving husband? Who's going to beat a cop to a bloody pulp, knowing the system bands together to collar a cop killer? Somebody hated our popular guy in a big, nasty way.'

'Somebody he'd busted?'

You couldn't worry about the ones you busted, Eve mused. But you always kept them in mind. 'A cop has a drink with and turns his back on someone he's busted, he's asking to have his head bashed in. Let's pump up the speed on getting all his records, Peabody. I want to see what kind of cop Taj Kohli was.'

Eve stepped into the squad room, had just turned toward her office, when a woman stood up from a bench in the waiting area.

'Lieutenant Dallas?'

'That's right.'

'I'm Rue MacLean. I've just heard about Taj. I . . .' She

20

lifted her hands. 'Roarke indicated you'd want to speak to me, so I thought I'd come in right away. I want to help.'

'I appreciate that. Just one moment. Peabody.' She stepped aside with her aide. 'Give the record drones a boost on Kohli, then run his financials.'

'Sir? His financials?'

'That's right. You run into any blocks on that, call Feeney in EDD. Do some digging. Find out who he was tight with in his squad. He didn't talk to his wife about work, maybe he talked to someone else. I want to know if he had any hobbies, side interests. And I want to know what case files he was working on or was looking into. I want his life in front of me by end of shift.'

'Yes, sir.'

'Ms MacLean? I'd like to take you into an interview room. My office is a little cramped.'

'Whatever you like. I can't believe this happened. I just can't understand how it *could* happen.'

'We'll talk about it.' *On the record*, Eve thought, as she led Rue through the warren of Central to the interview area. 'I'd like to record this,' she said and gestured Rue into the boxlike room with a single table and two chairs.

'Of course. I only want to help.'

'Have a seat.' Eve activated the recorder. 'Dallas, Lieutenant Eve, in interview with MacLean, Rue. Subject has volunteered to cooperate, on record, in the matter of Kohli, Taj. Homicide. I appreciate you coming in, Ms MacLean.'

'I don't know what I can tell you that might help.'

'You manage the club where Taj Kohli worked as part-time bartender?'

She was just the type Roarke would choose, Eve thought. Slick, sleek, lovely. Deep purple eyes, full of concern now, that shone like jewels against creamy skin.

Delicate features, close to elegant, with just a hint of steel in the line of the chin. Curvy, petite, and perfectly groomed in a plum-colored skirt suit that skimmed her body and showed off great legs.

Her hair was the color of sunlight and was drawn severely back in a fashion that required perfect confidence and good bones.

'Purgatory. Yes, I've managed the club for four years now.'

'And before that?'

'I was hostess at a small club downtown. Prior to that, I was a dancer. A performer,' she added with a thin smile. 'I decided I wanted to move off the stage and into management where I could keep my clothes on. Roarke gave me the opportunity to do so, first at Trends as hostess, then as manager of Purgatory. Your husband appreciates ambition, Lieutenant.'

That was an avenue best not traveled on record. 'Are part of your duties as manager of Purgatory the hiring of employees?'

'Yes. I hired Taj. He was looking for part-time work. His wife had just had a baby and was opting for professional mother status. He needed some extra money, was willing to work the late shift, and being happily married, wasn't likely to hit on the talent.'

'Are those the only requirements for employment at Purgatory?'

'No, but they matter.' Rue lifted her fingers. She wore a single ring, a trio of stones twisted together like snakes and studded with stones the same color as her eyes. 'He knew how to mix drinks, how to serve. He had a good eye for troublemakers. I didn't know he was a cop. His application stated he worked in security, and it checked out.'

'What company?'

'Lenux. I contacted the office, spoke with his supervisor – well, or so I assumed – and was given his employment record. I had no reason to question it, and his record was

22

solid. I hired him on a two-week probationary, he did the job, and we went from there.'

'Do you have the contact at Lenux in your files?'

'Yes.' Rue blew out a breath. 'I've already tried to call. All I got this time around was that the code had been discontinued.'

'I'd like it anyway. Just to follow up.'

'Of course.' Rue reached into her bag, took out a day book. 'I don't know why he didn't tell me he was a cop,' she said as she keyed in the code number on an e-memo for Eve. 'Maybe he thought I wouldn't hire him. But when you figure the owner's a cop—'

'I don't own the club.'

'No, well.' She shrugged and handed Eve the memo.

'He was in the club after closing. Is that standard?'

'No, but it isn't unheard of. Routinely, the head bartender on duty and one of the security team close up together. Taj was serving as head last night, and according to my records, it was Nester Vine's turn to close with him. I haven't been able to reach Nester as yet.'

'Are you in the club every night?'

'Five nights a week. Sundays and Mondays off. I was there last night until two-thirty. The place was clearing out, and one of the girls was having a bad night. Boyfriend trouble. I took her home, held her hand for awhile, then went home myself.'

'What time was that?'

'When I went home?' Rue blinked a moment. 'About three-thirty, quarter to four, I guess.'

'The name of the woman you were with until that time?'

'Mitzi.' Rue drew in a breath. 'Mitzi Treacher. Lieutenant, the last time I saw Taj, he was alive and working the bar.'

'I'm just putting the facts on record, Ms MacLean. Do you have a take on Detective Kohli's state of mind the last time you saw him?'

'He seemed fine. We didn't talk much last night. I stopped by the bar for some mineral water a couple of times. How's it going, busy night, that kind of thing. God.' She squeezed her eyes shut. 'He was a nice man. Quiet, steady. Always called his wife on his early break to see how she was doing.'

'He use the bar phone?'

'No. We discourage personal calls, barring emergencies, on the business line. He used his palm-link.'

'Did he use it last night?'

'I don't know. He always did. I can't say I noticed. No, wait.' This time she closed her eyes and seemed to drift. 'He was eating a sandwich, back in the break room. I remember walking by. The door was open. He was making cooing noises. Talking to the baby,' she said, opening her eyes again. 'I remember that because it was so sweet and silly, hearing this big bruiser of a guy make baby noises into the 'link. Is it important?'

'Just trying to get a picture.' There hadn't been a palm-link on or near the body, Eve recalled. 'Did you notice anyone who came in last night or any other night when he was on? Somebody he knew, hung out at the bar with him?'

'No. We've got some regulars, of course. People who come in several times a week. Taj got so he'd know their usual drinks. Clients appreciate that.'

'Did he get tight with anyone who worked there?'

'Not particularly. Like I said, he was a quiet guy. Friendly enough, but he didn't hang with anyone in particular. He did the bartender thing. Watched, listened.'

'Do you keep a metal bat behind the bar?'

'It's legal,' Rue said quickly, then paled. 'Is that what—'

'Did Taj ever have occasion to use it or threaten to?'

'He never used it.' She rubbed her upper chest with the flat of her hand in long, soothing strokes. 'He had it out once or twice, I guess. Tapped it on the bar as a deterrent. That's mostly all you need, especially with a guy his size.

24

The club's upscale. We rarely have any real trouble there. I run a clean place, Lieutenant. Roarke won't tolerate less.'

The preliminary report was straightforward, and for Eve, unsatisfactory. She had the facts. A dead cop, bludgeoned to death with serious overkill and the wild destruction that pointed to an addict popping on Zeus or some lethal combination of illegals. A sloppy attempt to cover with the look of attempted robbery, a missing palm-link, and thirty loose credit chips.

The victim was apparently moonlighting to supplement his family income, had no blemishes or commendations on his service record, was well liked by his associates, and loved by his family. He had not, at least as far as she had uncovered, lived above his means, engaged in extramarital affairs, or been involved with a hot case that could have led to his death.

On the surface, it looked like just bad luck. But she was damned if that suit fit.

She brought his ID photo up on her screen, studied it. Big guy, with a proud look in his eyes. Firm jaw, wide shoulders.

'Somebody wanted you out, Kohli. Who'd you piss off?'

She shifted, sat up again. 'Computer, run probability. Current case file, scheming cause of death and ME prelim, running primary's report on victim. What is the probability that victim Kohli knew his assailant?'

Working . . . Probability, given known data and primary's report is ninety-three point four percent that victim Kohli knew his assailant.

'Yeah, well, good for me.' She leaned forward, scooped her fingers through her hair. 'Who do cops know? Other cops, weasels, bad guys, family. Neighbors. Who do bartenders know?' She let out a short laugh. 'Every fucking body. Which hat were you wearing for your meet this morning, Detective?'

'Lieutenant?' Peabody poked her head in the door. 'I've got Kohli's current case load. There's no record of him asking for files other than apply to his open logs. I ran into a trip with the financials. Everything's jointly owned, so we need a warrant or spousal permission to poke around.'

'I'll take care of it. Full service record?'

'Right here. Nothing special caught my eye. He was in on a big bust about six months ago. Some dealer named Ricker.'

'Max Ricker?'

'Yeah. Kohli was down in the feeding chain, mostly leg or drone work. He didn't get the collar, that went to a Lieutenant Mills and Detective Martinez. They tied the warehouse of illegals to Ricker, got him indicted, but he slipped through. Still, they nailed six others in the cartel.'

'Ricker's not the type to ruin his manicure by getting blood on the polish. But he wouldn't think twice about paying for a hit, even on a cop.'

And the idea of it gave her a little ping of excitement. 'Find out if Kohli testified. Seems to me it got to court before the whole business was dismissed on techs. See just what his part was in the bust. Get it from Captain Roth, and if she hassles you over it, pass her to me. I'll be with the commander.'

Commander Whitney stood at his window while Eve reported on the status of her investigation. He had his big hands folded together behind his back and stared out at the sky traffic.

One of the new Cloud Dusters winged by close enough for him to see the color of its young pilot's eyes and in direct violation of traffic codes.

Ballsy, Whitney thought absently, *and stupid*, he added as he heard the high, whining beep of the air patrol.

Busted, he thought. It should always be so easy to uphold the law.

When Eve fell silent behind him, Whitney turned. His face

was dark and wide, his hair a close-cut military crop that was showing hints of gray. A big man with cool and sober eyes, he'd spent the first half of his career on the streets. Though he was spending the second half riding a desk, he hadn't forgotten what it meant to strap on a weapon.

'Before I comment on your report, Lieutenant, I want to inform you that I've had communications from Captain Roth of the One twenty-eighth. She's put in a formal request to have the Kohli homicide transferred to her squad.'

'Yes, sir. She indicated she would do so.'

'And your opinion of that request?'

'It's understandable. And it's emotional.'

'Agreed.' He waited a moment, inclined his head. 'You don't ask if I intend to grant Captain Roth's request.'

'There's no tactical reason to do so, and if you'd decided to put the investigation in Captain Roth's hands, you'd have told me up front.'

Whitney pursed his lips, then turned back to the window. 'Correct on both counts. The investigation remains on you. The case *is* emotional, Lieutenant. For Captain Roth's squad and for every cop on the NYPSD. It's difficult when one of us goes down, even though each of us knows the risks. But the nature of this killing takes it to another level. The excessive violence doesn't smack of a professional hit.'

'No. But I'm not discounting that angle. If Ricker's involved, whoever he hired may have been using or may have had instructions to make it messy. I don't know what kind of cop Kohli was yet, Commander. Whether he was foolish enough or cocky enough to put himself in a vulnerable position with one of Ricker's hammers. I have Peabody digging into his record and case load. I need to know who he was close to, the names of his weasels, and how involved he was in the Ricker investigation and trial.'

'It's not the first time Ricker's suspected of arranging a cop killing. But he's generally more subtle.'

'There was something personal in this, Commander. Whether for the badge or for Kohli, I don't know. But it was very personal. Roarke owned the club,' she added.

'Yes, so I've heard.' He turned back, skimmed his gaze over her face, and walked to his desk. 'Personal all around, Lieutenant?'

'It will be easier and quicker to obtain data on the club and on its staff and clientele. The manager's already come in voluntarily for interview. The fact that Kohli concealed his attachment to the NYPSD makes me wonder if he was on the job – on his own. He deliberately misrepresented himself and went so far as to arrange a cover. There's no indication he was working in soft clothes for the department, so it would have been unofficial.'

'I have no knowledge of any investigation, official or otherwise, that required Detective Kohli to go under in Purgatory. But I will pursue that matter with Captain Roth.' He held up a hand before Eve could object. 'It'll be smoother if that particular inquiry comes from this office rather than from you, Dallas. Let's keep it smooth.'

'Yes, sir.' But it grated. 'I want a warrant to open Kohli's financials. They're jointly held with his widow. At this time, I prefer not to request permission from Mrs Kohli.'

'Or alert her before they're open,' he finished. He spread his hands on the desk. 'You think he was taking?'

'I'd like to eliminate that angle, sir.'

'Do it,' he ordered. 'And do it quietly. I'll get your warrant. You get me a cop killer.'

Eve spent the rest of the day poring over Kohli's record, familiarizing herself with his case load, trying to get a handle on the man. The cop.

What she saw was an average officer who'd performed steadily, if slightly under his potential. He'd rarely missed a shift and just as rarely put in any overtime.

He'd never used his weapon for maximum force and therefore had never undergone extensive Testing. Still, he'd closed or been in on the closing of a good number of cases, and his reports on those closed and those open were efficient, carefully written, and thorough.

This was a man, Eve thought, who followed the book, did the job, then went home at night and put his day away.

How? she wondered. *How the hell did anyone manage that?*

His military record was similar. No trouble, no glow. He enlisted at the age of twenty-two, served six steady years, the last two in the military police.

Every t was crossed, every i dotted. It was, to her mind, a perfectly ordinary life. Almost too perfect.

The call to Nester Vine from Purgatory got her as far as his harassed-looking wife, who informed Eve that Vine had come home before the end of his shift the night before, dogsick. She herself had just gotten in from the hospital where she'd taken her husband at three that morning for what turned out to be appendicitis.

As alibis went, it was a beaut. The only tip she pried out of Mrs Vine was that she should get in touch with some stripper named Nancie, who'd apparently stuck around after Kohli had urged Vine to go home.

Still, she contacted the hospital and verified one Nester Vine had indeed had his appendix removed, in emergency, early that morning.

Scratch Nester, she thought, and put the stripper on her talk-to list.

Calls to Lieutenant Mills and Detective Martinez went unreturned. In the field and unavailable was the response. She left one last message for each, gathered the files, and prepared to go home.

She'd take a hard look at Kohli's financials that evening.

She caught Peabody in her cubicle in the bullpen dealing with the follow-up paperwork.

'Leave the rest of that until tomorrow. Go home.'

'Yeah?' Peabody's face lit up as she glanced at her wrist unit. 'Almost on time, too. I've got an eight o'clock dinner with Charles. Now I'll have just enough time to go snazz myself up.'

When Eve's response was a grunt, Peabody grinned. 'You know the problem with juggling two guys?'

'Do you consider McNab a guy?'

'On a good day, he's a nice contrast to Charles. Anyway, you know the problem with seeing both of them?'

'No, Peabody, what's the problem with seeing both of them?'

'There isn't one.'

With a hoot of laughter, Peabody grabbed her bag and shot out of her cubicle. 'See you tomorrow.'

Eve shook her head. One guy, she decided, was plenty problem enough for her taste. And if she got the hell out of Central, she might even beat him home for a change.

In a kind of test, she tried to click her mind off her case files. Traffic was ugly enough to keep her mind occupied, and the current blast of the billboards were hyping everything from spring fashions to the latest hot sports car.

When she caught a familiar face burst across one of the animated screens, she nearly sideswiped a glide-cart.

Mavis Freestone, her hair a riot of flame-colored spikes, whirled over the street at Thirty-fourth. She jiggled, spun, in a few sassy and amusingly placed scraps of electric blue. With each revolution, her hair changed from red to gold to blinding green.

It was, Eve thought with a foolish grin on her face, just like her.

'Jesus, Mavis. Would you just look at that? What a kick in the ass.'

A long way. Her oldest friend had come a long way from

the street grifter Eve had once busted, to performance artist in third-rate clubs, and now to bona fide musical star.

Musical, Eve thought, *in the broadest sense of the word.*

She reached for her car-link, intending to call Mavis and tell her what she was looking at, when her personal palm-link beeped.

'Yeah.' She couldn't take her eyes off the billboard, even when several impatient drivers honked rudely. 'Dallas.'

'Hey, Dallas.'

'Webster.' Instantly, Eve's shoulders tensed. She might have known Don Webster on a personal level, but no cop liked receiving a transmission from Internal Affairs. 'Why are you calling on my personal 'link? IAB's required to use official channels.'

'I was hoping to talk to you. Got a few minutes?'

'You are talking to me.'

'Face-to-face.'

'Why?'

'Come on, Dallas. Ten minutes.'

'I'm on my way home. Tag me tomorrow.'

'Ten minutes,' he repeated. 'I'll meet you at the park right across from your place.'

'Is this Internal Affairs business?'

'Let's talk.' He gave her a winning smile that only increased her level of suspicion. 'I'll meet you there. I'm right behind you.'

She narrowed her eyes, checked her rearview, and saw he meant it literally. Saying nothing, she broke transmission.

She didn't stop across from the gates of her home but drove another block and a half, on principle – then made certain she found the only convenient parking spot before she pulled in.

It didn't surprise her when Webster simply double-parked and, ignoring the snooty glares from an elegant couple and their three equally stylish Afghan hounds, flipped on his On Duty light and joined her on the curb.

His smile had always been a handy weapon, and he used it now, keeping his light blue eyes friendly. His face was thin, sharp-angled, and would probably be termed scholarly as he aged. His dark brown hair waved a little and was cut to flatter.

'You've come up in the world, Dallas. This is some neighborhood.'

'Yeah, we have monthly block parties and get crazy. What do you want, Webster?'

'How's it going?' He said it casually and started strolling toward the lush green and the trees still tender with spring.

Sucking in temper, she jammed her hands in her pockets and matched her steps with his. 'It's going fine. How about you?'

'Can't complain. Nice evening. You gotta love spring in New York.'

'And how about those Yankees? Now, that should conclude our period of small talk. What do you want?'

'You never were much on chat.' He remembered very well the one and only time he'd managed to get her into bed; they hadn't done any talking. 'Why don't we find a bench? Like I said, it's a nice evening.'

'I don't want to find a bench. I don't want a soy dog, and I don't want to talk about the weather. I want to go home. So if you don't have anything interesting to say, that's what I'm going to do.'

She turned, took three steps.

'You pulled the Kohli homicide.'

'That's right.' She turned back, and her inner alarm system flashed to red light. 'What does that have to do with IAB?'

'I didn't say it had anything to do with IAB, other than the usual run we do when a cop goes down.'

'The usual run doesn't mean a private meet, off duty, with the primary.'

'We go back a ways.' He lifted a hand. 'Hell, all the way back to the Academy. It seemed friendlier this way.'

She kept her eyes on his as she walked to him, stood toe to toe. 'Don't insult me, Webster. Where does IAB come into my investigation?'

'Look, I've seen the prelim. This is a rough one. Rough on the department, his squad, his family.'

Something started clicking in her brain. 'Did you know Kohli?'

'Not really.' Webster gave a thin smile, just a little bitter at the edges. 'Most detectives don't care to socialize with Internal Affairs. Funny how we all frown over a dirty cop, but nobody wants to rub elbows with the ones digging them out.'

'Are you saying Kohli was dirty?'

'I'm not saying that at all. I wouldn't be at liberty to discuss an internal investigation with you, if there was an internal investigation.'

'Bullshit, Webster. Just bullshit. I have a dead cop. If he was mixed up in something off, I need to know.'

'I can't discuss IAB business with you. It came to my attention that you've opened his financials.'

She paused a minute as her temper threatened to spike. 'I can't discuss a homicide investigation with you. And why would part of the procedure of that investigation come to the attention of the Rat Squad?'

'Now you're trying to piss me off.' He kept his composure, gave a little shrug. 'I thought I would give you a heads-up, unofficially and in a friendly manner, that the department, as a whole, will be better off if this investigation is closed quickly and quietly.'

'Was Kohli in bed with Ricker?'

This time a muscle jumped in Webster's cheek, but his voice stayed smooth. 'I don't know what you're talking about. Digging into Detective Kohli's financials is a dead end, Dallas, and will upset his family. The man was killed off duty.'

'A man was beaten to death. A cop. A woman's been widowed. Two children lost their father. And it's supposed to matter less that it happened when he was off duty?'

'No.' He had the grace or the wit to look uncomfortable. And then to look away. 'That's just the way it went down. That's all there is to it.'

'Don't tell me how to do my job, Webster. Don't ever tell me how to conduct a homicide investigation. You gave up cop work. I didn't.'

'Dallas.' He caught up with her before she reached the curb again. He gripped her arm and braced himself for the storm when she whirled on him.

Instead, she met his eyes, her own cold, flat, empty. 'Move your hand. Now.'

He complied, slipping his into his pocket. 'I'm just trying to tell you IAB wants this closed quiet.'

'What makes you think I give one good fuck about what IAB wants? You have something to say to me regarding my investigation into the death of Detective Taj Kohli, you do it in an official capacity. Don't tail me again, Webster. Not ever.'

She climbed into her car, waited for a break in the mild traffic, and swung into a U-turn.

He watched her cover the distance, then turn into the high gates of the world she lived in now. He took three deep breaths, and when that didn't work, kicked viciously at his own rear tire.

He hated what he'd done. And more, he hated knowing he'd never really gotten over her.

Chapter Three

She was steaming when she barreled down the drive to the great stone house Roarke had made his home. And hers.

So much, she thought, for checking your work at the door. What the hell were you supposed to do when it followed you to the damn threshold? Webster was up to something, which meant there was an agenda here, and the agenda was IAB's.

Now she had to calm herself down so she could filter out her annoyance at being waylaid by him. It was more important to puzzle out what he'd been trying to tell her. And more important yet, to calculate what he'd been so damn careful not to tell her.

She left the car at the end of the drive because she liked it there and because it annoyed Roarke's majordomo, the consistently irritating Summerset.

She grabbed her bag that held the files and was halfway up the steps when she stopped. Deliberately, she blew out a long, cleansing breath, turned, and simply sat down.

It was time to try something new, she decided. Time to sit and enjoy the pleasant spring evening, enjoy the gorgeous simplicity of the flowering trees and shrubs that spread over the lawn, speared into the sky. She'd lived here for more than a year now and rarely, very rarely took time to see. Time to appreciate what Roarke had built or the style with which he'd built it.

The house itself with its sweeps and turrets and dazzling

expanses of glass was a monument to taste, wealth, and elegant comfort. There were too many rooms to count filled with art, antiques, and every pleasure and convenience a man could make for himself.

But the grounds, she thought, were another level. This was a man who needed room, who demanded it. And commanded it. At the same time, he was a man who could appreciate the simple appeal of a flower that would bloom and fade with its season.

He'd decorated his grounds with those flowers, with trees that would outlive both of them, with shrubs that spread and fountained. And closed it all away with the high stone walls, the iron gates, and the rigid security that kept the city outside.

But it was still there, the city, sniffing around the edges like a hungry, restless dog.

That was part of it. Part of the duality of Roarke. And, she supposed, of her.

He'd grown up in the alleys and tenements of Dublin and had done whatever was necessary to survive. She'd lost her childhood, and the flickers of memory, the images of what had been, of what she'd done to escape, haunted the woman she'd become.

His buffer against yesterday was money, power, control. Hers was a badge. There was little either of them wouldn't do, hadn't done, to keep that buffer in place. But somehow, together, they were . . . normal, she decided. They'd made a marriage and a home.

That was why she could sit on the steps of that home, with the ugliness of her day smearing her heart, look at blossoms dancing in the breeze. And wait for him.

She watched the long, black car slide quietly toward the house. Waited while Roarke climbed out the back, had a word with his driver. As the car drove off, he walked to her in that way he had, with his eyes on her face. She'd never had anyone look at her as he did. As if nothing else and no one else existed.

No matter how many times he did so, just that long, focused look made her heart flutter.

He sat beside her, set his briefcase aside, leaned back as she was.

'Hi,' she said.

'Hi. Lovely evening.'

'Yeah. The flowers look good.'

'They do, yes. The renewal of spring. A cliché, but true enough, as most clichés are.' He ran a hand over her hair. 'What are you doing?'

'Nothing.'

'Exactly. That's out of character for you, darling Eve.'

'It's an experiment.' She crossed her scarred boots at the ankles. 'I'm seeing if I can leave work at Central.'

'And how are you doing?'

'I've pretty much failed.' Still with her head back, she closed her eyes and tried to recapture some of it. 'I was doing okay with it on the drive home. I saw Mavis's billboard.'

'Ah yes. Fairly spectacular.'

'You didn't tell me about it.'

'It just went up today. I figured you'd see it on your way home and thought it would be a nice surprise.'

'It was.' And remembering brought her smile back. 'I nearly clipped a glide-cart, and I was sitting there, grinning at it, about to call her, but I had a transmission come through.'

'So work intruded.'

'More or less. It was Webster.' Because the smile was gone again, and she was scowling at the trees, she didn't notice the slight tension in Roarke's body. 'Don Webster from Internal Affairs.'

'Yes, I remember who he is. What did he want?'

'I'm trying to figure that out. He called on my personal and asked for a private meet.'

'Did he?' Roarke murmured, his voice deceptively mild.

'He went out of his way for it, tailed me from Central. I met up with him just down the block from here, and after he got finished trying to make nice, he started a song and dance on the Kohli case.'

Just thinking about it again got her blood boiling. 'Tells me how IAB wants it put away quiet, doesn't like the idea that I'm going to look into Kohli's financials. But he won't confirm or deny anything. Claims it's just a friendly, unofficial heads-up.'

'And do you believe him?'

'No, but I don't know what he's feeding me. And I don't like IAB's sticky fingers poking into my case files.'

'The man has a personal interest in you.'

'Webster?' She looked over now, surprised. 'No, he doesn't. We blew off some steam one night years back. That's the beginning and end of it.'

For you, perhaps, Roarke thought, but let it go.

'Anyway, I can't figure if the meet was really about Kohli or if it's more about the Ricker connection.'

'Max Ricker?'

'Yeah.' Her eyes sharpened. 'You know him. I should've figured that.'

'We've met. What's the connection?'

'Kohli worked on the task force that busted Ricker about six months back. He wasn't a key player, and Ricker slithered through, but it had to cost him a lot of time and money. Could be Ricker put out contracts and is getting some of his own back by whacking cops.'

'What I saw in Purgatory today didn't seem like Ricker's style.'

'I don't figure he'd want his fingerprints on it.'

'There's that.' Roarke was silent for a moment. 'You want to know if I ever did business with him.'

'I'm not asking you that.'

'Yes, you are.' He took her hand, kissed it lightly, then got to his feet. 'Let's have a walk.'

'I brought work home with me.' She let him pull her up, smiled. 'So much for the experiment. I should get to it.'

'You'll work better if we clear this up.' He kept her hand in his, started across the lawn.

The breeze had shaken some of the petals from the trees so they lay like pink and white snowdrops on the green. Flowers, banks of them she couldn't name, flowed out of beds in soft, blurry blues and shimmering whites. The light was beginning to go, softening the air. She caught drifts of fragile perfumes, country sweet.

He bent, snapped off a tulip, its cup as perfect as something sculpted from white wax, handed it to her.

'I haven't seen or dealt with Max Ricker in a number of years. But there was a time we had business of sorts.'

She held the tulip and heard the city sniffing at the gates. 'What kind of business?'

He stopped, tipped her head back so their eyes met. Then saw, with regret, that hers were troubled. 'First, let me say that even one with my . . . let's call it eclectic palate . . . hasn't the taste for certain activities. Murder for hire being one of those. I never killed for him, Eve, nor for that matter, for anyone but myself.'

She nodded again. 'Let's not go there, not now.'

'All right.'

But they'd come too far to shy away now. She walked with him. 'Illegals?'

'There was a time in the beginning of my career, I couldn't . . . No,' he corrected, knowing that honesty was vital. 'When I wasn't particularly selective in the products I handled. Yes, I dealt in illegals from time to time, and some of those dealings involved Ricker and his organization. The last time we associated was . . . Christ, more than ten years back. I didn't care for his business practices, and I'd reached a point where I wasn't obliged to negotiate with those who didn't appeal to me.'

'Okay.'

'Eve.' He kept his hand on her face, his eyes on hers. 'When I met you, most of my business was legitimate. I made that choice long ago because it suited me. After you, I dispensed with or reconstructed those interests left that were questionable. I did that because I knew it would suit you.'

'You don't have to tell me what I already know.'

'I think I do, just now. There's little I wouldn't do for you. But I can't, and I wouldn't, change my past, or what brought me here.'

She looked down at the tulip, perfect and pure. Then back up at him. Not pure, God knew, but for her, perfect. 'I wouldn't want you to change anything.' She put her hands on his shoulders. 'We're okay.'

Later, after they'd shared dinner where they were both careful not to discuss his business or hers, Eve settled down in her home office and began to study the data on Taj and Patsy Kohli's financials.

She came at them from several different angles, drank three cups of coffee, reached certain conclusions, then rose. She knocked briefly on the door that adjoined her work space to Roarke's, then stepped inside.

He was at his console, and from what she could gather, he was talking to someone in Tokyo. He held up a hand, out of the range of his screen, in a signal for her to wait.

'I regret that projection will not meet my needs at this time, Fumi-san.'

'The projection is, of course, preliminary and negotiable.' The voice through his desk-link was precise and cool, but no cooler, Eve thought, than her husband's mild and polite expression.

'Then perhaps we should discuss it further when the figures are no longer preliminary.'

'I would be honored to discuss the matter with you, Roarke-san, in person. It is the feeling of my associates that such a delicate negotiation would be better served in this way. Tokyo is lovely in the spring. Perhaps you will visit my city, at our expense, of course, some time in the near future.'

'I regret that such a trip, as appealing as it may be, is impossible, given my current schedule. However, I would be happy to meet with you, and any of your associates, in New York. If this is possible for you, you have only to contact my administrator. She will be delighted to assist you in any travel arrangements.'

There was a slight pause. 'Thank you for your gracious invitation. I will consult with my associates and contact you through your administrator as soon as possible.'

'I look forward to it. *Domo*, Fumi-san.'

'What are you buying now?' Eve asked.

'That remains to be seen, but how do you feel about owning a Japanese baseball team?'

'I like baseball,' Eve said after a moment.

'Well then. What can I do for you, Lieutenant?'

'If you're busy buying sports teams, it can wait.'

'I'm not buying anything, at least not until negotiations are completed.' The wolf came into his eyes. 'And on my turf.'

'Okay, first a question. If I were to refuse to discuss any part of my work with you, or my professional business, what would you do?'

'Slap you around, of course.' He rose, amused, when she laughed. 'But, I imagine we can both be spared that unhappy event as the question doesn't apply. So, why do you ask it?'

'Let me put it another way, since I'm so terrified of being slapped around. Can two people be married, live in the same house, have a solid marriage, and one of them have no clue about the other's outside business?'

When he merely lifted his eyebrows, she swore. 'You don't apply. Nobody could keep up with your outside business. Besides, I know stuff you do. You buy everything you can get your hands on and manufacture and sell almost every product known to humankind. And right now, you're considering buying a Japanese ball team. See?'

'My God, my life's an open book.' He came around the desk. 'But to go back to your question, yes, I suppose it's possible for people to live together and not know the thrust, or at least the intricacies of the other's work or outside interests. What if I liked to fish?'

'To fish?'

'As an example. We'll hypothesize that fishing is a passion of mine, and I often toddle off for a wild weekend of dry fly fishing in Montana. Would you pay attention to my recitation of every cast and catch upon my return?'

'To fish?' she repeated and made him laugh.

'And there you have my point. So, yes to your question. Now, why do you ask?'

'Just trying to get a picture. Anyway, since you might be tempted to belt me – and then I'd have to take you down – I'm willing to share some of my professional business with you. How about taking a look at something?'

'All right. But you couldn't take me down.'

'Can and have.'

'Only when you cheat,' he said and walked by her into her office.

She'd left the financials on the wall screen. Roarke eased a hip onto her desk, angled his head, and scanned them.

Figures, they both knew, were like breath to him. He simply drew them in.

'Standard outlays for a typical middle-class lifestyle,' he commented. 'Reasonable rent payments, made in a timely fashion. Vehicle payments and maintenance costs, garage fees are a little on the high side. They ought to shop around

42

a bit. Taxes, clothing, food, entertainment are a bit light. They don't get out much. Deposits are regular bimonthly, which would coincide with salaries. You certainly couldn't accuse this family of living over their incomes.'

'No, you couldn't. Interesting though about the vehicle expenses. Seeing as Kohli had a city unit and neither he nor his wife own a personal vehicle.'

'Is that so?' Frowning, he refocused. 'So, there's some skimming or padding going on, but at just under four thousand a month, it's hardly big time.'

'Every little bit,' Eve murmured. 'Now take a look at this. Investment account. College funds, retirement, savings.' She flipped the screens and heard Roarke's quiet 'Ah.'

'Someone was looking to the future. A half million in the past five months, and earning decently. Though I'd advise a bit more diversity and more of the pie in growth areas if college tuition is, indeed, the goal.'

'He won't be needing a portfolio consult. A cop doesn't come up with a half million by watching his pennies. He comes up with it by being dirty.'

With anger simmering, she sat. 'He was taking. The question is, from who and why. The deposits and the accounts were down a couple of levels, but not buried deep, not covered up so a full scan didn't pop them right out. Pretty damn cocky.'

She rose again to pace. 'Pretty damn cocky. I don't think he was stupid. I think he was just sure of himself, sure he'd be covered.'

'If he hadn't been killed, no one would have been looking at his financials,' Roarke pointed out. 'His lifestyle wasn't sending up red flags. He lived within his means.'

'Yeah, he did his job, no more, no less. Went home at night to his pretty wife and pretty kids, then got up the next morning and did it all over again. No flash. The kind of cop nobody pays a lot of attention to and everybody likes. Nice guy, quiet guy. But IAB was looking at him.'

She stopped in front of the wall screen. 'They were looking, and they knew about the take. They don't want it coming out. Last time I looked, IAB didn't have a heart, so it's not concern for his grieving widow. So who's covering whose ass?'

'Perhaps they're simply being territorial. If they had him under investigation, they want to close that internal business up themselves.'

'Yes, could be. I wouldn't put it past them.' But it stuck in her craw. 'Dirty or not, I've got a dead cop. And he's mine.' She nodded at the screen. 'I want to talk to Max Ricker.'

'Lieutenant.' Roarke moved behind her, rubbed her shoulders. 'I have every confidence in your abilities, your intellect, and your instincts. But Ricker is a dangerous man, with a taste for the unpleasant. Particularly where women are involved. You'll appeal to him on several levels, not the least of which is your connection to me.'

'Really?' she murmured and turned around.

'We didn't sever our business association on the best of terms.'

'So, I can use that. If he's interested, it'll be easier to wade through his lawyers and set up a meet.'

'Let me do it.'

'No.'

'Stop and think. I can get you to him quicker and more directly.'

'Not this time, and not this way. You can't change your past,' she said, 'and he's part of that. But he's not part of your today.'

'He's part of yours.'

'That's right. Let's try to keep this, if not separate, sort of side by side. If he's part of it, you'll probably know before I do, because you won't leave it alone. But whatever kind of cop Kohli was, I'm the one standing for him now. I'll set up the meet when the time's right.'

'Let me look into it a bit first, then you'll have more in your pocket when you do.' And he'd have more time to do what needed to be done to keep her away from Ricker.

'Go ahead and look.' But she was careful not to agree. 'Tell me what you know about him. Give me an inside track.'

Troubled, Roarke walked away, poured a brandy. 'He's very smooth, educated, and can be charming when it suits him. He's quite vain and enjoys the company of beautiful women. When they please him, he can be very generous. When they displease him . . .'

Roarke turned, swirling the brandy. 'He can and will be brutal. He's the same with his employees and associates. I once saw him slit the throat of a servant over a chipped wine goblet.'

'It's hard to get good help these days.'

'Isn't it? His main income is through the manufacture and distribution of illegals on a wide scale, but he also dabbles in weapons, assassinations, and sex. He has several high-placed officials in his pocket, which keeps him protected. Within an hour of your contact with him, he'll know whatever there is to know about you. He'll know, Eve, things you would prefer no one knew.'

Her gut clenched, but she nodded. 'I can handle that. Does he have family?'

'He had a brother. Rumor is Ricker dispensed with him over some sibling dispute. In any case, his body was never discovered. He has a son about my age, perhaps a few years younger. Alex. I never met him as he was living primarily in Germany when I had dealings with Ricker. Word is he's kept close, and insulated.'

'Weaknesses?'

'Vanity, arrogance, greed. So far, he's been able to indulge himself in all three with relative impunity. But over the last year or so, there've been rumors. Quiet, very cautious ones, that his mental health is deteriorating, and as a result, some of his businesses are in mild distress. That's one of the avenues I'll explore more carefully.'

'If he's involved in Kohli's death, that impunity ends. If he's mentally defective, it won't keep him out of a cage. Do you figure he'll agree to meet me if I make an approach?'

'He'll see you because he'll be curious. And if you take a shot at him, he'll never forget it. He's cold, Eve, and he's patient. If he has to wait a year, ten years, to circle back to you, he will.'

'Then if I take a shot at him, I'll have to make it count.'

More, Roarke thought as he finished his brandy. If she went after Ricker, Ricker would have to die.

He, too, could be cold. And patient.

She turned to him in the night. It was rare for her to do so unless the dreams were chasing her. When she slept, she slept deep and unprotected. Perhaps she knew he needed it, needed to feel her wrapped around him in the dark, the intimacy of it that stated more truly than words what they'd come to be to each other.

Her mouth found his, offered, while her hands roamed up the solid length of his back, down again to his hips.

They shifted on the wide bed, a tangle of limbs, of warm flesh, of breath beginning to quicken with each touch.

The taste of her – lips, throat, breasts – filled him, as it always did, even as it stirred hunger for more. Her heartbeat under his hand, under his mouth, and her first sign of pleasure trailed off into a quiet moan.

She arched against him, strength and surrender. Opened for him, invitation and demand.

He slipped inside her – hot and wet and waiting – and it was he who moaned as she closed around him. Shadows in the dark, their bodies rose and fell together, a slow, silky rhythm to draw out the night.

Pleasuring her, pleasuring himself, he slipped his hands under her hips, lifted her. Gave her more.

She locked herself around him, rode the edge. And when she felt herself begin to fall, she said his name.

He lifted his head, saw the gleam of her eyes, open, on him. 'Eve,' he said, and let himself fall with her.

Into the night, in the dark, he lay beside her, listening to her breathe. He knew the varied and sundry reasons a man would kill. But none were more fierce, none were more vital than to hold safe what he loved.

Chapter Four

Lieutenant Alan Mills caught Eve on her communicator as she was grabbing her second cup of coffee. Her first thought was that he looked as though he could have used a good jolt of caffeine himself.

His eyes were sleepy and irritable, a watery gray in a pale face.

'Dallas. Mills, here. You looking for me.'

'That's right. I'm primary on the Kohli homicide.'

'Son of a bitch.' Mills snorted, sniffed. 'I'd like a piece of the dickweed who did Kohli. What have you got?'

'This and that.' She wasn't about to share investigative data with a man who looked like he'd yet to roll out of bed and had probably rolled into it with a little chemical enhancement, not strictly departmentally approved. 'You and a Detective Martinez worked with Kohli on a task force over the past year. Max Ricker.'

'Yeah, yeah.' Mills rubbed his face. She could actually hear the scrub brush sound of his stubble against his palm. 'Him and about a dozen other cops, and the slick bastard still oozed through the cracks. You think Ricker's tied to this?'

'I'm covering my bases here. I need a picture of Kohli, then maybe I'll get a picture of his killer. You got some time this morning, Mills, maybe you could hook Martinez and meet me at the crime scene. I'd appreciate any input.'

'I heard the case was being transferred to our house.'

'You heard wrong.'

He seemed to digest this information and not find it particularly to his liking. 'Kohli was one of ours.'

'And now he's mine. I'm asking for some cooperation on this. Are you going to give it to me?'

'I want a look at the scene anyway. When?'

'No time like the present. I'll be at Purgatory in twenty minutes.'

'I'll round up Martinez. Probably still taking her siesta. She's a Mex.'

He ended transmission and left Eve regarding her communicator thoughtfully before she stuck it in her trouser pocket. 'Gee, Mills. Nobody told me you were a complete and total asshole. Go figure.'

'The asshole is still going to want to prove he has harder balls than you,' Roarke commented. He'd stopped scanning the morning stock reports to watch her handle her colleague.

'Yeah, I got that.'

She snagged her weapon harness, strapped it on. In a way, Roarke thought, another woman clipped on earrings. He rose, slid a finger down the dent in her chin. 'He'll find out, very shortly, he's wrong. No one has harder balls than you, Lieutenant.'

She checked her weapon, settled it. 'Is that a compliment or a dig?'

'An observation. I'd like to take another look at the scene myself – for insurance purposes.'

For insurance purposes her ass, Eve thought. 'Not today, pal. But I'll try to clear it for you by tomorrow.'

'As property owner, I'm entitled to an on-site scan to determine damage costs.'

'As primary in a homicide investigation, I'm entitled to seal and preserve the crime scene until I'm satisfied all evidence has been gathered.'

'The sweep was completed yesterday afternoon, and the

scene was fully recorded.' He reached down to the table in the sitting area of the bedroom, lifted a file disc. 'At this point, the property owner is allowed admittance, in the company of a police representative and his insurance agent, to estimate repair and replacement costs. The memo from my attorney on the matter, Lieutenant.'

She snatched the disc he offered. 'Now who's rattling their balls,' she muttered and made him grin. 'Maybe I don't have time for you this morning.'

He strolled to his closet, selected a suit jacket from the vast forest of his wardrobe. She had never figured out how he knew what went with what when there was so damn much to choose from.

'Maybe you'll have to make time. I'll ride with you. I've made arrangements to be picked up at the club when I'm finished there.'

'You had this set up before you got home last night.'

'Hmmm.' He moved to her closet, found the gray vest that matched her trousers. If she'd thought to look for it herself, it would have taken her an hour not to find it. 'It's cool out this morning,' he said as he handed it to her.

'You think you're slick, don't you?'

'Yes.' He bent down, kissed her, deftly did up the vest buttons for her. 'Ready?'

'You don't talk to the other cops,' Eve warned as they approached the club.

'What in the world would I have to say to them?' He continued to read and respond to overnight correspondence on his PPC while she pulled to the curb.

'You don't go anywhere on scene unless you're accompanied by me, Peabody, or an officer I designate,' she continued. 'And you take nothing – that means nothing – off scene.'

'Are you interested in a small summer home in Juno, Alaska?' He glanced at her, met her narrowed eyes. 'No,

I see you're not. I don't believe I am, either. Ah, here we are.' He pocketed the miniunit. 'And we appear to be the first to arrive.'

'Roarke, no funny business.'

'Fortunately, I left my red rubber nose at the office.' He climbed out of the car. 'Shall I open it for you?' He gestured at the police seal on the club's entrance door.

'Don't start with me.' Struggling not to rise to the bait, she strode to the door, uncoded the seal. 'If you screw around, I promise I'm calling a couple of big, burly uniforms and having them remove you from the scene.'

'But darling, it's so much more arousing when the police brutality comes from you.'

'Keep it up, smart guy.' She shoved open the door. The light was dim through the windows, and she could still smell the unpleasant aroma of spilled liquor and stale blood that mixed with the chemical stench of sweeper dust.

'Lights on,' she ordered. 'Main bar area.'

Those that were still operational brightened and cast a cool white light over the destruction.

'Doesn't look any better today, does it?' Roarke scanned the room, felt the little stir of temper.

'Close the door.' She said it quietly, took a breath, and did what she did best. She put herself in the middle of murder.

'He comes in, after closing. He's been here before. He has to know the place, the setup, the security. Maybe he worked here, but if he did, and was last night, he left with everyone else. Nobody's going to tag him as being alone here with Kohli.'

She moved around and through the debris, toward the bar. 'He sits down, asks for a drink. Friendly, casual. They've got business to discuss, something to talk over. That needs privacy.'

'Why doesn't he have Kohli disarm the security cameras?' Roarke asked.

'He's not worried about the cameras. He's going to take

51

care of them. After. Just a friendly after-hours drink, a little conversation. Nothing that's going to set off Kohli's cop vibes. If he had any. Kohli gets himself a beer, stays behind the bar. He's comfortable. Eats some nuts. He knows this guy. They've probably had a drink together before.'

She glanced up, checking out the locations of the cameras. 'Kohli's not worried about the security cams either. So either they're not talking about anything that's going to jam him, or he has turned them off. All the while, this guy's sitting here thinking about how to make his move. He comes behind the bar, helps himself to a drink this time.'

She walked behind the bar, seeing it in her head. Kohli, big, strong and alive, wearing his Purgatory uniform. Black shirt, black slacks. Sipping at a beer, popping some bar nuts.

'The blood's pounding in his head, and his heart's thumping like a drum, but he doesn't let it show. Maybe he makes a joke, asks Kohli to get something. Just enough to make him turn his back for an instant. Long enough for him to grab the bat and swing.'

A second, she thought, no more. No more than that to close a hand around the bat, jerk it free. Swing.

'The first crack of it sings up his arms, right into the shoulders. Blood sprays, and Kohli's face smashes into the glass. Bottles crash, and it's like an explosion.

'An explosion,' she repeated, with her eyes slitted, flat. 'That screams in his head. It makes his blood swim, pump, boosts the adrenaline. He turned the corner now, no going back. He swings the second time, into the face. It's good to see Kohli's face, the pain and the shock in it when he takes him out. The third swing does the job, cracks his head wide open. Blood and brains. But it's not enough.'

She lifted her hands, fisted them one over the other like a batter waiting for a clutch pitch. 'He wants to obliterate. He strikes again and again, and the sound of snaps and crunches when bones go is like music. Raging through him. He tastes blood. His breath's whistling. When he pulls himself back, pulls back just enough to think again, he gets Kohli's shield out of the pocket, tosses it down in the blood. That means something, blood on the shield, then he rolls the body on top of it.'

She stopped a moment, thinking. 'He's covered with blood. His hands, his clothes, his shoes. But there aren't any signs of it in the rest of the club. He changed. He had the sense to clean up first. The sweepers found traces of Kohli's blood, skin, brain matter in the drain of the bar sink.'

She turned, looking at the bowl, covered with powder now, under the bar. 'He washed up right here, with the body behind him. Cold. Stone cold. Then he took care of business, went around smashing everything. Made a real party out of it. Celebrate. But he's still got his wits. He tosses the bat with Kohli behind the bar. Here's what I've done, and here's how I did it. Then he takes the security discs and walks away.'

'Do you know what it takes to put that kind of image inside your own head, Lieutenant? Courage. An amazing level of courage.'

'I'm just doing what has to be done.'

'No.' Roarke laid a hand over hers, found it cold. 'You do a great deal more.'

'Don't sidetrack me.' She drew away because she *was* cold, and faintly embarrassed. 'Anyway, it's just a theory.'

'A damn good one. You made me see it. Blood on the shield. If you're right about that meaning something, he was probably killed because he was a cop.'

'Yeah. That's what I keep circling back to.'

She glanced over as the door opened. She recognized Mills right away, though he was bigger than she'd assumed, and most of the big had run to fat.

Didn't take advantage of the department's physical fitness program, she thought, or the break they were given on body sculpting.

53

The woman beside him was small and lean, built for action. Her skin had the olive cast that always made Eve think of sun-baked countries. Her hair was black and glossy and tamed back into a long sleek tail. Her eyes were nearly as dark and seemed to snap with vibrancy.

Beside her, Mills looked like an overfed, sloppy mongrel.

'Word came down it was bad.' Martinez's voice was clipped and faintly exotic. 'But it's worse.' Her eyes skimmed over Roarke, lingered an instant, then locked on Eve. 'You'd be Lieutenant Dallas.'

'That's right.' Eve moved back across the room. 'Thanks for coming down. The civilian's the property owner.'

With barely a nod in acknowledgement, Mills lumbered to the bar. He moved like a bear. An overfed one. 'Bought it back here, huh? Shitty way to die.'

'Most ways are crap.' Martinez turned to the door, fingers dancing a little too quickly for Eve's taste toward her side arm.

'My aide,' Eve said when Peabody stepped in. 'Officer Peabody, Detective Martinez and Lieutenant Mills.' With a slight shift of her body, she tapped a finger to her collar, then turned back to follow Martinez to the bar.

Recognizing the signal, Peabody clipped on her recorder and engaged.

'How long did you know Kohli?' Eve asked.

'Me, a couple of years. I transferred to the One two-eight from Brooklyn.' She looked down at the mess murder had left behind. 'The lieutenant knew him longer.'

'Yeah, since he came in rookie. Spit and polish and by the book. Did some military time and brought that with him. He was a one-shift wonder.'

'Give him a break, Mills,' Martinez muttered. 'We're standing in his goddamn blood here.'

'Hey, just saying it like it was. The guy did his shift, clocked out. Couldn't get an extra minute out of him without it being a direct order from the captain. But he did his job while he was on.'

'How'd he get picked for the Ricker team?'

'Martinez wanted him.' Mills shook his head at the mess behind the bar. 'Last cop I'd've figured for getting taken out. I'da made book he'd have done his twenty-five and spent his retirement building birdhouses or some shit.'

'I tagged him for the task force,' Martinez confirmed. She angled her body away from Mills in a way that told Eve the detective wanted distance from the lieutenant. Bad. 'I was head investigator under Lieutenant Mills. Kohli was a detail freak. He never missed a word. You had him on surveillance, you got a report that described everything he saw for four hours, down to the garbage in the gutter. He had good eyes.'

She frowned at the blood splatter. 'If you're thinking Ricker ordered a hit on him, I can't see it. Kohli was background, he was a drone on that investigation. He was in on the bust, but he didn't do anything but record the scene. I took Ricker down, for all the fucking good it did.'

'Kohli was the one with the details,' Eve said. 'Anyway, some of those details could've gotten through to Ricker, helped him slide?'

There was a long pause. Eve saw Martinez's eyes meet Mills's before they both turned toward her. 'I don't like what I'm hearing coming out of your mouth, Dallas.'

Mills's tone was a jagged threat, like rusted metal in a sweaty hand. Out of the corner of her eye, Eve saw Roarke shift, and damn it, Peabody as well. She took a step forward as if to shake off the guard dogs. 'What you're hearing coming out of my mouth is standard.'

'Yeah, for some half-ass or lowlife who ends up in a bag. It's not fucking standard for a cop. Kohli carried a badge same as you, same as me. Where do you come off saying he was dirty?'

'I didn't say he was.'

'Hell you didn't.' Mills jabbed a finger at her. 'You start heading down that road, Dallas, you won't get any help from me. This is why the case belongs in our house and not with some bitch down at Central.'

'The case is with some bitch down at Central, Mills. Live with it.' At her easy response, Eve thought she caught Martinez biting back a grin. 'The question has to be asked, I asked it. I still haven't heard the answer.'

'Fuck you. There's your answer.'

'Mills,' Martinez murmured. 'Take it down.'

'And fuck that, too.' He rounded on her. His fists were clenched, and the blood had surged to his face. 'Goddamn skirts don't belong on the job anyway. You go ahead and play with Whitney's pet cunt, Martinez, and see where it gets you. No cop turns on another, no matter what he was, and gets by me.'

With a last vicious look at Eve, he stalked out.

Martinez cleared her throat, scratched her head. 'The lieutenant has a problem working with women and minorities.'

'Is that so?'

'Yeah. So you shouldn't take it more personal than that. Look, the Ricker deal was mine, and Kohli was a straight arrow. That's one of the reasons I tagged him for some of the drone work. I don't like your question either, but I figure it's like you said. It had to be asked. Kohli may not have been one to go the extra mile, but he respected his badge. He liked being a cop, standing for the law and order thing. I can't see him going on the take, Lieutenant. Just doesn't fit.'

It depended, Eve thought, on where you put the pieces. 'What did Mills mean, no matter what he was.'

'On Kohli?' Her eyes sparkled with what might have been humor or temper. 'Meaning Kohli was black. Mills is of the opinion the only real cop is male and white and hetero. Personality-wise, Mills is pretty much a flaming asshole.'

Eve waited until Martinez left. 'You get all that, Peabody?'

'Yes, sir.'

'Record off. Make a copy for my file, keep the other under wraps. Walk Roarke through the place so he can get his damage report. You've got fifteen minutes,' she told him. 'Then you're out, and the place is sealed until I say different.'

'She's lovely when she's annoyed, isn't she, Peabody?'

'I've always thought so.'

'Fourteen minutes,' Eve warned. 'And counting.'

'Why don't we start at the top?' He offered Peabody his arm. 'And work our way down.'

When they were out of earshot, she pulled out her communicator and called Feeney in the Electronic Detective Division. 'I need a favor,' she said the minute his worn and weary face floated on-screen.

'If it ties to the cop killing, we won't count it. Every man in my until'll put in whatever time you need on it. Son of a bitch thinks he can get off with doing a cop like that, he's gonna find out different, and the hard way.'

Eve waited until he'd run down. 'Switch this transmission to privacy mode, would you?'

Feeney frowned but made the switch and slipped on his headset. 'What's the deal?'

'You're not going to like it. Let's clear that up front so you don't have to give me grief on it. I need you to run two cops for me. Lieutenant Alan Mills and Detective Julianna Martinez, both in Illegals out of the One twenty-eight.'

'I don't like it.'

'I need a quiet run, Feeney. I don't want any flags going up.'

His already mournful face dropped into sags. 'I especially don't like it.'

'I'm sorry to ask. I'd do it myself, but you can do it faster and quieter.' She glanced up to where Roarke and Peabody walked along the top level. 'I don't like it either, but I've got to open the door before I can close it.'

Though he was alone in his office, Feeney lowered his voice. 'You just looking, Dallas, or are you looking for dirt?'

'I can't fill you in now, but I've got too many connections to ignore. Do this for me, Feeney, and when it's done, let me know. We'll hook up somewhere, and I'll bring you up to date.'

'I know Mills. He's an asshole.'

'Yeah, I've had the pleasure.'

'But I can't see him dirty, Dallas.'

'That's the problem, isn't it? We never want to see it.'

She pocketed the communicator, righted a bar stool, and sat. In her notebook she began listing names, putting Kohli's in the center with arrows out to Ricker, connecting his with Mills and theirs with Martinez. She added Roth, curving a line to all, then in the bottom corner she added Webster. IAB.

She arrowed his to Kohli and wondered if she would be connecting him to anyone else before it was done.

Then, because it had to be done, she added Roarke, hooked him to Kohli and to Ricker. And hoped to God that would be the end of it.

Death, she thought, left a picture, told a story, from both the victim's and the killer's point of view. The scene itself, the body, the method, time and place, what was left behind, what was taken away. They were all part of the story.

Illegals, she thought, continuing to scribble in her book. *Blood on the shield. Overkill. Strippers. Missing security discs. Vice. Sex? Money. Thirty credit chips.*

She continued to make notes, frown over them as Roarke and Peabody worked their way back to her. 'Why the credit chips?' she asked out loud. 'Because he died for money? Not to make it look like a robbery. Another symbol? Blood money. Why thirty chips?'

'Thirty pieces of silver,' Roarke said, watching Eve's

blank stare. 'Your state education, Lieutenant, wouldn't have included Bible study. Judas was paid thirty pieces of silver for betraying Christ.'

'Thirty pieces of silver.' It clicked with her, and she nodded as she pushed to her feet. 'We can figure Kohli stands for Judas. But who's standing as Jesus?' She scanned the scene one last time. 'Time's up,' she told Roarke. 'You'll want to call your ride.'

'He'll be outside by now.' Roarke opened the door himself, holding it. As Eve moved by him, he caught her, yanked her against him and closed his mouth warmly over hers. 'Thank you for your cooperation, Lieutenant.'

'Oh man, he can really kiss.' Peabody all but sang it as Roarke strolled to the limo waiting at the curb. 'You can tell, just by watching him do it, he's a seriously excellent kisser.'

'Just stop imagining he was kissing you.'

'I can't.' Peabody rubbed her lips together as Eve resealed the door. 'And I can tell you, that one's going to get me through the day and into the night.'

'You've got your own men now.'

'Not the same.' Peabody sighed as she trudged to Eve's car. 'Just nowhere near the same. Where are we going?'

'To see a stripper.'

'Tell me it's a male stripper and my day is made.'

'You're doomed to disappointment.'

Nancie lived in an attractive prewar building on Lexington. There were window boxes spilling with flowers on several of the upper levels, and a cheerful-faced uniformed doorman gave Eve a dazzling grin when she held up her badge.

'I hope there's no trouble, Lieutenant Dallas, ma'am. If there's anything I can do, you just let me know.'

'Thanks, I think we can handle it.'

'I bet he makes tons in tips,' Peabody commented as they

entered the small, dignified lobby. 'Great smile, nice butt. What else could you ask for in a doorman?'

She studied the lobby with its discreet name plaques, polished brass elevator, and attractive arrangement of spring flowers. 'I never figured a place like this for a nude dancer. It's more like what you'd think of for upper-level office drones and junior execs. I wonder what she makes a year.'

'Thinking of switching professions?'

'Yeah, right.' Peabody snorted as they stepped onto the elevator. 'Guys are lining up to see me naked. Though McNab—'

'Don't go there. I just can't take it.' Eve hurried off the elevator on six, made a beeline for apartment C. She was relieved when the door opened promptly and cut off any idea Peabody might have harbored about finishing the statement.

'Nancie Gaynor?'

'Yes.'

'Lieutenant Dallas, NYPSD. Can we come in and speak with you?'

'Oh, sure. This is about Taj.'

Nancie fit the image of the apartment. Tidy, attractive and pretty as a sunbeam. She was young, midtwenties by Eve's estimation, and cute as a damn button with a curling mop of golden hair, doll-baby lips painted rosy pink, and huge green eyes. The buttercup-yellow skin suit she wore showed off her talent and still managed to look sweet.

She stepped back into the room on bare feet, leaving a faint trace of lilies in the air.

'I'm just sick about it,' she began. 'Just sick. Rue called us all yesterday to tell us.' Those big eyes filled, swam like irrigated green fields. 'I just can't believe something like this could happen at Purgatory.'

She made a helpless gesture toward a long, curving sofa covered in velvety pink fabric and an avalanche of shimmering pillows. 'I guess we'd better sit down. Should I get you something, like to drink?'

'No, don't bother. Do you mind if we record this conversation, Miss Gaynor?'

'Oh. Oh. Golly.' Nancie bit her pretty bottom lip, clasped her hands together between her truly spectacular breasts. 'I guess not. Are you supposed to?'

'With your permission.' *A stripper who said golly*, was all Eve could think. *Just when you'd thought you'd seen it all.*

'Okay, gee. I want to help if I can. But we can sit down, right? Because I guess I'm a little nervous. I've never been involved in a murder case. I was questioned once, right after I moved here from Utumwa, because my roommate, she was an LC, and she'd let her license lapse, but I'm sure it was just an oversight. Anyway, I talked to the officer in charge of the licensing committee and all. But that was different.'

Eve just blinked. 'Utumwa?'

'Iowa. I moved here from Iowa four years ago. I was hoping maybe to be a dancer on Broadway.' She smiled a little. 'I guess girls move here thinking stuff like that all the time. I'm really a pretty good dancer, but well, so are a lot of other girls, and it can be pretty expensive to live here, so I took a job in a club. It wasn't a very nice club,' she confided, blinking those big eyes. 'And I was getting pretty scared and discouraged and thinking maybe I should just go back to Iowa and marry Joey, but he's sort of a cluck, you know, and then Rue came in to catch my act and got me a job at this better club. It was nice, and the pay was much better, and the customers didn't paw at you. Then when Rue went to Purgatory, she took some of us with her. That's a really classy club. I just want you to know that. Nothing hinky-dink goes on there.'

'Hinky-dink,' Eve repeated, slightly dazed by the tumble of words and information. 'I appreciate you telling me all that.'

'Oh, I want to help.' Nancie leaned forward, leading with her eyes. 'Rue said if any of us knew anything, we should contact you. Lieutenant Eve Dallas. And that we should answer all your questions and do whatever we could, because, well, it's the right thing and you're married to Roarke. He owns Purgatory.'

'I heard that somewhere.'

'Oh gee, I'd answer the questions even if you weren't married to Roarke. I mean, it's my civic duty and all, and Taj was a really nice guy. He respected your privacy, you know? Even in a classy club, some of the staff can take peeks when they're not supposed to. But you could walk right in front of Taj naked as a jay, and he never looked. I mean he looked because you were right there, but he never *looked*. He had a wife and kids, and was a real family man.'

How did you shut this one off? Eve wondered. 'Miss Gaynor—'

'Oh, you can call me Nancie.'

'Fine, Nancie, you were working last night. Was a dancer named Mitzie also on?'

'Sure. We work pretty much the same schedule. Mitzie left kind of early last night. She was blue, you know, because that asshole – excuse my French – of a boyfriend dumped her for some sky waitress. She kept breaking down and crying in the dressing room because like, well, he was the love of her life and all and was going to marry her and buy a house in Queens. I think, or maybe it was Brooklyn, and then—'

'Miss Gaynor.'

'I guess that doesn't matter, huh?' she said with a cheery smile. 'Anyway, Rue took her home. Rue's really good at taking care of us dancers. She used to be one. Maybe I should call Mitzie and see how she's doing.'

'I'm sure she'd appreciate that.' A tangle of information it might have been, Eve thought, but it corroborated Rue MacLean's alibi. 'Why don't you tell me about the last time you saw Taj.'

'Okay.' Nancie sat back, wiggled her butt into the cushions, and folded her hands, tidy as a schoolgirl, in her lap. 'I had two shows that night, plus the two group dances, and three private performances, so I was kind of busy. On my first break, I saw Taj eating a chicken sandwich. I said, "Hey, Taj, that looks good enough to eat." You know, like a joke, because you make a sandwich *to* eat it.'

'Ha,' Eve managed.

'So he laughed a little and said that it was, and that his wife had made it for him. I got a soda pop, a Cherry Fizz, and said how I'd see him later because I had to go change costumes.'

'Did you talk about anything else?'

'No, just his chicken sandwich. Then I went back to change, and the dressing room was a real zoo. One of the girls, that's Dottie, couldn't find her red wig, and like I told you, Mitzie—'

'Yes, we covered Mitzie.'

'Uh-huh. One of the other girls, I think it was Charmaine, was telling Mitzie how she should say good riddance, which only made Mitzie cry harder, so Wilhimena, who used to be a guy but opted for the sex change, told her to shut up. Charmaine, I mean, not Mitzie. And everybody was running around because we had a group dance coming up. So we did that, the group dance, then I had a private. I saw Taj working the bar, and I waved.'

Her ears were going to start ringing in a minute. Eve was sure of it. 'Was he talking to anyone in particular?'

'Not that I noticed. He had a way of working the bar so everybody had their drink and didn't get all huffy. So I did the private for this businessman from Toledo. He said it was his birthday, but sometimes they say stuff like that so you'll do extra, but Rue doesn't want any of the dancers doing extra unless they're licensed. He gave me a hundred tip anyway, then I had a turn in the spinner, that's the level that revolves. I don't really remember seeing Taj again till closing because we were pretty packed. I wanted another Cherry Fizz, and he got me one, and I sat at the bar for a little while after the place cleared out, just unwinding, sort of.'

She sucked in a breath, Eve opened her mouth. But Nancie recovered first. 'Oh, and Viney was sick. Um, Nester Vine. We girls call him Viney 'cause he's long and skinny. Isn't it funny how sometimes people look just like their names? Anyway, he was all pale and sweaty and kept going back to the john until Taj told him to go home and take care of himself. I was feeling a little blue because I heard how Joey got engaged to Barbie Thomas back home.'

'In Utumwa.'

'Right. She was always chasing after him.' Nancie frowned over it, then appeared to let it go. 'So Taj was being sweet and telling me not to fret over that. How I was a pretty young girl and would find the right man when the time came. He said how when you found the right person, that was just it, and you didn't even have to wonder about it. I'd just know. I could tell he was thinking about his wife, because he always got this soft look in his eyes when he thought about her. It made me feel good, so I stayed a little longer. Viney should have been there to close up with him, but he was sick. Did I tell you that?'

'Yes,' Eve said, a little dizzy. 'You did.'

'Okay, he was sick, like I said. We aren't *really* supposed to close up alone, but sometimes we do. Taj said to me how it was getting late, and I should go on home. He said he'd call me a cab, but I was going to take the subway. He wouldn't let me, because the streets can be dangerous at night, so I called a cab, and he waited at the door until I got in it. That was like him,' she said, and her eyes went damp again. 'He was sweet that way.'

'Did he tell you anything about expecting a friend to come by that night?'

'I don't think . . .' She trailed off, pursed her lips. 'Maybe. Maybe he did, when I was crying the blues a little over Joey, and missing my friends from home, I think he said something about how friends were always friends. I think maybe he said he was looking forward to seeing a friend later. But I didn't take it to mean that night, at the club. Anyway.' She sighed, dabbed under her eyes with a fingertip. 'A friend didn't hurt Taj that way. Friends don't do that.'

It depends, Eve thought. *It very much depends on the friend.*

Chapter Five

Eve calculated she could spend the next three days interviewing strippers, table dancers, customers, and club crawlers, or she could zero in on Max Ricker.

It wasn't a tough choice, but both areas had to be covered.

She walked into the detectives' squad room, scanned faces. Some cops worked the 'links, others wrote reports or studied data. A team was taking a statement from a civilian who appeared to be more excited than distressed. The scent of bad coffee and aging disinfectant stung the air.

She knew these cops. Some were sharper than others, but all of them did the job. Pulling rank here had never been her style, and she thought she could get what she wanted without resorting to it now.

She waited until the civilian, looking flushed and pleased with himself, left the bullpen.

'Okay, listen up.'

A dozen faces turned in her direction. She watched expressions shift. Every one of them knew the case in her hands. No, she thought when 'links were disengaged and screens ignored. She wouldn't have to pull rank.

'I've got over six hundred potential witnesses to either eliminate or interview in the matter of Detective Taj Kohli. I could use some help. Those of you who aren't on priority cases or who can see their way clear to put in a couple of extra hours over the next few days can see either me or Peabody.'

Baxter was the first to get to his feet. He was an occasional pain in the ass, Eve thought, but Christ, he was dependable as sunrise.

'I got time. We all got time.' He glanced around the room himself as if daring anyone to disagree.

'Good.' Even slipped her hands in her pockets. 'To give you an update on the investigation . . .' And here she had to step carefully. 'Detective Kohli was bludgeoned to death while moonlighting in a high-class strip club called Purgatory. The club was closed, and it appears Kohli knew his attacker. I'm looking for someone he knew well enough to be alone with, to turn his back on.'

Someone, she thought, *who was contacted by him or contacted him on his personal palm-link during his shift. That's why the killer removed it from the scene.*

'At this point, it doesn't appear that Kohli was working on a sensitive case or pursuing information regarding one. But it's possible the killer was a weasel or outside informant. Robbery isn't a motive that holds. This was personal,' she added, watching faces. 'A personal attack on the badge. The One twenty-eight thinks the investigation belongs with them. I say it stays here.'

'Damn right it stays here.' A detective named Carmichael lifted her coffee mug, scowled into it.

'The media's leaving this alone so far,' Eve continued. 'It's not a hot story. A bartender doesn't boost ratings, and the fact that he was a cop doesn't make much of a ripple on-screen. He doesn't matter to them.'

She waited, scanned faces. 'But he matters here. Any of you who want in can let Peabody know how many witnesses you feel you can handle. She'll assign. Copy all statements and reports to me.'

'Hey, Dallas, can I have the strippers?' Baxter teased. 'Just the well-stacked ones?'

'Sure, Baxter. We all know the only way you're going to

see a woman naked is if she's paid for it.' There was a chorus of snorts and whoops. 'I'll be in the field most of the day. Anyone pulls anything I need to know, tag me.'

As she headed toward her office, Peabody hurried after her. 'You're going in the field alone.'

'I need you here, coordinating the witness assignments.'

'Yeah, but—'

'Peabody, up until last year, I did most of my field work solo.' As she shoved back her desk chair to sit, she caught the gleam of hurt in Peabody's eyes. Nearly rolled her own. 'That doesn't mean you haven't aced the job, Peabody. Get a hold of yourself. I need you here right now, running this and scanning data. You're better at the tech stuff than I am.'

That appeared to brighten Peabody again. 'Yeah, I am. But I could hook up with you when I'm clear here.'

'I'll let you know. Why don't you get started while everyone's in the mood to put in extra time?' In dismissal, Eve turned to her desk unit. 'Let's get moving.'

'Yes, sir.'

Eve waited until Peabody left, then got up to close the door. Back at her desk she called up all known data on Max Ricker.

She didn't want any surprises.

She'd seen his picture before, but she studied it more carefully now. He had a powerful look, a strongly carved face with prominent planes that looked glass sharp. His mouth was hard, with the silver brush of a mustache doing nothing to soften it. His eyes were silver as well, opaque and unreadable.

The vanity Roarke had spoken of showed in the waving mane of dark hair tipped with silver wings, in the single diamond stud he wore in his right ear, and in the smooth polish of his white, white skin that showed neither line nor fold but looked as if it had been stretched taut as bleached silk over those ice-edged bones.

Subject Ricker, Max Edward. Height, six feet, one inch.

68

Weight two hundred two pounds. Caucasian. DOB 3 February 2000. Born Philadelphia, Pennsylvania. Parents Leon and Michelle Ricker, deceased. One sibling, deceased.

Educated University of Pennsylvania with degree in business.

No marriages or legal cohabitations. One son, Alex, DOB 26 June 2028. Mother listed as Morandi, Ellen Mary. Deceased.

Current residences include Hartford, Connecticut, Sarasota, Florida, Florence, Italy, London, England, Long Neck Estates on Yost Colony and Nile River Hotel on Vegas II.

Profession listed as entrepreneur with interests and holdings as follows . . .

Eve sat back now, closed her eyes, and listened to the rundown of Ricker's businesses. There had been another time she'd done a run on a man who had extensive and varied interests, who'd owned strings of companies and organizations. Who'd looked, as Ricker did, dangerous.

That run had changed her life.

She intended for this one to change Ricker's.

'Computer, list criminal record, all arrests and charges.'

Working . . .

She sat up again when the data began to roll, and her eyebrows lifted. There were a number of charges over the years, beginning with petty larceny in 2016, continuing with gun running, illegals distribution, fraud, bribery, and two conspiracies to commit murder. None of it had stuck, he'd slipped and slithered through, but his sheet was long and varied.

'Not as clever as Roarke, are you?' she murmured. 'He never got caught. There's the arrogance. You don't mind getting caught, not really.' She studied his face again. 'Because it gives you a kick to fuck the system. That's a weakness, Ricker. A big one. Computer, copy all data to disc.'

She turned to her 'link. It was time to find out just where Ricker was currently cooling his well-shod heels.

*

She considered it good luck that Ricker was spending some time in his Connecticut compound. She considered it his arrogance that he'd agreed to meet with her without making her dance through a sea of attorneys.

She made the drive in good time and was met at the gate by a trio of hatchet-faced guards who put her through an ID scan for form's sake. She was instructed to leave her vehicle just inside the gates and get into a small, sleek cart.

Its operator was an equally small and sleek female droid who drove her along the winding, tree-lined path to a sprawling three-story house of wood and glass that perched on a rocky slope over a restless sea.

There was a fountain at the entrance where a stone woman draped in a flowing gown gracefully poured pale blue water from a pitcher into a pool teeming with red fish. A gardener worked a plot of flowers at the east side of the house.

He wore baggy gray pants and shirt, a wide-brimmed hat, and a double-scoped distance laser.

Another female droid met her at the door, this one a comfortably built serving model in a starched black uniform. Her smile was welcoming, her voice warm.

'Good day, Lieutenant Dallas. Mr Ricker is expecting you. I hope you had a pleasant trip. If you'd follow me, please.'

Eve studied the house as they walked through. Here, the money all but dripped. It didn't have the class of Roarke's place where the mood was rich but somehow homey, with its polished woods and muted colors. Ricker went for the modern and the garish, surrounding himself with eye-searing colors, too much fabric, and not enough taste.

Everything was sharp-edged and accented by what she now concluded was his signature silver.

Thirty pieces of silver, she thought as she stepped into a room done in bloodred with a breathless view of the sea through the window-wall. The other walls were jammed with art, all of it modernistic or surreal or whatever the hell they called stuff that was nothing more than slashes of paint on canvas and pulsing slides of ugly colors on glass.

The scent of flowers was heavy here, and funereal, the light overbright, and the furniture all sliding, sinuous curves with glimmering cushions and silver limbs.

Ricker sat in one of the chairs, sipping something violently pink out of a long, slim tube. He got graciously to his feet, smiled.

'Ah, Eve Dallas. We meet at last. Welcome to my humble home. What can we offer you in the way of refreshment?'

'Nothing.'

'Oh, well, you've only to ask if you change your mind.' There was a roundness to his voice, something that reminded her of the dialogue in some of the old black-and-white videos Roarke liked to watch. 'That will be all, Marta.'

'Yes, Mr Ricker.' She backed out of the room, closing the doors behind her.

'Eve Dallas,' he said again, eyes sparkling as he gestured to a chair. 'This is absolutely delightful. May I call you Eve?'

'No.'

The sparkle turned cold, silver sleet now, even as he let out a hearty laugh. 'Pity. Lieutenant, then. Won't you sit down? I have to admit to some curiosity about the woman who married one of my old . . . I was going to say protégés,' he said as he sat again. 'But I'm sure Roarke would object to the term. So I'll say one of my former associates. I had hoped he would accompany you today.'

'He has no business here, or with you.'

'Not at the moment. Please sit. Be comfortable.'

Comfort wasn't one of the options in the ugly chair, but she sat.

'How attractive you are.' He spoke smoothly while his gaze crawled over her.

Men who looked at a woman in just that way wanted her

to feel sexually vulnerable, physically uneasy. Eve only felt mildly insulted.

'In a competent, unpretentious sort of fashion,' Ricker finished. 'Not what one expected of Roarke, of course. His taste always ran to the more stylish, more obviously female.' He drummed his fingers on the arm of his chair, and she noted he had his nails painted in his signature color. And the tips were filed to vicious little points.

'But how clever of him to have selected you, a woman of your more subtle attributes and profession. It must be very convenient for him to have such an intimate ally on the police force.'

It was meant to get a rise out of her, so she only angled her head. 'Really? And why would that be convenient for him, Mr Ricker?'

'Given his interests.' Ricker sipped his drink. 'Business interests.'

'And does his business concern you, Mr Ricker?'

'Only in an academic sense, as we were once connected. So to speak.'

She leaned forward. 'Would you like to speak, on record, about your connections?'

His eyes narrowed, snakelike. 'Would you risk him, Lieutenant?'

'Roarke can take care of himself. Can you?'

'Have you tamed him, Lieutenant? Neutered the wolf and made him a lapdog?'

This time she laughed, and meant it. 'The lapdog would rip out your throat without breathing hard. And you know it. I had no idea you were so afraid of him. That's interesting.'

'You're mistaken.' But his fingers had tightened on the tube.

She watched his throat work, as if he were struggling to swallow something particularly vile.

'I don't think so. But Roarke isn't the reason I'm here. It's your business I'd like to discuss, Mr Ricker.' She took out her recorder. 'With your permission.'

His lips curved, a hard line under that brush of silver that was nothing like a smile. 'Of course.' And he tapped a finger on the arm of his chair. Across the room a hologram swam into view. Six dark-suited men sat side by side at a long table, hands folded, eyes sharp.

'My attorneys,' he explained.

Eve set the recorder on the silver table between them, read off the necessary data, and recited the revised Miranda.

'You're thorough. Roarke would appreciate that. As do I.'

'You understand your rights and obligations, Mr Ricker?'

'I do indeed.'

'And you have engaged your right to have your attorneys – all six of them – present at this informal interview. You were arrested six months ago for . . .' She held up a hand, and though she knew the charges by rote, took out her memo book and read them off precisely. 'The manufacture, possession, and distribution of illegal substances including hallucinogens and known addictives, the international and interplanetary transportation of illegal substances, possession of banned weapons, the operation of chemical plants without a license, the—'

'Lieutenant, to save us both valuable time, I will state that I was aware of all charges levied against me at the time of my unfortunate arrest last fall. As I'm sure you are aware that most of those ridiculous charges were subsequently dropped, and those that were not resulted in a trial in which I was acquitted.'

'I'm aware that your attorneys and the prosecuting attorney of New York negotiated a deal in which several of the more minor charges against you were dropped. In return, the names of four arms and illegals dealers and information

73

against them were given to the PA's office through your representative. You're not overly loyal to your associates, Mr Ricker.'

'On the contrary, I'm exceedingly loyal to them. I have no associates who are arms and/or illegal dealers, Lieutenant. I'm a businessman, one who makes considerable donations to charitable and political causes every year.'

'Yes, I know about your political donations. You gave generously to an organization known as Cassandra.'

'I did.' He lifted a hand as one of his attorneys started to speak. 'And was shocked, shocked to the bone, when I discovered their terrorist activities. You did the world a great service, Lieutenant, by breaking open that ugly sphere, by destroying it. Until the story came out in the media, I had been deluded into believing the Cassandra group was dedicated to insuring the safety and rights of the American public; yes, through paramilitary means. But legal ones.'

'A pity you didn't research Cassandra more closely, Mr Ricker, as I would assume someone with your resources would do before he tossed in more than ten million of his hard-earned dollars.'

'A mistake I deeply regret. The employee who oversaw the donations has since been terminated.'

'I see. You were scheduled for trial on several of the charges, not within the scope of the deal with the prosecutor's office. However, evidence went missing, and certain data from the operation leading to and including the raid on the warehouse owned by you was damaged.'

'Is that the official word for it?' He tossed his head, causing his silver wings to flutter. 'The data was thin, incomplete, and ridiculously weighted with misinformation by the police in order to arrange for the attack on a warehouse which, though one of my properties, was run and operated by an independent contractor.'

His eyes began to gleam, she noted, his voice to rise, and

those lethally tipped fingers to beat a fast tattoo on the arm of the chair.

'The entire matter was nothing more than police harassment, and my attorneys are looking into a suit against the NYPSD as a result.'

'What is your connection with Detective Taj Kohli?'

'Kohli?' He continued to smile, the hard glitter bright in his eyes. 'I'm afraid that name doesn't ring a bell. I do have acquaintance with many in your profession, Lieutenant. I am a strong supporter of the men and women who serve. But that particular name . . . Wait, wait.'

He rubbed a finger against his lips, and damn him, she heard the light chuckle. 'Kohli, yes, of course. I heard about the tragedy. He was killed recently, wasn't he?'

'Kohli was on the task force that busted your New York warehouse and cost you several million dollars in goods.'

'Mr Ricker was never legally connected to the warehouse, labs, or distribution center in New York City, which was discovered by and closed down by the New York City Police and Security Department. We object to the statement claiming otherwise being read into this record.'

The lawyer's voice droned, but neither Ricker nor Eve bothered to glance in his direction.

'It's most unfortunate that your Detective Kohli was killed, Lieutenant. Am I to be questioned every time a police officer meets a tragic end? It could be construed as additional harassment.'

'No, it couldn't, as the request for this interview was granted without condition.' Now she smiled. 'I'm sure your fleet of lawyers will verify that. Kohli worked details, Mr Ricker. He was good at details. As a businessman, and man of the world, I'm sure you'll agree that the truth is in them – and the truth has a way of surfacing, no matter how deep it's buried. It just takes the right person to dig it out. I have a real fondness for the truth and a serious objection to having a low officer executed. So finding that truth, and finding the person who killed Kohli – or arranged for it – is going to be a personal mission of mine.'

'I'm sure it offends you to have had your colleague murdered, and brutally, in an establishment owned by your husband.' Excitement jangled in his voice, just a little off-key. 'Sticky, isn't it, Lieutenant? For both of you. Is that why you're troubling me with veiled accusations rather than calling your own husband into Interview?'

'I didn't say the murder was brutal or that it took place in an establishment owned by Roarke. How did you come by that information, Mr Ricker?'

For the first time, he appeared flustered, his stare going blank, his mouth drooping. All six lawyers began talking at once, a buzz of noise that was no more than cover and wasted air. It gave Ricker time to compose himself.

'I make it my business to know things, Lieutenant. My business. I was informed that there was an incident at one of your husband's properties.'

'Informed by who?'

'Another associate, I believe.' He waved a hand idly, but it curled into a fist before it rested on the arm of the chair again. 'I can't recall. Is it against the law to have that information? I collect information. A kind of hobby. Information on people who interest me. Such as yourself. I'm aware, you see, that you were raised by the state, found in considerable distress when you were but a child of eight.'

His hand uncurled as he spoke, but his eyes grew brighter. Hungrier, Eve thought. Like a man anticipating a particularly fine meal.

'Raped, weren't you, and quite violently. It must be difficult to live with a trauma such as that, to reconcile yourself to such viciously stolen innocence. You don't even have your own name, do you, but one given to you by a harried social worker. Eve, a rather sentimental choice, indicating the first

76

woman. And Dallas, a practical one, reflecting the city where you were discovered, broken, bruised, and all but mute in a filthy alley.'

It did the job. It took her back, slicked her insides with illness, chilled her bones. But she never took her eyes off his face. Never flinched. 'We play the cards we were dealt. I collect information, too. Mostly on people who disturb my sense of style. Dig up all the data you want on me, Ricker. It'll only help you get a good, clear picture of just who you're up against this time. Kohli's mine now, and I'll find the who and why and how for him. Depend on it. Interview end,' she said, and picked up her recorder.

Even as his lawyers erupted with warnings and objections, Ricker clicked off the hologram. If possible, he was paler than he'd been when she'd come in. 'Be careful, Lieutenant. Those who threaten me meet unpleasant ends.'

'Look at my data again, Ricker, and you'll see the unpleasant doesn't worry me.'

He rose as she did, took a step forward in a way that had her bracing and hoping, hoping he'd lose control just for an instant. An instant would be long enough. 'You think you can pit yourself against me? You think your badge is power.' He snapped his fingers in front of her face. 'Like that, you can be gone and forgotten.'

'Try it. And see.'

Muscles worked in his face, but he drew himself back. 'Perhaps you believe, mistakenly, that your connection to Roarke will protect you. He's weak, gone soft and sentimental, and over a cop. I had plans for him once. I have different ones now.'

'You'd better take a closer look at your data, Ricker, and you'll see I don't and never have needed anyone to protect me. But I'll tell you this: Roarke's going to get a real kick out of knowing just how much you fear him. We'll have a good laugh over it, over you, later.'

When she turned, he grabbed her arm. Her heart leapt in anticipation as she looked up coolly. 'Oh, please do,' she murmured.

His fingers dug in once, viciously, the nails drilling into her flesh before they released. Control? she thought. No, he wasn't nearly as controlled as he believed he was.

'I'll show you out.'

'I know the way. You'd better get to work, Ricker, make sure you've covered your tracks. I'm going to be turning up every rock you crawl under. I'm going to enjoy it.'

She strolled out, unsurprised to see the servant droid hovering close by and smiling homily. 'I hope you enjoyed your visit, Lieutenant Dallas. I'll see you to the door.'

As she walked away, Eve heard the unmistakable sound of glass smashing.

No, she thought and smiled herself. *Not nearly as controlled.*

She was taken back to her car and was watched carefully as she drove through the gates.

Ten minutes later, she spotted the first tail. They didn't even try to be subtle about it. She let them tag her, kept her speed just over the legal limit, and passed another twenty miles before the second car swung on from a ramp and pulled in front of her. Caged her in.

Let's play, she decided, and hit the accelerator.

She changed lanes, threaded through traffic, but didn't make it too hard for them. As she calculated the lay of the land, she made a call on her 'link. Almost casually.

With what she hoped looked like panic, she pulled off the freeway just over the New York line. 'I knew you wouldn't let me down,' she murmured as the cars closed in behind her. 'Morons.'

Satisfied the road was quiet enough, she punched the accelerator again, flew along. Then swung in a hard circle and drove headlong toward the pursuing cars. One veered right, one left, and at the speed they were traveling, they skidded off the road just as she hit her sirens.

She hopped out, weapon drawn.

'Police! Out! Everybody out, hands where I can see them.' She saw the passenger in the second car reach inside his jacket, and she shot a blast at the headlights.

Glass exploded even as the screams of other sirens joined hers.

'Get your asses out of those vehicles right now.' With her free hand, she whipped out her badge. 'NYPSD. You're under arrest.'

One of the drivers got out, looking cocky. But he kept his hands in sight as two black and whites pulled up behind. 'What's the charge?'

'Why don't we start with speeding and go from there.' She jerked a thumb. 'Hands on the roof. You know the position.'

The uniforms swarmed in like bees. 'Want them cuffed, Lieutenant?'

'Yeah, I think they were resisting. And would you look at this?' She stopped patting down the first driver and plucked out his side arm. 'Concealed weapon. Man, a banned weapon, too. Wow, you're in really big trouble.'

A quick search turned up more weapons, six ounces of Exotica, two of Zeus, a fancy set of burglary tools, and three short steel pipes, handy for spine cracking.

'Haul these losers into Central for me, will you?' she asked the uniforms. 'Book them on carrying concealed, possession of illegals, transporting banned weapons in a motor vehicle, and crossing state lines with same. Possession of suspicious merchandise.'

She grinned fiercely as she dusted off her hands. 'Oh, and don't forget speeding. Mr Ricker's going to be very unhappy with you boys. Very unhappy.'

She slid back into her car, rolled her shoulders.

Temper, temper, Ricker, she thought, and rubbed absently at the ache where his fingers had dug. *Never give orders when in emotional distress.*

Round one goes to me.

Chapter Six

Ian McNab tried to look casual as he wandered into the detectives' bullpen. It wasn't easy for a man sporting a waist-long braid and wearing orange flight pants to look casual, but he worked at it.

He had an excuse for being in that area. A few of the detectives had tossed run requests on the witnesses listed in the Kohli case over to EDD. That was McNab's story, and he was sticking to it.

He also had a reason for being in that area. And the reason was tucked into a skinny cubicle in the far corner, studiously doing tech work.

She looked so cute when she was studious. He was gone on her, all right. He wasn't particularly happy about it, as his plan had always been to scoop as many women into his life as humanly possible. He just plain loved women.

But then Peabody had marched into his life in her ugly cop shoes and spit-spot uniform, and that, as the historians say, was that.

She wasn't completely cooperating. Oh, he'd finally gotten her into bed – on the kitchen floor, in an elevator car, in an empty locker room – and anywhere else his fluid imagination could devise. But she wasn't moony over him.

He was forced to admit, though it grated daily, that he was well over that moon as regarded Officer Delia Peabody.

He squeezed into her cubicle, settled his skinny butt on the corner of her desk. 'Hey, She-Body. What's up?'

'What are you doing out of EDD?' She kept right on working, didn't even glance up. 'You break your chain again?'

'They don't lock us up in EDD like they do over here. How do you work in this cage?'

'Efficiently. Go away, McNab. I'm really swamped here.'

'The Kohli deal? It's all anybody can talk about. Poor son of a bitch.'

Because there was pity in his voice, she did glance up. And noted that his eyes, cool and green, weren't just sad. They were pissed. 'Yeah. Well, we'll get the slime who killed him. Dallas is working the angles.'

'Nobody does it better. Some of the guys here asked us to run some names. Everybody in EDD from Feeney down to the lowest drone's on it.'

She worked up a sneer. 'Why aren't you?'

'I was elected to swing over and see if I could wangle an update. Come on, Peabody, we're in it, too. Give me something to take back.'

'I don't have that much. Keep this part to yourself,' she said, lowering her voice and peeking through the narrow opening of her work space. 'I don't know what Dallas is up to. She went out in the field and didn't take me with her. Didn't tell me where she was going, either. Then a few minutes ago, I get a call from her. She's got uniforms bringing in four mopes, booking them on various charges, including carrying concealeds, and she wants me to run the names quick, fast, and now. She's on her way in.'

'What'd you find?'

'All four of them have been guests of various government facilities, mostly violent crimes. Assaults, assaults with deadlies. Spine-crackers and persuaders, from the sheets. But get this.'

She lowered her voice even more, so that McNab had to lean in, catch a teasing whiff of her shampoo. 'They're connected to Max Ricker.'

McNab opened his mouth, then sucked in the exclamation when Peabody hissed at him. 'You think Ricker's behind the Kohli deal?'

'I don't know, but I know Kohli was part of the team that busted him last fall, because Dallas had me get the case file and the trial transcript. I took a quick look, and Kohli was low level, didn't testify, either. Of course, the case was tossed out of court within three days. But Dallas has some reason for hauling in four of his goon squad.'

'This is good stuff.'

'You can pass on the mopes she's bringing in, but keep quiet about the Ricker connection until we've got more.'

'I could do that, but I want some incentive. How about you come by tonight?'

'I don't know what Dallas has planned.' He was grinning at her. For reasons Peabody couldn't figure, she was finding it harder and harder to resist that dopey grin. 'But I could probably swing by.'

'Speaking of swinging, when you get there, we could . . .' He started to lean closer, make a suggestion he thought would keep her revved through shift. Then he shot off the desk like a pebble from a sling. 'Jesus, it's the commander.'

'Chill down.' But Peabody came to attention herself.

It wasn't unprecedented for Whitney to make an appearance in the squad room. But he didn't make a habit of it, either.

'Oh man, he's coming over here.'

She saw it and had to resist the impulse to tug at her uniform jacket to make certain it was straight.

'Detective.' Whitney stopped, filled the entrance to the cubicle, and pinned McNab with dark, steely eyes. 'Have you transferred out of the Electronic Detective Division?'

'No, sir, Commander. EDD is working in conjunction with Homicide on the matter of Detective Taj Kohli. We're confident that this interdepartmental cooperation and effort will result in closing the case quickly.'

He was good, Peabody thought with annoyed admiration. Slick as cat spit.

'Then perhaps you should get back to your division and continue that cooperation, Detective, instead of disrupting this officer's work.'

But not, she thought, quite slick enough.

McNab nearly saluted but managed to restrain himself. Then vanished like smoke.

'Officer, do you have the data your lieutenant requested on the four individuals currently in booking?'

In booking? Already? Jeez. 'Yes, sir.'

'Hard copy,' he said and held out a hand.

Peabody ordered the printout. 'As ordered, Commander, I've sent copies of the data to Lieutenant Dallas's vehicle and office units.'

He merely grunted, then turned away already reading the data. He paused, glanced over as Eve walked in. 'Lieutenant, your office.'

Peabody winced at the tone. It was hard as granite. And courageously, she stepped out of her cubicle. She couldn't say she was disappointed when Eve signaled her back, then swung toward her office.

There was a fire being lighted, Peabody thought, but wasn't sure who was going to get burned.

'Sir.' Eve held the door open, waited for Whitney to pass through, then closed it behind them.

'Explain, Lieutenant, why you left the state, and your jurisdiction, interrogated Max Ricker without discussing your intentions or going through the chain of command?'

'Commander, as primary, I am not required to clear investigative interviews through any chain of command. And I am authorized to leave my jurisdiction to do so if the interview is pertinent to the case.'

'And to harass a civilian in another state?'

She felt the first sting of temper, ignored it. 'Harass, sir?'

84

'I received a call from Ricker's attorney, who has also contacted the Chief of Police, and who is threatening to sue you, this department, and the city of New York for harassing his client and for assaulting and detaining four of Ricker's employees.'

'Really? He's running scared all right,' she murmured. 'I didn't think I'd gotten to him that deep. Commander,' she said, bringing herself back. 'I contacted Ricker, requested an interview at his convenience, and was granted same.'

She pulled a sealed disc from a drawer. 'The request, made from this unit, and the agreement to said request, were recorded, as was my interview with Ricker, in his home where he was properly Mirandized in the presence of six of his attorneys by holograph.'

This time, she took a disc from her bag. 'Recorded, Commander, with his full knowledge. With respect, sir, he's pissing in the wind on this.'

'Good. I thought as much.' He took both discs. 'However, angling for Ricker on a cop killing is a dangerous and delicate matter. You'd better have a foundation you can stand on.'

'It's my job to pursue all possible leads. I'm doing my job.'

'And does your job include rousting four men on a public road, endangering their lives and the lives of innocent bystanders with reckless driving, and causing two vehicles to incur damage?'

Her training was too solid to permit her to snarl. But she thought about it. 'While in transit from Connecticut to New York City, I was tailed then pursued by two civilian vehicles containing two men each. While I took evasive maneuvers, said vehicles continued pursuit, exceeding the posted speed limits. Concerned at the possible danger to other civilians, I left the heavily traveled freeway for an empty stretch of road. At this time, the two pursuing vehicles further increased speed, shifting into a charge pattern. The vehicles crossed the state line. Unsure of their purpose, I called for backup, and rather than risk continuing a high-speed chase into a populated area, I engaged my sirens, executed a U-turn. As a result, the pursuing vehicles ran off the road.'

'Lieutenant—'

'Sir, I would like to complete my report of the incident.' Her temper might have been spiking, but her tone was very cool.

'Go ahead, Lieutenant. Complete your report.'

'I identified myself as a police officer, ordered them out of the vehicles. At this time one of the individuals made a suspicious move toward what I perceived, and later discovered was, in fact, a weapon. I fired a warning shot, which damaged a headlight. Two radio cars arrived as backup, and the four individuals were restrained. During the resulting search, which is permissible given the probable cause, banned weapons, two forms of illegals in small quantities, suspicious tools, and two weighted steel pipes were found to be in the individuals' possession or concealed in their vehicles. At this time, I requested that the uniformed officers transport the individuals to Central for booking on various charges, contacted my aide to execute a standard run on each man, and returned with the intention of writing my report and questioning the individuals I had so detained.'

Her voice remained flat, cool, and dead calm. She refused to allow any temper or triumph to glimmer in her eyes. Once again, she reached in her bag, took out two discs. 'All of the aforesaid was recorded, through my unit during the pursuit, and during the arrest by my collar clip. It is my opinion that proper procedure was followed as closely as possible.'

Whitney took the discs and allowed himself the tiniest of smiles as he pocketed them. 'Nice work. Damn nice work.'

She ordered herself to change gears, and change them smoothly. But her 'Thank you, sir' came out with a bite.

'Pissed off that I questioned you?' Whitney asked.

'Yes, sir. I am.'

'Can't blame you.' Idly, he tapped his fingers on the discs in his pocket, then wandered, as much as he was able, to her skinny window. 'I was confident you'd have covered yourself here, but not completely confident. Above that, you'll be hammered at by the lawyer, even with the record. I wanted to see how you'd hold up to it. You held, Dallas, as always.'

'I can handle myself with the lawyer.'

'No doubt.' Whitney drew a breath, studied the miserable view out her miserable window, and wondered how she stood working in that box of a room. 'Are you waiting for an apology, Lieutenant?'

'No. No, sir.'

'Good.' He turned back to her, his face closed and hard again. 'Command rarely apologizes. You followed procedure, and I'd expect no less. However, this doesn't negate the fact that by pulling Ricker into the case, you've put the department in a strained situation.'

'A dead cop makes a strained situation for me.'

'Don't second-guess me, Lieutenant,' he snapped. 'And don't underestimate my personal and departmental stand on the murder of Detective Kohli. If Ricker was involved in this, I want his ass more than you do. Yes, more,' he added. 'Now, tell me why, if he agreed to interview, he sent four assholes after you?'

'I got under his skin.'

'Specifics, Lieutenant.' Then he looked around. 'Where the hell do you *sit* in this hole?'

Saying nothing, she pulled out her creaky desk chair. He stared at it a moment, then in a gesture that popped the tension out of the room like a pin in a balloon, he threw back his head and roared.

'You think I don't know that's an insult? I put half my ass on that excuse for a chair, and I'm through it and on the floor. For Christ's sake, Dallas, you've got rank. You can have an office instead of this cave.'

'I like it here. You get something bigger, you end up putting more chairs in, maybe a table. Then people start dropping by. To chat.'

Whitney hissed through his teeth. 'Tell me. Let me have some of that coffee Roarke scores you.'

She moved to the AutoChef, programmed for two cups, hot, strong, and black. 'Commander, I'd like to speak off the record for a moment.'

'Give me that coffee, and you can speak any way you damn well want for the next hour. Jesus God, what a scent.'

She smiled to herself, remembering the first time she'd tasted Roarke's coffee. The real thing, not soy or any of that man-made bean crap. She should have known, then and there, he'd be it for her.

And because he was it for her, she turned with the coffee and put her faith in her commander. 'Roarke was connected to Ricker in some areas of business. Roarke ended the association more than ten years ago. Ricker hasn't forgotten it or forgiven it. He'd like to sting Roarke if he could, through me if it works that way. During the meet, I used Roarke to poke at him. It worked. He lost his cool a couple of times. I keep pressing that sore spot, he'll keep losing it.'

'How bad does he want Roarke?'

'Bad enough, I think, but he's scared of him. That scrapes at him more than anything, that underlying fear. Because, well, he doesn't see it as fear, but as intense loathing. He sent those morons after me because he wasn't thinking, he was reacting. He's too smart to order four piss-brains to hassle a cop, piss-brains that can be tracked back to him. But he lost control just long enough to send them out. He wanted me hurt because I sneered at him. Because I'm Roarke's cop, and I sneered at him.'

'You baited him. Consider this. He might have hurt you before you got clear of the house.'

'He wouldn't foul his own nest. It was a risk, but calculated.

If I can get one of those jerks to roll, we could bring Ricker in, put more pressure on him.'

'These types don't roll easy.'

'It wouldn't take much. I want Ricker inside. He skated on the illegals bust. He shouldn't have. I've studied the reports and transcripts. It looked like textbook, every angle covered. Then there were all these screw-ups. The mix in the chain of evidence, one of the primary witnesses disappearing when he was supposed to be under protection, some clerk in the PA's office misfiles a statement. Little holes make bigger holes, and he slides through.'

'I agree, and there's no one who'd like to nail Ricker more than I would. But his connection to Kohli is tenuous at best. I can't see your angle on it.'

'I'm working it' was all she would say. She thought of Webster, the hints, but she wasn't ready to talk about it.

'Dallas, Ricker can't be your personal vendetta.'

'He's not. Let me work it through, Commander.'

'It's your investigation. But watch your step. If Ricker was the trigger on Kohli, he won't hesitate to point at you. From what you've told me, he has more reason to.'

'I get in his face enough, he'll make a mistake. I won't make one.'

She went a round with the lawyers, one for each of the men she'd brought in. They were, she thought, slime in five-thousand-dollar suits. They knew every trick. But they were going to have a hard time weaseling around the fact she had everything on record.

'Records,' the head slime named Canarde said, with a lift of his perfectly manicured fingers, 'you alone had possession of. You have no corroboration that the discs were not manufactured or tampered with for the purpose of harassing my client.'

'What was your client doing riding my back bumper from Connecticut to New York?'

'It isn't against the law to drive a public road, Lieutenant.'

She simply flipped back, tapped her finger on the file. 'Carrying concealed and banned weapons.'

'My client claims you planted those weapons.'

Eve shifted her gaze toward the client, a man of about two hundred and fifty pounds with hands like hams and a face only a mother could love – if she were seriously nearsighted. As yet, he hadn't opened his mouth.

'I must've been pretty busy. So your client, who apparently has been struck mute, proports that I just happened to be carrying four self-charging hand lasers and a couple of long-scoped flame rifles in my police unit, with the hopes that some innocent civilian might come along and I could frame him. Seeing as, what, I didn't like his face?'

'My client has no knowledge of your motives.'

'Your client is a piece of shit who's been down this road before. Assault and battery, carrying concealeds, assault with a deadly, possession with intent. You're not standing for some choirboy, Canarde. With what we've got on him, he goes in, and he stays in. My best guess is twenty-five, hard time with no parole option, off-planet penal colony. Never been on an off-planet facility, have you, pal?'

Eve showed her teeth in a smile. 'They make the cages here look like suites at The Palace.'

'Police harassment and intimidation is expected,' Canarde said smoothly. 'My client has nothing more to say.'

'Yeah, he's been a real chatterbox up till now. You going to let Ricker make you the sacrificial lamb here? You think he's worried about the twenty-five you'll do in a cage?'

'Lieutenant Dallas,' Canarde interrupted, but Eve kept her eyes on the man, saw the faintest shadow of worry in his eyes.

'I don't want you, Lewis. You want to save yourself, you want to deal with me. Who sent you after me today? Say the name, and I cut you out of the herd.'

'This interview is over.' Canarde got to his feet.

'Is it over, Lewis? You want it over? You want to start your first night of twenty-five in a cage? Does he pay you enough, can anyone pay you enough to make you swallow sitting in a hole twenty hours every day for twenty-five years, with a slab for a bed, with security cams watching you piss in a steel toilet? No luxuries off-planet, Lewis. The idea isn't rehabilitation, no matter what the politicians say. It's punishment.'

'Be quiet, Mr Lewis. I have ended this interview, Lieutenant, and demand my client's right to a hearing.'

'Yeah, he'll get his hearing.' She rose. 'You're a sap, Lewis, if you think this mouth in a pricey suit's standing for you.'

'I got nothing to say. To cops or cunts.' Lewis looked up, sneered. But Eve saw the glitter of fear in his eyes.

'I guess that counts me out altogether.' Eve signaled to the guard. 'Take this sack of shit to his hole. Sleep tight, Lewis. I won't tell you to sleep, Canarde,' she said as she walked out. 'I hear sharks don't.'

She rounded the corner, slipped down a hall, and through a door where Whitney and Peabody stood in observation.

'The hearings are set for tomorrow. Starting at nine,' Whitney told her. 'Canarde and his team put on the pressure to get them in.'

'Fine, our boys'll still spend the night in a cell. I want to sweat Lewis again, before the hearing. We can push his hearing to the end of the group, give me some time with him tomorrow morning. He's the one who'll crack.'

'Agreed. You've never visited an off-planet rehabilitation center, have you, Lieutenant?'

'No, sir. But I've heard they're gutters.'

'Worse. Lewis will have heard, too. Keep playing that note. Go home,' he added. 'Get some sleep.'

'If I'd been in there,' Peabody said when they were alone,

'I'd've rolled over on my mother. Could he really cop twenty-five off-planet?'

'Oh yeah. You don't mess with a cop. The system frowns severely on it. He knows it, too. He's going to be thinking about it tonight. Thinking hard. I want you back here at six-thirty. I want to hit him again early. You can stand in, look mean and heartless.'

'I love doing that. Are you going home?' she asked, knowing how often her lieutenant sent her off and stayed on the job herself.

'Yeah. Yeah, I am. After rubbing shoulders with that bunch, I want a shower. Six-thirty, Peabody.'

'Yes, sir.'

She'd missed dinner and wasn't pleased to discover the candy thief who'd targeted her as patsy had found her newest stash. She had to settle for an apple someone had foolishly left in the squad's friggie.

Still, it filled the hole so that by the time she got home she was more interested in a long, hot shower than a meal. She was slightly disappointed that Summerset didn't slide into the foyer on her arrival so they could have their evening pissing match.

Shower first, she decided, jogging up the stairs. Then she'd track Roarke down. The shower would give her time to figure out just how much of her day she wanted to share with him.

Editing Ricker out of it, for the time being, seemed like the best path to marital harmony.

When she stepped into the bedroom, she saw the flowers first. It was difficult to miss them as there was a four-foot spread of them dead center of the room and the scent was sweet enough to hurt her teeth.

It took another moment to realize the flowers had long, skinny legs in black trousers.

Summerset. The shower could wait.

'For me? Gee, you shouldn't have. If you don't try harder to control your passion for me, Roarke's going to fire your bony ass and make my life complete.'

'Your humor,' the flowers said in a dry, faintly Slavic voice, 'eludes me as usual. This obnoxious and overstated arrangement just arrived by private messenger.'

'Watch the cat,' she began as Summerset stepped forward and Galahad strolled in his path. To her surprise and reluctant admiration, Summerset neatly sidestepped, avoided Galahad's tail by a, well, a cat hair, and neatly set the enormous bouquet on the wide table in the sitting area.

Galahad leaped up, sniffed at it, then padded over to butt his head on Summerset's leg.

'The flowers are for you,' Summerset said, and since she was looking, ignored the cat. 'And as of now, they become your problem.'

'Who sent them? They're not Roarke's style.'

'Certainly not.' Summerset sniffed, a great deal as Galahad had done, and eyed the elaborate arrangement with distaste. 'Perhaps one of your felonious acquaintances considers it a suitable bribe.'

'Yeah, right.' She snatched out the card, ripped it open, then snarled in a manner that had the cat leaping down and standing between Summerset's legs. 'Ricker, that son of a bitch.'

'Max Ricker?' Distaste turned to ice, the jagged sort that flayed skin. 'Why would he send you flowers?'

'To get my goat,' she said absently, then a ripple of fear worked into her belly. 'Or Roarke's. Get them out of here. Burn them, stuff them in the recycler. Get rid of them fast. And don't tell Roarke.' She grabbed Summerset's sleeve. 'Don't tell Roarke.'

She made it a point never to ask Summerset for anything. The fact that she was, and urgently, had alarm bells sounding in his brain. 'What's Ricker to you?'

'A target. Get them out, damn it. Where's Roarke?'

'In his office upstairs. Let me see the card. Have you been threatened?'

'They're bait,' she said impatiently. 'For Roarke. Take the elevator. Move. Get them gone.' She crumbled the card in her hand before Summerset could grab it from her. 'Now.'

Dissatisfied, Summerset lifted the arrangement again. 'Be very, very careful,' he said, then maneuvered them onto the elevator.

She waited until the doors closed before she smoothed out the card, read it again.

I never had the chance to kiss the bride.
M. Ricker

'I'll give you the chance,' she muttered and carefully tore the card to bits. 'The first time we meet in hell.'

She flushed the pieces, breathed a little easier, then stripped. She left her clothes where they fell, laid her weapon harness over the long counter, then stepped into the glass-walled shower.

'All jets full,' she ordered, closing her eyes. 'One hundred and two degrees.'

She let the water beat at her everywhere, warm away the little chill the flowers had brought with them. She would put that aside and calculate how she would drill at Lewis the next morning.

Feeling better, she turned the jets off, squeezed some of the water out of her hair, and turned. Yelped.

'Jesus. Jesus Christ, Roarke, you know I hate when you sneak up on me like that.'

'Yes, I do.' He opened the door to the drying tube, knowing she preferred it to a leisurely toweling off. While the fan whirled, he strolled over to take her robe from the hook on the back of the door.

But when she stepped out, he held onto it rather than offering. 'Who put those marks on you?'

'Huh?'

'Your arm's bruised.'

'Yeah.' She glanced down, had an image of Ricker, his eyes burning as his fingers dug into her flesh. 'You're right. Must've run into something.' She reached for the robe only to have him hold it out of reach. 'Come on, I'm not going to play your sick games in the bathroom.'

Such a statement usually made him smile. Her stomach began to quiver when his eyes stayed cool and steady on hers.

'They're finger marks, Lieutenant. Who handled you?'

'For God's sake.' Working up irritation, she snatched the robe. 'I'm a cop, remember? It means I tend to run into a number of nasty characters in any given day. Have you eaten? I'm starving.'

He let her walk back into the bedroom, stand and fiddle with the AutoChef. Waited until she punched in a request. 'Where are the flowers?'

Oh shit. 'What flowers?'

'The flowers, Eve, that were delivered just a while ago.'

'I don't know what you're talking about. I just got – Hey!'

He'd spun her around so quickly her teeth nearly rattled. Might have if they hadn't frozen solid at the fury in his eyes. The chill had turned to fire very quickly. 'Don't lie to me. Don't ever fucking lie to me.'

'Cut it out.' He had her arms. But even now, she realized, even when he was furious, he didn't hurt her, and was careful to keep his grip away from the bruise. 'Flowers come here all the time. What am I supposed to know about it? Now let me go. I'm hungry.'

'I'll tolerate, and by God do tolerate, a great deal from you, Eve. But you won't stand here and lie to my face. You have bruises on you put there since I last saw you, and by someone's hand. Summerset is downstairs feeding a bunch of flowers into the recycler. On your orders, I assume, since he brought them up here first. Goddammn it, I can still smell them. What are you afraid of?'

'I'm not afraid of anything.'

'Then who? Who put the fear behind your eyes?'

'You.'

She knew it was wrong, knew it was cruel. And hated herself for it when his eyes went blank, when he stepped just a little too carefully back from her.

'I beg your pardon.'

She hated when he used that rigid and formal tone, hated it worse than a shout. And when he turned to walk away from her, she gave up.

'Roarke. Damn it, Roarke!' She had to go after him, take his arm. 'I'm sorry. Look, I'm sorry.'

'I have work.'

'Don't freeze me out. I can't take it when you do that.' She dragged her hands through her hair, pressed the heels of them hard on her forehead where it had begun to throb. 'I don't know how to do this. Any way I do, it's going to piss you off.'

Disgusted, she stalked back to the sitting area, flopped on the couch, scowled at nothing in particular.

'Why don't you try the truth?'

'Yeah, all right. But you have to make me a promise first.'

'Which would be?'

'Oh, get the stick out of your ass and sit down, would you?'

'The stick in my ass is surprisingly comfortable just now.' He'd been studying her face, calculating, speculating. And he knew. 'You went to see Ricker.'

'What are you, psychic?' Then her eyes popped wide

and she was up and running again. 'Hey, hey, hey, you promised.'

'No. I didn't.'

She caught up to him in the hallway, considered trying to muscle him to the floor, then decided to go for his weak spot. She simply wrapped her arms around him.

'Please.'

'He put his hands on you.'

'Roarke. Look at me, Roarke.' She laid her hands on his face. The look in his eyes was murder. She knew he could accomplish it, hot or cold. 'I baited him. I've got my reasons. And right now, I've got him shaken. The flowers were just a dig at you. He wants you to come after him. He wants it.'

'And why shouldn't I oblige him?'

'Because I'm asking you not to. Because taking him down is my job, and if I play it right, I'm going to do that job.'

'There are times you ask a great deal.'

'I know it. I know you could go after him. I know you'd find a way to get it done. But it's not the right way. It's not who you are anymore.'

'Isn't it?' But the rage, the first blinding rush of it, was leveling off.

'No, it's not. I stood with him today, and now I'm standing with you. You're nothing like him. Nothing.'

'I could have been.'

'But you're not.' The crisis had passed. She felt it. 'Let's go in and sit down. I'll tell you all of it.'

He tipped her face back, a finger under her chin. Though the gesture was tender, his eyes were still hard. 'Don't lie to me again.'

'Okay.' She closed a hand over his wrist, squeezed there in silent promise where his pulse beat. 'Okay.'

97

Chapter Seven

So she told him, running through the steps and movements of her day in a tone very close to the one she'd used in her oral report to Whitney. Dispassionate, professional, cool.

He said nothing, not a word, stretching out the silence until her nerves were riding on the surface of her skin. His eyes never left her face and gave her no clue to what he was thinking. Feeling. Just that deep, wicked blue, cold now as Arctic ice.

She knew what he was capable of when pushed. No, not even when pushed, she thought as her nerves kicked into a gallop. When he believed whatever methods he used were acceptable.

When she was finished, he rose, walked casually to the wall panel that concealed a bar. He helped himself to a glass of wine, held up the bottle. 'Would you like one?'

'Ah . . . sure.'

He poured a second glass, as steadily, as naturally as if they'd been sitting discussing some minor household incident. She wasn't easily rattled, had faced pain and death without a tremor, had waded through the pain and death of others as a matter of routine.

But God, he rattled her. She took the glass he offered her and had to remind herself not to gulp it down like water.

'So . . . that's all there is to it.'

He sat again, gracefully arranged himself on the cushion.

Like a cat, she thought. A very big, very dangerous cat. He sipped his wine, watching her over the crystal rim.

'Lieutenant,' he said in a voice so mild it might have fooled another.

'What?'

'Do you expect me – honestly expect me – to do nothing?'

She set her glass down. It wasn't the time for wine. 'Yes.'

'You're not a stupid woman. Your instincts and intellect are two of the things I admire most about you.'

'Don't do this, Roarke. Don't make this personal.'

His eyes flashed, a hard glint of blue steel. 'It is personal.'

'Okay, no.' She could handle it. Had to. And leaned forward toward him. 'It's not, unless you let him string you. He wants it to be, wants you to make it personal so he can fuck with you. Roarke, you're not a stupid man. Your instincts and intellect are two of the things I admire most about you.'

For the first time in more than an hour, his lips curved in a hint of a smile. 'Well done, Eve.'

'He can't hurt me.' Seeing her opening, all but diving through it, she shifted onto her knees, put her hands on his shoulders. 'Unless you let him. He can hurt me through you. Don't let him do that. Don't play the game.'

'Do you think I won't win?'

She lowered to her heels. 'I know you will. It scares me knowing you will and what the cost could be to both of us. To us, Roarke. Don't do this. Let me work it.'

He said nothing a moment, looking in her eyes, studying what he saw there, felt there. 'If he touches you again, puts his mark on you again, he's dead. No, be quiet,' he said before she could speak. 'I'll stand back so far, for you. But he crosses the line, and it's over. I'll find the way, the time, and it's over.'

'I don't need that.'

'Darling Eve.' He touched her now, just a skim of his

fingertips over her jaw. '*I* need that. You don't know him. As much as you've seen, as much as you've done, you don't know him. I do.'

Sometimes, she reminded herself, you had to settle for what you could get. 'You won't go after him.'

'Not at the moment. And that costs me, so leave it at that.'

When he pushed off the couch, she felt the chill, swore under her breath. 'You're still pissed off at me.'

'Oh yes. Yes, I am.'

'What do you want from me?' Exasperated, she scrambled to her feet and wished she didn't want to punch a fist into his gorgeous face for lack of a better solution. 'I said I was sorry.'

'You're sorry because I pinned you.'

'Okay, right. That's mostly right.' Out of patience with him, with herself, she kicked viciously at the sofa. 'I don't know how to do this! I love you, and it makes me crazy. Isn't that bad enough?'

He had to laugh. She looked so baffled. 'Christ Jesus, Eve, you're a piece of work.'

'I ought to at least get some sort of handicap for . . . Damn it,' she hissed as her communicator beeped. She resisted the urge to simply pluck it out and wing it against the wall. Instead, she just kicked the sofa again. 'Dallas. What?'

Dispatch, Dallas, Lieutenant Eve. DOS reported, George Washington Bridge, eastbound, level two. Victim is preliminarily identified as Mills, Lieutenant Alan, assigned to Precinct One two-eight, Illegals Division. You are ordered to report to scene immediately, as primary.

'Oh God. Oh Christ. Acknowledged. Contact Peabody, Officer Delia, to act as aide. I'm on my way.'

She was sitting now, her head weighing heavily in one hand, her stomach dragging to her knees. 'Another cop. Another dead cop.'

'I'm going with you. With you, Lieutenant,' Roarke said when she shook her head. 'Or alone. But I'm going. Get dressed. I'll drive. I can get us there faster.'

The bridge sparkled, an arch teeming with lights against the clear night sky. In that sky, busy air traffic streamed, all but obliterating the tentative light of a thumbnail moon.

Life surged on.

On the second level of the bridge, closed now to traffic, a dozen black and whites and city units crowded together like hounds on a hunt. She could hear the 'link chatter, the mutters and oaths, as she cut through the uniforms and plain-clothes.

More lights, cold blue, iced white and blood red washed over her face. She didn't speak but walked to the dirty beige vehicle parked in the break-down lane.

Mills was in the passenger's seat, his eyes closed, his chin on his chest as if he'd stopped to take a catnap. From the chin down, he was blood.

Eve stood, coating her hands with Seal-It, and studied the position of the body.

Posed, she thought as she leaned in the open window. She saw the badge, facedown on the bloody floor of the car, and she saw the dull glint of silver coins.

'Who found him?'

'Good Samaritan.' One of the uniforms stepped forward, as if he'd been waiting anxiously for his cue. 'We got him stashed in a unit with a couple of cops. He's pretty shook.'

'You get a name, a statement?'

'Yes, sir.' Smartly, the uniform flipped out his notebook, keyed in. 'James Stein, 1001 Ninety-fifth. He was heading home from work – worked late tonight – and saw the vehicle in the break-down lane. Wasn't much traffic, he said, and he saw somebody sitting in the car. Felt bad about it. Stopped, went over to see if he could lend a hand. When he saw the deceased, he called it in.'

'When did the call come in?'

'Ah, twenty-one-fifteen. My partner and I were first onscene, and arrived at twenty-one-twenty-five. We recognized the vehicle as departmental, called it in, and transmitted the vehicle identification number and a physical description of the deceased.'

'All right. Have Stein taken home.'

'Sir? You don't want to question him?'

'Not tonight. Verify his address and have him taken home.' She turned away from the uniform and saw Peabody and McNab hustle out of another black and white.

'Lieutenant.' Peabody glanced toward the car, and her mouth went tight. 'I was with McNab when the call came through. I couldn't shake him off.'

'Yeah.' Eve looked over to where Roarke stood, dark against the lights. 'I know the feeling. Seal up, record the scene, all angles.' She didn't bother to bite back an oath when yet another car squealed up, and Captain Roth jumped out.

Eve walked over to meet her.

'Report, Lieutenant.'

Eve didn't report to Roth, and they both knew it. They studied each other a moment, a subtle flexing of muscles. 'At this point, Captain, you know what I know.'

'What I know, Lieutenant, is you fucked up, and I've got another man dead.'

The chatter around them cut off, as if someone had severed vocal chords with a knife.

'Captain Roth, I'll give you leeway for emotional distress. But if you want to try to set me down, you do it officially. You don't come at me on my crime scene.'

'It's no longer your scene.'

Eve simply sidestepped and blocked Roth from shoving by her. 'Yes, it is. And because it is, I have the authority to have you removed, should it become necessary. Don't make it necessary.'

'You want to take me on, Dallas?' Roth jabbed a finger between Eve's breasts. 'You want to go a round with me?'

'Not particularly, but I will if you put your hands on me again or try to interfere with my investigation. Now, you either back off, fall in, or remove yourself from the sealed area.'

Roth's eyes flared, her teeth bared, and Eve braced herself for what was to come.

'Captain!' Clooney pushed his way through the crowd of cops. His face was flushed, his breath short as if he'd been running. 'Captain Roth, may I speak with you, sir? In private.'

Roth vibrated another moment, then seemed to pull herself in. With a brisk nod, she turned and strode back to her vehicle.

'I'm sorry about that, Lieutenant,' Clooney murmured. His gaze slid past her, rested miserably on Mills. 'This cuts deep with her.'

'Understood. Why are you here, Clooney?'

'Word travels.' He sighed, long and deep. 'I'm going to be knocking on another door tonight, sitting with another widow. Goddamn it.'

He turned away, walked to where Roth waited.

'She's got no cause slapping at you that way.' McNab said it, from just behind her.

Eve shifted, stared at the scene Peabody meticulously recorded. 'That's cause,' she said.

He didn't think so but decided to let it go. 'Can I help out here?'

'I'll let you know.' She took a step away, looked back. 'McNab?'

'Yes, sir?'

'You're not always a complete asshole.'

It made him grin, and he slipped his hands into his pockets and wandered over to Roarke. 'Hey. You doing a ride-along, too?'

'Apparently.' Roarke had a low-grade urge for a cigarette, which annoyed him. 'What's the story on Captain Roth?' When McNab started to shrug, Roarke smiled. 'Ian, no one knows the gossip like an e-detective.'

'You got that right. Okay, maybe we poked around a little when we heard about Kohli, seeing as he was hers. She's a hard-ass, eighteen years on, got a shit-pot load of busts under her belt, a slew of commendations, and a couple minor reprimands for insubordination. They came early on, though. Moved up the ranks, and took a lot of crap work to do it. Been captain under a year, and word is she's holding onto it by her fingernails since the Ricker case blew up under her.'

They both glanced back to where Roth and Eve had squared off. 'And that,' Roarke said, 'makes her touchy.'

'Looks like. Had a little problem with alcohol a few years back. Did voluntary rehab before it became a big one. On her second marriage, and my source says it looks pretty shaky right now. She lives and breathes the job.'

He paused a minute, watching Roth talk to Clooney. 'You want my take, she's territorial and competitive. Probably have to be to wear captain's bars. Losing two men stings. Having another cop handle the cases is going to eat at her. Especially when it's a cop with a rep like Dallas.'

'And what would that rep be?'

'She's the best there is,' McNab said simply. He smiled a little. 'Peabody wants to be her when she grows up. Speaking of Peabody, I just wanted to say how that advice you gave me – you know about the romance angle – it's working pretty good.'

'Glad to hear it.'

'She's still seeing that slick-handed LC though. Burns my ass.'

Roarke glanced down as McNab held out a jumbo pack of wild grape bubble gum. *What the hell*, he thought, took a cube.

Chewing thoughtfully, they watched their women work.

Eve ignored the onlookers. She could have ordered the scene cleared except for essential personnel, but it felt wrong to do so. The cops were there, a kind of homage to the badge, and to reassure themselves they were alive.

Both were valid reasons to stand by.

'Victim is identified as Mills, Lieutenant Alan, attached to the One two-eight, Illegals Division. Caucasian, age fifty-four.'

Eve recited the data into the record as she gently lifted the chin. 'The victim was found by civilian Stein, James, in the passenger seat of his official vehicle, on the break-down lane on the George Washington Bridge, eastbound. Cause of death not yet determined. He'd been drinking, Peabody.'

'Sir?'

'Gin, from the smell of it.'

'I don't know how you catch it,' Peabody muttered, breathing between her teeth. 'With the rest of the stench here.'

With a sealed hand, Eve turned back Mills's jacket, saw his weapon still holstered. 'Doesn't look like he even went for it. Why wasn't he driving? It's his unit. Most cops have to have their hands pried off the wheel before they let somebody else man their ride.'

She wrinkled her nose. 'That's more than blood and bowels and gin I'm smelling.'

She released the seat belt, then jerked her hands back, an instinctive move, as his guts slithered out, sliding nastily from under his shirt.

'Oh. Oh Christ.' Peabody choked, went glassily pale, stumbled back. 'Dallas . . .'

'Get some air. Go on.'

'I'm okay, I . . .' But her head spun, her stomach revolted. She managed to get to the side of the bridge before she lost the cheese and bean tacos she'd shared with McNab.

Eve closed her eyes a moment, bore down and bore down hard. There was a dull roar in her head, like the sea cresting. She blanked her mind until she was certain the rumbles she heard were from the traffic on the level below and from the sky overhead.

With steady hands, she unbuttoned Mills's fouled shirt. He'd been sliced, one long wide swath, from breastbone to crotch.

She noted it into the record while Peabody retched.

Sickened, she straightened, stepped back, let the marginally fresher air fill her lungs. Her gaze skimmed over a sea of faces; some grim, some horrified, some frightened. Peabody wasn't the only cop leaning over the bridge.

'I'm all right, I'm okay.'

Through the pounding bells in her ears, Eve heard Peabody's weak voice.

'Come on, sit down a minute. Sit down, honey.'

'McNab, get her recorder. I need it here.'

'No, I can do it. I can.' Peabody nudged McNab's patting hands away, straightened her shoulders. Her face was dead white to the lips. She shuddered once, but she walked back. 'I'm sorry, Lieutenant.'

'There's no shame in it. Give me your recorder. I'll finish this.'

'No, sir. I can hold.'

After a moment's study, Eve nodded. 'Get him on record. Don't think about it. Close your mind to it.'

'How?' Peabody asked, but turned to do the work.

Eve lifted a hand, had nearly rubbed it over her face before she remembered what it was smeared with. 'Where the hell's the ME?'

'Lieutenant.' Roarke stepped to her, held out a pristine white silk handkerchief.

'Yeah, thanks.' She used it without a thought. 'You can't be here. You have to stay back.' She looked around for

106

somewhere to dispose of the smeared silk and ended up stuffing it into an evidence bag.

'You need to take a minute,' Roarke said quietly. 'Anyone would.'

'I can't afford it. I fold, even look like I'm going to, and I lose control of the scene.' She stayed crouched, added a fresh coat of sealant to her hands. She got to her feet, handed him the ruined handkerchief in its bag. 'Sorry about that.'

Then she planted her feet, legs spread, as Roth marched back to Mills's car with Clooney in her wake. Roth stopped short, as if she'd run into an invisible wall, and stared at what there was of the man who'd served under her command.

'Ah, holy mother of God.' It was all she said, her only sign of distress. While her eyes were burning dry, Clooney's misted with tears.

'Jesus, Mills. Jesus, look what they did to you.' He closed his eyes, breathed long and deep. 'We can't tell the family this. Can't give them the details of this. Captain Roth, we have to go inform next of kin before they hear some other way. We have to cover over the worst of this for their sakes.'

'All right, Art. All right.' She looked over as Eve took out her communicator.

'What are you doing?'

'Checking on the ME, Captain.'

'I've just done so. ETA is under two minutes. A moment, Lieutenant. In private. Clooney, assist the lieutenant's aide in keeping the scene secure. I don't want any of those cops moving closer.'

Eve walked away with her, away from the glare of lights into the softer shadows. The air cleared, the scent of exhaust and pavement was like balm after a burn.

'Lieutenant, I apologize for my earlier outburst.'

'Apology accepted.'

'That was very quick.'

107

'So was your apology.'

Roth blinked, then nodded slowly. 'I hate making them. I haven't gotten where I am on the job by indulging my temper or apologizing for it. Neither, I imagine, have you. Women are still more closely scrutinized in the department and more strictly judged.'

'That may be true, Captain. I don't let it concern me.'

'Then you're a better woman than I, Dallas, or a great deal less ambitious. Because it burns the living hell out of me.' She inhaled, hissed the breath out through her teeth. 'My coming at you as I have has been an emotional reaction, an indulgence again, that was both inappropriate and ill-advised. I'm going to tell you that I overreacted to Kohli's death because I liked him, very much. I believe I overreacted to Mills because I disliked him. Very much.'

She glanced back at the car. 'He was a son of a bitch, a mean-spirited man who made no secret that, in his opinion, women should be having babies, cooking pies, and not wearing a badge. He disliked blacks, Jews, Asians . . . hell, he disliked everyone who wasn't just what he was: an overfed white male. But he was my cop, and I want whoever opened him up that way.'

'So do I, Captain.'

Roth nodded again, and together they watched the ME arrive. *Morse*, Eve noted. *Only the top dog for one of the boys in blue.*

'Homicide isn't my sphere, Dallas, as Clooney in his calm, reasonable manner has pointed out to me. I know your rep, and I'm depending on it. I want . . .' She trailed off and seemed to bite down on impatience. 'I'd *appreciate* being sent a copy of your report.'

'You'll have it in the morning.'

'Thank you.' She looked back, her eyes skimming over Eve's face. 'Are you as good as they say?'

'I don't listen to what they say.'

Roth gave a short laugh. 'You want to wear bars, you'd better start.' And she held out a hand.

Eve took it. They parted ways, one to speak of death and the other to stand over it.

As she walked, Eve glanced up and spotted the first media copter.

That, she decided, was a problem for later.

'Well, they made a mess out of him, didn't they?' Morse took the time to pull on a protective gown, then placidly sealed his hands and shoes while Eve waited beside him.

'Push the tox reports. I'm betting he was unconscious when he was sliced. His weapon's still on safety, and there aren't any defensive wounds. I could smell gin on him.'

'Take a hell of a lot of gin to take a man his size under far enough that this could be done to him without his objection. You think he was killed while he sat there?'

'Too much blood for otherwise. The killer got him drunk, doped, whatever, took the time to unbutton his shirt, sliced him right down the middle. Then he buttoned him up again, strapped him in. Even tipped the seat back just enough so that his insides would stay in, more or less, until some lucky winner unstrapped him.'

'Bet I can guess who that lucky winner was.' Morse smiled at her with a great deal of sympathy.

'Yeah, I rang that bell.' She was, damn it, going to feel the sensation of Mills's intestines slopping over her hands for a long, very long time. 'The killer drove Mills here,' she continued, 'and walked away. We won't find any prints.'

She scanned the area. 'Ballsy. Ballsy again. He'd have to sit here. Maybe he even did it here, but I'm thinking he's not that much of a fucking daredevil. But he'd have to sit here and wait until he was sure it was clear enough for him to get out of the car. He had to have another transpo close by.'

'An accomplice?'

'Maybe. Maybe. I can't rule it out. We'll check with the

traffic cops, see if they spotted another car in the breakdown lane tonight. He didn't just walk off the goddamn bridge. He had a plan. He knew the steps. Get me the tox, Morse.'

Peabody was standing by the rail, McNab beside her. She'd gotten her color back, but Eve thought she knew the kind of images her aide would see when she closed her eyes that night.

'McNab, you want in on this?'

'Yes, sir.'

'Go with Peabody, get the traffic discs from the toll booths. All discs, all levels, for the last twenty-four hours.'

'All?'

'We're going to be thorough, and maybe we'll get lucky. Start scanning them, starting backward with this level from twenty hundred hours. Find me this vehicle.'

'You got it.'

'Peabody, do a standard background on James Stein, the Good Samaritan. I don't expect you to find anything, but let's clear him out. Report, my home office, oh eight hundred.'

'You've got Lewis in the morning,' Peabody reminded her. 'I'm scheduled for six-thirty at Central.'

'I'll handle Lewis. You're going to be putting in a long night.'

'So are you.' Peabody's face turned mulish. 'I'll report to Central as ordered, Lieutenant.'

'Christ, have it your own way.' Eve dragged a hand through her hair and reorganized her thoughts. 'Have the first uniforms on-scene provide your transpo. One of them's a hot dog. He needs something to do.'

She turned away from them, strode to Roarke. 'I have to ditch you.'

'I'll ride with you to Central, then find transportation home.'

'I'm not going to Central straight off. I have some stops to make. I'll have one of the black and whites take you back.'

He looked toward the units with mild disdain. 'I believe I'll find my own transportation, thanks all the same.'

Why, she thought, was everyone arguing with her tonight? 'I'm not going to just leave you on the damn bridge.'

'I can find my way home, Lieutenant. Where are you going?'

'Just some things I have to do before I write my report.' His voice was so damn cool, she thought. His eyes so detached. 'How long are you going to be pissed off at me?'

'I haven't decided. But I'll be sure to let you know.'

'You're making me feel like a jerk.'

'Darling, you managed that perfectly well on your own.'

Guilt and temper tangled inside her, had her glaring at him. 'Well, fuck it,' she said, then grabbed him by the lapels of his coat, yanked him to her, and kissed him hard. 'See you later,' she muttered and stalked away.

'Count on it.'

Chapter Eight

Don Webster was awakened out of a dead sleep by what he initially took to be a particularly violent thunderstorm. When the clouds cleared from his brain, he decided someone was trying to beat through the walls of his apartment with a sledgehammer.

As he reached for his weapon, he realized someone was pounding on his door.

He pulled on jeans, took his weapon with him, and went to look through his security peep.

A dozen thoughts ran through his head, a morass of pleasure, fantasy, and discomfort. He opened the door to Eve.

'Just in the neighborhood?' he said.

'You son of a bitch.' She shoved him back, slammed the door behind her. 'I want answers, and I want them now.'

'You never were much on foreplay.' The minute it was out, he regretted it. He covered that with a cocky grin. 'What's up?'

'What's down, Webster, is another cop.'

The grin vanished. 'Who? How?'

'You tell me.'

They stared at each other a moment. His gaze shifted first. 'I don't know.'

'What do you know? What's IAB's angle on this? Because there is one. I can smell it.'

'Look, you come barging in here at . . . Christ, after one

in the morning, jump down my throat, and tell me a cop's dead. You don't even tell me who or how it happened and I'm supposed to be some fount of fucking information for you.'

'Mills,' she snapped. 'Detective Alan. Illegals, same squad as Kohli. You want to know how? Somebody sliced him wide open from neck to balls. I know because his guts spilled out on my hands.'

'Christ. Christ.' He rubbed both hands over his face. 'I need a drink.'

He walked away.

She stormed after him. She remembered, vaguely, his old place, the one he'd had when he'd worked the streets. This one had a lot more space, and more of a shine on it.

IAB, she thought bitterly, paid well.

He was in the kitchen, at the refrigerator, pulling a beer out. He looked back at her, took out a second. 'Want one?' When she simply stared at him, he put it back. 'Guess not.' He flipped off the top, let it fly, then took one long swallow. 'Where'd it happen?'

'I'm not here to answer questions. I'm not your goddamn weasel.'

'And I'm not yours,' he countered, then leaned back against the refrigerator door. He needed to get his thoughts in order, his emotions under control. Unless he did, she'd spring something out of him he wasn't free to say.

'You came to me,' she reminded him. 'Either fishing or smelling bait. Or maybe you're just IAB's messenger boy.'

His eyes hardened at that, but he lifted the bottle again, sipped. 'You got a problem with me, you take it to IAB. See where it gets you.'

'I solve my own problems. What do Kohli and Mills and Max Ricker have in common?'

'You're going to stir up a hornet's nest and get stung if you mess with Ricker.'

'I've already messed with him. Didn't know that, did

113

you?' she said when his eyes flickered. 'That little gem hasn't dropped in your lap quite yet. I've got four of his storm troopers in cages right now.'

'You won't keep them.'

'Maybe not, but I might get more out of them than I'm getting from one of my own. You used to be a cop.'

'I'm still a cop. Goddamn it, Dallas.'

'Then act like one.'

'You think because I don't get all the press, don't go out closing high-profile cases so the crowds cheer, I don't care about the job?' He slammed the bottle on the counter. 'I do what I do because I care about the job. If every cop was as hard-line straight as you, we wouldn't need Internal Affairs.'

'Were they dirty, Webster? Mills and Kohli. Were they dirty?'

His face closed in again. 'I can't tell you.'

'You don't know, or you're not saying.'

He looked into her eyes. For an instant, just an instant, she saw regret in his. 'I can't tell you.'

'Is there an ongoing investigation in IAB involving Kohli, Mills and/or other officers in the One two-eight?'

'If there was,' he said carefully, 'it would be classified. I wouldn't be at liberty to confirm or deny that, or to discuss any of the details.'

'Where did Kohli get the funds he's funnelled into investment accounts?'

Webster's mouth tightened. Spring it out of him? She'd pry it out, he thought, with her fingernails. 'I have no comment regarding that allegation.'

'Am I going to find similar funds in an account under Mills's name?'

'I have no comment.'

'You should be a fucking politician, Webster.' She turned on her heel.

'Eve.' He'd never used her first name before, not out loud. 'Watch your step,' he said quietly. 'Watch your back.'

She never stopped, never acknowledged the warning. When she'd slammed the door behind her, he stood for a moment while a war waged inside him.

Then he walked to his 'link and made the first call.

Her next stop was Feeney's. For the second time, she woke a man from a dead sleep. Heavy-eyed, more rumpled than usual, and wearing a ratty blue robe that had his pale legs sticking out like a chicken's, he answered the door.

'Jeez, Dallas, it's going on two o'fucking clock.'

'I know; sorry.'

'Well, come in, but keep it down before the wife wakes up and thinks she has to come out and make coffee or some damn thing.'

The apartment was small, several steps down from Webster's in size and style. A big, ugly chair sat in the center of the living area, facing the entertainment screen. The privacy screens on the windows had been pulled, giving the place the feeling of a tidy, and well-worn box.

She felt more at home immediately.

He went toward the kitchen, a short, skinny space with a battered counter running along one wall. She knew he'd added that on himself because he'd bragged about it for weeks. Saying nothing, she boosted herself on one of the stools and waited while he programmed the AutoChef for coffee.

'I thought you were going to tag me earlier. Waited around awhile.'

'Sorry, I got held up on something else.'

'Yeah, I heard. Taking Ricker on. That's a big chunk to chew.'

'I'm going to swallow him down before I'm finished.'

'Just make sure he doesn't give you permanent indigestion.'

He set two steaming mugs on the counter, settled onto the other stool. 'Mills is dirty.'

'Mills is dead.'

'Well, shit.' Feeney paused, thinking while he drank some coffee. 'He died rich. Found two and a half million tucked into different accounts so far, and there may be more. He did a good job of burying them, used names of dead relatives mostly.'

'Can you trace where it came from?'

'Haven't had any luck with that yet. With Kohli either. Money's been through the wash so many times, it oughta be sterilized. But I can tell you Mills started pumping up his goddamn pension fund and portfolio big time two weeks before the Ricker bust. There were dribbles before that, but that's when it started rolling.'

He rubbed his hand over his face where the nightly complement of chin hair itched.

'Kohli started later. Months after. Don't have anything on Martinez yet. She's either clean or more careful. I took a look at Roth.'

'And?'

'She's had some sizable withdrawals over the last six months. Big chunks taken out of her accounts. On the surface, it looks like she's damn near broke.'

'Any of the withdrawals connect?'

'I'm still looking.' He blew out a breath. 'Thought maybe I'd see if I can work into their logs and 'links. Take a little time, since I have to be careful.'

'Okay, thanks.'

'How'd Mills go down?'

She sat, drank her coffee, and told him. It was still raw inside her, but by the time she'd finished, it was easier.

'He was an asshole,' Feeney said. 'But that's ugly. Somebody he knew. You're not going to get that close in on a cop, open him up that way, without some solid resistance unless the cop's relaxed.'

116

'He'd been drinking. My hunch is he'd been drinking with somebody. Just like Kohli. Taking a meet in his ride maybe, having a drink. He gets sloppy, gets drugged, gets dead.'

'Yeah, most likely. You did good putting McNab on the traffic scans. He'll do the job.'

'I've got him and Peabody in my home office at eight. Can you come in on it?'

He looked at her, smiled his sorrowful basset-hound smile. 'I thought I already was.'

It was nearly four when she got home, and a soft spring rain had started to fall. In the dark she showered off the greasiness of the night. Resting her forehead on the tiles until she stopped smelling blood and bile.

She set her wrist alarm for five. She meant to hit at Lewis again, and that meant another trip to Central in just over an hour. For that hour, she promised herself she'd sleep.

She climbed into bed, grateful for Roarke's warmth. He'd be awake, she thought. Even if he'd slept before she got home, he slept like a cat and would have sensed her.

But he didn't turn to her as he usually did, didn't reach out or say her name to help her slip into comfort.

She closed her eyes, willed her mind to blank and her body to sleep.

And when she woke an hour later, she was alone.

She was out in her car, nearly ready to pull out, when Peabody ran out of the house behind her.

'Nearly missed you.'

'Missed me? What are you doing here?'

'I bunked here last night. Me and McNab.' In a bedroom, she thought, she'd dream about for the rest of her life. 'We brought the traffic discs back here. Roarke said it'd be easier to do that instead of running us back to McNab's, then all of us coming here this morning.'

'Roarke said?'

'Well, yeah.' She settled into the passenger's seat, strapped in. 'He rode along with us to pick up the discs, then he'd called for a car, so we drove back here with him and got to work.'

'Who got to work?'

Peabody's brain had engaged enough now to catch the edginess in Eve's tone. She'd have squirmed if it hadn't been so undignified. 'Well, me and McNab . . . and Roarke. He's done some tech consults with us before, so I didn't think anything of it. Are we in trouble?'

'No. What would be the point?'

There was a weariness in the answer Peabody didn't like. 'We broke off about three.' She infused her voice with cheer as they headed down the drive. 'I never slept in a gel bed before. It's like sleeping on a cloud, except I guess you'd fall through a cloud. McNab was snoring like a cargo tram, but I fell out about two seconds after I hit the bed anyway. Are you mad at Roarke?' she blurted out.

'No.' *But he's mad at me. Still.* 'Did you spot Mills's vehicle on the disc?'

'Oh, man, I can't believe I didn't tell you. Yeah, we got it. Passed the toll through the e-pass at twenty-eighteen. You'd swear he was just sleeping until you enhance and see the blood.'

'The driver, Peabody?'

'That's the not-so-good news. There was no driver. McNab said you'd need to go over the in-dash computer, but it looks like it was on auto.'

'He programmed it.' She hadn't thought of that. Very slick, very confident. Took Mills out somewhere else, then programmed the auto. If it ran into a snag and there was nobody in the vehicle to correct, what did he care?

'Yeah, that's what we came to. McNab started calling it the Meteor of Death. You know, it was a Meteor model,' Peabody said lamely. 'Gets to be that late, you start making stupid jokes, I guess.'

'You need a code to program a police unit. You need a code, or you need clearance. It'll have security override to keep it from being boosted, even by electronic-savvy car-jackers.'

'Yeah, Roarke said.' Peabody yawned comfortably. 'But if you know what you're doing, it can be finessed.'

He'd know, Eve thought sourly. 'If it was finessed, it'll show.' She snagged her 'link, called Feeney, and asked him to go down to vehicle impound and run the test personally.

'If it doesn't show,' she said, thinking out loud as she swung into Central's garage, 'he had the code or clearance.'

'He couldn't have had clearance, Dallas, that would make him . . .'

'Another cop. That's right.'

Peabody goggled at her. 'You don't really think—'

'Listen to me. Murder investigation doesn't just start with a body. It starts with a list, with potentials, with angles. You close the case by cutting down that list, narrowing the potentials, working the angles. You take that, the evidence, the story, the scene, the victim, and the killer. And you put it together as many different ways as you have to, until it fits.

'You keep this to yourself,' Eve added. 'You don't say anything. But if we put it together and it fits a cop, then we deal with it.'

'Yeah, okay. A lot of this one's making me kind of sick.'

'I know it.' Eve pushed out of the car. 'Call in, have Lewis brought up to interview.'

She fueled herself with coffee, took her life in her hands and bought what was reputed to be a cherry danish from vending on the Interview level. It tasted more like cherry-flavored glue over sawdust, but it was something in her stomach.

She strolled into Interview, carrying an oversized mug of her own – or Roarke's own – coffee because she knew the smell of it could make a grown man beg. She settled down, all smiles, while Peabody took up her post by the door and glowered. She set the recorder, read in the current data.

'Morning, Lewis. Beautiful day out there.'

'I heard it's raining.'

'Hey, don't you know the rain's good for the flowers? So how'd you sleep?'

'I slept just fine.'

She smiled again, sipped from her mug. He had circles layering the circles under his eyes. She doubted he'd gotten much more sleep than she had. 'Well, as we were saying when last we met—'

'I don't have to say dick to you without my lawyer.'

'Did I ask you to say *dick?* Peabody, replay the record and verify that I at no time requested that the subject say *dick*.'

'That shit don't work on me. I got nothing to say. I'm sticking with silence. It's one of my civil rights.'

'You hold onto those civil rights, Lewis, while you can. They don't count for a whole hell of a lot on Penal Station Omega. That's where I'm sending you. I'm going to make it my mission in life to put you in one of their smaller concrete cages. So you stick with that silence, and I'll do the talking. Conspiracy to kidnap a police officer.'

'You can't prove that. We never touched you.'

'Four armed men in two vehicles, pursuing poor little me, at high rates of speed, over the state line. You shouldn't have gone over the state line, ace. I can make that federal, and my guess is the FBI would just love a shot at you. With your record, the concealeds are enough to shoot you on the next transit to Omega. Add the illegals.'

'I don't use no drugs.'

'They were in the vehicle you were driving. That was another mistake. You know, if you'd been a passenger, you might have had a better chance to cut back on that hard time. But being the driver, the driver with concealeds, with illegals, that makes you my favorite patsy. Ricker's not even going to wave bye-bye when you're strapped in the prison transport.'

'I got nothing to say.'

'Yeah, I heard that.' But he was starting to sweat. 'I bet the lawyer's made you promises. I bet I can list them right off for you. You'll do some time, but you'll be compensated. They'll work the politics and get you into a nice, cushy facility. Five years, seven tops. And you walk out a rich man. I bet that's real close.'

She could see by the worry in Lewis's eyes that it was more than close. It was bull's-eye. 'Of course, he's a lying sack of shit, and I think you're smart enough to have figured that out during the night. Once you're in, you're in, and if you're unhappy with the arrangement and make noises, one of your upstanding fellow inmates is going to get a message. Poison sprinkled in your rehydrated mashed potatoes. A shiv in the kidneys during your single hour a day in the yard. An accident in the showers where you slip on the soap and break your neck. You won't know where it's coming from until you're dead.'

'I talk to you, I'm dead before I get there.'

That was it, she thought, leaning forward. The first crack. 'Witness protection.'

'Fuck that. He can find anybody anywhere.'

'He's not a magician, Lewis. I'm offering you a nice ride, Lewis. You give me what I need, I can get you immunity, a free walk, a new life anywhere you want to go, on or off planet.'

'Why should I trust you?'

'Because I've got no reason to want you dead. That's a big one, isn't it?'

Lewis said nothing, but he licked his lips.

'I got the impression Ricker's not real stable. He strike you as real stable, Lewis?' She waited a moment while he thought about it. 'Ricker's going to tell himself you screwed up. Doesn't matter, won't matter that he sent you out after

121

me. That he was stupid. He's going to blame you for missing me and for getting caught. You know it. You know that, and you know he's just a little crazy.'

He'd stewed about it all night, tossing, turning as best he could on the narrow bunk in the dark cell. He'd come around to that himself, and he didn't like the fish-eye look of Canarde. Ricker wasn't known for forgiving what he considered employee mistakes.

'I don't do any time.'

'That's what we're going to work on.'

'Work on? Screw that. You get me immunity. I don't say squat until I see the PA and the paperwork. Immunity, Dallas, a new name, a new face, and a hundred fifty thousand in seed money.'

'Maybe you'd like me to arrange a pretty wife and a couple of rosy-cheeked children while I'm at it.'

'Hah. Funny.' He was feeling better now, better than he had in hours. 'You get me the PA, get me the deal. Then I'll talk to you.'

'I'll start on it.' She got to her feet. 'You might have to go through the hearing. Keep cool about it, and try out that silence as a civil right. You let Canarde get a whiff of this, he'll go straight to Ricker.'

'I know how it works. Get me the deal.'

'You called that one right,' Peabody commented as they headed down the hall.

'Yeah.' Eve was already calling the PA's office, and was disgusted when she got the snooty recording listing working hours. 'Looks like I'm getting somebody else out of bed today. Let's head back while I start the wheels rolling on this. I want a look at the disc. Then everyone needs to be briefed.'

'Everyone?'

'Feeney's coming in on it.'

*

122

She expected to find Roarke there, huddled with McNab over her office unit, working some of his magic. When she found McNab alone, she was surprised, irked, and disappointed. A glance at their adjoining doors showed the red locked light engaged.

Damn if she'd knock.

'I can't get you more than I've got, Lieutenant,' McNab told her. 'I cleaned up the image, and it's crystal now. But all you see's a dead guy riding in a car.'

She picked up the hard copy he'd printed out for her, studied Mills. 'Go through the discs, following this segment. I want you to freeze and enhance every car, van, scooter, and fucking jet bike that came through that level from this point until the area was blocked off.'

'You want every vehicle that crossed eastbound on the GW on level two for over an hour?'

She shot him a cool look. 'That was my order, Detective. Do you have a problem understanding it?'

'No. No, sir.' But he allowed himself one weighty sigh.

She went to her 'link, contacted Dr Mira's office, and set up a conference for the next day with the department's top profiler. After a moment's hesitation, she put through a transmission to her commander.

'Sir, I've requested that Captain Feeney and Detective McNab assist in the electronics work as regards my current case.'

'You're cleared to enlist EDD or any assistance you deem appropriate or necessary. That's standard, Lieutenant, and per your judgment. What is the current status on the Mills homicide?'

'I would prefer to report that in person, sir, when I have more data to offer. In the meantime, I'd like to have Detective Martinez, from the One twenty-eight, put under surveillance.'

'Is it your opinion that Detective Martinez is connected to these deaths?'

'I have no data supporting that, Commander. But it is my opinion that Martinez, if not connected, may be a target. I intend to interview her more extensively, but in the meantime, I have some concerns.'

'Very well, Lieutenant. I'll see to it.'

'Commander, are you aware of any investigation involving Kohli, Mills, and/or Martinez currently being run through IAB?'

His eyes went to slits. 'I am not. Are you aware of any such investigation?'

'I am not . . . but I have concerns.'

'So noted. I want a report, by noon. The media's sniffed this out, and they're clamoring. Two cops dead is news.'

'Yes, sir.'

She put the next call through to Nadine Furst from Channel 75, and caught the reporter at home. 'Dallas, great minds. I just got an interesting lead from a source. Who's killing cops?'

'My office . . .' Eve checked her wrist unit, calculated time. 'Ten-thirty, sharp.' She would finish with Feeney, zip down to Lewis's hearing, and back to Central. 'You get what I've got to give, before any scheduled press conference, in a one-on-one.'

'And for this, I have to kill who?'

'We won't take it quite that far. I want a story planted . . . leaked, let's say. From an unnamed police source. You scare easy, Nadine?'

'Hey, I dated a dentist. Nothing scares me.'

'Well, you're going to want to cover your pretty ass anyway. The leak's going to involve Max Ricker.'

'Jesus Christ, Dallas. Let's get married. What have you got on him? Is it confirmed? What's that I smell? Hey, I think it's an Emmy, or no, no, it's a Pulitzer.'

'Slow down. Ten-thirty, sharp, Nadine. And if I hear anything about this before then, deal's off, and I fry your ass.'

'My pretty ass,' Nadine reminded her. 'I'll be there. Bells on.'

She broke the connection, mulled over what she was about to do, then turned to see both Peabody and McNab staring at her. 'Problem?'

'No, sir, working away here. I've already got the first ten minutes run.'

'Work faster.'

'Maybe if I had some breakfast.'

'You've been here about eight hours. There's probably nothing left to eat.' She looked toward Roarke's door again. Tempted, very tempted. Then was saved from making the decision as Feeney came in.

'Got the breakdown.' He laid discs on her desk, took a chair, stretched out his legs. 'Diagnostics, computer analysis. Ran it through up, down, and sideways. The programming wasn't jumped. I'll swear to that.'

'Was Mills's code used?' Eve demanded.

'No. If it had been, I'd've figured whoever killed him got the code from him first, one way or the other.' Feeney rattled in his pocket and began to nibble mournfully from a bag of nuts. 'It was an emergency clearance code – an old one, but it still works on that unit. It's one Maintenance used to go by to transport or run scans on disabled units. They've got a new system the past few years, but the older units still respond to this one. Thing is, he had to have a master to tie it in. He didn't bypass.'

'Mills's master was still in his pocket.'

'Yeah.' Feeney sighed. 'Yeah, you said. Anyway, the killer went right through the stages. I can follow it like a map.'

She nodded because it fit, and the dread in her stomach was ignored. On Feeney's face she read her own thoughts and her own conflict.

'Okay, odds are we're looking for a cop, retired or active.'

Feeney crunched down on an almond. 'Hell.'

'Both victims knew their killer and trusted him or considered him no particular threat.' She moved behind her desk, brought up a wall screen. 'Kohli,' she began, drawing a diagram. 'To Mills. Mills to Martinez. Roth connects to all three. At the center of it is Max Ricker. Who else connects?' As an answer, she brought up a list of the names of the task force from Illegals who worked on Ricker's case. 'We run all these cops.'

She paused long enough to scan faces. 'Inside and out. I want it done without sending up any flags. Concentrate on financials. Both Kohli and Mills had suspicious funds. Follow the money.'

'Sucks,' McNab commented. His eyes were cool and flat as he studied the names. 'Lieutenant, if these two were dirty, taking money from Ricker or one of his sources, why take them out? Why would another cop on the take go after them?'

'You think there's honor among thieves, McNab?'

'No . . . well, sort of. I mean what would be the point?'

'Self-protection, covering your ass. Guilt, remorse.' She lifted a shoulder. 'Or it could be as simple as Ricker paying one more to cut down the field. Thirty pieces of silver,' she mused. 'Ricker's really fond of silver. You may not find the killer on this list. But you may find the next target. Thirty pieces of silver,' she said again. 'A symbol of betrayal. Maybe whoever killed these men wanted us to know they were wrong cops. We need to find out why. You start by finding out how many more are wrong.'

'Shit's going to hit the fan when this comes out,' Feeney told her. 'Some aren't going to be happy you tossed mud on the badge.'

'There's already blood on it. I've got to get to Central, then over to court. We'd better work out of here today. I'll get another computer brought in so you can network.'

The lock light was still on the adjoining door. She wasn't about to humiliate herself by knocking on it in front of her associates. Instead, she went out, walked down the hall and, swallowing pride, knocked from there.

Roarke opened it himself, briefcase in hand. 'Lieutenant. I was just heading out.'

'Yeah, well, me, too. My team's going to set up here today. It'd be helpful if they had another computer unit or two.'

'Summerset will get them whatever they need.'

'Yeah, good. Well . . .'

He touched her arm, turning her so that they walked toward the steps together. 'Was there something else?'

'It's really distracting trying to work and knowing you're still torqued at me.'

'I imagine so. What would you like me to do about it?'

It was said so pleasantly, she wanted to kick him. 'I said I was sorry. Damn it.'

'So you did. How rude of me to still be . . . what was it? Torqued.'

'You're better at this than I am,' she said grimly. 'We're not on even ground.'

'Life has very little even ground.' But he couldn't hold out against her misery and stopped halfway down the stairs. 'I love you, Eve. Nothing changes that, nothing could. But Christ, you piss me off.'

The wash of relief at hearing him say he loved her warred with irritation that she should be slapped, again, for doing what she'd thought best. 'Look, I just didn't want you involved in—'

'Ah.' He tapped a finger on her lips to silence her. 'There it is. There's quite a world of trouble with that single statement. As I doubt you have time, and know I don't, to explore that world right at the moment, why don't you, between your quests for justice today, give it some thought.'

'Don't talk to me like I'm a moron.'

He kissed her, which was something, but did so lightly before continuing down the steps. 'Go to work, Eve. We'll talk about this later.'

'How come he's in charge?' she muttered. She heard him

say something to Summerset, something quick and careless before the door opened. Closed.

She started down, replaying the scene in her head, with all the sharp, pithy, and clever things she *would* have said if she'd had a few minutes to think about it.

'Lieutenant.' Summerset stood at the base of the stairs, holding out her jacket. It was something he never did. 'I'll see to it that your associates have the equipment they require.'

'Yeah, great. Fine.'

'Lieutenant.'

She shoved her arms into the jacket, snarled at him. 'What, goddamn it?'

He didn't so much as blink. 'Regarding your actions of last evening—'

'Don't you start on me, hatchet-face.' She shoved by him, wrenched open the doors.

'I believe,' he continued in the same mild tone, 'those actions were quite correct.'

He might as well have stunned her with her own weapon. Her mouth fell open as she looked back at him. 'What did you say?'

'I also believe your hearing is unimpaired, and I dislike repeating myself.' That said, he walked down the hall and left her staring at him.

Chapter Nine

Nadine Furst was precisely on time, and ready to roll live. Eve hadn't agreed to a live feed, but she didn't object. It was a minor point, but one that Nadine noted.

They were friends, which didn't surprise either of them as much as it once had. They settled into the one-on-one interview in Eve's office with the smooth rhythm of practice. There were no bombshells. Nadine was fully aware Eve Dallas dropped no ammunition unless she intended to use it for her own purposes.

Still, the early interview with the primary investigator and the precise and carefully edited data put her report and her ratings considerably higher than her competition.

'With the available information,' Nadine concluded, 'it would appear that Detective Kohli and Lieutenant Mills were killed in broadly different manners. Is it their attachment to the same precinct, the same squad, that leads you to believe their deaths are connected?'

Smart, Eve thought. She had no doubt Nadine had done a quick crash course on both victims and knew of their work on the Ricker bust. But she was clever enough not to bring up the man's name before Eve gave her the signal.

'That connection, and certain evidence the department is not able to make public, leads us to believe both Detective Kohli and Lieutenant Mills were killed by the same individual. In addition to their attachment to the One twenty-eighth, these officers had worked on some of the same cases. Those avenues are being pursued. The New York Police and Security Department will employ all available means to track down, identify, and bring to justice the killer of two of its own.'

'Thank you, Lieutenant. This is Nadine Furst reporting live from Cop Central for Channel 75.' She tossed the playback to her station, nodded at her camera operator, then sat back.

Much like, Eve thought, *a cat preparing to feast on a fat canary.*

'Now,' she began.

'I'm running a little short on time here. I have to be in court.'

Nadine popped out of the chair. 'Dallas—'

'Why don't you walk me over?' Eve said casually, and gave the camera person a bland stare.

'Sure. It's a nice day for a walk. Lucy, go on back to base. I'll catch transpo.'

'Whatever.' Always affable, and perfectly aware something more was up, Lucy hauled her camera out.

'Talk to me,' Nadine demanded when they were alone. 'Ricker.'

'Not here. Let's walk.'

'Oh. You actually meant that.' Nadine glanced down at her stylish but impractical heels. 'Hell, how I suffer to give the public their right to know.'

'You only wear those torture devices because they make your legs look hot.'

'Damn right.' Resigned, Nadine followed Eve out of the office. 'So how are things on a personal front?'

Eve took the glide down, surprised at how nearly she skimmed toward telling Nadine about her problem with Roarke. Nadine was a woman, after all, and Eve had a feeling she needed to talk to a female about strategy or something.

Then it occurred to her that Nadine, for all her polished

looks, sharp brains, and basic good humor, wasn't one of the top runners in the successful race of male-female relationships.

'Fine.'

'Well, that certainly took some time. A little trouble in paradise?'

There was just enough sympathy in the tone to have Eve skirting a little closer to the edge. 'I'm just distracted.'

She stepped outside, opting to take the long way around. She wanted the air, she wanted the time. And she wanted the relative privacy of a crowded street.

'An anonymous police source, Nadine.'

'I'll give you that, Dallas, but I have to tell you that coming so hard on the one-on-one, it's going to be fairly easy to pin you as that source.'

'No kidding?'

Nadine studied her friend's face. 'Excuse me for being one step behind. I'll just catch up now. You want certain parties to tag you, or at least suspect you, as the source of the information you're going to give me.'

'I'm not going to give you information so much as supposition. You do what you like with it. You already know, or I'm wasting my time talking to you, that Kohli and Mills were on the task force that busted Max Ricker.'

'Yeah, I've picked that up. But then again, there were more than a dozen cops and various official drones on that task force. Ricker's bad news, but it's a long stretch to think he'd scrape his knuckles having a whole group of cops taken out. And for what? The annoyance factor? He lost a big pile of money, but he got off.'

'There's reason to believe he had a connection to at least one of the victims.' *Keep it vague*, Eve thought. *Let the reporter do the digging.* 'There are four men coming up for a hearing this morning who are allegedly employed by Max Ricker. They are charged with various crimes, including

131

the unlawful vehicular pursuit of a police officer. Seems to me if Ricker's ballsy enough to send goons after a cop in broad daylight, he wouldn't stick at arranging for the murder of cops.'

'He came after you? Dallas, as a reporter, that tip makes me incredibly hot and excited.' But she laid a hand on Eve's arm. 'As your friend, I'd like to advise you to take a vacation. Far, far away.'

Eve stopped at the steps of the courthouse. 'Your police source can't tell you that Ricker is a suspect in the murder, or the conspiracy to murder, two NYPSD officers. But your source can tell you that the investigation is taking a cold, hard look at the activities, associations, and businesses of one Max Edward Ricker.'

'You won't nail him, Dallas. He's like smoke, just keeps shifting and vanishing.'

'Watch me,' Eve invited, and strode up the steps.

'I'm going to,' Nadine murmured. 'And I'm going to worry, damn it.'

Eve pushed through the doors and tried not to sigh over the line for the security scan. She chose the shortest for police and city officials, inched her way forward, and had just cleared when all hell broke loose.

She heard the shouts from the second level where Lewis's hearing was scheduled and, charging up the stairs, pushed her way through the crowd of lawyers and court groupies that had already gathered.

Lewis was on the floor, his face gray, his eyes rolled back.

'He just keeled over!' someone called out. 'Just keeled right over. Somebody call the MTs. Get a doctor.'

She was swearing as she charged forward, crouched down.

'Ma'am, you'll have to move back.'

She looked up at the uniform. 'Dallas, Lieutenant Eve. This one's mine.'

'Sorry, Lieutenant. I've called for medical.'

'He's not breathing.' She straddled him, ripped open his shirt, and started CPR. 'Get these people back. Lock down the area—'

'Lock down—'

'Lock it down,' she ordered, and gave her breath to Lewis, knowing it was futile.

She worked on him until the medical techs arrived and pronounced him. Disgusted, she cornered his guard. 'Report. I want to know everything that happened from the time you got him out of his cell.'

'Standard, sir, right down the line.' The uniform was ready to be resentful that anyone would point the finger at him because some hired hammer's heart went bad. 'Due to the charges, the subject was cuffed, then transported here.'

'Who was in the transport?'

'Myself and my partner. The orders were that he wasn't to come into contact with the other three suspects. We walked him through, walked him up to this level.'

'You didn't use the secured elevator?'

'No, sir.' He twitched very slightly at that. 'It was jammed, Lieutenant. We brought him up the steps. He didn't give us any trouble. His lawyer was here and asked us to wait a moment until he'd finished up a consult with another client, via palm-link. We stood by, then the subject staggered and fell. He gasped for breath, and while my partner checked him over, I attempted to keep the crowd at a distance. Shortly thereafter, you arrived on the scene.'

'What precinct are you with?' She skimmed a glance over his nameplate. 'Officer Harmon.'

'Sir, I'm assigned to Central, Security Division.'

'Who approached or had contact with the subject?'

'No one, sir. My partner and I flanked him, per procedure.'

'Are you telling me no one came close to this guy before he dropped?'

'No. That is, we went through security, as required. There were a number of people on line, and a number moving through the area. But no one spoke to the deceased or had physical contact with him. Someone stopped my partner and inquired about directions to the civil court area.'

'The person who wanted directions – how close did he get to the subject?'

'She, sir. It was a female. She appeared to be in some distress and stopped as we were walking by each other.'

'Get a good look at her, Harmon?'

'Yes, sir. Early twenties, blonde, blue eyes, fair complexion. She'd been crying, sir, was crying but trying not to, if you understand me. She was visibly distressed, and when she dropped her handbag some of the contents scattered.'

'I bet you and your partner were very helpful picking up those items for her.'

Her tone alerted him, and Harmon began to feel slightly ill. 'Sir. It couldn't have taken more than ten seconds, and the suspect was restrained and never out of our sight.'

'Let me show you something, Harmon, and you can tell your partner once he finishes jerking off.' She signaled the MTs aside. 'Come down here,' she ordered, once again crouching by the body. 'Do you see this faint red mark, the small circular mark over the deceased's heart?'

He had to look hard, but since he was now close to terrified, Harmon all but jammed his nose against Lewis's chest. 'Yes, sir.'

'Do you know what that is, Officer?'

'No, sir. No, sir, I don't.'

'It's the mark left by a pressure syringe. Your weepy blonde assassinated your charge under your goddamn nose.'

She had every corner of the building searched for a woman matching the description Harmon gave her, but she expected to find nothing. And found exactly that. She called in a crime scene unit to start the process of a homicide investigation and gave herself the pleasure of interrogating Canarde.

'You knew he was going to roll, didn't you?'

'I have no idea what you're talking about, Lieutenant.' Back at Central, idly examining his manicure, Canarde sat placidly in Interview Three. 'I will remind you that I'm here voluntarily. I was nowhere near my unfortunate client this morning, and you have yet to determine whether his death was other than by natural causes.'

'A healthy man, under fifty, keels over from a heart attack. Convenient, particularly since the PA's office was prepared to offer him immunity for turning evidence against another of your clients.'

'If immunity was being offered, Lieutenant, I am unaware of it, as I was uninformed of such an offer. As the deceased's attorney of record, it would have been required that such an offer be made through me or in my presence.'

He had small teeth, perfect little teeth. And he showed them when he stretched his lips in a smile. 'I believe you've stepped over, or certainly around, a line of legal procedure. It doesn't appear to have worked out well for my client.'

'You got that right. You can inform your client, Canarde, that all he's done here is piss me off. I work harder when I'm pissed off.'

Canarde gave her another of his snakelike smiles. 'My client, Lieutenant, is beyond caring. Now, if you'll excuse me, I must do my duty by the tragic Mr Lewis. I believe he had an ex-wife and a brother. I'll offer them my condolences. And, if by some quirk of fate, you happen to be correct about Mr Lewis being helped into the grave, I will advise his family to sue the NYPSD for negligence and wrongful death. It would be a great personal pleasure to represent them in the civil case.'

'I bet he doesn't even have to pay you, Canarde. He just tosses you the fish, and you jump up, squeal, and dive into the muck to get it back.'

The amusement faded from his eyes, though his mouth continued to smile. He got to his feet, nodded, then left the room.

'I should have anticipated it,' Eve told her commander. 'I should have figured Ricker had sources in the department and in the PA's office.'

'You covered yourself.' A low, burning anger simmered inside Whitney. He would use it like fuel. 'Only necessary personnel were informed of the plans to grant immunity.'

'Still, it leaked. And with Lewis taken out this way, I'll never turn any of the others on Ricker. I can't even assure myself they'll do the maximum time. I need a lever, Commander. I got under his skin once, and I can do it again. But I need something, no matter how minor, to justify bringing him in to Interview.'

'That won't be easy. He's too well insulated. Mills,' Whitney said. 'You have no doubt he was taking.'

'No, sir. I don't. But as to connecting the funds back to Ricker, I don't know. Feeney's on it, and I have several different angles I'm going to pursue.'

'From this point on in this investigation, I want daily reports of every step you and your team makes. Every step, Lieutenant.'

'Yes, sir.'

'I want the names of every cop you're looking at, the ones you've cleared to your satisfaction, and the ones you haven't.'

'Yes, sir.'

'If you believe the involvement in the department goes beyond Mills and Kohli, IAB will have to be informed.'

They watched each other a moment, treading a line.

'Sir, I would hesitate to inform Internal Affairs until such time as I have evidence substantiating what, at this point in the investigation, is only a suspicion of further involvement.'

'And how much time do you estimate your hesitation will encompass?'

'If I could have twenty-four hours, Commander.'

'One day, Dallas,' he said with a nod. 'Neither of us can afford to dance around it longer than that.'

She didn't waste time but tracked down Martinez, contacted her, and requested a meeting. Off police territory, Eve thought, would make it easier all around.

She met Martinez at a small coffee shop between both their bases. Far enough away from each location to insure it wasn't a cop hangout.

Martinez arrived a few minutes late, giving Eve the opportunity to observe, to judge. Going by body language, it was clear Martinez's defenses were up.

'I had to take personal time for this.' Her shoulders as stiff as her voice, Martinez slid into the booth across from Eve. 'And I don't have a lot of it.'

'Fine. My clock's ticking, too. You want coffee?'

'I don't drink it.'

'How do you live?'

Martinez gave a sour smile, signaled the serving droid, and ordered water. 'And don't pour it from the tap,' she warned. 'I'll know and fry your circuits. Let's just cut through the crap,' Martinez continued, turning back to Eve. 'You're looking for me to hang something on Kohli and Mills, and it ain't gonna happen. You're looking to dig up dirt, doing scut work for IAB. That turns my stomach.'

Eve picked up her coffee and watched Martinez placidly over the rim. 'Well, that covers that. Now, just where do you get all this information?'

'Word gets around when one cop's hunting others. It's all over the One two-eight. We've got two dead cops. It seems to me you'd be more interested in finding out who did them than in turning up muck before they're even in the fucking ground.'

That kind of temper, while Eve respected it, wasn't going

to help Martinez work her way up the chain in rank. 'Whatever you've heard, whatever you think, finding out who did them is my priority.'

'Yeah, right. Your priority is covering your husband's ass.'

'Excuse me?'

'He owns Purgatory. I figure maybe something was up there, and Kohli tuned into it. They didn't know he was a cop, so maybe they weren't careful. And when he got too close, they took him out.'

'And Mills?'

Martinez shrugged. 'You're the one saying they're connected.'

'You know, Martinez, when I first met you and Mills, I figured he was the moron of the pair. Now, here you are, seriously damaging my self-esteem by showing me my character judgment stinks.'

'You're not my commanding officer.' Martinez had dark eyes. Now they fired like black suns. 'I don't have to take crap from you.'

'Then take some advice from someone who's been on the job longer. Learn when to jab and when to wait. You've been here under five minutes and told me more than I've asked.'

'I haven't told you dick.'

'You told me that someone's starting talk at your precinct. That word's already out – likely through that source – that there's reason to believe Kohli and Mills were taking. Ask yourself where that came from? Who'd want to put cops on their guard and looking sideways at me? Think, Detective.'

To give her a minute to do so, Eve sipped at her coffee. 'I don't have to cover for Roarke. He's been handling himself for a long time. Nobody but someone who'd have something to worry about has cause to suspect or know that part of my investigation is turning up dirt on the two victims.'

'Word gets out,' Martinez said, but her tone wasn't quite

so confident. She reached for her water the minute it was on the table.

'Yeah, especially when someone wants it to. You think I arranged to put over three million dollars in Kohli's and Mills's accounts to cover my husband's ass? You think I've maybe been funneling it there for months to try to create a scandal involving fellow cops?'

'You're the one saying the money was there.'

'That's right. I'm saying it.'

Martinez said nothing for a moment, just staring back into Eve's eyes. Then she closed her own. 'Hell. Oh, hell. I'm not turning on another cop. I'm fifth generation. There's been a cop in my family for over a hundred years. That means something to me. We have to stand up for each other.'

'I'm not asking you to judge. I'm asking you to think. Not every one of us respects the badge. Two of the men on your task force are dead. Both of them had more money stashed away than most cops can save in a lifetime on the job. Now they're dead. Somebody got close enough to them to take them out before they could blink. Are you ready to be next?'

'Next? You see me as a target?' The fire came back into Martinez's eyes. 'You think I've been taking.'

'I haven't seen anything to make me think that. And I've looked.'

'Goddamn bitch. I worked my ass off to make detective. Now you're going to toss me to IAB?'

'I'm not tossing you anywhere. But if you're not straight with me, you're going to hang yourself. One way or another. Who's at the core of this?' Eve demanded, leaning forward. 'Be a detective, for Christ's sake, and figure it. Who connects Kohli and Mills and has the money to turn a cop into a weasel?'

'Ricker.' Martinez's fingers curled on the table until her fist ran white across the knuckles. 'Goddamn it.'

'You had him, didn't you? You went into that bust knowing

you had everything you needed for an arrest, an indictment, and a conviction. You were careful.'

'It took me months to set it up. I lived with that case twenty-four/seven. I made sure I didn't miss anything. Didn't rush it. Then to have it all fall apart. I couldn't figure it. I kept telling myself the son of a bitch was just too slick, too well covered. But still . . . Part of me knew he had to have somebody inside. Had to. But I didn't want to look there. I still don't.'

'But now you will.'

Martinez lifted her glass, drank water as though her throat was scorched. 'Why am I being tagged?'

'Spotted the surveillance, did you?'

'Yeah, I spotted it. I figured you were going after me next.'

'If I find out you're in bed with Ricker, I will. Right now, the tag's for your protection.'

'I want it off. If I'm going to throw in with you, I need to move without somebody breathing down my neck. I have a personal copy of all the data, all my notes, every step leading up to Ricker's bust. After the case fell apart, I looked over them, but my heart wasn't in it. It will be now.'

'I'd like a copy.'

'It's my work.'

'And when we take him down, I'll see to it you get the collar.'

'It means something to me. The job means something to me. This case . . . the captain said I'd lost my objectivity. She was right,' Martinez added with a twist of her lips. 'I did. I ate that case for breakfast every morning and I slept with it every night. If I'd kept the right distance, I might have seen all this coming. I might have seen how Mills insinuated himself into it until he was calling shots. I just took it as his usual macho bullshit.'

'We're supposed to stand for each other. You had no reason to look his way.'

'Kohli's memorial's scheduled for day after tomorrow. It comes to me, without doubt, that he was looped with Ricker, I'll spit on his grave. My grandfather went down in the line of duty during the Urban Wars. He saved two kids. They're somewhat older than I am, and they write my grandmother every year at Christmas, and again on the anniversary of the day it happened. They never forget. It's not just about the collar, Dallas. It's about being a cop.'

Eve nodded, and after a moment's hesitation, leaned in again. 'Martinez, I worked on one of Ricker's spine crackers, had him ready to roll. The deal was going through the PA's office for immunity. He had a hearing this morning. Walking down the hall in the courtyard, between two cops, he got hit. He's dead. Just like that. There are leaks, and I don't know where to begin to plug them. I want you to know before you start on this that I may not be able to keep a lid on it. I may not be able to keep your name out of the mix. And that could put you in the crosshairs.'

Martinez pushed her empty glass aside. 'Like I said. It's about being a cop.'

Eve spent the rest of the day backtracking, reading data until her eyes stung. She went back to Patsy Kohli under the pretext of a follow-up. After twenty minutes, she was convinced the grieving widow had known nothing.

That's what her gut told her, Eve thought as she got into her car again. She just wasn't sure she could trust her gut anymore.

She had a new list working in her brain, the one McNab was shooting her every few hours. A line of cops he'd cleared, another line of those who remained suspect.

Because Central was closer, she slipped back to her office there and ran a series of probabilities using the new data and the new list of names.

No matter how she juggled it, she found nothing conclusive.

And would find nothing, she thought, until she dug deeper. They would have to pick the lives of these cops apart, like crows on fleshy bones. Every time they cleared one, it would put more weight on the rest.

She knew what it was to undergo an internal investigation, to have the hounds of IAB sniffing at her heels. Being clean didn't make it less nasty. Being clean didn't wash the vile aftertaste out of your throat.

She couldn't go deeper without sending up flags. Unless she made use of Roarke's unregistered and illegal equipment. She couldn't make use of it without his help. She didn't have the skill to peel those layers away on her own.

And she couldn't ask him for help when she'd made such a big damn deal about wanting him uninvolved.

She put her head in her hands, unsurprised, in fact almost pleased that it was throbbing. A good, solid headache would give her something else to be unhappy about.

She decided to head home. And on the way passed Mavis's billboard. Before she could think about it, she'd engaged her 'link and tried Mavis at home, without any real hope of catching her there.

'Hello. Hey! Hey, Dallas!'

'Guess what I'm looking at?'

'A naked, one-armed pygmy.'

'Damn. Okay, you're too good at this. Talk to you later.'

'Wait, wait.' Giggling, Mavis shifted in front of her own 'link as if that would somehow give her the angle of Eve's view. 'What is it really?'

'You. About a million times bigger than life over Times fucking Square.'

'Oh! Is that iced, or what? Is that beyond Arctic? I keep finding excuses to go down and look at it. I want to give your husband a big, wet, sloppy kiss. Leonardo says it's all right with him, under the circumstances, but I thought I should clear it with you.'

142

'I don't tell Roarke who he can kiss.'

Mavis's eyebrows, currently a neon magenta, rose straight up into her blueberry-colored hair. 'Oh oh. Are you having a fight?'

'No. Yes. No. I don't know what the hell we're having. He's barely speaking to me. Are you – never mind.'

'Am I what?' She put a hand over her screen, made Eve roll her eyes while she had a whispered conversation with someone else in the room. 'Sorry. Leonardo's trying out a new stage costume. Hey, why don't you come by?'

'No. You're busy.'

'Uh-uh. Come on, Dallas, you never come by the old place. If you're in Times Square, you can be here in a heartbeat. I was just thinking I was going to make a big batch of screamers. So I'll see you in a few.'

'No – I—' She hissed a breath at the blank screen, nearly called back and made excuses. Then she shrugged, felt her back go up when she remembered that coolly distant tone Roarke had used on her that morning. 'What the hell,' she muttered. 'Just for a few minutes.'

Chapter Ten

Mavis Freestone and her lover Leonardo cohabited in Eve's old apartment.

What a difference a year made.

Eve had lived in the single-bedroom unit contentedly enough with a few basic pieces of furniture, no decor to speak of, and an AutoChef that was empty more often than stocked. She'd preferred to think of her lifestyle as simple rather than bland.

Then again, compared to Mavis, a surf on Saturn's outer rings in a comet buster was bland.

The minute Mavis opened the door, Eve was struck with color. Blasts of it. Every hue and tone on the palette was turned up to scream level, in patterns and textures that boggled the eye.

And that was just Mavis.

The living area of the apartment was draped with miles of fabrics. Some, she supposed, were art of some kind; others, Leonardo's designs in progress. The rather lumpy sofa Eve had left behind when she'd moved in with Roarke was covered now with a bright and nervy pink material that shimmered like polished glass. If that wasn't enough, it was heaped with pillows and throws of clashing colors that seemed to drip onto the floor where more cloths were cleverly tossed in lieu of rugs.

Beads and spangles and ribbons, and God knew what, rained

down the walls, tinkled gaily from the ceiling, which had been painted a high-sheen silver studded with crimson stars.

Even the tables were fabric, arty lumps of shape that could be called in for seating in a pinch. Eve didn't think there was a hard surface or a right angle left in the place.

And while she was vaguely concerned that staying there for any length of time might bring on a stroke, it was a frame that suited the picture of her oldest friend perfectly.

The effect was something like a storm-edged sunrise. On Venus.

'I'm so glad you came by.' Mavis dragged Eve into the psychodelia, then turned a stylish circle. 'What do you think?'

'Of what, exactly?'

'Of the new gear?'

Tiny, slim, and bright as a fairy wand, Mavis turned again, showing off a short-skirted . . . you couldn't call it a dress, Eve decided. A costume, she supposed, of crossed diagonal stripes that ran from deep purple to neon pink and back again. The bodice scooped low, just tucking the nipples under and left Mavis's shoulder – adorned now with twin pansy tattoos – bare.

Sleeves – they had to be sleeves because as far as Eve knew, gloves had hands – skimmed down her arms. Needle-heeled boots, in the same dizzy stripes, rode up her legs to just under crotch level.

'It's—' She had no idea. 'Amazing.'

'Yeah, isn't it? TTT. Too totally terrific. Trina's going to do my hair to match. Leonardo's a complete genius. Leonardo, Dallas is here. He's making a batch of screamers,' she told Eve. 'You came by at the exact moment. I hate drinking alone, and you know how Leonardo can't.'

She kept up the chatter, pulling Eve toward the pink couch. She wasn't giving her friend a chance to escape until she knew what was going on.

'Here he is.' Her voice went to coo, her eyes went gooey. 'Thanks, honey love.'

Leonardo, a giant of a man with long, glossy braids, gold eyes, and the smooth copper skin of a mixed-race heritage, swirled into the room. He moved with uncanny grace for a man topping six-five and wearing a hooded ankle duster of Atlantic blue. He beamed at Mavis, and the ruby studs beside his mouth and just under his left eyebrow winked flirtatiously.

He cooed right back at her. 'You're welcome, turtledove. Hello, Dallas. I put together a little snack, in case you haven't had dinner.'

'Isn't he TTT?'

'You bet,' Eve said as Mavis cuddled up against him. Even in the boots, she didn't make it to his breastbone. 'You didn't have to go to any trouble, Leonardo.'

'None at all.' He set down a tray loaded with food and drink. 'It's nice you came by so Mavis won't spend the evening alone. I have some appointments.'

Mavis sent him an adoring look. Their plans had been to have a rare quiet evening together. When she'd told him Eve was coming by and something was wrong, he'd agreed without a murmur to her request that he make himself scarce.

He was, Mavis thought with a sigh, perfect.

'I can't stay long,' Eve began, but Leonardo was already scooping Mavis up in his long arms, kissing her in a deep and intimate way that had Eve wincing and looking away.

'Enjoy yourself, my dove.'

He sent Eve a quick, flashing smile and managed to glide out of the apartment without running into anything.

'He didn't have any appointments.'

Mavis started to protest, then grinned, shrugged, and plopped down to pour the first round of screamers. 'I told him we wanted a little girl time. He was ultracool with it. So . . .' She passed Eve a glass the size of a small bird-bath, filled to the rim with emerald green liquid. 'You wanna get a buzz on, then tell me about it, or just dive in?'

Eve opened her mouth, then closed it and pursed her lips. It had been a hell of a long time since she'd downed a batch of screamers with Mavis. 'Maybe I can get a buzz on while I tell you.'

'Solid.' Mavis tapped her glass against Eve's and knocked back the first of what promised to be many.

'So . . .' Mavis was on her third screamer, and most of the soy chips, whey-cheese dip, and corn doodles Leonardo had arranged were long consumed. 'Let me sort of put this in a box. You went to square off with some bad guy who used to have business with Roarke, without telling Roarke you were going.'

'It's police business. It's my job.'

'Okay, okay, I'm just scoping it down. Then the bad guy sent second-string bad guys after you.'

'I handled it.'

Mavis glanced over with a gimlet look in her eye. 'You want my take or just your own?'

'I'm shutting up,' Eve muttered and poured another screamer.

'When you got back home, there were flowers from the bad guy and a smarmy card.' Because Eve's mouth opened again, Mavis held up a purple-tipped finger. 'You figured he did it to rile you up and to get Roarke's goat, so you had Summerset ditch the posies. But Roarke saw them and called you on it. Then you were like: "Duh, what flowers?"'

'I didn't say "duh."' The screamers were doing the job. 'I never say that. I think, maybe, I said "Huh." That's entirely different.'

'Whatever. You . . . what's a word that means lie, but's nicer than lie?' Mavis closed one eye as if to sharpen her focus. 'Fib. You fibbed because you didn't want Roarke to go out and

147

crush the bad guy like a bug and maybe get messed up in the process.'

Eve actually preferred the word lie to the word fib but decided not to make an issue of it. 'More or less.'

'Well, that was stupid.'

Eve's mouth fell open. 'Stupid? You're saying I was stupid? You're supposed to tell me I was right. That's how this works.'

'Dallas.' Mavis leaned over, then slid gracefully to the floor. 'You didn't figure the man factor. They got dicks. You can't ever forget the dick when you're dealing with a man.'

'What're you talking about?' Eve slid to the floor as well, sucked down the rest of her drink. 'I know Roarke has a dick. He uses it every chance he gets.'

'The dick's connected to the ego. It's medical fact. Or maybe it's the other way around.' With a shrug, Mavis emptied the last of the screamers. 'It's a mystery to all womankind. You didn't trust him to handle himself.'

'He didn't trust me to handle myself.'

'Dallas, Dallas.' Shaking her head, Mavis patted Eve's thigh. 'Dallas,' she said a third time, with great pity. 'Let's make more screamers. We'll need them when we get to the men are pigs stage.'

Halfway through batch two, Eve lay on the floor staring up at the beads raining from the silver ceiling. 'If men are pigs, why do so many of us have one?'

'Because women work on an emotional level.' Mavis hiccupped delicately. 'Even you.'

Eve rolled over, eyed Mavis narrowly. 'Do not.'

'Do, too. First he got you by the hormones. I mean, Jesus, look at him. The man's a sexual . . . Gimme a minute. A sexual . . . banquet. Yeah, that's a good one. Then he clicked into your head, because he's smart and interesting and mysterious and all that stuff you'd really go for. But then, the whammer was when he jammed right into your heart. Whatcha gonna do then? A guy's got his hooks in your heart, he just reels you right in.'

'I'm not a goddamn fish.'

'We are all fish,' Mavis said in rounded tones, 'in the great sea of life.'

Eve had swallowed enough screamers to find that hysterically funny. 'You moron,' she managed when she got her breath back.

'Hey, I'm not the one in emotional crisis here.' On her hands and knees, Mavis crawled over and kissed Eve, smackingly, on the cheek. 'Poor baby. Mommy's gonna tell you just what to do to make it all better.'

She crawled off for the screamers, crawled back, and poured them out into the glasses, somehow managing not to spill a single potent drop.

'Well, what?'

'Fuck his brains out.'

'That's it? That's Mommy's best advice?'

'It's the only advice. Men, being pigs and having the dick factor, will usually forget what they were pissed about if you lay them right.'

'So I'm supposed to use sex to fix this?' Somewhere in her alcohol-dulled brain there was a glimmer of a thought that this approach was seriously marred. But she couldn't quite grab onto it. 'It could work,' she decided.

'Guaranteed. But . . .'

'I knew there was a but. I could almost feel it.'

'It's only a . . . what do you call it, a temporary measure. Dallas, you've got like, you know, issues. So you gotta figure out why you went behind his back. Not that there's anything really wrong with that, 'cause sometimes you just gotta do what you do. But what you got here are two really rock heads that are rapping up against each other.' She demonstrated by banging her hands together, and spilled some screamer after all. 'Oops.'

'You're saying I'm a rock head?'

'Sure you are. That's why I love you. And when you got those rock heads smacking together like that, you're gonna have something crack now and again.'

'He's hardly speaking to me.'

'He's so mean.' Mavis polished off the screamer, then gave Eve a hard hug. 'Want some ice cream?'

'I'll be sick. What kind?'

They ended up back on the floor with enormous bowls of Triple Fudge Decadence topped with clouds of pink whipped cream.

'I wasn't wrong,' Eve said between bites.

'Of course you weren't. We're women. We're never wrong.'

'Even Summerset went on my side, and he hates me.'

'Doesn't hate you.'

'I love the stupid son of a bitch.'

'Aw, that's so sweet.' Mavis's eyes, seriously blurred, went moist with sentiment. 'If you'd tell him, you guys would get along better.'

It took Eve a minute. 'Not Summerset. Jeez. Roarke. I love *that* stupid son of a bitch. You'd think he could cut me a break when this case is hammering at me, and I don't know what I'm doing.'

'You always know what you're doing. That's why you're Dallas, Lieutenant Eve.'

'Not with the job, Mavis. I know what I'm doing with the job. With Roarke, with the marriage deal, with this love crap. You must be drunk.'

'Of course I'm drunk. We each drank an entire batch of Leonardo's – isn't he the cutest thing – special screamer mix.'

'You're right.' Eve set her empty bowl aside, pressed a hand to her stomach. 'I have to go throw up now.'

'Okay. I'm next, so let me know when you're done.'

As Eve stumbled to her feet, staggered out of the room, Mavis simply curled up, tucked one of the satin throws under her head, and went blissfully to sleep.

Eve washed her face, studied her pale, sloppy-eyed reflection in the mirror. She looked soft, she thought. Soft, a little stupid, and more than drunk. With some regret, she raided Mavis's supply of Sober-Up. After brief consideration, she decided to take only one. She wasn't quite ready to give up the buzz a full dose would dull.

When she found Mavis asleep on the floor, like a doll among a forest of colorful toys, she grinned. 'What would I do without you?'

She leaned down, gave Mavis's shoulder a little shake. When she got a sexy little purr as a response, she decided to forgo her plan to help Mavis to bed. Instead, she plucked one of the many fabric throws off the sofa, tucked it around her sleeping friend.

And straightening again, had her head spin.

'Yep, still half drunk. Good enough.'

She left the apartment, rolling her shoulders like a boxer prepping for a bout. She would deal with Roarke all right, she thought. She was more than ready for it.

The fresh air hit her, knocked her back. She stood a moment, breathing slowly, then walked, in mostly a straight line, to her car. She had wit enough to program it to auto and let it take her home.

She was going to straighten this out, she told herself. Yes, she was. And if she had to get Roarke into bed to do it, well . . . the sacrifices she had to make.

That made her snort with laughter and settle back to enjoy the ride.

New York looked so cheerful, she decided. The glide-carts were doing brisk business, as the pedestrian traffic was thick.

The street thieves, she thought with mild affection, were having a field day plucking the tourists and the unwary.

Greasy smoke stinking of overcooked soy dogs and rehydrated onion bits plumed in front of her car. Two street LCs were in a shoving match on the corner of Sixth and Sixty-second while a hopeful john cheered them on. One Rapid Cab tried a sneak maneuver around another, missed, and scraped fenders. The two drivers were out of the cars like jacks from the box, squaring off with fists.

God. She loved New York.

She watched a flock of the head-shaven Pure Sect, well out of their bailiwick, herd each other uptown. An ad blimp, past curfew, glided overhead and touted the delights of a package trip to Vegas II. Four days, three nights, round-trip and deluxe accommodations for two, all for the low-low-low price of twelve thousand and eighty-five.

What a deal.

The blimp chugged its way downtown as she continued up.

The pedestrian traffic thinned out and trimmed up. The glide-carts took on a sheen.

Welcome to Roarke's world, she thought, amused at herself.

As she approached the gates, a figure stepped into the path of her vehicle. Eve let out a yelp, and fortunately, the programming accessed the obstruction and hit the brakes. Mild annoyance turned to disgust when Webster stepped out of the shadows.

She rolled down her window, glared at him. 'You got a death wish? This is a city vehicle, and I was on auto.'

'Good thing, as you look a little impaired.' Sleepy, he thought. Sleepy, smashed, and sexy. 'Night on the town?'

'Bite me, Webster. What do you want?'

'I need to talk to you.' He glanced at the gates. 'It's not easy getting into this place. How about a lift?'

'I don't want you in my house.'

The engaging smile he'd fixed on his face hardened. 'Ten minutes, Dallas. I promise not to steal the silver.'

'I have an office at Central. Make an appointment.'

'If it wasn't important, do you think I'd be hanging out in front of your house waiting to give you a chance to bust my balls?'

She wished she didn't see the logic of that. Wished she wasn't sober enough to resist the urge to roll the window up and leave him outside the gates. She jerked a thumb toward the passenger seat. While he walked around the car to get in, it occurred to her that for the last few hours, murder hadn't entered her head.

'It better be important, Webster. If you're hosing me, I'm going to do a lot more than bust your balls.'

She completed the turn toward the gates. Her vehicle ID was scanned, and they opened silently.

'Pretty heavy security for a residence,' he commented.

She didn't nibble at that particular bait, but she wished she'd gone for both Sober-Ups so her mind would be absolutely clear.

She left the car at the end of the drive, led the way up the steps. He was doing his best not to gape at the house but didn't manage to swallow the low whistle when she opened the front door.

'I've got a meeting,' she said, even as Summerset stepped into view and opened his mouth.

With her hands jammed in her pockets, she headed upstairs. Webster gave up, stared down at the elegant butler, scanned what he could see of the lower floor. 'Some place. I'm trying to picture you in this palace. You never struck me as the princess type.'

But when he stepped into her office, one Roarke had modeled to reflect her previous apartment, he nodded. 'This is more like it. Streamlined and practical.'

'Now that I have your approval, spill it. I've got work to do.'

'You had time to go out and knock a few back tonight.'

She angled her head, folded her arms. 'Are you under the impression you have any say in what I do with my time, on or off the job?'

'Just an observation.' He prowled the room, picking up, setting back, items at random, then nearly jolted when he saw the enormous cat curled up in his sleep chair and watching him out of narrowed bicolored eyes.

'Palace guard?'

'Damn right. One word from me, and he'll claw your eyes out and eat your tongue. Don't make me set him off.'

He laughed, ordered himself to relax. 'Got any coffee?'

'Yes.' She stood just where she was.

He laughed again, a short, resigned sound. 'I was going to say you used to be friendlier, but you weren't. Something about that mean streak of yours always did it for me. I must be sick.'

'Get to the point, or get out.'

He nodded, yet still he stalled, walking to her window, staring out. 'Your current avenues of investigation are infringing on an IAB movement.'

'Aw, I feel so bad about that.'

'I warned them about you. They didn't listen. Had this idea that you could be handled.' He turned back, met her eyes. 'I'm here to order you off Ricker.'

'You have no authority to order me off anything.'

'Request,' he amended. 'I'm here to request you back off your investigation of Max Ricker.'

'Request denied.'

'Dallas, you push the wrong buttons, you could screw up an investigation that's been in the works for months.'

'An internal investigation?'

'I'm not at liberty to confirm or deny.'

'Then leave.'

'I'm trying to give you a hand here. If you just back off, we'll both end up getting what we're after.'

She eased a hip on the edge of her desk. 'I want a cop killer. What do you want?'

'You think it doesn't matter to me.' His voice took on heat. His eyes flashed with it. 'The way those two men went down?'

'I don't know what matters to you, Webster. Why don't you tell me?'

'Doing the job,' he shot back. 'Making sure the job gets done right, and it gets done clean.'

'And Mills and Kohli were dirty.'

He started to speak, then jammed his fists in his pockets. 'I can't comment.'

'I don't need your comments. IAB might have its reasons for wanting to keep that information under wraps for now. Fine. As it happens, so do I. But it's not going to stay under. The connection to Ricker's going to explode before much longer. How many more dead cops do you want me to stand over while you guys dick around with your internal investigation? You knew they were dirty, and you left them out there.'

'It's not as black and white as that.'

'You knew,' she repeated, heating up. 'And that they were in Ricker's pocket, that they'd helped him slide on charges that should have put him in for the rest of his unnatural life. How long have you known?'

'Knowing isn't proving, is it, Lieutenant?'

'Bullshit, Webster. That's just bullshit. In a matter of days I've put together enough on those two cops to have pulled them in and taken their badges. You left them out for a reason. Now you want me to back off Ricker. How do I know he hasn't made room in his pocket for you?'

His eyes flashed again, and he was on her before he could stop himself, dragging her off the desk. 'That's low.'

155

'IAB gives lessons in low.'

'You want to go through the door with a dirty cop? With one who might hesitate just long enough to have you on a slab? There's a reason for what I do, and I don't have to justify it to you. You used to draw a hard, straight line, Dallas. When did it start to go crooked? About the time you hooked up with Roarke?'

'Step back. Now.'

But he didn't. Couldn't. 'Mills was garbage. You want to risk destroying the case we've been building for months so you can stand for him? He'd have sold you out for pocket change.'

'Now he's dead. Is that IAB's sense of justice, to have your guts spilled out for being on the take? If Ricker took him out, he used another cop to do it. Does that balance it in your world?'

His eyes flickered. 'That's reaching.'

'No. No, it's not.' She watched him closely now. 'It's accurate. And you knew it. You knew it, starting with Kohli, and that's why you . . .'

She trailed off as pieces began to shift and fall into another pattern. One that made her stomach churn. 'Kohli. You didn't mention him. Just Mills. Because Kohli wasn't garbage, was he, Webster? He was just a tool. You set him up. You used him.'

'Leave it alone.'

'The hell I will.' Her fury was like a living thing, and it was clawing at her brain. 'He was under for you. He wasn't taking, you were giving. To make him look wrong, so he could pick up information for you, get closer to Ricker's police contacts.'

She closed her eyes as she worked it out. 'You picked him because he was clean, and more, because he was average. Almost invisible. A data cruncher who had a strong sense of right and wrong. You'd have played to him, recruited him,' she murmured, opening her eyes again and studying Webster's.

'His background in the MPs, that was on his side. He was good at taking orders. You probably offered him extra pay, help him save for the bigger place he wanted for his family while his wife stayed home with the kids. Put a real package deal together, appealing to his sense of duty, sense of family. Then there was the Ricker edge. He'd put in a lot of time on that, had to be bummed when it fell apart. You set him up.'

'Nobody held a blaster to his head.' Webster's voice was raw as guilt ate at him. 'There's a serious problem at the One twenty-eight. Kohli fit the profile for what we needed. All he had to do was say no.'

'You knew he wouldn't *because* he fit the fucking profile. Goddamn it, Webster, goddamn it, he was killed because somebody believed the setup. Somebody killed him for being dirty.'

'Are you going to stand there and tell me we should have anticipated that?' He had plenty of fury of his own, and mixed with it was a sticky guilt that made a bitter brew. 'It came out of the fucking blue. He was on the job, Dallas. He knew the risks. We all know them.'

'Yeah, we know the risks, and we live with them. Or we die with them.' But she stepped closer, shoved her face into his. 'You used me, Webster, the same way. And nobody asked. You came to me, all friendly, all unofficial, to toss just enough garbage in my path so I'd look in the right places, so I'd find the money Kohli'd put away, just like you told him to. So I'd look and I'd paint him dirty. You had me looking at a good cop and tossing muck at him.'

'You think that doesn't make me sick?'

'I don't know what makes you sick.'

She started to turn away, but he grabbed her arm. 'He'll be exonerated when the time comes. He'll be put in for a posthumous promotion. His family will be taken care of.'

At her side, her hand bunched into a fist. But she didn't

157

use it. Instead, she used frigid disdain. 'Get away from me. Get out of my house.'

'For God's sake, Dallas, nobody meant for this to happen.'

'But you jumped right on it when it did. He wasn't even cold.'

'It's not my choice.' Enraged, he took her other arm, shook her once. 'I'm not supposed to be here tonight. I'm not supposed to have told you any of this.'

'Then why did you?'

'The bureau will find a way to kick you off the case, or if it suits better, to put you right in Ricker's path. Either way, you're going to walk around with a target on your back. You matter to me.'

He jerked her against him, and she was too shocked to block the move. 'Hey.'

'You matter. You always have.'

She slapped both hands on his chest, felt the rapid pump of his heart. The heat. 'Jesus, Webster. Are you crazy?'

'I'd prefer that you take your hands off my wife before I break them,' Roarke said from the doorway. 'But either way works for me.'

Chapter Eleven

The voice was rigidly pleasant and didn't fool Eve for an instant. She knew the sound of savagery when she heard it, however elegantly it was cloaked. Just as she recognized it in the frigid blue of Roarke's eyes.

She felt the punch of fear, like a blow to her solar plexus. As a result, her voice was sharp and clipped as she broke Webster's hold and stepped deliberately between him and her husband.

'Roarke. Webster and I are in the middle of a meeting, and a professional disagreement.'

'I don't think so. Go find something to do, Eve. Elsewhere.'

Insult worked hard to kick fear aside but didn't manage the job. She felt her muscles begin to tremble and had an image of capping off the evening by arresting her husband for murder.

'Get a grip.' She did her best to plant her boots. 'You've mistaken the situation here.'

'No, he hasn't. Not on my end.' Webster moved away from Eve. 'And I don't hide behind women. You want to do this here?' he said with a nod toward Roarke. 'Or outside?'

Roarke smiled, much Eve thought, like a wolf might before a kill. 'Here and now.'

They leapt at each other. Charged, she would think later when her brain engaged again, like a couple of rams in rutting season. For a moment, she was too stunned to do more than goggle.

She watched Webster fly, come heavily down on a table, which crashed under the weight. Galahad sprang up, hissing, and took a vicious swipe at his shoulder.

He was up quickly, she'd give him that, bleeding. Fists flew with the ugly sound of bone against bone. A lamp shattered.

She was shouting, she could hear herself calling out in a voice that seemed oddly unlike her own. At wit's end, she drew her weapon, hastily checked to insure it was on lowest stun, then fired a stream between them.

Webster's head whipped around in shock, but Roarke didn't so much as flinch. And his fist, already swinging, smashed into Webster's face.

Another table went, splintering into toothpicks. And this time Webster stayed down. Or would have if Roarke hadn't leaned over and hauled him up by the collar.

'Roarke.' Her hand steady, Eve kept her weapon trained. 'That's enough. Let him go or I'll stun you. I swear I will.'

His eyes met hers, hot now, hot enough to burn. He released Webster so the half-conscious man crumpled in a heap. Even as Roarke started toward Eve, Summerset slid into the room.

'I'll just show your guest out.'

'Do that,' Roarke said without taking his eyes from Eve's. 'And close the door. Stun me, will you?' He murmured it, silkily, when he was a foot away.

She backed up, all but hearing her nerves fray. 'If you don't calm down, yes. I'm going to go see how bad he's hurt.'

'You're not, no. That you're not. Stun me then,' he invited, and she heard the alleyways of Dublin in his voice. 'Do it.'

She heard the doors close, the locks click. Fear had her by the throat, infuriating her even as she took another step in retreat. 'There was nothing going on here. It's insulting for you to think there was.'

'Darling Eve, if I thought there'd been anything, on your part, going on here, he wouldn't have left breathing.' There was no change in his expression as his hand snaked out and knocked the weapon from hers. 'Yet you stood between us.'

'To try to avoid this.' She threw out her arms. 'This testosterone explosion. Damn it, you wrecked my place and assaulted an officer, and over nothing. Over my having a professional disagreement with a colleague.'

'A colleague who was once a lover, and what I walked in on was personal.'

'Okay, all right, maybe. But that's no excuse. If I jumped every one of your old lovers, I'd be bashing every female face in New York and the known universe.'

'That's entirely different.'

'Why?' She had him now, she thought with satisfaction. 'Why is it different for you?'

'Because I don't invite those former lovers into my home and let them put their hands on me.'

'It wasn't like that. It was—'

'And because.' He fisted a hand at the front of her shirt, haul-ing her up until she was forced to her toes. 'You're mine.'

Her eyes all but bulged out of her head. 'What? What? Like property? Like one of your damn hotels?'

'Aye. If you like.'

'I don't like. Not one damn bit.' She shoved at his hand, twisted, and only succeeded in ripping the shoulder seam of her shirt. Alarm bells went off in her head even as she tried to break his hold with another counter maneuver. She ended up with her back pressed into him and her arms pinned.

'You've crossed a number of lines in a short time, Lieu-tenant.' His voice was warm against her ear. Warm and dangerous. Erotic. 'Do you think I'm a man who'll go meekly about your bidding? Do you think loving you has taken my teeth?'

As if to prove otherwise, he sank them lightly in her throat.

161

She couldn't think, not with the red haze covering her brain. She quite simply couldn't get her breath. 'Let go of me. I'm too mad to deal with you tonight.'

'No, you're not mad.' He whipped her around again, slammed her back to the wall, and yanked her arms over her head. And his face, the face of a condemned angel, was close to hers. 'Intrigued is what you are, and reluctantly aroused. Your pulse is pounding, and you tremble. Some of it's fear, just a touch of it to add an edge.'

He was right. She could have damned him for it, but need was crawling through her like savage little ants.

'You're hurting me. Let go of my hands.'

'No, I'm not, but perhaps I've been too careful, too often, not to hurt you. Have you forgotten what you took on with me, Eve?'

'No.' Her eyes skimmed down to his mouth. God help her, she wanted it on her.

'You're mine, and you'll say it before we're done tonight.' He reached out with his free hand and ripped her shirt down the center. 'And now I'll have what's mine.'

She resisted, but that was pride, and pride was weaker than lust. She twisted her body, hooking a foot behind his in an attempt to overbalance him. He merely shifted his weight into the move and took her down with him.

The shock of the fall knocked the breath out of her, but her knee came up, an automatic jerk of defense. He rolled away from it, still gripping her hands. Pinned her. She bucked, swore at him, whipping her head to the side as his mouth came down.

He settled for her throat. Savaged it, and sent the pulse beneath his teeth and lips bounding.

He might have stopped himself. The civilized veneer he'd coated over himself was hard set and hard won. But the beast inside him had been teased to raging. He wanted it loose. And the scent of her, of his mate, was humming in his blood.

She was strong. He'd pit his strength and his will against hers before, but always with a sense of fair play underneath. *Not this time*, was all he could think.

Not this time.

He clamped a hand over her breast, found the skin hot and damp. She made some sound between a snarl and a moan, and when he crushed his mouth to hers, she bit.

The quick flash of pain only appealed to the primal lust surging inside him. When he lifted his head, his eyes were wild and fierce. *'Liomsa.'*

He'd said it to her once before, in the language of his youth. *Mine*. She struggled, fighting herself now, but when his mouth came to hers again, hot and hard and hungry, she lost.

Desire, with its more primitive barbs, scraped through her. She wanted. Wanted. And now her body arched not in protest but in demand, and her mouth met his with feral force.

He released her hands only to jerk her up, yanking what was left of her shirt over her shoulders. Her weapon harness tangled, locking her arms as effectively as restraints. And now the fear leaped back. She was defenseless.

'Say it back to me. Damn you, Eve. Say it.' His mouth fused to hers again, then streaked down her throat, over her breasts. His teeth raked at her. And his hands.

On a sharp cry, her head fell back. Pleasure, its edge as keen as razors, sliced at her, leaving what was left of pride in tatters.

Then she was rolling with him over a floor littered with splintered wood in something too fierce to be surrender.

She fought free of the harness and tore at his shirt. She wanted flesh, his flesh. The feel of it, the taste. Every breath she took was a desperate gasp.

His hands took, possessed, bruising as they moved over her. Those long, skilled fingers arousing mercilessly until she was mad for more. He yanked her trousers down her

163

hips, flung them aside. And ruthlessly used his mouth on her.

Release gushed through her, a flood that scorched her system. Floundering, she dug her fingers into the rug, tried to find some anchor to hold her. But she was flying, catapulted out of control.

And still he wouldn't stop.

Couldn't stop.

The small, mad sounds she made inflamed him, whipped his already crazed blood into a fever of greed. Every gulp of air he took in was full of her, the hot, sharp taste of woman. His.

His mouth raced up her shuddering body, feasted on her breasts while he plunged his fingers into her.

She came again, brutally, and her shocked cry was a dark thrill to him, the sudden bite of her nails on his back a vicious pleasure.

'Say it. Say it back to me,' he demanded while his breath heaved, while he watched her eyes go blind as he pushed her to the edge yet again. 'Damn it, I'll hear it from you.'

Somehow, through the madness ruling her, she understood. Not surrender, even after this, it wasn't surrender he asked for. But acceptance. Her throat burned, her system screamed to mate. As she opened for him, lifted to him, she fumbled out the Gaelic.

'Mine,' was what she said. 'You're mine, too.' And her mouth rose to his as he drove himself inside her.

She lay beneath him, enervated, stupefied. Her ears were ringing, making it impossible to think. She wanted to find herself in this body that had responded so primitively. But more, she simply wanted to wallow in the echoes of sensations that still rippled through her.

When he shifted, she would have rolled to her stomach, the position she assumed when exhaustion ruled. But

164

he plucked her off the floor, into his arms. 'We're not done yet.'

Leaving the wreckage of her office behind, he carried her out, and took her to bed.

When she woke, light was streaming through the sky window, her body pulsed with a thousand sly aches. And he was gone.

She lay where she was, on a bed that had been well used, on sheets that were tangled to ropes, and let the tug-of-war between shame and pleasure play out inside her. Nothing was resolved, she realized. Nothing was balanced. She rose, went in to shower wondering if they'd fixed anything or only damaged it further.

She managed to dress for the day without once meeting her own eyes in the mirror. Her harness and weapon were on the table in the sitting area. Wondering when he'd put them there, she strapped it on.

And with her weapon in place, she felt steadier. Or did until she walked into her office and found Peabody staring at the carnage.

'Ah . . . some party,' Peabody said.

'We had an incident.' Eve kicked the broken lamp aside, strode directly to her desk. Her only goal at that moment was to stay in charge. 'I have information that needs to be considered in the investigation. Sit down.'

Peabody cleared her throat, righted a chair. It was the first time in her memory her lieutenant had started a morning briefing without a cup of coffee in her hand. But Peabody sat, took out her memo book.

'An IAB operation has come to my attention,' Eve began, and told her aide what she needed to know.

When she was done, Peabody set her book on her knee. 'If I can offer an opinion, sir, that sucks.'

'Your opinion is noted and agreed with.'

165

'They've been impeding two homicide investigations by withholding pertinent data. Even IAB doesn't have that right.'

'No, they don't, and I'm going to deal with it. In the meantime, I'd like you to contact Dr Mira and request that our consult be moved here. I don't want IAB catching any scent. Call McNab in. I want a harder, closer look at the list from the One twenty-eight, and I want that done here, too. Until we've worked out the feeding chain, officially, we give Internal Affairs nothing.'

'So much for solidarity,' Peabody muttered. 'Those rat bastards.'

'Put your personal feelings aside. Cops are being murdered. We can't afford the indulgence of resentment.' But she felt it, deep and dark inside her. 'I want to inform Whitney of this new information in person. I'll be back within two hours or contact you if I'm delayed.'

'Yes, sir. Would you like me to clean up in here?'

'That's not your job,' Eve snapped, then squeezed her eyes shut, took a breath. 'Sorry. Personal distraction. Don't worry about it unless something's in your way. Relay to Mira that this consult is now a priority. Have the backgrounds on as many from the One twenty-eight as possible before that consult.' She hesitated, then shrugged as she walked toward the door. 'And I'd appreciate it if you'd inform Roarke's offices that we'll clear Purgatory by end of day.'

He wasn't the least bit interested in Purgatory, even the time he assumed he'd spend there for his sins. Nor was Roarke overly surprised to find Don Webster waiting for him in the reception area of his midtown offices.

Roarke's admin, an exceptional woman of great efficiency and insight, moved into reception, cutting neatly between the two men. 'Your schedule is quite full this morning. This gentleman would like to see you and is reluctant to make an appointment for later in the week.'

'I'll make time for him now. Thank you, Caro. Webster.'

He gestured toward the corridor that led to his office and wasn't displeased to note Webster sported a violent bruise running from under his right eye to his cheekbone and a split lip that had yet to be treated.

His own ribs were aching like a bitch, something he'd refused to see to as a matter of pride. He stepped into his office, moved directly to the desk, but didn't sit. With his hands lightly in his pockets, his body balanced on the balls of his feet, he measured his adversary.

'You want another round, mate?'

'More than I want to see the sunrise,' Webster replied, then shook his head when the light came into Roarke's eyes. 'But I'm going to have to pass. I hate saying this, but you had every right to pound the shit out of me last night.'

'And there,' Roarke said smoothly, 'we're in perfect accord. And if I find your hands on what's mine again, you'll lose them. That's a promise.'

'She'd have taken care of that herself if you'd been five minutes later. Shit, five seconds later. I want you to know that.'

'Eve's fidelity was never in question.'

'Okay.' Webster felt part of the weight that had hung on him through the night lift. 'I didn't want you to get the idea that she . . . hell.' He raked a hand through his hair. 'We have a professional problem, which I used to move on a personal one. A problem I have,' Webster elaborated. 'I think I'm in love with your wife.'

'That's indeed a problem. I have to admire your courage in saying that to my face.' Considering, Roarke chose a chair, took out a cigarette. He caught Webster's quick glance at it, lifted a brow. 'Would you like one?'

'I haven't had one in five years. Three months, and . . . I think it's twenty-six days. I've managed to lose track of the

167

hours. Fuck it.' He took one, drew deep until his eyes all but crossed. 'I don't know you,' Webster continued, 'but I know about you.'

'I can say the same.' Roarke replied. 'Did you think Eve hadn't told me you'd once had a night together?'

Doing his best to shrug, Webster sat as well. 'It didn't mean anything to her. I knew it then, and I know it now. I know your rep, Roarke. If you want to come after me, that's what you'll do. I'm up for that. I just didn't want Dallas to take any heat for it.'

'An attempt like that to protect her would tempt her to kick your balls into your throat.'

For the first time, Webster smiled, then swore as the cut lip burned like fire. 'Yeah, well.' He pressed a finger gingerly to his lip. 'When I screw up, I don't like anybody else catching the flak.'

'Whatever you know or think you know about me, know this: I don't strike out at women, particularly when they've done nothing but be who they are.'

He thought of the way he'd handled her the night before, then ruthlessly pushed that aside again. For later.

'And going after you would make Eve unhappy. I might risk that, but I've no reason to.'

Webster stared down at his cigarette. 'You're not what I expected.'

'I could have been.'

'Could have beens don't mean squat.' Biting back a sigh, Webster took one last drag. 'It's what is that counts. That's ah . . .' He tapped his bruised cheek. 'Something I needed to be reminded of.' He crushed out the cigarette before getting to his feet. Meeting Roarke's eyes, he held out a hand. 'I appreciate the time.'

Roarke rose. He felt a stir of pity, another of respect. Each as unexpected as the other. He accepted the hand, smiled. 'I've a fucking bruise the size of a dinner plate on

168

my ribs, and my kidney feels like it's been slammed with a brick.'

Despite the split lip, Webster grinned. 'Thanks.' He started for the door, turned back briefly. 'You fit, you know, you and Dallas. Christ, the two of you fit.'

They did, yes, Roarke thought when the door closed. But the fit wasn't always comfortable.

Commander Whitney didn't explode when Eve relayed the information she'd come by, but it was a close thing.

'Can you verify?'

'No, sir, not at this time. But my information is accurate. My source unimpeachable.'

'And that source is?'

She'd considered this, debated it, and saw no choice. 'I regret, sir, that I'm unable to reveal the name of my source.'

'I'm not a goddamn reporter, Dallas.'

'Commander, this information was given to me in confidence. I have no compunction about using the information but can't name the source.'

'You're making it more difficult for me to kick ass in IAB.'

'I'm sorry about that.'

'I'll hit them with it,' he continued, drumming his fingers on his desk. 'They'll deny, stall, prevaricate. If, as you relate, this operation has been in place some time, they're going to be very reluctant to open it, even with this office.'

He sat back, eyes slitted with concentration. 'Politics is a dirty little game. I'm very good at it.'

'Yes, sir.' Eve allowed herself the barest hint of a smile. 'You are.'

'Be prepared to be called into The Tower to discuss this matter, Lieutenant,' he said, referring to the offices of the police commissioner. 'I'll start the wheel rolling.'

'I'll be available, Commander. At this time, and until this

area of my investigation is resolved to our satisfaction, I'll be working with my team at my home office.'

He nodded, already turning to his 'link. 'Dismissed.'

As she jogged through the garage toward her vehicle, Carmichael hailed her.

'Got a little something that might interest you. I've been through most of the witnesses on my list, and hit with one of the waitresses.'

'Hit what?'

'Seems this server did some short time for running scams. Nothing major, a little bait and switch. But it gave her a good eye for cops. She claims she made Kohli as one but didn't think anything of it. Didn't make much of the other cop who came in from time to time and sat at the bar sucking down whiskey sours.'

'What other cop?'

'Yeah,' Carmichael said with a grin. 'That was my question. And the answer was the lady cop. The good-looking blonde. When I nudged her a little more, she gave me a pretty fair description of Captain Roth of the One two-eight.'

'Son of a bitch.'

'Yeah. The general description could have fit a few hundred women, but it rang bells. So I pulled some photos and had her do a match. She plucked Roth's out, first shot.'

'Thanks. Keep this quiet, will you?'

'Can do. I was on my way up to drop the record of the interview on your desk.' Carmichael pulled a disc out of her bag. 'Want it now?'

'Yeah. Thanks again.'

Eve jammed the disc in her pocket, hurried to her car. She was going to squeeze in time for a trip to the One two-eight.

'Peabody.' She tagged her aide on the run. 'Pull up data on Roth and dig. Don't worry about flags, I want them to wave.'

'Yes, sir. Your consult with Dr Mira is set for your home office at ten-thirty.'

'I'll try not to keep her waiting. Pull the data now, make it noisy.'

Eve didn't expect a brass band welcome when she walked into the One twenty-eighth. What she got was a number of cool stares, muttered asides. One particularly inventive officer oinked.

Rather than ignoring it, she strolled over to his desk, smiled. 'You've got a lot of talent there, Detective. Do you hire out for parties?'

He curled his lip. 'I got nothing to say to you.'

'That's good, because I don't have anything to say to you, either.' She kept her eyes on his until he shifted, looked away. Satisfied, she made her way back to Captain Roth's office.

It was a corner room, one Eve imagined had been hard won, with a pair of windows, a good solid desk, and a thriving vining plant on the sill.

The door was glass, and through it Eve saw Roth surge to her feet when their eyes met. Eve didn't bother to knock.

'How dare you run my personal file without notification?' Roth began. 'You're over the line, Lieutenant.'

'One of us is.' Eve closed the door at her back. 'Why are you worried about what I might find in your personal?'

'I'm not worried. I'm furious. There's a matter of professional courtesy, which you've summarily ignored in some vendetta you have to smear my house. I intend to report your conduct to Commander Whitney and all the way up to The Tower.'

'Your privilege, Captain. Just as it's mine, as primary on two homicides, to ask you why you concealed the fact from me that you had visited Detective Kohli at Purgatory – a number of times,' she added when she saw Roth flinch.

'Your information is inaccurate.'

171

'I don't think so. We talk about it here, Captain, or at Central. Your choice – as a professional courtesy.'

'If you think I'm going to let you ruin me, you're mistaken.'

'If you think I'm going to let you hide behind your captain's bars, you're mistaken. Where were you on the night Detective Kohli was murdered?'

'I don't have to answer your insulting questions.'

'You will if I pull you into Interview. And I will.'

'I was nowhere near Purgatory the night Kohli was killed.'

'Prove it.'

'Oh, I hope you rot in hell.' Roth marched around her desk, snapped her privacy screens into place to block the view from the bullpen. 'My whereabouts on that night are personal.'

'Nothing's personal in a murder investigation.'

'I'm a cop, Lieutenant, a good one. Better at the desk than on the street, but a goddamn good cop. My having a drink at a club now and then has nothing to do with Kohli's death or my position as captain of this squad.'

'Then why did you withhold the information?'

'Because I'm not supposed to drink.' Her color came up, a flag of mortification. 'I have a problem with alcohol, and have already been through rehab. But you know that,' she muttered and walked back behind the desk. 'I'm not going to have a lapse in my recovery endanger my job. I didn't know Kohli was moonlighting in Purgatory when I went in the first time. I went back because he was a familiar face. I didn't mention it because it was irrelevant.'

'You know better than that, Captain.'

'All right, goddamn it, I was protecting myself. Why shouldn't I?'

They were squared off again, with Roth planted behind the desk. Defending her territory. She'd do whatever it took to hold what she'd worked to win.

172

'I know damn well you're trying to say Kohli was dirty, that Mills was dirty. You won't say I am.'

'There have been a number of substantial deposits in your husband's financial accounts.'

'Goddamn it. I'm calling my rep.' She reached for her 'link, then curled her hand into a fist. The room was silent as Eve watched her battle for control. 'I do that, and this goes on record. You've got me by the short hairs.'

She took a deep breath, expelled it. 'A few months ago I began to suspect my husband was involved with someone else. The signs were there. Distraction, disinterest, late arrivals, missed appointments. I confronted him, he denied. Some men have a talent for turning such an accusation around until you're at fault. Even when in your gut you know better. Very simply, Lieutenant, my marriage was falling apart, and I found myself unable to stop it. You're a cop, a woman, married. You know it's not easy.'

Eve didn't reply nor did Roth expect her to. 'I was upset, edgy, distracted. I told myself it wouldn't hurt to smooth out the nerves with a drink. Or two. And I ended up in Purgatory. Kohli was working the bar. We both pretended it was no big deal for either of us to be in there. Meanwhile, my marriage was crumbling. I discovered that my husband was not only rolling around on someone else's sheets but had been steadily transferring funds from our account to one under his own name. Before I could stop it, he'd ruined me financially, had me heading right back into the bottle, and was adversely affecting my work performance.

'About two weeks ago, I pulled myself together. I kicked his lying, lazy ass out and put myself back into rehab. I did not, however, report my counseling, which is a violation of procedure. A minor one, but a violation. Since that time, I have not been back to Purgatory nor had I seen Detective Kohli outside of the job.'

'Captain Roth, I sympathize with your personal difficulties

during this period, but I need to know your whereabouts on the night of Kohli's death.'

'Until midnight I was at an AA meeting in a church basement in Brooklyn.' She smiled thinly. 'Not much chance of running into anyone I know there, which was the point. After that, I went out for coffee with several of the other participants. We tell war stories. I returned home, alone, about two, and went to bed. I have no alibi for the time in question.'

Steadier now, Roth looked into Eve's eyes. 'Everything I told you is off record and inadmissible, as I wasn't Mirandized. If you take me in, Lieutenant, I'm going to make it very hard on you.'

'Captain, if I decide to take you in, I can promise, it'll be a lot harder on you.'

Chapter Twelve

She needed time to absorb and access, to let the new pieces shift into patterns. And she needed to consider, carefully, whether she wanted to damage another cop's career before she was certain that cop had done more than be careless.

But under it she was afraid her own marital strain made her too sympathetic to another's.

She would have her consult with Mira, input the new data, run probabilities. She would do it all by the book.

When she walked into her home office, she saw Mira sitting in a chair in the now tidy office, while Peabody and McNab worked back-to-back at their individual keyboards.

'I'm sorry I kept you waiting.'

'That's perfectly all right.' Mira set aside a cup of what Eve assumed was tea. 'Peabody explained you might be delayed.'

'Do you mind if we take this in another room?'

'Not at all.' Mira rose, elegant as always in a sleek suit of spring leaf green. 'I always enjoy seeing parts of your home.'

Though she wasn't sure if it was strictly appropriate for a consult, Eve led the way to one of the lounging rooms. Mira sighed in appreciation. 'What a lovely space,' she murmured, studying the soft colors, the gracious lines of the furniture, the gleam of wood and glass. 'My God, Eve, is that a Monet?'

Eve glanced at the painting, something in that same soft

pallette that seemed to flow together and form a garden. 'I have no idea.'

'It is, of course,' Mira said after she'd walked over to admire the painting. 'Oh, I do envy you your art collection.'

'It's not mine.'

Mira only turned and smiled. 'I envy it nonetheless. May I sit?'

'Yeah, sure. Sorry. I'm sorry, too, that I've dumped so much data on you in such a short time.'

'We're both accustomed to working under pressure. These killings have ripples radiating throughout the department. Being in the center of those ripples is a very difficult position.'

'I'm used to that, too.'

'Yes.' *Something else here*, Mira thought. She knew Eve too well to miss the small signs. But that would wait. 'I concur with your analysis that both victims were killed by the same hand. The methodology notwithstanding, there is a pattern. The coins, the victims themselves, the brutality, and the knowledge of security.'

'It's another cop,' Eve said. 'Or someone who used to be.'

'Very likely. Your killer is enraged but controlled enough to protect himself by removing evidence. The rage is personal. I'd go as far as to say intimate. This may substantiate your cop-to-cop profile.'

'Because he believed Mills and Kohli were dirty, or because he is?'

'The former, I believe. This isn't the act of someone protecting themselves but one of avenging. Your killer is systematic and sees himself as dispensing justice. He wants his victims marked as Judas, wants their crimes to be revealed.'

'Then why not simply expose them? The data's there if you want to find it.'

'That isn't enough. The loss of the badge, the disgrace. It's

176

too easy. Their punishment must come from him. He or she was punished in some way, very likely through the job, in a manner that is perceived as unjust. Perhaps he was falsely accused of some infraction. The system somehow failed him, and now cannot be trusted.'

'They knew him, or her.'

'Yes, I'm sure of it. Not only because the victims seem to have been unprepared for the attack but because, psychologically, this connection only increases the rage. It's very likely they worked with their killer. Possibly, some act of theirs was responsible, at least in the killer's judgment, for the injustice that occurred to him. When you find him, Eve, you'll find connections.'

'Do you see him in a position of authority?'

'A badge is a position of authority.'

'Of command, then?'

'Possibly. But not as one who's confident of command, no. His confidence comes from his rage, and his rage, in part, from his disillusionment in the system he's represented. In the system his victims had sworn to represent.'

'The system screwed him, they screwed the system. Why blame them?'

'Because they profited by its flaws, and he lost.'

Eve nodded. It jelled for her. 'You're aware now that the One twenty-eight is suspected of having a serious internal problem. The connection with organized crime. With Max Ricker.'

'Yes, your report to me made that clear.'

'I have to tell you, Dr Mira, that it's been established that Detective Kohli was clean, and part of an IAB operation attempting to uncover this corruption.'

'I see.' Her clear eyes clouded. 'I see.'

'I don't know if the killer is aware of this as yet, but I doubt it. What will his reaction be when he learns Kohli was clean?'

Mira got to her feet. Her training and her position made it necessary for her to put herself into the mind of murderers. As she did so, she wandered to the wide band of windows and looked out on the gardens where a sea of candy-pink tulips danced. She saw beyond them to the sweeps of shape and color, very much as Monet had reflected them in oil.

There was nothing so comforting, she thought, as a well planted garden.

'He will disbelieve it initially. He's not a killer but a servant of justice. When he can't deny it, he'll turn to rage. It's his salvation. Once again, the system has betrayed him and tricked him into taking an innocent life. Someone will pay. Perhaps someone in Internal Affairs, where it began. Perhaps you, Eve,' she said and turned back. 'As you are the one who has, indirectly at least, shoved this horror into his face. He'll be doubly fueled now. For himself, and for Kohli. Very shortly after he learns, and accepts, he'll kill. He'll kill, Eve, until he's caught.'

'How do I make him turn to me, specifically?'

Mira walked back, sat down. 'Do you think I would help you with that, even if I could?'

'It's better to know his target than to guess.'

'Yes, you'd think so,' Mira said placidly. 'Particularly if you can make yourself that target. But you can't direct his mind, Eve. His logic is his own. He's already selected his next victim. This information, when he learns of it, may alter his plans. He'll have to grieve, then he'll have to balance his scales.'

Eve frowned. 'He has a conscience.'

'Yes, and Kohli will weigh on it. Kohli will cost him. But who he'll blame? That's the shading I can't give you.'

'Why the hell doesn't he go after Ricker?'

'He may, but first he'll clean his own house.'

'How do you protect and investigate every cop in a precinct?' Eve murmured. 'And how do you manage it when they look at you as if you're the enemy?'

'Is that what's troubling you? Having your own step away from you?'

'No.' She shrugged it off. 'No, I can handle it.'

'Then, since there's little to nothing more I can give you on this profile at the moment, I wish you would tell me what is troubling you.'

'I have a lot on my mind.' In dismissal, Eve got to her feet. 'I appreciate you taking the time to come here. I know it's an inconvenience.'

Eve wasn't the only stubborn woman in the room. 'Sit down; I'm not finished.'

A little surprised by the authoritarian tone, Eve sat. 'You said—'

'I said to tell me what's troubling you. You're unhappy and distracted, and I suspect its cause is personal.'

'If it's personal,' Eve said coolly, 'then it has no place in this consult.'

'Have the nightmares increased? Are you having more flashbacks?'

'No. Damn it. This has nothing to do with my father, with my past, with any of that. It's my business.'

'You need to understand something. I care very much about you.'

'Dr Mira—'

'Be quiet.' And the command, in that warm, pleasant voice, brooked no argument. 'I care, on a very personal level. However much it may discomfort you, Eve, I look on you as a kind of surrogate daughter. It's a pity that causes you embarrassment,' she said mildly when that emotion ran over Eve's face. 'You don't know my children, but I can promise you that they would tell you I am relentless when concerned about their happiness. While I will try not to interfere, I will know the cause.'

Eve was dumbfounded, and she was chased by so many emotions they ran over themselves on their way to clog

179

her throat. She had no mother, no memory of one. And no defense against the offer from the woman who watched her and seemed so determined to stand as one.

'I can't talk about it.'

'Of course you can. If it's not your past, it's your present. If it's personal . . . it's Roarke. Have you had a disagreement?'

The term, so tame, so civilized, caused a reaction Eve never expected. She laughed, laughed until her sides ached and she realized to her utter shock the sound was coming perilously close to sobs. 'I don't know what we had. He's not speaking to me, basically.'

'Eve.' Mira reached for her hand, clasped it. The gesture snapped the last lock.

It poured out of her, everything from the time she'd walked into the bedroom and seen Summerset staggering under the weight of the flowers.

'I went to see Mavis,' Eve continued. 'And got drunk. That sounds stupid, but—'

'On the contrary, it sounds perfectly sensible. You went to a trusted friend, one who knows both of you and is herself in a committed, monogamous, and loving relationship. Getting drunk was a release valve, but talking it over with her was an avenue.'

'She said I should . . .' Eve couldn't quite bring herself to repeat Mavis's descriptive phrase. 'Seduce him.'

'Again, sensible. Sex opens doors to communication and relieves tension. It didn't work?'

'I didn't really get the chance to try it out. There was an individual, I can't give you the name, who has a connection with the case and an older one with me, who was waiting outside. I brought him up to my office to discuss the case, and . . . Jesus . . . I don't know what got into him. I guess you could say he made a move on me, which I was about to repel, with some violence, when Roarke . . .'

'Oh dear. I imagine he was seriously displeased.'

Eve simply stared for a minute, stunned by the phrase. She was afraid to laugh again. Afraid she wouldn't stop. 'You could say that. Words were exchanged, and then they went at each other. The worst is, for a minute, I just stood there with my mouth open. They're breaking furniture, and blood's flying and I stand there, stupid.'

'Not for long, I take it.'

'No, but still. Anyway, I drew my weapon.'

'Good God, Eve.'

'It was on stun.' She made a defensive move with her shoulders. 'I fired a warning, which Roarke ignored. Unfortunately for . . . for the other individual, he didn't and Roarke cold-cocked him. Summerset got the guy out, and I'm telling Roarke to calm his ass down or I'll stun him. I meant it.'

'I'm sure you did.'

'He didn't seem to care. He sort of backed me into a corner, and I couldn't seem to . . . Then he, hmmm, he . . .'

'Oh.' Mira felt something flutter in her belly. 'I see.'

'No, no, he didn't punch me or anything.'

'That's not what I thought. He . . . made love to you.'

'No. That's not the way it was. He just took me over. I wasn't going to stand for it. I told myself I wouldn't, but I was . . . Damn it, I was aroused, and he knew it, and he was ripping my clothes and we were sort of struggling a little, then we were on the floor and I was ripping his clothes and we were on each other like animals or something. I couldn't stop him, or myself, or any of it, and I didn't want to because, God, I was so hot I'd have let him eat me alive.'

'Oh my,' Mira managed.

'I shouldn't have told you.' Mortified, Eve squeezed her eyes shut. 'What was I thinking?'

'No, no, sweetheart, that was a very unprofessional reaction, and I apologize. But it was a very female one.' And she thought her husband was going to be quite delighted with the aftereffects of this heart-to-heart with Eve.

'I didn't just let him take me, I helped him. I enjoyed it.' She looked down, miserably, at her empty hands. 'That's got to be sick.'

'*Not* enjoying what you just described to me might be. Enjoying it was completely healthy. Extremely healthy, if I might say so. Eve, you love each other. Passionate sex—'

'It went over the top of passionate.'

'Please, my system can only handle so much.' And now Mira laughed. 'You and Roarke are two strong, stubborn, physical people who are wildly in love. He was angry with you for your attempt to protect him at your own risk. As you would be if he did the same.'

'But—'

'You know that's true. As much as you know you'd do the same thing again, just as he would. You dented his ego, always a tricky proposition with a man, particularly a man like him. Then, before he could come to full terms with it, he walks in on you being hit on by another man.'

'He had to know that I wouldn't have—'

'He did, of course. But he wouldn't stand for two slaps at his ego. Think a moment, and answer honestly. Would you really want him to stand for it?'

'I . . . maybe not,' she admitted, grudgingly. Then she blew out a breath, surprised that she felt considerably better. 'No, I wouldn't want him to stand for it.'

'Of course not. And his reaction was, given who he is, physical. The fight reasserted his ego. Territoriality, Eve. This woman is mine.'

'That's what he said,' she muttered.

'Naturally enough. You are. Just as he's yours. Then you stand there, holding your weapon on him. Oh, what a sight that would have been. So he, metaphorically speaking, drew one of his own.'

Eve's lips quivered. 'Dr Mira, I think that's crude.'

'Nonetheless. Both of you reacted as natural for you,

engaged in a bout of rough, sweaty sex that no doubt satisfied you.'

'You'd have thought so, but we hadn't even cooled off when he picked me up off the floor and carried me into bed and did it all over again.'

Mira stared, rather blankly. 'Does he have a particular diet? Vitamins?'

Eve felt her grin spread and the muscles that had been tied all day loosen. 'Thanks. And I don't even have to throw up like I did after drinking screamers and eating ice cream with Mavis.'

'That's a plus. The man loves you with everything he has, everything he is. Eve, that means you can hurt him. Make the time, and go talk to your husband.'

'I will.'

'I have to get back to the office.' Mira rose. 'I plan to finish up early today, go home, and ravish my husband.'

Amused, Eve watched Mira, dignity and grace, walk to the door. 'Doctor?'

'Yes?'

'The, um, mother thing? That was weird. But nice.'

'It's nice for me, too. Good-bye, Eve.'

Recharged, Eve walked into her office and ordered Peabody and McNab to take a twenty-minute break. But when McNab made a beeline for the kitchen in her office, she headed him off.

'No, downstairs, upstairs, outside. Somewhere else. I want quiet. Stay out of the bedrooms,' she added when she caught the gleam in his eye.

She settled down, contacting Feeney first. If and when she was called to The Tower, she wanted him along.

'Computer, run probability using all available data re Roth, Captain Eileen, as perpetrator in homicide cases in file.'

Working . . .

Eve wandered the room while the computer crunched data and percentages. Recharged, yes, she thought. She was also restless, energized, ready to move.

She thought of Roth, desperately trying to blend her professional and personal lives. Failing at one, endangering the other.

'That's not going to happen to me.'

Whatever it took, she thought, she was going to make it work. On both sides.

Requested analysis as follows . . . Using available data, probability Roth, Captain, committed homicides on file is sixty-seven point three percent.

Low, Eve thought, *but not out of the running.*

'Computer, recalibrate with additional data, for my eyes only. Captain Roth's recurrent alcohol addiction, failing marriage, and financial crisis. In addition, subject Roth was aware of victim's employment at Purgatory and had visited the scene in the weeks prior to the incident.'

Working . . . Additional data increases probability by twelve point eight percent for a total percentage of eighty point one.

'Yeah, it makes a difference. That puts you on the short list, Captain. Who else have we got?'

Before she could move on, her 'link beeped. 'Dallas.'

'Martinez.'

There was background noise, a great deal of it. Air and street traffic, Eve decided. Martinez wasn't calling from the squad room.

'You got anything for me?'

'I've got holes in the data files, holes that don't match my own records. I've backtracked, cross-referenced, but I can't pin down who did the shifting. Somebody sure as hell messed with the reports, just a little twist here and there.'

'You get me a copy, I'll have a friend – a discreet friend

– in EDD pin it down. He's a bloodhound. He'll smell it out.'

'I don't want to send it through the system at Central.'

'Home office.' Eve rattled off the proper identification code.

'Got it. Hey, I thought you were going to pull the tag on me.'

'I did.'

'Well, if you did, I've picked up another one. And they're cops. I know a cop tag.'

'Just go about your routine. Don't contact me on any departmental line.'

'I know the drill, Lieutenant.'

'Right. You need to talk to me, contact through my home or my personal 'link. Ready?' She reeled off the numbers. 'Don't take any chances, don't be a hero. And don't trust anybody.'

'I don't. Not even you.'

'Fine,' Eve murmured when the transmission ended. 'Just so you keep breathing.'

She turned away from the 'link. She scanned through Peabody's current runs and results and found an additional three potentials in the One twenty-eighth. Wanting a visual impression, she called up ID photos, stopped, smiled a little, and focused on one.

'Well, well, if it isn't our oinking detective. Vernon, Jeremy K. I don't like your face, Jerry. Let's have a closer look at you, and the hell with the flags.'

She dug through his financials and saw nothing to ring alarms. She did a search and scan on connecting accounts, keying in variations of his name, trying for the numbers by using date of birth, address, his precinct, his badge number.

She was well into it when Peabody strolled back in. 'Did you know you have paella? With honest-to-God shellfish? I've never had paella for lunch.'

'Yum yum.' Eve didn't bother to look up. 'Use the other unit and copy the data on Detective Jeremy Vernon.'

'You got something?'

'Yeah, I got me a nibble here. How many cops have numbered bank accounts in another city?' Now she did glance up, giving Peabody a speculative look.

'Not me. By the time I pay the first of the months, factor in transpo costs and food allowance, I'm lucky to have enough left over for new underwear, which I'm in desperate need of at the moment. Having a sex life is great, and a nice change, but you have to have decent drawers.'

'Detectives make more than uniforms,' Eve speculated, 'but unless the pay scale's gone up since my day, this guy shouldn't be able to tuck away three hundred grand and change. But it's not enough. Dead relatives,' she murmured. 'Mills used dead relatives. Where the hell's McNab?'

'He was still stuffing his face. You also have strawberry shortcake. Don't make me go get him. I'm weak, and it looked really mag.'

Eve turned to her 'link. She'd never used the house intercom, but now seemed like a good time to start. She flipped it to full open. 'McNab! Get your bony ass up here. Now.'

'It's not bony so much as tight,' Peabody offered and earned a killing look from Eve.

'I've told you about that.'

'Just saying,' Peabody muttered. 'Do you want me to start a search for ancestors?'

'Let McNab do it. He's faster than both of us.'

And delegating, she thought, would give her time to balance those scales. She rose.

'I want him to do the run, then the two of you split the names. Look for current accounts. If the names crap out, go for numbers. DOBs, DODs, IDs, driver's license, and anything else that comes to you. All combinations. I'm taking an hour personal time.'

She headed out as McNab rushed in. 'Man, Dallas, it was like hearing the voice of God. You nearly scared me to death.'

'You've got strawberry gunk on your lip. Clean up and get to work.'

'Where's she going?' McNab demanded when Eve breezed out.

'An hour personal time.'

'Dallas? Personal time? Maybe it was the voice of God and this is the end of the world.'

That got a smirk out of Peabody, but she told herself she'd been too nice to him lately and refused to let the laugh loose. 'She's entitled to a life like everybody else. And if you don't get that bony ass in gear, she's going to kick it to New Jersey when she gets back.'

'I didn't get my coffee.' But he wandered to the desk on his way to the kitchen. 'What's she running?'

'This guy. She wants a financial search.'

'Hey, I know him. Vernon.'

'You do?'

'Yeah, yeah, I remember him. I got called on-scene, backup for an illegals bust, when I was in uniform. He's an asshole.'

'Why's that? Wasn't he properly awed by the brilliance of your mind?'

He gave her a sour look. 'He's a strutter. Preening around. Hitting on the LCs we hauled in during the bust. Made a big deal out of himself, and it was a penny-ante bust, too. Bunch of street hookers, couple of johns, and a couple kilos of Exotica. Acted like he'd just taken down some major cartel, and he treated the uniforms like slaves. I heard one of the LCs yelled sexual harassment and he got called in on it. Took a knuckle rap.'

'Nice guy.'

'Yeah, a prince. Seems I heard a rumor that he liked to bust the hookers for Exotica because he could skim a couple ounces

187

for personal use. Well, Jerry old pal, what goes around comes around.'

He forgot the coffee, dramatically flexed his fingers, and got to work.

Chapter Thirteen

Roarke's midtown offices were in his own sleek black tower that speared up from the street like a shaft into the blue belly of the sky. That sheer ebony lance was a favorite image on the tourists' postcards and holocubes.

Inside, it was just as sleek, with edges of the lush, in banks and pools of stunning flowers, tropical trees, acres of animated maps, and an ocean of glossy tile.

Not all the businesses housed in the tower were his. But he owned a piece of most that were, including the shops, restaurants, and chic salons.

He worked on the top floor, which Eve could access through a private elevator. She arrived, unannounced and unexpected, and with a chip the size of a meteor on her shoulder.

The receptionist beamed at her. Because she was a clever and experienced woman, that welcoming smile stayed in place even when she caught the combative expression on Eve's face.

'Lieutenant Dallas, how nice to see you again. I'm afraid Roarke's in a meeting at the moment and can't be disturbed. Is there anything I can do to—'

'Is he back there?'

'Yes, but – Oh, Lieutenant.' She scrambled up from her post as Eve marched past her. 'Please. You really can't—'

'Watch me.'

'It's an extremely *important* meeting.' The receptionist

risked her very attractive face by throwing herself in Eve's path. 'If you could just wait, possibly ten minutes. They should be breaking for the lunch portion very shortly. Perhaps I can get you some coffee. A pastry.'

Eve gave her a considering look. 'What's your name?'

'I'm Loreen, Lieutenant.'

'Well, Loreen, I don't want coffee or a pastry, but thanks. And I'll be sure to tell Roarke you tried. Now move.'

'But I—'

'Tried really hard,' Eve added, then simply shouldered Loreen aside and yanked open the door.

Roarke was in front of his desk, leaning back against it, looking cool, casual, and completely in control with the staggering view of the city behind him. He was listening with polite interest to something one of the six people, all sober-suited and seated, said to him. But his gaze shifted to the door as it burst open, and Eve had the pleasure of seeing surprise flash into his eyes.

He recovered instantly. 'Ladies, gentlemen.' With lazy grace, he straightened. 'My wife, Lieutenant Dallas. Eve, the representatives, attorneys, and financial advisers of Green Space Agricultural Port. You know Caro, my admin.'

'Yeah, hi. How's it going? We have to talk.'

'Excuse me a moment.' He walked to the door, took her arm firmly, and pulled her through.

'I'm sorry, sir,' Loreen began, nearly stuttering. 'I couldn't stop her.'

'Don't worry about it, Loreen. No one can. It's all right. Go back to your desk.'

'Yes, sir. Thank you.' With obvious relief, Loreen fled, with the single-minded intensity of a woman fleeing a burning building.

'This isn't a convenient time, Eve.'

'Then you'll have to settle for an inconvenient time, because I have things to say, and I'm saying them now.' She peered past him. 'Want me to say them in front of the representatives, attorneys, and financial backers of Green Space Agriculture Port and your trusty admin, Caro?'

He didn't care for her mood or the position she put him in. And his hand stayed, a not particularly subtle warning, on her arm. 'We'll talk at home.'

'We haven't been doing a lot of that lately. I say we talk now.' She lifted her chin. A not particularly subtle challenge. 'And if you think you can call security and have them change my mind, I'll haul you downtown on some trumped-up charge. In fact, I like the idea of that. I'm making time,' she said, quietly now. 'You make it.'

He studied her face. If he'd seen only temper, he'd had met it with his own or dismissed it. But he saw something more. 'Give me ten minutes. Caro?' When his hand ran down Eve's arm like a caress, she felt the clutch in the gut that came with relief. 'Would you show my wife to Conference Room C, please?'

'Of course. This way, Lieutenant. Shall I get you some coffee?'

'I got an offer of a pastry with that before, when I scared Loreen.'

Caro's smile remained polite as she steered Eve through the corridors, but her eyes twinkled with humor. 'I'll make good on that offer. I'm sure you'll be quite comfortable in here.' She opened one of a pair of double doors and escorted Eve into a pretty, almost homey room with two cozy seating areas, a gleaming wood bar, and a spectacular and lofty view of the city.

'Doesn't look like any conference room I've ever seen.'

'Amazing, really, how much business can be done in comfortable surroundings. What kind of pastry would you like, Lieutenant?'

'Hmm? Oh, I don't know. Whatever. Are you allowed to tell me what that meeting was about?'

'Certainly.' Placidly, Caro programmed the AutoChef behind the bar. 'Green Space is floundering, though they claim otherwise. Their costs of maintaining the space port have steadily overrun their profits for the past three years. Their production level is down, though the quality of their produce remains very high. Transportation costs, in particular, are taking an enormous bite and causing their overhead to soar.'

She removed a china cup and saucer steaming with coffee and a pretty matching plate with a selection of flaky pastries.

'So, is he making them a deal on transpo?'

'Quite possibly. I imagine he'll have done so, and have a controlling interest in the port, with his hand-selected team assigned to restructure Green Space from the ground up, so to speak, before he joins you.'

'Caro, do they want to sell him controlling interest?'

'They didn't.' She set the tray on a table. 'They will before it's done. Is there anything else I can get you, Lieutenant?'

'No. Thanks. Does he always win?'

Caro's smile didn't shift by a single degree. She didn't even blink. 'Of course. Just ring Loreen if you need anything.' She walked to the door, then turned back, her smile warming a little. 'You surprised him, Lieutenant. That's not easy to do.'

'Yeah, well,' Eve muttered when Caro quietly closed the door, 'you ain't seen nothing yet.'

She was revved, edgy, and didn't have any interest in the damn pastries. But she ate one anyway, decided the sugar rush could only help, and started on another.

She was licking flakes from her thumb when Roarke walked in. He aimed those eyes at her, closed the door at his back.

Pissed, she thought. *Not just surprised but seriously pissed. Good.* When you were dealing with the richest and potentially the most deadly man in the world, you needed every advantage you could get.

'I'm pressed for time, so let's save some,' he began. 'If

you're here for an apology regarding last night, you won't get it. Now, is there something else you need to discuss with me? I've people waiting for me.'

That's how he worked it, she mused. *All those deals, all those wheels. Draw your line in cold, cold sand, then intimidate.* He was good at it, but there were any number of cons doing time who could have vouched that Eve Dallas was a bitch in Interview.

'We'll get to that, but since I'm pressed for time myself, let's start right at the beginning and move along. Going to see Ricker was my job, and I'm not apologizing for that.'

He inclined his head. 'That's one each.'

'Okay. I don't know if I'd have told you about it or not. Probably not, if I thought I could skate by it. And I didn't intend to tell you about him sending his hammers after me because I dealt with it.'

He could feel temper fighting to get out of his belly and into his throat but said nothing. He merely walked to the bar and got himself a cup of coffee. 'I have no dispute over your job, Lieutenant. But the fact is, Ricker and I were connected. You knew that going in. We discussed it.'

'That's right. That's right exactly. And we discussed the fact that I would set up a meet.'

'You didn't indicate you'd move on that intention immediately, without preparation.'

'I don't have to indicate anything when it comes to my work. I just have to do the job. And I was prepared. I knew after five minutes with him that his fondest wish was to get to you. Using me to do that wasn't going to be an option I tossed in his lap.'

He studied the pretty pattern on his china cup, even as he fantasized about hurling it against the wall. 'I'm quite able to take care of myself.'

'Yeah, well, me, too. So what? Did you tell me about your plans to corner the market on broccoli?'

He shot her a look of mild interest. 'Excuse me?'

Oh, she hated when he used that formal, adult-to-idiot-child tone on her. And he knew it. 'This deal with the Green Space people. Did you bring me in on it?'

'Why would I? Have you developed a stirring interest in fresh produce?'

'It's a big deal, taking them over. It's what you do. You didn't consult me about it. I don't have to consult you about what I do.'

'It's an entirely different matter.'

'I don't see it that way.'

'The representatives of Green Space aren't likely to put out a contract on my life.'

'The way you work, they may want to. But yeah, that's a point. On the other hand, dealing with the criminal element is part of the package with me. You married a cop. Live with it.'

'I do. This is different. It's my head he wants. Taking yours would simply be a bonus.'

'Oh, I got that. I got that as soon as I saw the flowers. Why do you think I panicked?' She strode over, slapped her hands on the bar. 'Okay, I panicked, and I don't like knowing it. When I read the card, I was annoyed. And then, it hit me, hit hard what you might do. What he was hoping you'd do, and all I could think was to get rid of them. To make them go away so you wouldn't see them or know about them. Maybe I wasn't thinking at all but just reacting. I was afraid for you. Why isn't that allowed?'

He had no answer for that and, setting the coffee aside, struggled to put his own thoughts in order. 'You lied to me.'

'I know it, and I said I was sorry. But I'd do it again. I wouldn't be able to stop myself. I don't care if it put your dick in a twist.'

He stared at her now, torn between annoyance and amusement. 'Do you really think this is about my ego?'

'You're a man, aren't you? I have it on good authority that what I did put a big dent in your ego, which is the same as a kick in the groin to a man.'

'And who,' he said with deceptive sweetness, 'is this authority?'

'I talked to Mavis.' She caught the glint in his eye and narrowed her own. 'She made sense, and so did Mira. I had a right to talk to somebody since you were freezing me out.'

He had to take a minute, had to walk it off. He paced to the window, stared out until reason could make its way through the haze of temper. 'All right. You had every right, and every reason to talk to friends. But whether or not some of my reaction had to do with ego isn't the sticking point, Eve. You didn't trust me.'

'You're wrong.' And if the kick to his ego had made him believe that, she had to fix it. 'Altogether wrong. I've never trusted anyone the way I trust you. Don't turn away from me again, damn it. Don't do that. I was afraid,' she said when he turned back to her. 'I don't deal well with fear. I don't let it in, but it snuck up on me. I wasn't wrong, and neither were you. We were just right on different levels.'

'That's an amazing and accurate analysis. One I'd nearly reached myself before I happened upon that little scene last night.' He walked to her then, until they were face-to-face. 'Do you expect me to take two kicks in the groin, Eve, then just sit meekly, like a puppy when ordered?'

Another time she might have laughed at that image. The man in front of her would never be meek. He would do as he pleased when he pleased, and hang the consequences.

'That was about work.'

He took her chin in his hand, fingers strong and firm. 'Don't insult me.'

'It started out that way, I don't know how it got where it did. Webster had information, confidential, the kind that could get his ass burned for passing it to me. We were going

195

around about it, arguing, then . . . I don't know what the hell got into him.'

'No,' Roarke murmured, not particularly surprised. 'I see you don't.' She was refreshingly, sometimes frustratingly, oblivious to her own appeal.

'He caught me off balance,' she continued, 'but I'd've dealt with it. Next thing I know, there you are. And the two of you are like a couple of rabid dogs fighting over a bone. Talk about insulting.'

'You pulled your weapon on me.' He couldn't get over that one. Wasn't sure he ever would.

'That's right.' She shoved his hand away from her chin. 'You think I'm stupid enough to jump physically between two crazy men trying to break each other's faces? I had it on stun.'

'Oh, well then, what am I whining about? You had it on stun.' He had to laugh. 'Christ, Eve.'

'I wouldn't have used it on you. Probably. And if I had, I'd've been really sorry.' She tried a smile, thought she saw the hint of one in return. It made her decide to give him the rest of it.

'Then you were standing there, sweaty and messed up and mad as hell. And so fucking sexy. I wanted to jump you, bite you right . . . there,' she said, tracing a finger on the side of his neck. 'It wasn't a reaction I was expecting. Before I could work it out, you had me against the wall.'

'Slugging you seemed like the less enjoyable of the two options.'

'Why weren't you there this morning? Why have you only touched me twice since I've been here?'

'I said I wouldn't apologize for what happened between us last night. I won't. I can't. Still . . . Still,' he repeated and touched her now, just a brush of his fingers on the ends of her hair. 'I took your choice away. If not physically,' he said before she could argue, 'then emotionally. I meant to.

196

It's given me some bad moments since, some concern that it might have reminded you of your childhood.'

'My childhood?'

She could have no idea what her confused expression did to him. How it cooled and smoothed every hot and ragged edge inside him. 'Your father, Eve.'

Now confusion turned to shock. 'No. How could you think that? I wanted you. You knew I wanted you. There's nothing between us that would make me . . .' It stirred hideous images to think of it, but she faced them. 'There was no love there, no passion, not even need. He raped me because he could. He raped a child, his own child, because he was a monster. He can't hurt me when I'm with you. Don't let him hurt you.'

'I won't say I'm sorry.' He lifted his hand, skimmed his fingers over her cheek. 'I wouldn't mean it. But I will say I love you. I've never meant anything more.'

He drew her into his arms. She pressed her face to his shoulder and held on. 'I've been so messed up.'

'So have I.' He brushed his lips over her hair, felt his world balance again. 'I've missed you, Eve.'

'I won't let the job screw this up.'

'It doesn't. We manage that on our own.' He drew her back, touched his lips gently to hers. 'But it keeps things lively, doesn't it?'

She sighed, stepped back. 'It's gone.'

'What is?'

'I've had this low-grade headache for a couple of days. It's gone. I guess you were my headache.'

'Darling. That's so sweet.'

'Yeah, I'm sugar. Did I queer this Green Space deal for you?'

'Well now, what's a few hundred million in the grand scheme of things?' He'd have played with that awhile, but she looked so appalled. 'Just kidding. It's fine.'

'Glad you found your sense of humor. Anyway, I've got

a lot going on. Maybe, unless you want to talk more about that broccoli, we could go into it later.'

'I think we've said all there is to say about broccoli already.'

'Good. You know, even though we're all mushy again, it's hard to say this. But I could use some help. Your kind of help on this case.'

'Why, Lieutenant, you've made my day.'

'I thought it would, though it doesn't do a lot for mine.'

Her communicator sounded. She pulled it out, listened to Whitney's aide order her immediately to The Towers. 'Acknowledged. There's the bell for the next round,' she told Roarke.

'My money's on you.'

'So's mine.' She rose on her toes, kissed him hard before she broke away to stride to the door. 'By the way, ace, you owe me a new lamp.'

She was revved and ready to do battle when she entered The Tower. Chief Tibble ruled here, with a steady, if an occasionally ruthless hand.

A great many cops feared him. Eve respected him.

'Lieutenant Dallas.' He wasn't behind his desk but stood in front of it. The style, the positioning, made her think of Roarke. Standing put him in control of the people who sat in the room and of the situation that brought them there.

At his signal, she took a seat between Whitney and Captain Bayliss from IAB. Captain Roth sat rigidly on the other side of Bayliss. Feeney lounged, or appeared to lounge, on Roth's far side.

'We'll begin with information that has come to my attention regarding an internal investigation, centering most specifically on the Illegals Division of the One hundred and twenty-eighth Precinct.'

'Chief Tibble, I wish to state my objection that such an investigation was initiated and proceeded without my knowledge.'

'So noted,' he said, nodding at Roth. 'However, it is within the authority of the IAB to conduct such an investigation without informing the squad captain. However,' he continued, shifting his hard gaze to Bayliss, 'neglecting to inform the commander and myself of the operation exceeds that authority.'

'Sir.' Bayliss started to get to his feet, but Tibble gestured him down.

Good move, Eve mused. *Keep the little rodent in his place.*

Bayliss kept his seat, but a faint wash of color stained his cheeks. 'The Internal Affairs Bureau is allowed some leeway on technical procedure when it deems an investigation warrants secrecy. After consideration of the information, the suspicion of certain leaks and confirmation of others, it was agreed that this operation be held within the confines of IAB and its chosen officers.'

'I see.' Tibble leaned back against his desk in a way that forced Eve to bite back a small, satisfied smile. 'And may I ask, Captain, who made this agreement?'

'It was discussed between myself and several high-ranking members of my division.'

'I see. You decided among yourselves to disregard the chain of command.'

'Yes, sir.' He said it stiffly, stubbornly. 'We had reason to believe that the leaks reached up that chain. By informing other departments, we would compromise that investigation before it began.'

'Then am I given to understand that Commander Whitney is under suspicion in your division?'

'No, sir.'

'Perhaps I am part of your internal investigation.'

Bayliss opened his mouth, wisely closed it again to

give his brain time to engage. 'Sir, you are under no suspicion.'

'Any longer?' Tibble finished silkily. 'That's a comfort, Captain. And having established that neither myself nor the commander were suspected of infractions or crimes that warrant IAB action, you still neglected to inform either of us of this investigation.'

'Witch hunt,' Roth said under her breath and earned a glare from Bayliss.

'It seemed unnecessary to do so, sir, until the operation was satisfactorily completed.'

'Shall I explain to you, *Captain*, why you are mistaken?'

Bayliss bore up under the penetrating stare. 'No, sir. I regret the oversight. And as ordered, Chief Tibble, all records, all documents, all notes on said operation are now in your possession.'

'Including, I presume, all data pertaining to the homicide investigations currently under the hand of Lieutenant Dallas?'

Stubbornness set like concrete on Bayliss's face. 'It is my opinion that the two matters do not connect.'

'Really? Do you have an opinion on that, Lieutenant, Dallas?'

'Yes, sir. My opinion is that Captain Bayliss has made another error in judgement. Two police officers, both from the One two-eight, have been murdered in under a week by the same hand. I believe that one, Lieutenant Mills, was under IAB investigation and will prove to be guilty of accepting bribes, tampering with evidence, and conspiring to undermine a criminal case. Detective Kohli, an IAB plant, agreed to pose as an NYPSD officer who was also taking. While this portion of the operation is acceptable, the investigation into his death was compromised and tampered with by the withholding of Kohli's status. There is no precedent that I'm aware of that gives IAB the authority to compromise a homicide investigation in order to protect one of its own operations.'

'I am also unaware of such a precedent. Captain?'

'Our operation was at a delicate point.' He was beginning to ruffle, badly, and swerved in his chair to scowl at Eve. 'Look, Kohli went into this eyes open. Nobody pressured him. He wanted the extra duty and the extra pay. We had no reason to believe his life was in danger and every reason to believe that he would, in his position at Purgatory, connect with Ricker.'

She wanted to ask what Ricker had to do with Purgatory, but she didn't dare. Not here and now. 'And when he was dead, Captain?'

'We couldn't change that, but we felt if we maintained Kohli's cover, let it leak to the primary that he was dirty, it would open opportunities to uncover other leaks in the One twenty-eight.'

'You used one of my men,' Roth shot out. 'Do you think I've got the only squad with a Mills? Cops on the take aren't the exclusive property of my house.'

'You've got more than your share of them.'

'I was given false information,' Eve cut in. 'That's a violation of code. Above that – above it, beyond it, over it, and under it – trying to push the investigation of a murdered fellow cop into a dead end, using that dead cop as a blind, is contemptible. As far as I'm concerned, Kohli died in the line of duty. He damn well deserved respect.'

'Lieutenant,' Whitney muttered, but without heat. 'Enough.'

'No, sir, it's a long way from enough.' When she got to her feet, Tibble said nothing. 'IAB has a purpose, because a wrong cop smears all of us. But when some tin desk soldier takes on his own agenda, using his position to order those under his authority to circumvent procedure, tries to twist a homicide investigation for his own purposes, he's as dirty as the cops he purports to hunt.'

'You're over the line.' Bayliss surged to his feet. 'You think you can point the finger at me. I've spent fifteen years keeping the department clean. You're not lily white, Lieutenant. Your husband's link to Ricker may be buried, but it can be dug up. You shouldn't be on this case.'

'You will back away from my officer,' Whitney said quietly. He held up a hand to waylay Feeney, who'd come out of his chair and was moving toward Bayliss.

'And you will cease and desist any comments on her personal life or her professional abilities. If I were to indulge myself in personal snipes, I would say, with pleasure, that you can only aspire to achieve half the integrity Lieutenant Dallas has. But . . . I won't so indulge. Chief Tibble, I'd like to make a statement.'

Tibble spread his hands. 'Commander.'

'After reviewing the documentation belatedly provided by Internal Affairs, it is my opinion that Captain Bayliss seriously overstepped his authority and should face disciplinary action. Further, while said data is being analyzed and confirmed, and until the decision is made whether to continue or abort the internal investigation, it's my recommendation that Captain Bayliss take a leave of absence.'

'There are cops feeding Ricker,' Bayliss objected. 'I'm on the point of breaking that network open.'

'Be that as it may, Captain, there can be no law without order.' Tibble watched him. 'Particularly with those of us who have sworn to uphold that law. You'll take leave, with pay and without the suspension of benefits. Disciplinary action will be considered. You are advised to consult your union rep and/or your private attorney. You are dismissed.'

'Chief Tibble—'

'Dismissed, Captain. Believe me when I tell you, you don't want me to indulge myself in personal comments at this time.'

Bayliss set his teeth, turned on his heel. His eyes burned over Eve before he strode from the room.

'Captain Roth.'

'Sir. If I might speak.' She got quickly to her feet. 'I request that the documentation on the investigation into my squad be made available to me. My men are under suspicion, my house under the gun.'

'Captain Roth, your house is a mess. Request denied. You have until noon tomorrow to write a full report and a complete analysis of the status of your squad. I'm making your house my personal business and will expect you in this office with that report and analysis at noon.'

'Yes, sir. Chief Tibble?'

'Yes, Captain.'

'I accept full responsibility for that status. Mills was under my hand, and I can't claim to have held that hand steady. If, after this situation is resolved, you wish for my resignation—'

'Let's not jump our fences, Captain. Noon tomorrow.'

'Yes, sir.'

When she left, Tibble once again leaned on his desk. 'Now, Lieutenant. Just how deep into this mess are you, and who is your informant? You are required to give me that name when ordered to do so. Consider this such an order.'

'Sir, I am hip deep and regret I am unable to follow orders and divulge the name of my informant.'

Tibble shot a look at Whitney. 'I owe you fifty, it seems. Your commander bet me, and I was foolish enough to accept, that you'd hold the name. It's come to my attention you did a deep search on Captain Roth.'

'Yes, sir. I initiated the search as part of my investigation into the homicides of Kohli and Mills. It's my belief they were killed by one of our own.'

'So I gather. That's a very serious avenue to walk.'

'Yes, sir.'

'You suspect Roth?'

'She captains the squad. It would have been negligent not

to consider her. I've questioned her, analyzed her data, and run a probability.'

'And the result?'

'In the sixties.'

'Low, but troubling. I won't take up your time or mine by asking you to go through the steps of your investigation. At this time,' he qualified. 'But I will ask you, Lieutenant, if your husband is connected to Max Ricker, on a personal level or a business one, and if that connection should concern this office.'

'My husband is not connected to Max Ricker on a business level. It is my understanding that at one time, over a decade ago, there may have been some business between them.'

'And on a personal level?'

This was tougher. 'It was my impression, sir, during my interview with Ricker, that he held a personal grudge against Roarke. He did not specify this, but intimated. Roarke is a successful man, and a glamorized one,' she said for lack of a better term. 'Such status invites resentment and envy in certain types of individuals. However, I see no reason why a potential grudge held by Ricker for Roarke should concern this office.'

'You're honest, Dallas. Carefully so. Almost politically so. And my saying that, I see, insults you.'

'Somewhat,' Eve managed.

'Do you have any conflict of feeling or loyalty in pursuing a killer who may be a fellow officer, even though the victims were dirty or perceived to be so?'

'None whatsoever. Law and order, Chief Tibble. We uphold the law. We are not allowed to nor are we equipped to judge and sentence.'

'Good answer. She does you credit, Jack. Lieutenant,' he continued while she dealt with the sheer surprise of his comment, 'you'll report your findings to your commander and keep him closely apprised of your progress. Go to work.'

'Yes, sir. Thank you.'

'One last thing,' he said as she reached the door. 'Bayliss would like your skin on a rack – roasted.'

'Yes, sir, I'm aware of that. He wouldn't be the first.'

When the door closed, Tibble went behind his desk. 'It's a fucking mess, Jack. Let's pick up some shovels and start cleaning it up.'

Chapter Fourteen

'Nice job, Dallas.' Feeney rode down with her to lobby level. 'Now I'm going to tell you what they didn't. If Bayliss gets back behind his desk, he's going to be gunning for you.'

'I can't let a rat turd like Bayliss worry me. I got two cops and one witness in the morgue. Until I work through the layers of that, Bayliss can blow all the hot air he wants.'

'Enough hot air blows at you, you get scalded. Just watch your back. I'm going over to your place, switch off with McNab for awhile.'

'I'll meet you back there. I want to swing by Kohli's, have another talk with the widow. I'll pull Peabody. You know an Illegals Detective, Jeremy Vernon?'

Lips pursed, Feeney ran through his head files. 'Nope. Doesn't ring for me.'

'He's got an attitude – and a fat bank account. I'm probably going to pull him in for a chat, tomorrow latest. You want in on that?'

'I always like sitting in on one of your chats.'

They separated, with Eve moving through the late-lunch pedestrian traffic to her vehicle. She waited for a maxibus to clear, contacting Peabody as she pulled away from the curb.

'I'm on my way to Kohli's. Meet me there. I want a follow-up with the widow.'

'I'll head out now. Dallas, McNab's picked up three more

accounts for Detective Vernon. We've got a total of two million six, and still counting.'

'Isn't that interesting? Look, Feeney's on his way over there. I want McNab to pick his way through Vernon's financials. Make certain the son of a bitch didn't win some lottery or inherit a bundle from one of those dead relatives. Pin down his income and his outlay. I don't want to give him any wiggle room when I pull him in.'

'Yes, sir. I'll report to the Kohli residence as soon as our city's marvelous public transportation system will get me there.'

'Take a cab. Put it on expense account.'

'Do I have one?'

'Jesus, Peabody, put it on mine. Get moving.'

She cut transmission and let her mind wander through the tiers of her case while she cut across town.

There was a corruption problem in the One two-eight. In the Illegals Division and potentially elsewhere. The corruption pointed at Max Ricker, and two of the detectives on the task force formed to take him down were dead. One of them had been in Ricker's pocket.

IAB had conducted an unauthorized and clandestine operation involving the other of those detectives as a plant.

In Purgatory, she reminded herself. Roarke's place. What did Ricker have to do with Roarke's club?

Had Bayliss been fishing there, trying to dig up the old connection? The man struck her as a fanatic, but that was reaching.

Still, IAB had sent Webster, an old connection of hers, to feed her misinformation on Kohli.

The captain of the squad had either let her men get beyond her control or was part of the corruption. She had a problem, or she was one. Either way, Eve had a ranking officer on her short list of murder suspects.

Ricker was a key, maybe *the* key. He'd lured the cops

and most certainly knew which members of the department were on his payroll. His businesses, she imagined, depended heavily on them. If she found enough of them, pulled them out of the loop, would he come out? Come after her?

As much as she'd enjoy that, and emptying the dirty cops out of his pocket, those were second-level goals. Her first was to flush those cops in order to find a killer.

Avenging a loss or betrayal, Mira had said. Not revenge, *avenge*. And the difference was, in Eve's mind, another key. Scouring off the badge with blood to purify it.

A fanatic? she wondered. *On a parallel line with Bayliss. One who tossed the rules aside when it suited his agenda.*

She scouted out a parking place, pleased to find one on street level less than half a block from the Kohli residence.

Even as she pulled in, a car rolled up beside her. Distracted, she glanced over. As the doors of the blocking car swung open, her instincts kicked in. She was out of her vehicle on a forward roll and came up with her weapon drawn.

There were four of them, and she saw with one sweeping glance they were better and more heavily armed than the ones Ricker had sent after her the first time.

'No point in making a fuss here, Lieutenant.' The man on the far left spoke politely and held his long-nosed laser pistol just under the open flap of a natty spring topcoat.

Out of the corner of her eye, Eve saw the one on the far right begin to circle. She considered trying for a stun-sweep; her finger all but quivered on the trigger.

And a boy of about ten zipped behind the group of men on a dented street bike. One of them plucked him off. The bike skidded down the street, and while the boy yelped, the man nudged his stunner against the young throat at the pulse.

'Him or you.'

It was said almost offhandedly, and it enraged her.

'Let him go.' Deliberately, she clicked the power up on her weapon.

The boy's eyes were wide and terrified. He made sounds like a small cat being choked. She couldn't risk looking at him.

'Get in the car, Lieutenant. Quietly and quickly, before innocent civilians are injured.'

She had a choice to make and made it fast. The weapon seemed to leap in her hand as she fired it, struck the man holding the boy between the eyes. She saw the kid fall, heard with sweet relief his screams of terror and, diving for cover, fired again.

She rolled under the car, grabbed the boy by the foot, and scraped off a few layers of his skin when she dragged him under. 'Stay. Shut up.'

Even as she rolled again to block his body with hers and come out on the other side, she heard the whine of another weapon.

'Drop it! Drop it, fucker, or what's left of your brains'll be leaking out of your ears.'

Webster, she thought, then came out from under the car like a lightning bolt, hit her target midbody with a full tackle, and sent him crashing to the street. She lifted his head, bounced it smartly off the pavement, then looked up to see that Webster had the only remaining problem standing, unarmed, with his hands lifted.

'You trailing me again, Webster?'

'I needed to talk to you.'

She got to her feet, winced a little, and glanced down to see a long, nasty gash in her knee. 'You sure run off at the mouth a lot lately. You got that one?'

'Yeah.' He smiled a little at the sound of sirens. 'There's the backup. I took the liberty of calling for some.'

She limped over, picked up weapons, scanning the three unconscious men. Then she went back, crouched, and peered under the car.

The kid had shut up, she gave him that. And big, fat tears ran down his freckled face. 'Come on out. It's okay.'

209

'I want my mom.'

'Can't blame you. Come on.'

He crab-walked out, swiped his hand under his nose. 'I wanna go home.'

'Okay, in a minute. You hurt much?'

'No.' His lip trembled. 'Did I wreck my bike?'

'I don't know. We'll get somebody to look at it for you.'

'I'm not supposed to ride in the street. My mom said.'

'Yeah, well, next time, listen to your mother.' She gestured to a uniform the minute the black and white pulled up. 'Send somebody after the kid's bike. Give your name to this policeman,' she told the boy. 'He's going to take you home. If your mom wants to talk to me . . .'

She dug in her pockets, mildly surprised when she discovered she'd remembered her cards. 'Tell her to call me at this number.'

''Kay.' He sniffed again, studying her with more interest than fear now. 'Are you a policeman, too?'

'Yeah.' She pulled her restraints out of her back pocket. 'I'm a policeman, too.'

She rolled the first man over, checked for a pulse, lifted one of his eyelids. She wasn't going to need restraints for this one.

'You couldn't risk a stun,' Webster said from behind her. 'You had to take a kill shot to insure the safety of the civilian.'

'I know what I had to do,' she said. Bitterly.

'You'd been slower, less accurate, or if you'd lowered your weapon, that kid wouldn't be going home to his mother.'

'I know that, too. Thanks for the help here.'

He nodded, then stood back and waited while she organized the scene and had one of the uniforms disperse the small crowd that had gathered.

The MTs rolled up, and right behind them a cab. He saw Peabody leap out, rush to her lieutenant. To his surprise, she

210

shook her head when Eve gestured her aside. What appeared from his viewpoint to be a short, snarly argument took place. In the end, Eve threw up her hands, then hobbled over to one of the MTs to have her leg treated.

Amused, he wandered up to Peabody. 'How'd you manage that?'

She was surprised to see him, and it showed, but she shrugged. 'I threatened her with Roarke.'

'What do you mean?'

'Reminded her that if she went home without having that gash seen to, he'd be pissed, treat it himself. And pour a pain blocker into her. She hates that.'

'So, he handles her.'

'They handle each other. It works for them.'

'I noticed. Will you give me a minute with her?'

'It's not up to me.' But Peabody walked away to oversee the transportation of the suspects.

Webster strode over to the medi-van, crouched down, and studied the gash being treated. 'Not so bad, but those pants will never be the same.'

'It's a scratch.'

'Got grit in it,' the MT stated.

'Got grit in it,' she mimicked and scowled at him as he closed the cut. 'I hate you guys.'

'Oh, we know. My partner paid me twenty so I'd treat you instead of him.' He finished the job while she sat and stewed, then stepped back. 'There now. Want a lollitape?'

Because her lips quivered she didn't risk cursing him but simply got to her feet. 'Easiest twenty you ever made, pal.'

She walked away, still limping a little, and Webster fell into step beside her. 'Now that we've had our little party, can I have a minute?'

'I've got a follow-up to do, then I've got to go in and hammer these guys, write a report . . .' She sighed. 'What do you want?'

211

'To apologize.'

'Okay. Accepted.' But before she could walk away he took her arm. 'Webster.'

'Just a minute.' Cautiously, he removed his hand, put both in his pockets. 'I was way over the line last night, and I'm sorry for it. I put you in a bad spot. I was pissed, at myself a lot more than you, but it gave me an excuse to . . . Okay truth, goddamn it. I never got over you.'

He could probably have given her a quick roundhouse kick in the face and shocked her less. 'What? What was to get over?'

'Well, ouch. That should have my ego limping for the next couple of weeks. Let's just say I got hung up. It's not like I thought about you every waking minute for the past few years, but there were moments. And when that shit came down on you last winter and we had a few face-to-faces, it got stirred up again. It's my problem, not yours.'

She considered, strained for something, but her mind stayed blank. 'I don't know what I'm supposed to say.'

'Nothing. I just wanted to clear it up, get it out of my gut. Roarke has every right to kick my teeth in.' Experimentally, Webster ran his tongue around them now. 'Which he damn near did. Anyway.' He tried a shrug. 'I'd like to set that aside if it's just the same to you.'

'Yeah, let's do that. I've got to—'

'One more thing while I'm clearing my conscience. I was following orders when I came to you on Kohli. I didn't like doing it. I know you had a meet at The Tower, with Bayliss.'

'Your captain's an asshole.'

'Yeah. Yeah, he is.' He sucked in a breath. 'Look, I went into IAB because I wanted to do good work, because I believed in keeping a clean house. I'm not going to give you a song and dance on abuse of power, but—'

'Good, because I could sing a hell of a tune about your captain.'

'I know it. I didn't come to you last night just because I was hung up on you. This operation, the direction it's taken, has stuck in my craw. Bayliss says look at the big picture, but if you don't see the details, what the hell's the point?'

He looked back as the medi-vans and their police escort headed out. 'I'm adding up the details, Dallas, and they're making a whole new pattern. You're going after a cop killer, and it's going to swing you right into Ricker's face.'

'Tell me something I don't know.'

'Okay, I will.' He looked back at her. 'I want in.'

'Forget it.'

'If you don't think you can trust me, you're wrong. And if you think I'll give you any personal grief, you're wrong there, too.'

'I'm not worried about personal grief. Even if I wanted you in, I don't have the authority to sanction it.'

'You're primary. You pick your team.'

She stepped back, hooked her thumbs in her front pocket, and measured him with a deliberately insulting up-and-down glance. 'When's the last time you've been on the street, Webster?'

'Awhile, but it's like sex. You don't forget the moves. I just saved your ass, didn't I?'

'I was saving my own, thanks. Why the hell should I bring you in?'

'I've got information. I can get more. It may be my last duty in IAB. I'm thinking about transferring out, maybe putting back in for Homicide or Violent Crimes. I'm a good cop, Dallas. We worked together before. We did all right. Give me a shot. I could use some redemption.'

There were a dozen reasons to refuse. But there were one or two offsetting those. 'I'll think about it.'

'Good enough. You know how to reach me.' He walked away, then turned, walking backward as he grinned at her. 'Don't forget. I share the collar for these assholes.'

She stood frowning after him, trying to figure the angles.

'We're cleaned up here, Lieutenant.' Peabody, curiosity burning, walked up to her. 'The uniforms are taking the single subject who was still standing into booking. Weapons are confiscated. The dead guy's on his way to the morgue, the other two en route to the hospital under guard. I have the name and address of the little boy. Should I notify child services so a rep can be present while you take his statement?'

'Hold off on that. Let's have a female uniform take his statement later today. Since maximum force was used, it's better, cleaner, if I don't take it myself. I'll write it up when I get back and report to Whitney after I talk to the scum who's still standing. Let's go on and do what we came for.'

'How's the leg?'

'It's fine.' Because Peabody was eyeing her, she made a concerted effort not to limp.

'Sure was handy Webster was around, huh?'

'Yeah, handy. Let's leave it at that for now.'

'You're the boss.'

'Try to remember that next time,' Eve said with some heat as they entered Kohli's building. 'And don't nag me about medical treatment in front of a bunch of uniforms and gawking civilians.'

Got the job done, Peabody thought, but she was wise enough to button her lip.

A woman Eve didn't recognize opened the door of the Kohli apartment.

'Yes?'

'Lieutenant Dallas, NYPSD.' Eve held her badge to eye level. 'I'd like to speak with Mrs Kohli.'

'She's indisposed.'

'I'm sorry to disturb her at this difficult time, but I'm in charge of her husband's case. I need to ask Mrs Kohli some questions that may aid in my investigation.'

'Who is it, Carla?'

Patsy came to the door, peered out.

'It's you.' She wrenched open the door while the other woman made helpless, soothing noises. 'How dare you come here? How *dare* you show your face in my house.'

'Patsy, come on now, Patsy. You should go lie down. Go away,' the woman said to Eve. 'Just go away.'

'No, no, let her in. I have things to say.'

As Eve stepped in, Sergeant Clooney hurried to the group by the door. 'Patsy, you have to stay calm.'

'I'm supposed to stay calm when I'm burying my husband tomorrow and this woman is trying to smear him? To ruin his reputation? Everything he worked for.'

There were no tears, but there was fury. Eve preferred it. 'Mrs Kohli, you're mistaken.'

'You think I haven't *heard?* You think I don't *know?*' She sneered as Eve's glance shifted to Clooney. 'No, not from him. He says you're doing your job. But I know what you're doing.'

'Patsy.' Clooney laid a hand on her back, kept his voice low and calm. 'You don't want to upset the children.'

And there were plenty of them, Eve noted. A couple of babies, and one of those bigger babies who waddled around on shaky legs and made her nervous. The young boy Peabody had taken to the park on their first visit sat on the floor with a girl of about the same age. Their eyes were wide and focused on her.

She much preferred the four men with guns she'd just dispatched.

'Carla.' With rigid control, Patsy turned to the woman Eve now identified as her sister. 'Would you take the children to the park? Would you do that for me?'

'I don't like to leave you alone.'

'I'm all right. Just take the children. They've been cooped up too long.'

Eve stood where she was and watched what appeared to be

215

a well-rehearsed if chaotic circus. Babies were packed into some sort of rolling cart where they wiggled and shook pudgy fists. The one who could walk, more or less, tumbled onto his padded butt, laughed uproariously, and was hooked into a safety harness.

The older children were ordered to hold hands. There was a short but desperate moment until the little boy's jacket was discovered. The noise level reached a dangerous peak, then cut off abruptly when the entire contingent trailed out the door.

'I will not ask you to sit down,' Patsy said stiffly. 'I will not offer you refreshment. My husband was a good man.' Her voice trembled, nearly broke. But she continued. 'An honest man. He would do nothing to shame his name, or me, or his children.'

'I know that, Mrs Kohli,' Eve said and stopped what promised to become a tirade in its tracks. 'Everything I've learned in my investigation of your husband's death confirms that he was a solid cop.'

'Then how can you spread vicious lies about him? How can you let people think – his own coworkers believe – he was taking money?'

'Patsy.' Before Eve could speak, Clooney took the woman's arm. 'Lieutenant Dallas is doing her job, just as Taj did his job. Come sit down now.'

'I want answers.' But she went with Clooney now, let him guide her to a chair. 'I deserve answers.'

'Yes, ma'am, you do. I'm only able, at this time, to tell you that I've learned Detective Kohli was working under cover, and part of that cover involved the pretense that he was accepting illicit funds. He was part of an operation formed to expose corruption in the department. His death, Mrs Kohli, was, in my opinion, in the line of duty. And that will be stated in my official findings.'

'I don't understand.' Tears threatened as she lowered her face into her hands. 'I don't understand any of this.'

'I can't explain it to you in detail at this time. Mrs Kohli, I intend to find your husband's killer. You can help me.'

'I don't know how to help. I'm sorry, please sit down. I'll get coffee.'

'There's no need—'

'I have to settle myself.' She drew herself up. 'I need a moment to think. Excuse me.'

'She's been holding up so well,' Clooney muttered when Patsy left the room. 'Almost too well. For the children, I imagine. Then this.'

'What this, Clooney?' Eve didn't sit but turned her full attention on him. 'What have you been telling her?'

'That her husband was a good man,' he shot back. 'And that you're doing your job.'

He paused, held up a hand as he took the time to compose himself. 'Look, I don't know where she got the information that you were heaping dirt on him. She won't tell me. All I know is I got a call from her a few hours ago. She was close to hysterical.'

He picked up a little toy truck from the cushions of the couch, turned it over in his hand. 'Kids,' he said, as if to give himself a moment to calm down as well. 'You never know what you're going to sit on when you've got kids in the house.'

'What did she want from you, Sergeant?'

'Reassurance. That's all survivors want in the end. And that's what I've tried to give. I'd heard the talk around the squad the last day or two but didn't put much credence in it.' He paused another moment. 'I don't know you, so I didn't discount the talk, either. But it's not my function here to stir up the survivors. I've been working to calm her down since I got here.'

'Fair enough. Can you think of any reason I'd decide to smear an honest cop I didn't even know?'

'No.' Clooney sighed. 'That's what I've been telling her.

217

That's what I've been telling myself.' What, he thought it would be unwise to admit, he'd been telling his captain. 'But you've stirred up a lot of bad feelings in the One two-eight. It's hard to ignore that.'

Patsy came back with a tray, set it on the table. 'Taj would want me to try,' she said quietly. 'He'd want me to cooperate. I didn't know about this . . . operation. He never told me. I know about the money now, the other accounts. I . . . I thought you'd put it there. You have a rich husband. I was so angry.'

'Now we both are.' Eve sat. 'I don't like being used to bring you pain or to damage the reputation of the man I've sworn to stand for. Who told you I put the money there?'

'No one told me, exactly.' She looked tired again, and embarrassed. The heat of fury had burned away and left her empty and confused. 'It was just one of the things some people were saying in the heat of the moment. He had a lot of friends in his squad. I didn't know he had so many. They've been so kind. His captain came here herself, to assure me that Taj would have an official memorial.'

'Did Captain Roth tell you I was going after your husband's reputation?'

'No, no, not really. Just that no matter what anyone said, I could be proud of Taj. It meant a lot to me for her to say that, to my face. Most of the squad's come by, to pay their respects, and to offer to help in any way.'

'But someone contacted you today?'

'Yes, but he was only trying to help. He only wanted me to know the squad was behind Taj a hundred percent. I didn't understand at first, then he said that I shouldn't let any of the trash coming out of your office concern me. It was all a setup. He even backed off when he saw I didn't know anything, but I pushed. Then he told me.'

'Who told you?'

'I don't want him to get in trouble.' She clasped her hands

218

together, all but wrung them as she weighed confidentiality against justice for her husband. 'Jerry Vernon. Detective Vernon. But he was only trying to help.'

'I see. Was he a close friend of your husband's?'

'I don't think so. Not particularly. Taj didn't socialize a great deal with his coworkers. There were a few who came here to dinner, and some whose wives I got together with now and then.'

'It would help me to know who his friends were.'

'Oh, all right.' She listed off a few names, seemed to relax a little more as she spoke.

'You're going to hurt my feelings, Patsy,' Clooney said.

'Of course, you, Art.' She took his hand, seemed to anchor to it.

'Taj was friendly with my son,' Clooney explained. 'Now and again they let the old man tag along for a beer on a boys' night out. For the most part, Taj was a homebody.'

'Mrs Kohli, you told me Taj called you that night, told you he was meeting someone after he'd finished at Purgatory.'

'Yes, but he didn't tell me who, and I didn't ask. I guess I was getting a little tired of the long hours he was putting in. I was a bit short with him at first, but he brought me around. He always could,' she said with a smile. 'He promised it wouldn't be for too much longer, that he was close to having what he needed. I thought he meant the extra money for the new place we wanted. Then he told me to kiss the babies for him, and he said, "I love you, Patsy." It was the last thing he said to me. It was like him for that to be the last thing.'

Chapter Fifteen

The assailant with the polite voice and the natty topcoat went by the name of Elmore Riggs. A quick search proved that it had been the name he'd been born with, some thirty-nine years before, in Vancouver, Canada.

There had been a small dispute with the Canadian authorities over smuggling explosive devices across the border, and Elmore had done some time before he'd been considered rehabilitated and had moved to New York.

His address was listed in a tidy, moderately wealthy enclave north of the city, and his profession was reported to be security consultant.

A fancy name for a hired hammer, Eve decided.

Armed with this data, she headed toward the Interview level to link up with Feeney and put Elmore Riggs through his paces.

Vernon stepped in front of her when she reached the top of the glide.

'A little out of your territory, aren't you, Detective?'

'You think you can shake me?' He gave her a body bump that had a number of the cops moving through the area pausing.

Eve simply waved the hand she held at her side to keep them back. 'I don't know, Jerry. You look shaken.'

'Everybody knows you're trying to throw trash at the squad. IAB sow's what you are. If you think you can dump on me like you're doing on Kohli and Mills, think again. I've contacted my union rep, and we're coming down on you.'

'Gee, Vernon, now you're scaring me. Not the union rep.' She gave a deliberate shudder.

'You won't be so smart when you're hit with a lawsuit, and I start bleeding that rich husband you hooked.'

'My God, Peabody, a lawsuit. I feel faint.'

'Don't worry, Lieutenant, I'll catch you.'

'They'll take your badge.' Vernon sneered. 'Like they did before, only this time they'll keep it. Before I'm done, you'll wish you never heard my name.'

'We aren't close to done, and I already wish that, Jerry.' She grinned at him. 'I've got you cold, and when Ricker gets wind of it, when he starts worrying how I'm tracing those numbered accounts you set up back to him, he's going to be very unhappy with you. I don't think your union rep's going to be much help where he's concerned.'

'You got nothing. You're just trying to set me up. I figure you want Roth's job over the One two-eight, so you're messing us up so she gets the boot, and you can sail in. That's what she thinks, too.'

'Make sure you put that in your lawsuit. How I pulled your name out of a hat and decided to dedicate myself to destroying you and your squad, so I can sit behind a desk. That ought to fly.'

She shifted a little closer, her eyes drilling into his. 'Only you'd better start thinking how to cover yourself. The money you've been taking isn't going to help much, since I'm arranging to have those accounts frozen. And while you're dealing with that, remember I'm the only one coming at you who has even a marginal interest in keeping you breathing. While I'm coming at your face. Ricker's going to be at your back. And there's a cop killer hunting dirty cops. You won't know which direction he's coming from.'

'That's a rash of shit.'

He lifted his fists, she cocked her chin. 'I wouldn't,' she said softly. 'But you go right ahead.'

'I'm taking you down.' He stepped back, clenched those fists at his sides. 'You're finished.' He shoved past her, hopped on the downward glide.

'No, but I'm getting there,' Eve murmured. 'Let's put some men on him. I don't want him rabbiting.' She rolled her shoulders. 'You know what I'm in the mood for now?'

'Kicking righteous ass, sir?'

'Got it in one. Let's go sweat Riggs.'

'You're limping again.'

'I am not. And shut up.'

She limped, damn it, to Interview A, where Feeney was waiting and popping nuts in his mouth. 'What kept you?'

'Just a little kissy-face with a close personal friend. Did Riggs lawyer?'

'Nope. Made his phone call. Claimed it was to his wife. I gotta say, he's a cucumber. And polite with it. Cool and well mannered, that's our boy.'

'He's Canadian.'

'Oh. I guess that explains it.'

They walked in to where Riggs sat patiently in a miserably uncomfortable chair.

'Good afternoon, Mr Riggs,' Eve said and moved to the table.

'Lieutenant. Nice to see you.' He glanced down at the rip in her pants. 'A pity about those trousers. They look so well on you.'

'Yeah, I'm pretty torn up about it. Record on.' She read in the information as she took her seat. 'No lawyer, Riggs?'

'Not at this time, though thank you for asking.'

'You do, then, understand your rights and obligations in this matter?'

'Perfectly. First let me say I'm full of remorse for my actions.'

Clever, she thought. This was no moron. 'Are you?'

'Absolutely. I regret what happened today. It was, of course, never my intention to cause any injury. I see now how reckless and foolish it was to approach you in the manner I did. I'd like to apologize.'

'That's really big of you. How did it happen you were armed with banned weapons while traveling on a New York street with the intention of abducting and/or assaulting a police officer?'

'I fell in with bad companions,' he said with a soft smile, 'I have no excuse for having illegal weapons in my possession. I would like to say, however, that in my line of work, security consultation, it's often part of the routine to rub shoulders with criminal elements and to find oneself in possession of illegal weapons. Naturally, I should have turned those weapons over to the proper authorities.'

'Where did you acquire those weapons?'

'From the man you killed. I was hired by him, you see, just this morning.'

'The dead guy hired you.'

'Yes. I was unaware, of course, that you were a police officer when I accepted the commission. I was told that you were a dangerous individual who had threatened him and his family with bodily harm. Obviously, I was deceived, and I'm afraid I accepted his story and the weapons at face value. Very poor judgement on my part.'

'If you weren't aware I was a police officer, why did you call me Lieutenant at the scene?'

'I have no recollection of having done so.'

'So you just took this job. What was the name of the guy who hired you?'

'Haggerty, Clarence Haggerty. Or so he told me at the time. Imagine my shock when I discovered his purpose was not, as he told me, to frighten away by show of force, a woman who was endangering his family.'

'I'm trying to do just that,' Eve said mildly. 'I guess having him grab some innocent kid and hold a stunner to his throat where it could cause permanent paralysis or death, seemed like a fine way to frighten me.'

'It happened so fast. I was shocked when he grabbed the boy. I'm afraid my reaction was slow. Obviously Haggerty – or whoever he was – was not the man I believed him to be. Anyone who would endanger a child in that manner . . .'

He trailed off, sadly shaking his head. 'I'm quite glad you killed him, Lieutenant.' He smiled again. 'I can't begin to tell you how glad I am.'

'I'm sure you're dancing.' She leaned forward. 'Do you really think this lame story is going to fly, Riggs?'

'Why shouldn't it? If you require any documentation to corroborate my brief employment by Mr Haggerty, I'll be happy to supply it. I keep excellent records.'

'I'll just bet you do.'

'This, of course, in no way negates my responsibility for what took place. I will, no doubt, lose my security license. I face a prison term, or at the very least home incarceration. I'm prepared to take my punishment, as the law demands.'

'You work for Max Ricker.'

'I'm afraid I don't recall the name. If a Mr Ricker has hired me as a consultant at any time, it would be in my records. I'll be happy to sign an authorization so that you can search those records.'

'You're looking at twenty-five years, Riggs. Minimum.'

'I hope the courts won't be too harsh, as I was unaware of the true purpose when I was hired. And I certainly did nothing to harm that little boy. I was duped.' He lifted his hands, his face still placid. 'But I stand prepared to accept the punishment due me.'

'You figure that's better than ending up like Lewis.'

'I'm sorry? Do I know a Lewis?'

'He's worm food. And we both know Ricker may cut his losses with you so you end up the same.'

'I just don't understand, Lieutenant. I'm sorry.'

'Let's run it through again, in words of one syllable.'

She worked him for more than an hour, shifting over to Feeney to change the pace, coming back hard, leading in soft.

Riggs never broke a sweat, never varied his story by an iota. It was, she thought, like interrogating a goddamn droid with perfect programming.

'Get him out of here,' Eve ordered in disgust, then stalked out of the room.

'This guy won't roll,' she said when Feeney joined her. 'Ricker sent brains this time. But Riggs wasn't completely in control. He didn't expect that creep to grab the kid. So while he's got brains, there's no saying the others do. I want to double the guards on the two in the hospital, get an update on their condition.'

'Riggs gets a decent lawyer, using that line, holds to it, won't even do five years.'

'I know it, and so does he. Self-satisfied son of a bitch. Let's get a run on the two in the hospital, find a level.'

'I'll take that. We don't need the smoke now, so I'd as soon work out of my office.'

'Okay. I'm going to go write this up, then head home. I've got some lines to tug on that end.'

By the time she was finished, it was well after shift. She cut Peabody loose, then headed down to the garage. Her leg hurt, which pissed her off. Her head throbbed, which was only a minor annoyance.

But when she reached her parking level and saw the condition of her vehicle, she was ready to spit rock.

'Goddamn it. Goddamn it.'

She'd had this unit – one that actually worked – for less than eight months. It was ugly, had already been wrecked once and repaired, but it was hers, and she'd kept it in decent shape.

Now the hood, the trunk, the doors on both sides were smashed in, the tires slashed, and the rear glass looked like it had been attacked by lasers.

And all, she thought, in a police garage with full security cams.

'Whoa.' Baxter strolled up behind her. 'I heard you had a little trouble earlier, but didn't know you'd wrecked your vehicle. Maintenance isn't going to be happy with you.'

'I didn't wreck it. How the hell did somebody walk in here and beat the crap out of my ride?' She took another step toward it, and Baxter grabbed her arm.

'Let's just keep some distance. Call the bomb squad. You've got a very temperamental enemy at the moment. Could be rigged.'

'You're right. Yeah, you're right. If it blows up, they'll never issue me another one. They hate me in Requisitions.'

It wasn't rigged, and she managed to cop four new tires. Because Baxter called down for them and sweet-talked Maintenance. While they were being changed and two crabby Maintenance men were doing something to the doors to make them open and close again, she checked with Garage Security.

A blip, she was told, in the disc run.

'What's the verdict?' Baxter asked when she came back.

'A blip, fifteen minutes of snow and blocked audio. This level only. They didn't notice.' Her eyes narrowed into tawny glints. 'I guarantee they'll notice the next time. You didn't have to hang, Baxter.'

'This may be your game, Dallas, but we all want part of the ball. You should take something for that leg. You're limping.'

'I am not.' She sighed as she wrenched open her dented car door. 'Thanks.'

'Don't I get a kiss good-bye?'

'Sure, honey. Come on over here.'

He laughed, backed away. 'You'll hit me. You heading home?'

'Yeah.'

He wandered to his vehicle. 'I'm heading uptown, myself.' He said it casually and didn't fool her for a minute. 'I'll follow you up.'

'I don't need a baby-sitter.'

'I'm heading uptown,' he said and got in his car.

She wanted to be annoyed with him but couldn't quite pull it off. On the drive, she stayed alert, watching for tails, preparing for ambush. Other than her vehicle making ominous whining noises when she got over thirty miles an hour, and thumping ones when she turned left, the trip home was uneventful.

She waved Baxter off at her gates, figured she'd raid Roarke's liquor supply for a bottle of unblended scotch as payment for the favor.

She wanted a drink herself, she thought as she walked up the front steps. A nice cool glass of wine, maybe a quick swim to work out the kinks.

She had a feeling it was going to be a long night.

'I assume,' Summerset began while the cat streaked between his legs to greet Eve, 'you've been involved in some sort of vehicular accident.'

'You assume incorrectly. My unit was involved in some sort of vehicular accident.' She bent, picked up Galahad, and found a little comfort by rubbing her cheek against his fur. 'Where's Roarke?'

'He is not yet home for the evening. If you had consulted his schedule, you'd be aware he isn't expected for another hour. Those trousers are ruined.'

'People keep telling me that.' She set the cat down, stripped off her jacket, and tossed it over the newel post. She walked past him, intended to go down to the pool house.

227

'You're limping.'

She kept going, but she did indulge herself in a single short scream.

The swim helped, and once she was alone and naked, she took a good look at the wound on her leg. The MT had done a good job, she had to admit. It was healing up well, even if it did ache like hell.

There were a number of scrapes and bruises to go along with it. Some of which, she decided, she'd gotten during the jungle sex with Roarke. It didn't seem so bad when she backed those out of the mix. Feeling better, she tugged on a robe and, giving in to her knee, took the elevator up to the bedroom.

And coming out, nearly rapped straight into Roarke on the point of going in.

'Hello, Lieutenant. I was coming down to join you.'

'I took a long swim, but I could sit and watch you take one. If you're naked.'

'Why don't we take one together later?' He drew her into the bedroom. 'What happened to your car?'

'I can't prove it, but my guess is Ricker. It was like that when I got down to the garage. We seem to keep annoying each other.' She started toward her closet.

'Why are you limping?'

She rolled her eyes but resisted banging her head against the wall. 'I rapped my knee. Look, I want to get dressed, have a drink. I'll tell you about it.' She started to tug off the robe, remembered the range of bruises and scrapes. 'I ran into some trouble today, took a roll on the street. I'm a little banged up, so don't go crazy on me.'

'I'll try to retain my sanity.' His only reaction when she stripped was a sigh. 'Very colorful. Lie down.'

'No.'

'Eve, lie down so I don't have to knock you down. I'll treat them, and it'll be done.'

She grabbed out a shirt. 'Listen, ace, I missed a very much desired ass-kicking round today. I can substitute you for my intended target.' But when he took a step toward her, she tossed down the shirt. 'All right, all right. I'm not in the mood to fight. But if you're going to play doctor, I want a drink.'

She stalked to the bed, flopped onto her stomach, and said in a tone she hoped would irritate him a little, 'Wine. White and cold.'

'We're here to serve.' He got the glass, slipped a pain blocker into it, knowing it would irritate her when she figured it out. He retrieved the medication for her injuries, set them down, and flipped her over.

'Sit up, and no whining.'

'I don't whine.'

'Rarely,' he agreed. 'But when you do, you make up for the lack of quantity with quality.'

She picked up the glass while he ran the healing wand over the worst of the bruises. 'Why don't you crawl up in here with me, doc?'

'I intend to, a bit later. That's how I collect my fee.'

She'd finished half the glass before she noticed the effects. 'What did you put in here?' she demanded. 'You put a blocker in here.' When she started to set the glass aside, he simply plucked it out of her hand, gave her hair a yank to pull her head back, and poured the rest down her throat.

She choked, sputtered. 'I *hate* that.'

'Yes, I know, but I so enjoy it. Turn over.'

'Kiss my ass.'

'Darling, I will, once you turn over.'

She had to laugh. She rolled, forced to admit, at least to herself, that the worst of the pain had eased. Better yet, she decided with a sigh, when that wonderful mouth of his brushed over her butt. 'Keep going,' she invited.

'Later. I want these aches to settle down first.'

'I feel okay.'

'I want to make love with you, Eve.' He turned her over again, gently this time, leaned over her. 'Slowly, thoroughly, and for a very long time. I want you to feel much better than okay before that happens.'

'I'm starting to feel really good.' She reached for him, but he took her hands, tugged her up.

'Tell me what happened.'

'Well, if you're not going to jump me, I'm getting dressed.'

'The robe.' He held it out. 'You'll be more comfortable in something loose. And it'll be less for me to take off you later.'

Finding it hard to argue with his logic, she put the robe back on, then walked to the AutoChef. 'You want something?'

'Whatever you're having's fine.'

She ordered pasta for two, going for the spicy sauce. She sat with him, began to eat to fuel herself for the night to come, and told him about her day.

He listened, and the fact that he made no comments while she spoke had the nerves dancing at the base of her neck. Even when the delicate pasta began to taste like paste in her throat, she continued to eat.

'I've got some angles I want to play, and it takes a load off knowing I have the full support of the chief of police. It did my heart good to watch him skew Bayliss. Bloodlessly. You have to admire that.'

'Eve.'

She met his eyes, cold as winter, blue as an iced ocean. Odd, she thought, how facing down four armed men only hours before had merely kicked her adrenaline into gear. One look from Roarke was a great deal more potent.

'He's gone after you three times. However much you dislike it, disapprove of it, I will deal with him.'

'Two times,' she corrected. 'The third was just my car, and the score's been in my favor every time. But,' she continued,

'I anticipated your reaction. It's not going to do any good, but I'm going to point out that given my job, I've been gone after before and will be again. This personal thing between the two of you shouldn't enter into it.'

'You're mistaken.' And his voice was terrifyingly mild.

'But since it does, I want you to work with me on this.'

She could sense his underlying fury.

'Do you think you can placate me, Eve?'

'No. Hell, no. Stop staring at me that way. You're spoiling my appetite.' She tossed down her fork. 'I could use your help. I asked for it before this happened today, didn't I? All that's changed is he sent another goon squad after me, and I took them down. He's got to be royally burnt by that. If we go at this from the same angle, work together, we can both get what we want.

'Well, you won't get *exactly* what you want, which is, at my guess, eating Ricker's liver after you've roasted it on a spit over a slow fire. But we can get as close to that as the law allows.'

'The law's your yardstick, not mine.'

'Roarke.' She put a hand over his. 'I can get him without you, but it wouldn't be as quick and it sure as hell wouldn't be as satisfying. You could get him without me. Maybe quicker, and maybe more satisfying to you. But think about this: Wouldn't you rather picture him living a long, miserable life in a cage than just throwing the switch on him?'

He considered it. 'No.'

'You're a scary guy, Roarke. A very scary guy.'

'But I'll work with you on this, Lieutenant. And I'll contemplate, depending on how that work goes, settling for that image. I'll do that for you. I promise you, it costs me more than I can tell you.'

'I know that. So, thanks.'

'Don't thank me until it's done. Because if it doesn't work your way, it will work mine. What do you need?'

231

She let out a breath. 'First I need to know why IAB sent Kohli into Purgatory. What is there in the club or who is there they wanted? Bayliss said something today about Ricker's connection to it, but you told me you severed business with him over ten years ago.'

'That's right, I did, taking some of his more lucrative accounts with me. I've sold them off since, or adjusted them. As for Purgatory, he has no connection to it. But he did. I bought it from him five years ago. Or I should say,' he added when she gaped. 'My representatives acquired it from his representatives.'

'He owned the place? And you didn't tell me?'

'Lieutenant, I have to point out, you didn't ask.'

'For God's sake,' she grumbled and got to her feet to pace, to think.

'And at the time your Kohli was murdered, I didn't think of it, see a connection, or consider it relevant. It's been mine for a number of years and has been completely overhauled, remodeled, and restaffed.'

'If he used it for a front, it could be some of his people still come in. Do business.'

'None that's ever been reported to me. If that's the case, it's very minor business.'

'A cop died there. That's not minor.'

'Point taken.'

'Why did he sell it?'

'My research at the time indicated that it was becoming a little too warm. He often dispenses of businesses and property when they've outlived their usefulness to him. It's basic business practice.'

'If he's got this hard-on for you, why did he sell it to you?'

'He didn't know until after the fact. I assume he was displeased, but the deal was done.' He sat back, doing some thinking himself. 'Possibly he put out word that there was outside business being done there, or had some of his people come in to do some. He may have hoped to take a swipe at me that way. I can see that. He'd have waited until the club was well established, until it was running smoothly, then tried to disrupt it. He's a patient man. A few years wouldn't have been any time to wait.'

'And with his connections in the department, he'd have had a funnel for the rumors. IAB picked up on them, started looking into it, and put Kohli in. It plays. And it's looking more and more like the poor guy died for nothing.'

'You'll fix that.' Roarke got to his feet.

'Yeah, I'll fix it. I want to look at some data, data I'm not supposed to see, without anyone knowing I'm looking.'

He smiled now. 'Lieutenant, I believe I can help you with that.'

In his brilliantly lit lounging room in his expansive Connecticut estate, Max Ricker stomped viciously on the face of a house droid he'd called Marta.

She would never be the same.

Canarde wisely kept his distance during this torrent of temper. He'd seen it before, and it wasn't always a droid Ricker broke to pieces when the rage was on him.

For a time, the only sounds in the room were harsh, ragged breathing and the distressing crunch of plastic and metal. Canarde had seen it before, yes indeed. But these lapses of control were getting much worse.

He began to think it would soon be time to put his carefully outlined escape plan into action, and spend the rest of his days in the relative peace and elegance of the home he'd purchased under a false name on the Paradise Colony.

But for now, he was confident he could weather the storm.

'One woman, one single woman, and they can't deal with her? Can't *deal* with her? I promise you, promise you, *they* will be dealt with.'

He kicked what was left of Marta's head out of his way. The air stank with the stench of fried circuits. Calmer, as he always was after an . . . episode, he walked to the bar, filled a glass with his favored pink liquid that was sweetened rum with a heavy lacing of barbiturates.

'One dead, you say?' His voice was mild now, as were his eyes as he glanced toward Canarde. He might have said, 'Two for dinner?' for all the inflection in the tone.

'Yes. Yawly. Ines and Murdock are being treated for injuries. Riggs has been booked and has followed my instructions as to his story. He'll stick to it. He's an intelligent man.'

'He's a fool, like the rest of them. I want them disposed of.'

Prepared for this directive, Canarde stepped forward. 'That may be prudent with Ines and Murdock. I believe, however, that if you act on Riggs when he proves himself to be loyal, it will seriously damage your organization's morale.'

Ricker sipped, and his silver eyes slithered over Canarde's face. 'Why would you be under the impression I'm the least bit concerned with morale?'

'You should be,' Canarde said, knowing he risked a great deal. 'By demonstrating goodwill, even lenience, to an employee under these circumstances – as you showed instant discipline to Lewis under different circumstances – you send a clear message to those who work for you. And,' he added, 'Riggs can always be handled after a period of time has passed.'

Ricker continued to drink, continued to calm. 'You're right. Of course, you're right.' His smile was quick and almost terrifyingly brilliant. 'Thank you. I'm afraid I let the matter of this annoying cop influence my better judgment. Some things are worth waiting for.'

He thought of Roarke. He'd waited there. Years now. And hadn't he found just the right place to strike?

But it was harder to wait, harder to see clearly, when he could almost taste the blood.

'Assure Mr Riggs that his loyalty is appreciated and will be rewarded.'

He started toward the window-wall, saw the droid debris scattered over the floor. For a moment he was blank, for another simply puzzled. Then, dismissing it from his mind, he walked around it, slid open the glass, and stepped out on the deck overlooking his lawns.

'I spent a lifetime building what I have, and will one day pass it all to my son. A man needs a legacy to pass on to his son.' He was mellowing now, his tone turning dreamy. 'But I have a number of goals to reach before that time comes. And one I intend to achieve very soon is to crush Roarke. To have him on his knees. I will accomplish that, Canarde. Make no mistake.'

He sipped his bright drink and looked out over the grounds, a man satisfied and still vital. 'I'll accomplish that,' he said again, 'and have his cop begging for mercy.'

Chapter Sixteen

In the sealed room of Roarke's private office, the equipment was state of the art, expansive, and unregistered. The wide, searching eye of CompuGuard was blind to it. Nothing generated on it or scanned from it could be detected by any outside factor.

And in the hands of a man with Roarke's talents, there were no data that could not, eventually, be unearthed.

Despite the fact that besides Roarke, only Eve and Summerset had ever been through the secured doors, and the purpose of the area was business, it was a handsome room with generous privacy-screened windows and a floor of beautiful tile.

She'd often thought the glossy U-shaped control deck resembled the bridge of a particularly well-designed spacecraft. And when he was behind those controls, Roarke was very much captain of the ship.

Here, she would bend the rules. Or let Roarke bend them for her.

'Roth first,' Eve began. 'Her story is her husband's been bleeding out her financial accounts, setting up a nest egg for himself and his on-the-side piece. Roth, Captain Eileen. Her address is—'

'That isn't necessary.'

He enjoyed this type of work nearly as much as he enjoyed the annoyed look on Eve's face when he easily danced through the blocks and obstacles even the brains and talents in EDD couldn't budge. He put the data on a wall screen rather than commanding the computer to read it off.

'Not a very impressive nest egg,' he commented. 'But enough, one supposes, to set himself and his on-the-side piece up cozily enough. He's an unemployed writer. Some women are attracted to the struggling artist type. All those pale, Byronic moods.'

'Is that so?' Eve said in a voice dry as dust.

'Indeed. In my experience. She isn't his first,' he added, shooting more data to a second screen. 'He has two marriages and three cohabitations under his belt, and repeats this pattern of tapping into his partner's financial resources toward the end of the run.'

'You'd think she'd be too smart for that kind of con. Christ, she's a cop.'

'Love,' Roarke said, 'is blind.'

'The hell it is. I see you clear enough, don't I?'

His grin was quick and gorgeous. 'Why, Lieutenant, you've made my heart flutter.' He grabbed her hand, kissed her knuckles lavishly.

'No funny stuff.' She slapped him aside, an absent gesture that only made him smile again.

It was good, he thought, to be back in synch.

'She's got two payments to a Lucius Breck,' Eve noted. 'Three thousand a pop. Who's Breck?'

Because she hadn't realized he'd cued her into the system, she nearly jumped when the computer's polite voice answered.

Breck, Lucius. Substance abuse counselor, Private practice. Office address 529 Sixth Avenue, New York City. Residence—

'Never mind. That jibes with the story she gave me. Jesus, she's close onto flat busted financially and still paying through the nose for private counseling when she could get it through departmental sources for nothing. And she's going to lose anyway. She won't keep her squad command when this all washes down.'

And she thinks I'm bucking for her desk. Eve shook her head. No, thanks. Eve would wear captain's bars one day, but damn if they'd drag her off the street by them.

'You can't find any other accounts linked to her?'

'I can't find what's not there,' Roarke said reasonably. 'As you've seen for yourself, your Captain Roth is very nearly in financial ruin. She's borrowed from her retirement account in order to pay Breck's fee. Her living expenses are otherwise frugal.'

'So she's clean, and her squad's dirty, which may go to motive. She commanded both victims and had visited Kohli at Purgatory. Her probability scan's still fairly low, but that could change if I can add in her personality analysis from the department files and my own take on her.'

'And your take is?'

'She's hard, got a mean temper, and she's been so busy rising up the ladder, she's been missing details. She's covering up personal mistakes in a scramble to protect her position. Could be she's covered up more, in her squad, to keep her superiors from yanking her out. A lot of temper went into that first murder. Like I said, she's got a mean one.'

She turned back to Roarke. 'Vernon, Detective Jeremy. I've already got enough on him to haul him in – after I let him sweat awhile.'

'What do you need from me?'

'I want to connect the money to Ricker. Getting it this way, I won't be able to use it as evidence. But I can make him think I can. I break Vernon, I've got new lines to tug. He's connected to both victims and to Roth. And to Ricker.'

'Ricker's going to be insulated, thickly. Any funds he disperses in that manner would have been washed.'

'Can you find it?'

His brow winged up. 'That is, I assume, a rhetorical question. It'll take time.'

'Then why don't you get started? Can I use this subunit to check a few other names?'

'Hold on.' He issued some commands she didn't understand, keyed in something manually. The computer acknowledged him and began a low hum. 'It'll sift through the initial layers on auto,' he explained, 'as quickly as I could do it. What are the other names?'

She looked at him. 'Rue MacLean.'

If he was annoyed or surprised, he didn't show it. 'You suspect her?'

'She manages Purgatory, knows or should know what goes down there. Now you tell me Ricker used to own the place, and we know IAB suspects or suspected a connection. If he's doing any business there, she should've known about it. And,' she concluded, 'you already thought of that.'

'I did a run on her yesterday. Deep search. Computer, results of search on MacLean, Rue, on screen three. You can study the data yourself,' he told Eve. 'I found nothing to alarm me. Overmuch. But then again, if she's playing with Ricker, she'd be careful. She knows me.'

'Would she risk it?'

'I wouldn't have thought so.'

Eve scanned the financial first. 'Jesus, Roarke, you pay her a goddamn mint.'

'Which traditionally inspires loyalty. She essentially runs the club. She earns her salary. You'll see she enjoys the financial rewards and doesn't pinch her credits. She took a vacation to Saint Barthélemy this winter. Ricker's known to have a base near there.'

He paused for a moment, strolling over to pour himself a brandy. 'I intend to ask her about that tomorrow.'

'Just ask her?'

'That's right, and I'll know if she's lying.'

Eve studied his face: cool, hard, ruthless. Yes, he would know, and God help MacLean if she lied. 'I'd rather you didn't. I'll ask her.'

'If she's connected in any way to Ricker, it's a very tenuous connection to your case. She's my employee, and I deal with my own.'

'If you scare her off—'

'If she has reason to be frightened, she'll have nowhere to go. Then she'll be yours to question. Do you have more names?'

'You're not cooperating.'

'On the contrary.' He spread his hands, indicating the room and the busy equipment. 'Let me ask you a question, Lieutenant. Are you after a killer or Max Ricker?'

'I'm after a killer,' she snapped. 'And since Ricker's hooked to it somewhere, I intend to haul them both.'

'Because he's connected to the case, or once was, to me?'

'Both.' She shifted her stance, an unconscious move into combat. 'So what?'

'Nothing. Unless, when the time comes, you intend to stand between us.' He studied his brandy. 'But why borrow trouble? Names?'

She didn't intend to borrow anything. But she fully intended to get to Ricker first. 'Webster, Lieutenant Don.'

The faintest smirk touched his mouth. 'Well now, isn't that interesting? What do you suspect him of? Being the killer or being a target?'

'At the moment, neither, which is the same as both. He tailed me today. Maybe it was like he said, to apologize for being an idiot. Or maybe that whole business was staged. I want all the facts before I decide to trust him.'

Saying nothing, Roarke tapped keys and had data shooting onto a screen.

'You already ran him?'

'Did you think I wouldn't?' Roarke said coolly. 'Webster appears to be as clean as the traditional whistle. Which, using the standard you applied to Roth, puts him on your suspect list.'

'Except for one thing.' She moved closer to the screen, frowning over the data. 'He knew about Kohli, helped set it all up. Why take out a straight cop? Going from evidence, from my own instincts, and from Mira's profile, I'm looking for someone avenging themselves. Someone who's taking out cops who went wrong. Webster was one of the few who knew Kohli hadn't. So no, I'm not looking at him for this, not if he's clean.'

'And if he wasn't?'

'Then maybe I could've stretched it that he took Kohli out because Kohli was clean and knew Webster wasn't. What are these payments here? Steady outlay every month for the last two years to LaDonna Kirk.'

'He's got a sister, divorced. She's going to medical school. He's helping her out.'

'Hmmm. Could be a blind.'

'It's legitimate. I checked. She's in the top ten percent of her class, by the way. He gambles occasionally,' Roarke continued, sipping his brandy. 'Small stakes, typical entertainment gambling pattern. He springs for season tickets for arena ball every year and has an affection for suits made by an overpriced and, in my opinion, woefully inferior designer. He doesn't put much away for a rainy day, but lives within his means. Which isn't difficult. He makes twice as much as you do, at the same rank. I'd complain about that.'

'Desk jockeys,' Eve said with obvious disdain. 'Who can figure it? You went awfully deep on him.'

'I prefer being thorough.'

She decided, under the circumstances, to leave it at that. 'He wants in.'

'I beg your pardon?'

'On the case, Roarke. He wants me to let him in on the homicide investigation. He's feeling used and abused at the way it was set up. I believe him.'

'Are you asking me my opinion?'

Relationships, she thought darkly, were so often a major pain in the ass. 'I'm asking you if it's going to cause any problems around here if I let him in.'

'If I said yes?'

'Then he stays out. He'd be useful, but I don't need him.'

'Darling Eve. You needn't worry about . . .' He remembered her phrase, and her tone when she'd used it. 'About my dick getting in a twist. Do what suits you. This needs my attention,' he said as the computer signaled a pause. 'Do you have more names?'

'A few.'

'Be my guest.' He gestured to the side unit, then took his seat behind the console.

Marriage, Eve thought as she took her seat, was a puzzle she didn't think she'd ever solve. Too many damn pieces. And the shapes of them were constantly changing on her. He seemed perfectly fine with the idea of her working with Webster, a man he'd pounded on gleefully the night before.

But maybe he wasn't, and this complacent agreement was just a ruse.

She'd just have to worry about it later.

She got down to work. At least that was something she understood. She ran the names Patsy Kohli had given her. Her husband's cop friends. Detectives Gaven and Pierce and an Officer Goodman, along with Sergeant Clooney.

On her first pass, every one of them looked clean enough to glint. Gaven, Detective Arnold, had a nice pocketful of commendations and a solid number of closed cases. He was tidily married, had a five-year-old daughter, and was lead-off batter in the squad's softball team.

Pierce, Detective Jon, ran along a parallel route, only he had a son, age three.

Goodman, Officer Thomas, was younger by two years, and considered a shoe-in for a detective's shield. He was recently married and a lay minister at his church.

Religion, she thought. Thirty pieces of silver.

Clooney, a twenty-six-year vet, had been attached to the One two-eight for the last twelve years. He'd partnered with Roth at one time, Eve noted, intrigued. Then Roth had sprinted past him up the brass ladder. That could piss a certain type of individual off.

He had a wife, and though her residence listed was different than his, there was no record of a legal separation or divorce. His son, Thadeus, had been killed in the line of duty while attempting to prevent a robbery.

Walked in on in progress, Eve noted, frowning. According to witness reports, he'd drawn his weapon, stepped in to shield one of the civilians, and had been attacked from behind. He'd suffered numerous stab wounds and had been pronounced dead on the scene.

His assailants had cleaned out the 24/7 store and escaped. The case remained open.

Thadeus Clooney had left behind a wife and infant daughter.

Suffered a loss, she considered. A big one. Could that turn a twenty-six-year vet with a spotless record into a killer?

But why blame other cops for the loss?

Last, she ran Bayliss, Captain Boyd.

Oh, he was clean, she thought as she read his data. If you looked only at that slick surface. Churchgoer, community volunteer, chaired a couple of charitable organizations, had his two kids in posh private schools. Married for eighteen years to a woman who'd come to him with money and social status.

Never worked the streets, she mused. Even in uniform, which he'd shed quickly, he'd been assigned to a desk:

administration, evidence management, office aide. A born drone.

But a smart one. He'd moved up, then over, into IAB.

And there, she thought, he'd found his calling.

Interesting, she noted, that this last business wasn't his first official sanction. He'd been warned before about his methods. But whatever his means, he'd dug the dirt. The department had stepped nimbly aside, with a frown perhaps, but no serious block.

He'd skirted the rules: entrapment, illegal tapping, and surveillance. His favored ploy was to set cop against cop.

Cop against cop. How big a leap was it from destroying a career to taking a life?

Most interestingly, she discovered that shortly after the Ricker debacle, Bayliss had found himself under review, and had earned another sanction, for his attempt to discredit the sergeant in charge of the evidence area.

He'd gone so far as to harass the man's wife and children, to haul the sergeant into an IAB interview room and keep him there, without benefit of counsel or representation, for over four hours.

The IRS had received an anonymous tip, and though it hadn't been traced to Bayliss or his crew, it had resulted in a full audit of the sergeant's financials. Nothing suspicious had been found, but the audit had cost the unlucky cop thousands of dollars in legal fees and lost time.

She would have to take a much closer look at Bayliss, and now at the beleaguered Sergeant Matt Myers.

She wanted to go deeper but lacked the tech skill. She glanced over at Roarke, but she knew from his intent and focused expression that he wouldn't welcome the interruption.

Rather than humiliate herself with failure by attempting to access Bayliss's personal files, she tried another route.

She contacted Webster.

'Bayliss,' she said without preamble. 'Talk to me.'

'A fanatic disguised as a crusader. A disguise I bought, I'm sorry to say, for a considerable amount of time. Dedicated to his particular mission. Charismatic along with it, like some prophet preaching a new religion.'

She sat back, hummed. 'Really?'

'Yeah, gets you hyped, which is what can pull you along before you realize you've just stepped knee-deep in a pile of shit. On the other hand, he's exposed corruption and moved a lot of dirty cops out of the system.'

'By any means necessary.'

'Okay.' Webster sighed, rubbed the back of his neck. 'That's true, particularly over the last year. His methods have been making me uneasy. I'm pretty sure he has files, extensive ones, on every cop in the department. Not that he shares them with me. He crosses over the line, privacy and procedure wise. I used to think it was justified.'

'What changed your mind?'

'Sergeant Myers. He was officer of record on the Ricker evidence that mysteriously vanished or became corrupted. Jesus, Bayliss hounded him to death. He was convinced Myers was in Ricker's pocket, though there was no evidence, overt or covert, to substantiate it. My take is he figured he'd get Myers off the job one way or the other, but the guy stood up. He just wouldn't break, he wouldn't shake. When the department cleared him, he transferred to a house in Queens. Bayliss never forgot it, and he's been burning low over the slap on the wrist he took from The Tower.'

'Tibble rapped him.'

'That's the word. Right after the rap, he started the operation with Kohli. Maybe he figured he'd vindicate himself and end up with a shine. I don't know, Dallas, he's a hard one to figure.'

'Do you know if this Myers is still alive and well in Queens?'

'I never heard otherwise.' Webster's eyes widened. 'Christ, Dallas, you don't think Bayliss is out there killing cops?'

'It would get them off the job, wouldn't it?' she countered. 'One way or the other. You said you wanted in, Webster. Did you mean it?'

'Yeah. Yeah, I meant it.'

'Then here's your first assignment. Check out Myers, make sure he hasn't met with any recent accidents. And if he's still breathing, see if you can find out if he's been visiting our fair city.'

He hadn't worked Homicide for years, but he picked up fast. Nodded. 'He'd have plenty of reason to resent dirty cops. What angle are you working?'

'I've got plenty of them. Right now, I'm going to get a warrant for Bayliss's personal files.'

'I'll believe that when I see it,' he muttered.

'When I do,' she continued coolly, 'I want your help sorting through them. I'll be in touch.'

She cut transmission, then turned to see Roarke watching her. 'Are you looking at Bayliss for this?'

'There's dirty and there's dirty. He's got grime under his manicure. How much distance is there between deliberately ruining lives and taking them?' She shrugged. 'Webster can keep busy getting me some data on Myers, and we'll see where that goes. I can't say Bayliss is my first choice. I don't think he's got the stomach for blood – and we've still got Kohli being clean. But one way or the other, he's a connection.'

'It's a simple matter to access his personal files.'

'It would be, for you. I'll get a warrant, do it straight. If I'm going to bring Bayliss into Interview, and I am, I want it straight, and I want it clean.'

'Then you may want to ask for another warrant while you're at it. On Vernon.'

'It's already on my list,' she began, then got slowly to her feet. 'You followed the money.'

'I did indeed, through a circuitous, convoluted, and tedious route, back to Max Ricker Unlimited. That doesn't give you Ricker personally passing funds from his hand to Vernon's, but it does involve his corporation. He's not as clever as he once was,' Roarke murmured. 'Or as careful. It should have taken me twice this long to trace it back to him.'

'Maybe you're more clever than you once were.' She walked over to study the screen, laying a hand on Roarke's shoulder. Most of what she saw was a jumble of accounts, names, companies. But one name in particular jumped out, made her smile.

'Canarde, am I reading this right? He's attorney of record for Northeast Manufacturing, a subsidary of Ricker's main deal?'

'That's right.'

'And am I reading this one? Canarde authorized the electronic transfer of funds, funneled through the main deal, into Northeast, over into this other corporation, up into the casino in Vegas II, where Vernon picked it up, ostensibly as gambling winnings.'

'I'm so proud.' He took the hand on her shoulder, pressed his lips to her palm.

'Thanks, but you've diagramed it here so a moron could connect the dots. I wanted a shot at that smug son of a bitch Canarde. Now I've got one. Except I can't use it,' she said in disgust and paced away. 'Unless I can get Vernon to roll.'

She'd get him to roll, she promised herself, then moving away from the control center so that her communicator screen would show nothing but the screened window, she contacted her commander.

She wanted some brass knuckles.

Roarke sat where he was, watching her, listening to her make her case: clear, he thought, concise, detailed, and dispassionate. He knew her like a book and could already see the steps she planned to take.

He wasn't the least surprised when she pressed Whitney

after he agreed to throw his weight into her request for a warrant in the morning.

'Sir, I want to move on Captain Bayliss tonight.'

'Lieutenant, Captain Bayliss remains a ranking officer in the NYPSD. Convincing a judge to grant an immediate warrant ordering him to submit to interrogation regarding two homicides is going to be tricky.'

'I realize that, Commander. Which is why I contacted you, in the hopes that you will, in turn, contact Chief Tibble.'

'You want me to call Tibble in on this?'

'Certain information has come into my hands that leads me to believe Chief Tibble will be receptive to this request. I cannot at this point in my investigation ascertain whether Captain Bayliss is a suspect or a target. However, I have no doubt he falls on one side of the line. If he's a target, quick action may save his life. If he is a suspect, that same action may save another.'

'Dallas, your personal feelings—'

'Do not apply, sir, and have not influenced my current findings.'

'Be damn sure of it,' Whitney muttered. 'I'll contact the chief.'

'Thank you, Commander. At this time, I request a second warrant for Detective Jeremy Vernon of the One two-eight, requiring him to report for a formal interview at nine hundred tomorrow morning, regarding the same investigation.'

'Christ.' It was his first and only exclamation. 'You've been busy.'

'Yes, sir,' she said so coolly he let out a short laugh.

'I'll get the warrants, Lieutenant. Expect me, and in all probability Chief Tibble, in observation during these interviews. Let's take some care here. We're going to look like we've taken a page from IAB's book.'

'Understood. I'll await verification and receipt of the warrants.'

'Well done,' Roarke said quietly when she ended the transmission.

'Not close to done. I have to go get dressed. Thanks for the help.'

'One moment.' He rose and walked to her. He took her face in his hands and lowered his mouth, taking hers in a kiss of quiet, somehow desperate tenderness.

She felt it in her heart, that answering flutter; in her stomach, that slow, sliding drop. Her hands came up to settle at his waist. 'Roarke—'

'Just be quiet a minute.' He changed the angle, taking the kiss deeper, a long, lazy trip into glory.

Her hands slid around him, her arms wrapped to bring him close. And she understood he was showing her, offering her, the other side of passion. The sweetness of it, and the promise.

When he drew back, she found herself smiling, even as her head spun. 'I could probably spare one more minute.'

'Come home soon.' This time he pressed his lips to her forehead. 'And we'll take all the time we want.'

'Good thinking.' She started for the door, then with a half laugh turned back to look at him. 'Whenever you do that, you know, like you just did, I always feel a little drunk after. I kind of like it.'

She watched his grin flash before she slipped out the door.

In just over an hour, she was standing, with Peabody, at another door. Bayliss lived in a stylish neighborhood in a stylish suburb of New York. His home was a graceful if unimaginative two-story dwelling in a tidy forest of others like it. Lawns were rigorously mowed, tastefully fenced, and security lighted.

The house itself was dark and silent, with a discreet plaque by the door warning that the premises was guarded by Alarm Dog Security Systems, Inc.

Still, when she rang the bell, the summons was almost immediately answered by a polite request for indentification.

'Police.' Eve held up her badge. 'I have a warrant. You're required to open the door.

It was opened, quickly, by an attractive house droid in a simple gray maid's uniform. 'I'm sorry, Lieutenant, neither Captain nor Mrs Bayliss are at home this evening.'

'And where would they be?'

'Mrs Bayliss is in Paris on a spring shopping trip with her sister. She has been from home for three days. I am unable to tell you where Captain Bayliss is this evening. He is not at home.'

'This warrant allows me to enter the premises and ascertain that for myself.'

'Yes, Lieutenant. I am fully programmed on the law.' She stepped back. 'But you will find the captain is not at home this evening.'

Eve stepped in. 'Has he been home today?'

'Oh yes. He arrived home at shortly after four o'clock this afternoon. He left approximately fifty-eight minutes later. I do not expect him to return tonight.'

'And why is that?'

'The captain left with a suitcase.'

'Where's his room? His bedroom?'

'On the second level, first door to the left. Would you like me to escort you?'

'No.' Eve bounded up the stairs, shoved into the room, swore.

He'd been in a hurry, she thought. The closet door was open, two drawers were open as well.

'Another clothes horse,' she muttered. 'Hard to say how much he took. Peabody, find out where the wife's staying in Paris. He's got a weekend place, vacation home, whatever. I think it was the Hamptons. Get the address.'

'Do you think he's gone under?'

'I think he's gone,' Eve said sharply. 'Get the addresses. He's got to have an office in this place. I'm going to check it out.'

She found his office on the first level and had already formed an opinion of Bayliss's lifestyle by the time she reached it. The house was as cold and as organized as a computer. Everything in its place.

And, she'd noted, he and his wife didn't share a bedroom. Or, she assumed, a bed, as the bedroom down the hall from Bayliss's was an obvious feminine retreat, complete with dressing area, two-level walk-in closet, and a sitting area that had contained a desk holding fancy writing paper with his wife's name at the top.

His office was ruthlessly organized as well, and she saw immediately he'd run through it quickly. The desk chair was pushed back, and a file box of discs stood with its cover not quite straight.

Nerves, she thought. Nerves that made him not quite so smart and not quite so careful this time. What are you afraid of, Bayliss?

She pulled out her palm-link and, using her badge and identification, ran checks on transportation to Paris. Though she found nothing under Bayliss's name, she couldn't be sure he hadn't used an alias.

She walked to the door, gave a shout to Peabody, who came on the run. 'I have the information for you.' She ran it off.

'Good. We're going to stretch the warrant to its limit. I want you to contact Feeney. That unit,' she said, jerking her thumb back. 'I want it gone over with microgoggles. He took data with him, but Feeney will find what's on the machine. While he's doing that, I want you going over this house inch by inch.'

'Yes, sir. Where are you going?' she asked as Eve strode out.

'I'm going to the beach.'

Chapter Seventeen

Eve checked the fit of her safety harness and resisted the urge, the increasingly desperate urge, to simply close her eyes. 'I'm not really in that much of a hurry.'

Roarke cocked a brow in her direction while piloting the new Air/Land Sports Streamer through a sky turning soft with evening. 'That's not what you said when you asked me to get you there.'

'I didn't know you had some new toy you were dying to try out. Jesus.' She made the mistake of glancing down and saw the coastline and its complement of houses, hotels, and beachfront communities whiz by. 'We don't have to be this high, either.'

'We're not that high.' If Eve had one phobia, it was heights. To his way of thinking, she'd feel better as soon as they landed, so why not open the ALS up and see what it could do?

'High enough to crash,' she muttered and ordered herself to think of something – anything – else. It would have taken her a great deal longer to make the trip to Bayliss's beach hideaway in her city unit, particularly now that it was acting up.

Even if she'd used one of Roarke's spiffy cars, the distance couldn't have been covered so quickly by road.

The most logical solution was to draft him to fly her there. Logical, she thought, if she lived.

'Bayliss is up to something,' she said over the smooth roar

of the ALS's engines. 'He was in and out of his place too fast, didn't reprogram his house droid, and he took files.'

'You'll be able to ask him what he's up to yourself in a few minutes.' Testing the controls, Roarke took the sleek little streamer up another twenty feet, executed a turn.

Eve cut her eyes in his direction as he fiddled with controls, manually, then through voice command. 'What are you doing?'

'Just checking. I'd say this baby's ready for production.'

'What do you mean *ready* for?'

'This is just the prototype.'

She felt the color drain out of her face. Actually felt it. 'As in *experimental?*'

With his dark hair whipping in the air blowing through his open window, he tossed her a wide, delighted grin. 'Not anymore. We're going down.'

'What?' She braced every cell in her body. 'What?'

'On purpose, darling.'

If he'd been by himself, he'd have taken the streamer into a dive to check the responses, but in consideration of his wife, he kept the descent slow and smooth, targeting the road, hovering over it.

'Switch to landing mode,' he ordered.

Switch in mode confirmed. Flaps lowering. Retracting.

'Touching down.'

Touchdown confirmed. Switching to land drive.

There was barely a bump as the silver streamer set its wheels on the road. And barely, Eve noted sourly, a decrease of speed.

'Slow down, hotshot. This is a posted area.'

'We're on official business. When the weather warms up a bit more, we can try this with the top down.'

As far as Eve was concerned, hell wouldn't be warm enough to induce her to skim along in the fancy little two-seater without a roof. But she looked at the dash map, impressed

253

that it not only had Bayliss's house targeted, but that Roarke had set down less than a mile from their destination.

Logic, she thought now that she was on solid ground again, had its uses.

She could hear the water, a steady rise and slap of sound to the east. Houses, predominately of glass and recycled wood rose and spread, each seeming to try to outdo the next with how many decks they could manage to jut out toward sand and sea. The patches between them were manicured with sea oats, sand roses, and odd little sculptures that carried over the ocean theme.

Lights twinkled here and there, but for the most part, the houses were dark. This was where the rich and the privileged escaped from New York on weekends or during the long, hot summer.

'How come you don't have a place here?'

'Actually, I do have a string of properties that rent out, but I never had a yen to stay in one. Too ordinary and obvious.' He smiled at her. 'But if you'd like one . . .'

'No. It's too much like a neighborhood or something. You'd come down to kick back and probably have to talk to people. And have, I don't know, get-together and stuff.'

'Hideous thought.' Amused, he turned off and pulled into the drive behind a hulking black sedan. 'Do we assume that's his car?'

'Yeah.' She scoped out the house. Not so different from the others lining the coast. Big arches filled with glass that opened to decks and were loaded with enormous urns of enormous flowers or potted trees. The structure was blond and gleaming in the half light and came to triple points on the third level where another deck ran in a ring.

'Pretty snazzy for a cop,' she commented. 'But then he's got a rich spouse.' She glanced at Roarke. 'That kind of thing comes in handy.'

'So I've heard.'

'If he's in there, he's in the dark. I don't like it.' It had been her plan to convince Roarke to wait in the car. Something she'd assumed would take some doing. Now her gut told her to try a different plan.

They got out opposite sides and walked up a narrow boardwalk to the front door. There were tall, glass panels flanking it, etched with stylized seashells. Through them she could scan the main living area with its soaring ceilings and pale walls.

Instinctively, she hitched her jacket back so her weapon would be more accessible. And rang the bell. 'You'd think the place was empty, wouldn't you? Except for the car.'

'He might've taken a walk on the beach. People tend to do that here.'

She shook her head. 'He wouldn't be in the mood to stroll through the surf.' She made the decision, bent down, and took her clinch piece from her ankle holster.

'I need you to go around, cover the back. Don't use this, okay? Do not use this unless you're in immediate jeopardy.'

'I know the rules.' He slipped it in his pocket. 'Do you think Bayliss is dangerous?'

'No. No, I don't. But someone is. I'm going up to the second level. I'll circle around, left to right. Watch your back.'

'Same goes.'

They separated, each confident the other could handle whatever came. Eve moved to the side, up the open steps, over the deck. The doors here were clear sheets of glass and fully secured with their privacy shields lowered. She started to the left, moving slowly, her eyes tracking.

The gleam at her feet had her pausing, crouching. Water, she mused. Someone had slopped water on the deck, a path of it, she noted as she straightened to follow the trail.

The sound of the sea rose, a sly thrash and suck. Stars were beginning to come out, adding faint light to a sky going indigo. Ears cocked, she heard the footsteps mounting the steps to her right. Her fingers danced to her weapon.

It was in her hand when Roarke rounded the building.

'There's water on the steps,' he told her.

'Here, too.' She lifted a hand, signaled. The side doors were open.

Roarke nodded, moved to the far side of them, and she to the near. Their eyes met, she took a breath, held it. They went through. He took high, she low.

'Take the right,' she ordered. 'Lights on.' When they appeared, she adjusted her eyes to the change, sidestepped left. 'Captain Bayliss,' she called out. 'This is Lieutenant Dallas. I have a warrant. I need you to make your location known.'

Her voice echoed off the high ceilings, off the sand-colored walls.

'Bad feeling,' she muttered. 'Very bad feeling.' Sweeping with her weapon, she followed the tracking water. She saw Bayliss's suitcase open on the bed, a jacket tossed carelessly beside it.

She glanced toward Roarke, watched him check a roomsized closet, did the same herself on the other side, then moved along the wet to a door.

She signaled again, waiting until he'd joined her. With her free hand, she turned the knob, then shoving it open went in under Roarke's arm.

Music blared. It gave her a jolt to hear Mavis's voice screeching out into the opulent bathroom. All white and gold, the room almost hurt the eyes with its sheer white walls, gilt pools of mirrors, twin sinks large enough to bathe in.

Under the music she heard the rumble of a motor. She crossed the floor, damp and gleaming white, to the leg of the L-shaped room.

The tub was waist high and white as the Alps, but for the wet river of blood that ran down the side, just below a single hand. Red dripped onto the badge tossed on the floor.

'Damn it. Goddamn it.' She leaped to the tub and saw immediately it was far too late for the MTs.

Bayliss lay on the lounging level, his head pillowed on a silver cushion, his body strapped down with long ribbons of adhesive.

His eyes stared up at her, wide and horrified, and already filmed over with death.

Glinting on the floor of the tub were credits. She knew there would be thirty.

'I wasn't fast enough. Somebody wanted him dead more than I wanted him alive.'

Roarke lifted a hand to the base of her neck, rubbed once. 'You'll want your field kit.'

'Yeah.' Her assent was a sound of disgust. 'Whoever did this is gone, but be careful anyway.' She reached for her communicator. 'I have to contact the locals. Protocol. Then I'm calling it in. Meanwhile, you're drafted as aide. Seal up before you come back in, and don't—'

'Touch anything,' he finished. 'Hell of a way to die,' he added. 'He'd have been kept alive, aware, strapped down there while the water level rose. The room's soundproofed. No one would have heard him screaming.'

'The killer heard him,' Eve said and, turning away, opened transmission.

She recorded the scene and did a preliminary sweep before the local police arrived. Knowing she had to balance authority with diplomacy, she requested rather than ordered the sheriff to send his men out to knock on doors.

'Not many people around here just now,' Sheriff Reese told her. 'Come June, it'll be a different story.'

'I realize that. Maybe we'll get lucky. Sheriff, this is your turf, but the victim comes from mine. The killer, too. As this murder links to my ongoing investigation, it falls under my authority. But I need all the help I can get. And your cooperation.'

'You'll have it, Lieutenant.' He studied her for a moment. 'Some people might think we're in the boondocks here, but we're not boobs. Don't get your city crimes too much, but we know how to handle them when we do.'

'I appreciate it.' She passed him her Seal-It. 'Did you know Captain Bayliss?'

'Sure.' Reese sprayed his shoes, his hands. 'He and his wife were regulars. They spent the month of August here most every year, and about a weekend a month rest of the year. Popped in now and again otherwise. Had parties, spent some money in the village. Didn't have much to do with the locals but were friendly enough. Didn't cause any trouble.'

She started upstairs with him. 'Did Bayliss make a habit of coming here alone?'

'Not really. He'd come down on a Friday night now and again – once, twice a year – stay till Sunday. Went out on his boat, did some fishing. The wife didn't care for fishing. You notify her?'

'My information is that she's in Paris. She'll be contacted. Bayliss ever bring anybody here other than his wife?'

'Can't say he did. Some do, men bring a buddy or a side piece, you'll pardon the expression. Women do the same. Bayliss stuck with his wife. Never heard of him bringing any . . . entertainment with him.'

She nodded, walked to the tub with him. Reese stared down, blew out a breath. 'Jesus, that's a sorry sight. I don't mind saying I'm glad this is yours, Lieutenant.' Reese scratched his head. 'If he was trying to make it look like suicide, why'd he leave the man strapped in there?'

'He wasn't trying to mock a self-termination. He just needed the blood on the badge. It's pattern. I've got the scene recorded, and now that you've officially witnessed it, I'm going to drain the tub, examine the body.'

'You go right on.' He stepped back and watched Roarke come in.

'My temporary aide,' Eve explained. 'This is Sheriff Reese.'

'I know who you are,' Reese said. 'Seen your face onscreen often enough. You own some property around here.'

'That's right.'

'You keep it in good maintenance. We appreciate that around here. That your rig out front?'

'Yes.' Roarke smiled a little as Eve turned off the motor. 'It's a new line.'

'Slick.'

'I'll give you a closer look before we go,' Roarke offered.

'I'd appreciate that.'

'Victim is male, Caucasian,' Eve began. 'Identified as Bayliss, Captain Boyd, age forty-eight. Cause of death appears to be drowning. Single laceration in left wrist is potentially life-threatening.'

She fit on her microgoggles. 'No visible hesitation marks,' she reported, then pushed them off again. 'Victim is wearing a gold wedding ring and a gold wrist unit. A strong adhesive tape has been used to strap the victim to the tub at throat, left forearm, chest, torso, waist, hips, and on both thighs and ankles. No defensive wounds are evident.'

The water drained out, little sucking sounds, while she spoke. As the level lowered, Bayliss's hair and genitals floated toward the surface.

'I need to get in to examine the body. Sheriff, will you record?' She slipped the recorder off her jacket, held it out.

'I like my job better than yours.' He fixed it to his shirt, moved closer.

She stepped onto the platform, swung a leg over the edge. Already in her mind, the scene played out. He'd have been unconscious, she was sure of that. It wouldn't have been possible to get a healthy, well-built, adult male into the tub and restrained without signs of a struggle.

She planted her feet on either side of the body as she imagined the killer had done. Bending, she began to work at the tape. 'Strong stuff. It looks like that tape used for packing cargo and heavy shipments. He used a smooth-bladed tool to cut it. No ragged edges. Probably shears or scissors. Neat, patient work. He took his time.'

The tape screeched a little as it pulled away from the smooth, damp surface of the tub. She took her time with it, carefully sliding the tape into evidence bags.

With his head free, Eve lifted it, turned it. And saw no signs of a blow.

Stunned him, she thought. Used a weapon. Probably a standard police issue. Damn.

She worked her way down the body, handing Roarke the bagged tape as she freed it.

Her movements were brisk and efficient, Roarke thought. Her eyes were flat. Distancing herself, as much as she was able, focusing her mind, her skill on the job.

She wouldn't have called it courageous, but he did. To give herself over, to stand over death and work doggedly to balance the scales, even for a man he knew she had disliked.

'Microgoggles,' she ordered, and Roarke passed them back to her.

With them on, she crouched, examining the abraded skin where Bayliss had futilely fought against the tape. *Yeah*, she thought, *wanted him alive and awake while the water churned up. Screaming, begging, sobbing.*

Did he call you by name? I'd lay odds on it.

She turned him, her hands unconsciously gentle. On his back, his buttocks, she saw faint marks where his body had pressed and rubbed against the tub.

And on his hips was a small tattoo, gold and black, a replica of the shield that was now smeared with his blood.

'A cop through and through,' she commented. 'At least that's what he considered himself. He'd have hated dying like this. Naked, helpless, and undignified.'

She gathered the coins littering the bottom of the tub. 'Thirty,' she said, jingling them in her palm before dropping them into the bag Roarke held out for her. 'He deviates his method but not his symbolism. Bayliss hasn't been dead long. We didn't miss this one by much. The blood barely started to settle to its lowest level, and what's been spilled out there's still wet. I need the gauge to get time of death.'

'Lieutenant.' Roarke held out the gauge. 'I believe your team's here.'

'Hmm?' She took the gauge. She heard it now, the muted voice traveling from below up the stairs and through the open door. 'Okay. I'm almost done in here. An hour,' she said in disgust when she read the gauge. 'We didn't miss him by more than an hour.'

She climbed back out of the tub as Peabody strode into the room. 'Lieutenant.'

'Record on. See that he's bagged and transport's arranged, Peabody. Get some sweepers started in here. Did you bring EDD?'

'Feeney and McNab are right behind me.'

'When they get here, have them start on the security, then the 'links. For what it's worth. Thank you, Sheriff.' She held out a hand for her recorder. 'This is my aide, Officer Peabody. She'll handle the scene, if you have no objection.'

'None at all.'

'I want to go through the house. Bayliss had files with him. I need to find them.'

'First-level office,' Roarke put in, bringing her eyes to his. 'I can show you where it is.'

Something in his tone told her he didn't want to show her with company. She blocked off the automatic annoyance that he'd gone through the house without her and turned to Reese.

'I'd like you to check with your men doing the door-to-doors. Also, if you could contact your patrols, inquire as to whether anyone noticed a strange vehicle in this area tonight.'

'I'll get right on it. Outside, if it's all the same to you. I'd like some air.'

'Thanks.' She started out with Roarke, waited until the first wave of the crime scene unit passed them on the stairs. 'What's the idea of poking around the house on your own? We're on official business. I can't have civilians making themselves at home.'

'I was acting in my capacity as temporary aide,' he said smoothly. 'All of the other doors and windows were secured, by the way. The alarm system's one of mine, and top of its line. It wasn't tampered with. Whoever bypassed it had a code. And I located the security control,' he continued. 'Feeney's going to find that system was also bypassed. There won't be a recording of tonight's activities, in or out of the house, after seven o'clock.'

'Busy boy.'

'Me or your killer?'

'Ha ha. He doesn't panic, he doesn't rush, he covers his tracks. And he does all that with rage working through him. Must be a damn good cop.'

She moved through the door Roarke indicated, into a large office space with views of the sea through the glass wall in the rear.

Here there were signs of hurry. Here there were things out of place. A glass turned over on the desk, its contents spilled out on the brushed chrome surface. A jumble of discs, a disordered pile of clothes heaped on the floor. She recognized the suit Bayliss had been wearing at the meeting.

'He took him out here, from the front,' she began. 'Surprised him at work. Bayliss had fixed himself a drink.' She lifted the glass, sniffed. 'Smells like scotch. Settled himself down to go through his files. He hears something, looks up, sees someone in the doorway. Jumps to his feet, spills his drink. Maybe he even has time to say a name, then he's out.'

She walked around the room, around the desk. 'The killer undresses him here. He's already got the plan. He came in upstairs, checked the place out. Hell, maybe he's been to parties here before and knew the setup. He went out, disarmed the security cam, took the discs that recorded him. Did he bring the packing tape with him?'

She began opening compartments, drawers. 'No, look. Here's a roll of the same stuff, unopened. He got what he needed right here in Bayliss's office. He'll dispose of the rest of the roll and what he used to cut the tape. We won't find it.'

'Lieutenant,' Roarke said quietly. 'Look at the discs.'

'I'm getting to them. Then he carried Bayliss upstairs. He's strong. I didn't notice any signs the victim was dragged, no bruising or scrapes on the heels. Laid him in the tub. Didn't toss him in. No bruising again. Laid him out, strapped him down. Took his shoes off to do it, but not his clothes. No scuff marks in the tub, and too much water outside of it for him to have dried off.'

Yes, she could see it that way. Patience, while the rage ate inside you. Meticulous patience coated over murderous fury.

'Then he waited for Bayliss to come around. When he did, a little conversation. This is why you're going to die. This is why you deserve to die. To suffer fear and humiliation. And he starts the water, a hot gush, and listens to Bayliss plead for his life. As the water rises, and the motor kicks in churning into a hot froth, he stays cold. Ice cold. That's how it is when you stand over death. You stay cold so it can't get inside you. He stands there, right over it, and watches it come.

'It doesn't thrill him, doesn't make him sad. It's just a job that needs to be done, and done well. Done with purpose. When water fills Bayliss's lungs, when he stops struggling and his eyes are fixed and staring, he takes the coins and throws them in the water, over the body. The Judas coins.

'Then he gets out of the tub, dripping, picks up his shoes, and leaves the way he came in. He leaves the door open because he doesn't want the murder to go undiscovered for long. He wants it known. Announced. Discussed. The job isn't done until the department knows another cop is dead.'

'I can't re-create the way you can,' Roarke said. 'It's admirable.'

'It's basic.'

'Not the way you do it,' he murmured. How many scenes such as she'd described had a place in her memory? How many victims lived there with how many killers?

Stay cold, she'd said, so that it doesn't get inside of you. That, he knew, was one skill she lacked. The very fact that it all got inside her was what made her brilliant. And haunted.

'Look at the discs, Eve.'

'I saw them.'

There were dozens, many of the names she recognized. Cops. Bayliss's little rat file of cops. Reaching, she noted, all the way to The Tower.

'At least he was democratic in his witch hunt.' She saw the one with her name on the label. 'We'll bag them all. It's going to be a tedious and nasty job to go through them. His machine's still on.' She sat down, frowned at the blank screen.

'There's a disc in. And not, I think, one of the victim's.'

'You touched this?' She whirled in the chair, snarled at him. 'I told you not—'

'Shut up, Eve, and run the disc.'

She had more to say, a great deal more. But it could wait until they were alone and she could pound on him in private. She turned back to the screen. 'Run current disc,' she ordered.

Words swirled silently onto the screen. There was no audio backup or readout, but simply clear, cool letters on a smoke-gray background.

Lieutenant Dallas, as you are primary in the investigation of the deaths of Kohli, Mills, and now Bayliss, I address this message to you.

I deeply regret the death of Detective Taj Kohli. I was misled, largely by the efforts of the man I am about to execute for his crimes. Crimes against the badge he has misused in his own thirst for power. Is that any less a sin against his oath than that of Mills, who betrayed his badge for money?

Whether or not you agree with me is not my concern. I have pledged to do what I have done and will continue to do.

Because of our connection, I took the time to read the file Bayliss generated on you. If the allegations, the accusations, the data he has compiled is based in fact, you have dishonored your badge. I am not willing to trust the words of a liar, of a twisted, power-hungry cop. But they must be considered.

I will give you seventy-two hours to exonerate yourself. If you are involved with Max Ricker through your husband, you will die. If these allegations are false, and you are as skilled and dedicated as your reputation indicates, you will find the way to break Ricker and his organization in the time allotted. It will require your full focus and all your skills. To be fair, as fairness is my goal, I give you my word that I will make no move against you or anyone else during this time period.

Take down Max Ricker, Lieutenant. Or I will take you.

Chapter Eighteen

Eve made copies of the message, took the disc and the files into evidence, and turned the computer over to Feeney. He'd haul it into EDD, take it apart, run his scans and checks. That was for form, she knew. The killer had left nothing of himself on the machine but his single personal message to her.

Ricker was on her list, and she meant to take him down. But he couldn't be, wouldn't be a priority. Whatever his connection to the killer, Ricker wasn't the one at the controls.

She was after a rogue cop, and if he wanted to go head-to-head with her, that was fine. But he wouldn't threaten her into shifting her focus. There was a process to be gone through, and she meant to take it step by meticulous step.

She harassed the sweepers, called the lab personally and issued a few threats of her own along with her demand for priority on the samples she was sending in. As far as she was concerned, if she had to work twenty-four/seven until the case was closed, she would do so. And so would everyone on her team.

Roarke had a different process to work through, a different priority. And an entirely different style. He hadn't wasted time asking what Eve intended to do or arguing with her over taking precautions for her personal safety.

He left her with her work and made the trip back to New York alone. By the time he'd arrived, he'd already begun the groundwork on his own plans.

He pulled up in front of Purgatory, uncoded the door. The wreckage had been removed, and the first layers of repair were already under way. It wasn't the elegant arena of sin it had been, but it would be. Very soon.

The lights were on, shimmering over the floor with its newly laid squares of reflective silver squares and circles. The mirrors behind the bar had been replaced, in a deep blue glass per his instructions. The overall effect was somewhat otherworldly.

Or perhaps, he thought, underworldly, which was his intent.

He moved to the bar and was pouring two snifters of brandy when Rue MacLean came down the long, curving stairs.

'I ran a security check,' she said, smiling a little. 'We're up and running. You work fast.'

'We'll be open for business within seventy-two hours.'

'Seventy—' She picked up the snifter he nudged over the bar, blew out a breath. 'How?'

'I'll deal with it. I want you to put the staff on notice in the morning, get the work schedules done tonight. We reopen Friday night, and we reopen with a bang.' He lifted his snifter, watching her.

'You're the boss.'

'That's right.' He took out his cigarettes, left the case on the bar as he lighted one. 'How did he get to you?'

He saw just the barest glint of panic before puzzlement slid over her face. 'What?'

'He's been using my place to do a little business. Oh, nothing too overt, nothing too important. Just enough so he can sit smug in his little fortress and imagine fucking me over with my own. He'll get sloppy after a bit, if he hasn't already. That's his pattern. Makes him dangerous, that carelessness of his. Might be that the cop who died here began to sniff something, just a whiff of it. Then he was dead before he could follow through.'

She'd gone pale, so pale her skin was nearly translucent. 'You think Ricker had the cop killed?'

He drew in smoke, watching her through the veil of it as he exhaled. 'No, I don't, at least not directly. But the timing's interesting. Bad timing for the cop. Potentially for me, and certainly for you, Rue.'

'I don't know what you're talking about.'

She started to step back, but Roarke simply laid a hand over hers, the pressure firm enough to warn her to hold her place. 'Don't.' He spoke softly, and she shivered. 'You'll only piss me off. I'm asking how he got to you. I'm asking because we've been in the way of being friends for a considerable amount of time now.'

'You know there's nothing between me and Ricker.'

'I'd hoped there wasn't.' He angled his head. 'You're trembling. Do you think I'll hurt you? Have you ever seen me strike a woman, Rue?'

'No.' One tear, huge, glistening, spilled over and trailed down her white cheek. 'No, you wouldn't. It's not your way.'

'But it's his. How did he hurt you?'

It was shame now that pushed tears from her eyes, had her voice choked with them. 'Oh God, Roarke. I'm sorry. I'm so sorry. He had me picked up off the street, two of his men, right on the street. They took me out to his place, and he – Jesus, he had lunch, this fancy lunch all spread out in his solarium. He told me how it was going to be, and what would happen to me if I didn't go along.'

'So you went along.'

'Not at first.' She fumbled one of his cigarettes out, tried to light one. Roarke took her hand, held it steady until the flame caught. 'You've been good to me. Treated me with respect and with fairness. I know you don't have to believe me, but I told him to go to hell. I told him that when you found out what he'd tried to do, you'd . . . well, I made up all sorts of interesting, nasty things you'd do. He just sat there, that vicious little smile on his face, until I ran down. I was scared. I was so scared, the way he watched me. Like I was a bug he was contemplating squashing if the mood struck. Then he said a name, and an address. My mother's name. My mother's address.'

Her breath hitched as she picked up the snifter, drank quick and drank deep to steady herself. 'He showed me videos. He'd had her watched – her in the little house upstate I bought her – that you helped me buy her. Shopping, going to a friend's house, just day-to-day stuff. I wanted to be enraged, I wanted to be furious, but I couldn't get through the terror of it. I would go along, he told me – and really, he said, what harm was it – and my mother wouldn't be raped and tortured and disfigured.'

'I would have seen her safe, Rue. You could have trusted me to see her safe.'

She shook her head. 'He always knows the weak spot. Always knows. It's his gift. And he presses down on that spot, until you'd do anything to make him stop. So I betrayed you to make him stop.' She brushed tears away. 'I'm sorry.'

'He won't touch your mother, I promise you. I've a place she can go and be safe until we're done with this.'

Rue stared at him. 'I don't understand.'

'You'll feel better once she's seen to, and I need your energies focused on the club for the next few days.'

'You're keeping me on? After this?'

'I don't have a mother, but I know what it is to love beyond yourself, and just what you'd do to keep that love safe from harm. I'll say you should have trusted me, Rue, and so you should. But I don't blame you.'

She sat then, buried her face in her hands. He topped off the brandy as she wept soundlessly, then got a bottle of water, opened it, set it in front of her.

'Go on, drink that first, clear your head a bit.'

'This is why he hates you.' Her voice was raw but steady. 'Because of everything you are, everything he could never be. He can't understand what's inside you, what makes you.

So he hates. He doesn't just want you dead. He wants you ruined.'

'I'm counting on it. Now, I'm going to tell you what it is we're going to do.'

Eve figured she'd been playing the marriage game for going on a year, so she knew the moves. The easiest way to dodge a problem with Roarke over her handling of the case was not to talk to him about it for as long as humanly possible.

To buy time, she called home on her car-link, shifting to silent mode. She channeled the call to the bedside 'link, figuring he'd most likely be in his office. This way when the message light blinked on, he wouldn't be there to see it and intercept.

'Hey.' She gave the screen a quick, distracted smile. 'Figured I should let you know I'll be at Central. I'll catch some sleep there. Mostly I'll be working straight through after a swing by the lab to nag Dickhead for results. I'll tag you when I get a chance. See you.'

She broke transmission and wasn't aware she let out a quiet, relieved breath until she caught Peabody's gimlet stare. 'What?'

'Want a single woman's take on that marriage-go-round?'

'No.'

'You know he's going to have some choice words to say about you ignoring the threat,' Peabody went on, unperturbed by Eve's scowl. 'So you're dancing around him. Too busy to talk, don't wait up.' She couldn't resist a snort. 'Like that's going to work.'

'Shut up.' Eve shifted in her seat, tried biting her tongue, then gave up. 'Why won't it work?'

'Because you're slick, Dallas, but he is way slicker. He might even let you tango awhile, then . . . bop.'

'Bop? What the hell is bop?'

'I don't know, because I'm not as slick as either one of you. But we'll both know it when we see it.' Peabody stifled a yawn as they pulled up to the lab. 'I haven't ridden in a black and white for awhile.' She patted the thin, miserably uncomfortable seat. 'I haven't missed it.'

'It was the best I could do. I'm going to get grief for commandeering this at the scene, but my unit's trash.'

'Nah.' Peabody yawned again, rubbed her eyes. 'The uniform you snagged it from's too much in awe. He'll probably put a plaque in this thing. *Eve Dallas sat here.*'

'Give me a break.' But the idea made her snicker as they climbed out. 'I want you to contact Maintenance. They don't hate you as much as me. Yet. Get them to put my unit back in shape.'

'It'll go quicker if I lie and put in the request under another badge number.'

'Yeah, you're right. Use Baxter's. You're punchy,' she added when Peabody yawned again. 'When we're done here, take an hour's down time, or pop some Wake-Up, whatever. I need you focused.'

'I'll get my second wind.'

The guard at the door looked as if he'd missed his second wind altogether and was sliding under his third. His eyes were half closed, his uniform wrinkled, and he had a sleep crease deep into his right cheek.

'You're coded in,' was all he said and lumbered back to his station.

'This place is like a tomb at night.' Peabody gave a little shudder. 'Worse than the morgue.'

'We'll liven things up.'

She didn't expect Dickie to be happy to see her. But then again, she hadn't expected to once again hear Mavis's voice blasting into the air when she stepped into the main lab.

Chief Lab Tech Berenski, not so affectionately known as

271

Dickhead, was hunched over a compu-scope, his skinny butt twitching as he sang tunelessly along.

At that moment, Eve knew she could ask for the moon and the stars. She had a solid-gold bargaining chip.

'Hey, Dickie.'

'That's Mister Dickie to you.' He lifted his head and she saw she'd been right. Happy, he was not. His eyes were puffy, his oversized lips snarling. And, she noted, his shirt was on inside out. 'Get me out of bed middle of the night. Everything's always an emergency with you, Dallas. Everything's priority one. Just keep off my ass. You'll get results when I got results and not a minute before. Go somewhere and stop breathing down my neck.'

'But I get off just being near you.'

He slid his eyes up and over, studied her dubiously. Usually she came in with both feet poised to kick him in the ass. You just couldn't trust her when she was smiling and joking around.

'You're in a pretty chipper mood for somebody who's got bodies piling up and the brass ready to crawl down your drawers.'

'What can I say? This music just gives me happy feet. You know Mavis has a gig coming up here next week. I heard it was sold out. Did you hear it was sold out, Peabody?'

'Yeah.' She might have been tired, but Peabody clued in quickly. 'A one-night-only, too. She's pretty hot.'

'She's beyond hot,' Dickie said. 'I got me two tickets. Pulled a few strings. Second balcony.'

'Those kind of strings make your nose bleed.' Eve examined her fingernails. 'I can get two in the orchestra, with backstage passes. If I had a pal, that is.'

His head shot up, and his clever spider's fingers gripped her arm. 'Is that straight shit?'

'The straightest. If I had a pal,' she repeated, 'and that pal

272

was busting his ass to get me data I needed, I'd get him those tickets and those passes.'

Dickie's puffy eyes went moist. 'I'm your new best friend.'

'That's so sweet. Start feeding me results, Dickie, within the hour, and those tickets are in your greedy little hands. You find me something, anything that gives me a line on this guy, and I'll see to it Mavis plants a big, wet kiss right on your mouth.'

She patted his head, started out. At the door she glanced back saw him standing, staring, his mouth still hanging slack. 'Fifty-nine minutes, Dickie. Ticktock.'

He all but leapt at his scope.

'Slick,' Peabody said as they headed out. 'You are so slick.'

When they got back to Central, Eve sent Peabody off to write the intial report from the record and notes on-scene. And Eve made the miserable call to the next of kin.

It took longer than she had to spare, did little more than depress her. Bayliss's wife had no answers for her, and if there were any buried in the shock, it would take too long to dig them out.

The widow declined the option of making a video identification of the deceased, became increasingly hysterical, until her sister took over the 'link.

Eve could hear the woman sobbing in the background as a pretty, pale-cheeked brunette came on-screen. 'There's no mistake?'

'No, there's no mistake. I can arrange for a counselor from the local police department to come by your hotel.'

'No, no, she'll do better with me. She'll do better with family. Strangers only make it worse. She bought him cuff links this afternoon. God.'

The brunette shut her eyes, took a breath. She seemed to steady, which did a great deal for Eve's peace of mind. 'We'll

273

arrange to come back immediately. I'll take care of it. I'll take care of my sister.'

'Contact me as soon as possible. I'll need to speak with Ms Bayliss again. I'm sorry for your loss.'

Eve sat back, stared at the blank screen.

Kohli, Mills, Bayliss. She took a mental step away from the evidence and tried to see the people. Cops. Though they'd all carried badges, each one had carried his differently. All, she was certain, had known their killer. The first two had known him well enough to trust him.

Especially Kohli. A late-night chat over drinks in an empty club. That was something you did with a friend. Still, he'd talked of a meeting with his wife. If he meant that literally, perhaps it had been more an associate than a friend. One he'd respected. Someone he'd felt he could ask advice. Informally. Over a beer.

Someone, she thought, from his own house. Someone, she suspected, who had some link to Ricker.

'Computer, compile roster from Precinct One two-eight, this city, including any retirees within the last two, no correction, within the last three years. Run a search and scan for any cases or investigations connected to any police officer of said precinct regarding Max Ricker. Secondary search and scan, same parameters regarding . . . what was his name, the son. Alex. Alex Ricker. Final search and scan, include any investigation wherein Canarde acted as representative during interview or court appearance.'

Working . . . multitask request of this nature will require minimum of four hours-twenty minutes to complete . . .

'Then you'd better get your ass in gear.'

Command unknown. Please rephrase command . . .

'Christ. Begin task.'

She fueled up on coffee and let the computer hum while she ducked out and into the conference room. On that unit, she brought up all the current data on Vernon. She should've been able to run the data on her machine while the search and scan was in progress. It was a new one, a gem compared to the whining, stuttering heap she'd been stuck with before.

But she didn't trust her luck.

She spent an hour going over Vernon's data. She'd be pulling him into interview shortly. She intended to hit him and hit him hard.

The coffee was wearing off and the words beginning to blur when her communicator beeped.

'Dallas?'

'I'm going to get me a big sloppy tongue kiss.'

'I never said anything about tongues,' Eve said, and made a mental note to warn Mavis to keep her mouth locked tight when Dickhead was backstage. 'What have you got, Dickie?'

'Something that should make even your cold, cold heart pitty-patter. I got a little swab of Seal-It off the edge of the tub.'

'Jesus, tell me you got a print, I'll kiss you myself.'

'Cops always want a miracle.' He hissed out a breath, deflated. 'What I got is Seal-It. My guess is he used it to protect his hands and feet, but he got a little carried away with it. You know what happens if you hit it too thick?'

'Yeah it glops some. You can knock or scrape it on something and end up leaving some behind. Damn it, Dickie, what the hell does a swab of Seal-It give me?'

'You want to hear this, or you want to mouth off? He knocked some of the seal off, probably when he was getting your guy thrust up for the last spin in the bubble tub. That's why it's pretty damn likely this little piece of fingernail I got, which my diligence and sharp skills located, is your killer's.'

She held herself level. 'Have you checked the DNA against Bayliss's?'

'What do I look like? A moron?'

She opened her mouth, reminded herself she needed him,

and virtuously shut it again. 'Sorry, Dickie, it's been a long night.'

'Tell me. It doesn't match Bayliss. I got it – and I mean it's barely a sliver, the little darling – off the underside of the tape. Got Bayliss's hair with it. You figure that came off his arm, as that's the location label on the evidence bag, but you don't figure to get a piece of the dead guy's nail on the *under* side of the tape, do you?'

'No, no, you don't. Goddman, Dickie, that's good. That's beautiful. I think I'm falling in love with you.'

'They all do, in the end. Got the prelim data coming through now.' He shot across the room on his favored rolling chair. 'Male. Caucasian male. Can't give you much more than that right now. You want me to try to pin down approximate age and heritage and all that happy stuff, it's going to take time. And I ain't got a lot of this sucker to work with. Could be I'll find more. He broke the seal one place, might be he broke it another. So far, the only hair is from Bayliss.'

'Keep on it. Good work, Dickie.'

'Yeah. You know what, Dallas? You bring this guy in, we'll nail him in court. Get it? *Nail* him.'

'Yeah, I get it. That's a real knee-slapper.'

She cut transmission, sat back.

A sliver of a fingernail, she thought. Sometimes a man could hang for nothing more than that.

A sliver of a fingernail. Carelessness. The first small chink of it.

Thirty pieces of silver. Symbolism. Religious symbolism. If the victims were Judas, who was the Christ figure? Not the murderer, she decided as her mind drifted. Christ was the sacrifice, he was the pure. The Son. What was the phrase?

The only begotten Son.

A personal message to the primary. Conscience. The killer had a conscience, and his mistake with Kohli troubled him enough that he needed to soothe it by explaining, by justifying. And by setting up an ultimatum.

Bring down Ricker. It circled back to Ricker.

Ricker. The Son. Purgatory.

Roarke.

Business, she thought. Old business.

She was in bed, in the dark, but she wasn't sleeping. It wasn't safe to sleep, to let herself hide in dreams.

He was drinking, and he wasn't alone.

She could hear words when their voices raised, and they raised often. It was her father's voice she focused on, because he was the one who might slide into the dark with her if he didn't drink enough. Just enough. He would come in, make a shadow in the doorway with the light hard and bright behind him.

If he was angry with the man, and not drunk enough, he would hurt her. Maybe just slaps, maybe. If she was lucky.

But if she wasn't lucky, his hands would bruise and squeeze – and his breath, candy-scented – would begin to come fast and hard. The ragged T-shirt she wore to sleep in would be no defense. Her pleas and struggles would only make him mad, make him mad so his breathing got faster, faster, like a big engine.

Then he would put his hand over her mouth, cutting off her air, cutting off her screams as he pushed his thing into her.

'Daddy's got something for you, little girl. Little bitch.'

In her bed she shuddered and listened.

She was not yet eight.

'I need more money. I'm the one taking the risks. I'm the one putting my ass out there.'

His voice was slurred, but not enough. Not yet enough.

'We made the deal. Do you know what happens to people who fuck with me? The last employee who tried to . . .

277

renegotiate terms didn't live long enough to regret it. They're still finding small pieces of him in the East River.'

This voice was quiet; she had to strain to catch it. But he wasn't drunk. No, no, she knew the sound of a man who'd been drinking, and this wasn't it. Still, the tone had her shivering. There was a nasty undercurrent to the cultured voice.

'I'm not looking for trouble, Ricker.' There was a whine now, which had her cringing. If he was afraid, he'd hurt her. And he'd use his fists. 'I got expenses. I got a daughter to raise.'

'I'm not interested in your personal life but in my merchandise. See that it's delivered tomorrow night, at the appropriate time and place, you'll get the rest of your fee.'

'It'll be there.'

A chair scraped the floor. 'For your sake – and your daughter's – it better be. You're a drunk. I dislike drunks. See that you're sober tomorrow night.'

She heard footsteps, the door opening, closing. Then silence.

It was broken by the smashing of glass, of roaring oaths. In her bed she trembled and braced for the worst.

The walls shook. He was pounding his fists on them. Better than on her, was all she could think. Let him beat the walls, let him find another bottle. Please, please, let him go out to find more to drink, to find someone else to punish.

Please.

But the door of her room burst open. He stood, a shadow, big, dark, with the light bright and hard behind him.

'What're you staring at? You been listening to my private conversations? You been poking your nose in my business.'

No. No. She didn't speak, only shook her head fast and fierce.

'I ought to leave you here for the rats and the cops. Rats'll chew your fingers off, and your toes. Then the cops'll come. You know what they do to little girls who don't mind their own?'

He lumbered to her, dragging her up by the hair so fire burst in her scalp and she cried out despite her efforts to stay quiet.

'They put them in dark holes in the ground and leave them there so bugs crawl into their ears. You wanna go into a little dark hole, little girl?'

She was crying now. She didn't want to, but the tears simply spurted out. He slapped her. Once, twice, but it was almost absentminded, and she began to hope.

'Get your lazy ass out of bed and pack your junk. I got places to go, people to see. We're heading south, little girl.'

He smiled then, a big, toothy grin that left his eyes wild. 'Ricker thinks he scares me. Well, hell. I got the first half of his money and his goddamn drugs. We'll see who has the last laugh. Mother fucking Max Ricker.'

As she scrambled to obey, stuffing what clothes she had into a bag, she could only think she was saved, for one night, she was saved. Thanks to a man named Max Ricker.

Eve shot out of sleep with her heart pounding, her throat dry.

Ricker. Oh God. Ricker and her father.

She gripped the arms of the chair to steady herself, to keep herself in the now. Had it been real or just a product of fatigue and imagination?

Real. When those little flashes of the past came to her, they were always real. She could see herself, a tangle of hair, huge eyes, skinny arms, huddled in the bed like an animal in a cave.

She could hear the voices.

Leaning forward, she pressed her fingers to her temples. Max Ricker had known her father. In New York. Yes, she was sure they'd been in New York that night. How long had it been before they'd landed in Dallas? How long before the night she'd found the knife in her hand when her father was raping her?

How long before the night when she'd killed him?

Long enough for the money to run low. Long enough, she realized, for Ricker to have been hunting, to have set wolves on the trail of the man who'd stolen from him.

But she'd ended it first.

Rising, she paced the room. What had happened then didn't apply now, and she couldn't allow it to interfere with her investigation or influence her.

And yet, what sneering twist of fate had brought this circle around again? Ricker to her father. Ricker to Roarke.

And without question, Ricker to herself.

What choice did she have but to end it again?

Chapter Nineteen

She needed more coffee. She needed some sleep. Dreamless sleep. And she needed the rest of the data from the search and scan.

But something had rooted in her brain, something that had her leapfrogging over the current data and running yet another search.

She'd just begun when the summons came from The Towers.

'I don't have time for this. Goddamn politics. I don't have time to go running up to Tibble and giving him updates he can pass to the media.'

'Dallas, you go up to The Towers. I'll finish the run for you,' Peabody said.

Eve wanted to do the run herself. It was personal. And that was the whole damn problem, she admitted. She'd let it get personal. 'Vernon's due in an hour. If he's thirty seconds late, send uniforms, have him picked up. Familiarize yourself with his profile,' she added as she grabbed her jacket. 'Contact Feeney. I want him and McNab in on the interview. I want the room full of cops.'

She hesitated, looked back at the computer. No point in wasting time, she reminded herself. No point in it. 'Add the data I'm compiling to the file, and run a probability on our three homicides.'

'Yes, sir. On who?'

'You'll know,' Eve said as she stalked out. 'If you don't, you're in the wrong business.'

'I live for pressure,' Peabody muttered and sat down.

She was going to make it short, Eve told herself. And she was going to make it direct. Tibble might have to be concerned about departmental image, about politics, about the drooling and slathering in IAB, but she didn't.

She had one job, and that was to close her case.

She wasn't going to sit still for having to squeeze another damn press conference into her schedule. And if he thought he could yank her off the investigation to make the proper noises to the media, he could just . . .

Oh boy.

It wouldn't help matters for her to march into Tibble's office leading with attitude. Any more, she thought, than this underlying pity would help if her suspicions regarding the killer's identity proved out.

Her job *was* to close the case. And the dead, whoever they were, deserved her best.

As for Ricker, she intended to close that circle as well.

Tibble didn't keep her waiting. That surprised her a little. But it was nothing compared to the jolt she got when she stepped into his office and saw Roarke sitting there, cool-eyed and comfortable.

'Lieutenant.' From his desk, Tibble gestured her inside. 'Have a seat. You've had a long night,' he added. His face was calm, blank. As was that of her commander who sat with his hands on his thighs.

It was, Eve thought, like coming in late to a high-stakes poker game. And she didn't know the price of the damn ante.

'Sir. The preliminary report on Bayliss has already been updated with initial lab reports.' She glanced meaningfully toward Roarke. 'I am unable to specify regarding the evidence in the presence of a civilian.'

'The civilian came in handy last night,' Tibble said.

'Yes, sir.' She, too, knew how to hold her cards close, and merely nodded. 'It was vital to arrange the fastest transportation to Bayliss's weekend home.'

'Not quite fast enough.'

'No, sir.'

'That wasn't a criticism, Lieutenant. Your instincts regarding Captain Bayliss were correct. If you hadn't followed them as you did, we might still, at this point, be unaware of his murder. As I admire your instincts, Lieutenant, I'm about to follow them myself. I've made Roarke a temporary civilian attaché as regards the investigation of Max Ricker, concurrent with your investigation of these homicides.'

'Chief Tibble—'

'You have an objection, Lieutenant?' Tibble spoke smoothly. If her head hadn't been busy exploding, she might have heard the whiff of humor in the tone.

'A number of them, beginning with the fact that the Ricker matter is not priority. I am on the point of analyzing new evidence and data that I believe will lead to an arrest in the matter of my current investigation. The connection to Ricker exists,' she continued, 'is key, but it has no bearing on these leads or on the anticipated arrest. The connection is, I believe more emotional than tangible. Therefore, the pursuit of Ricker is secondary, and it is my belief that this pursuit can and will be continued subsequent to interview with the suspect in the homicides. I request that any steps in the Ricker area be postponed until my current case is closed.'

Tibble watched her. 'You're now a target.'

'Every cop's a target. The killer is attempting to shift my focus from him onto Ricker. I don't intend to accommodate him. And respectfully, sir, neither should you.'

There was just enough heat in the last of her statement to cause Tibble's brows to lift. Just enough to have the corners of his mouth lift in what could never be mistaken for amusement.

'Lieutenant Dallas, in my observations of your work, I have never perceived your focus shifting one degree once set on course. But perhaps I've missed something, or perhaps these current matters are more than you can reasonably handle. If that's the case, I'll assign the Ricker matter to another officer.'

'That's my second ultimatum in the last few hours. I don't like ultimatums.'

'You're not required to like it. You're required to do your job.'

'Chief Tibble.' Roarke, voice quiet, interrupted. 'We've taken the lieutenant off guard, after a difficult night. My presence here adds a personal level. I wonder if we might explain the reason I'm here before this goes any farther.'

It was nearly out of her mouth, the pissy little snipe that would tell Roarke in no uncertain terms she didn't need him defending her. But Whitney got to his feet, nodded.

'I think we might take a breath here, calm ourselves down. I'd like some coffee, sir. With your permission, I'll get some for all of us while Roarke outlines the basic plan for Lieutenant Dallas's benefit.'

Tibble gave a brief nod, gestured to Roarke, then sat back in his chair.

'As I've told you and have informed your superiors, I once had a brief business association with Max Ricker. An association,' Roarke added, 'which I severed upon discovering not all of Ricker's dealings were legal.

'We did not have a friendly parting of the ways. My ending of our association cost Ricker a considerable amount of money, and a number of accounts – clients. He's known to hold a grudge over much less, and to bide his time in seeking retribution. I can't say this worried me overmuch, until recently.'

He glanced up at Whitney as the commander offered him a cup of coffee. *Cop coffee*, Roarke thought with an inward wince but took it just the same. 'As you know, I purchased, through a representative, a property owned by Ricker. I remodeled, restaffed, and renamed the club Purgatory. It does good business, legal business, but since the time of the murder of your associate, I discovered that Ricker has been using my property, and some of my staff, to do business of his own.'

MacLean, Eve thought. She'd been sure of it.

'Illegals, primarily,' Roarke added. 'As he hardly needs one of my properties for this purpose, his goal was to build up these illegal activities, essentially under my nose, and eventually connect me to them. Causing me and my wife a great deal of trouble and discomfort.'

'She sold you out.' Eve felt fury bubbling in her throat. 'Rue MacLean.'

'On the contrary.' He never missed a beat. 'She discovered Ricker's infiltration and reported it to me only last night.'

That was bullshit, Eve thought, but she'd let it pass for now. 'IAB had a tip on it – no doubt through one of Ricker's sources – set Kohli up to sniff it out. He had a good nose. He'd have caught the scent.'

'I believe he did. Sooner than Ricker might have wanted. He was only doing minor business. But killing a cop, having a cop killed in my place, changes the level.'

'It wasn't Ricker.' It was out thoughtlessly, almost defensively; then she made herself consider. 'He lit the fuse,' she murmured. 'Connections inside the department, inside the One twenty-eight. He knew which buttons to push, which wounds to pour salt in. He couldn't have known what he was starting. Couldn't have anticipated that, but he's been sucking it in, just the same.'

She paused, then continued at Tibble's gesture. 'He'd have been distracted, angry, at the bust last fall. It shifted the balance. Martinez had him, all her data clicked. But Mills moved in and undermined the bust and the subsequent evidence. Ricker slid through, but the whole deal twisted him up.'

'And with his need to prove he still had the power, he offset that annoyance by arranging for a cop in my place. His reasoning there will come out eventually. And really, does it matter? I can get him for you. Isn't that enough?'

Too much, she wanted to say. She was afraid it would be too much. 'I can get him myself.'

'I don't doubt it,' Roarke admitted. 'However, I can help you do it quickly, without taking your energies and your considerable skills away from your homicide investigation. Or taking them only minimally. Purgatory reopens at eight on Friday night. Ricker will be there at ten.'

'Why?'

'To do business with me. Business I'll agree to do because I'm concerned about my wife's safety. Eve,' he murmured, 'surely you can swallow your pride long enough to let me set him up so you can kick his ass.'

'He won't believe you.'

'He will, yes. First because it's true, and second because I'll pretend it isn't and let him see through. He expects deceit because he's a liar himself. I'm bored, you see, towing the line. Want a bit of excitement back. Then there's the money. So much money to be made when you don't worry about the refinements.'

'You already own half the universe.'

'Why settle for half when you can have all?' He took a sip of coffee, found it just as bitter and bad as expected. 'He'll believe me because he wants to. Wants to believe he's won. And because he's not as clever as he once was, or as careful. He'd like me, at least, under his thumb so he can pick me apart at his leisure. We'll lead him to believe that can happen. When the deal's made, you'll have him.'

'We'll put men in the club.' Whitney picked up the plan. 'And Roarke is arranging for his security system to record the entire discussion. His club manager will be acting as liaison, setting up the meet. I need you to brief Roarke on Kohli so that he can steer Ricker in that direction. If he had any involvement in that murder, I want him to go down for it.'

'He'll know it's a setup,' Eve insisted. 'Why should he talk business off his own turf? He'll insist on having his men do a security sweep.'

'He'll talk,' Roarke corrected, 'because he won't be able to resist. Because he still considers the club his turf. And he can do his sweep. He won't find what I don't want him to find.'

She turned from him, got to her feet. 'Sir, Roarke lacks objectivity in this matter, and he's not trained. It's probable that under these conditions Ricker will attempt to cause him physical harm. Most certainly a plan along these lines will put a civilian in serious jeopardy and could cause him considerable legal difficulties.'

'Let me assure you, Lieutenant Dallas, the civilian has covered himself in all legal areas. He'll have his immunity regarding any information or allegations stemming from any areas discussed, past, present, or future, in this operation. As for physical jeopardy, I imagine he can handle himself every bit as well there as he has in the legal arena. His cooperation in this matter will save the department untold man-hours and financial resources. Objectively, Lieutenant, this is an opportunity we can't afford to miss. If you feel unable to head the team or be a part of the operation, you have only to say so. Under the circumstances, it won't be held against you.'

'I'll do my job.'

'Good. I'd have been disappointed to hear you say otherwise. Coordinate your schedule. Make time to brief Roarke on Kohli and to be briefed by him on the security setup at

Purgatory. I want every member of the team linked and locked within twenty-four hours. There'll be no leak, no mistake, no legal loophole for Ricker to slip through this time. Bring me his goddamn head on a plate.'

'Yes, sir.'

'Full updates, on my desk, concurrent cases, by sixteen hundred. Dismissed.'

When Roarke walked out with her, she said nothing. Didn't dare. Anything that spilled out would be hot and lethal and likely burn them both.

'Noon.' She snapped it out when she felt she had some measure of control. 'My home office. Have your security diagrams, all data. A list, with all background data on any and all staff members who'll be on duty Friday night. You've already planned to broach some sort of deal to Ricker, I want to know every angle of it. I don't want any more goddamn surprises. Don't talk to me now,' she ordered in a his. 'Don't even speak. You ambushed me. You fucking ambushed me.'

He took her arm before she could stalk away, and she rounded, one fist clenched and ready.

'Go ahead.' The invitation was mild. 'Take a shot if it'll make you feel better.'

'I'm not doing this here.' It took every scrap of control to keep her voice down. 'It's bad enough already. Just let go. I'm late for Interview.'

Instead, he simply yanked her into the elevator. 'Do you think I would do nothing? Stand back and do nothing?'

She was trembling, and she knew it. What the hell was wrong with her? She was trembling and tired and riding too close to panic. 'I think you have no right poking into my job.'

'Only when it suits you? Only when I come in handy. Then it's all right for me to poke in. Invitation only.'

'Okay, fine! Fine, fine!' She threw up her hands, furious because he was right, and that made her wrong. 'Do you know what you've done? Do you know what you've risked?'

'Can you imagine what I wouldn't risk for you? You can't, because there's nothing. There's bloody nothing.' He took her by the shoulders, fingers hard and tense.

It was always a weird sort of fascination to see him lose control, to hear his voice take on that jagged edge. But she wasn't in the mood to be fascinated. 'I was handling it, and I would've finished it.'

'Well, now *we're* handling it. And *we'll* finish it. When you swallow that pride, Eve, take care you don't choke on it.' Leaving it at that, he strode off the elevator when the doors opened and left her fuming inside.

It was Vernon's bad luck that she was ready to chew glass. He leaped to his feet when she walked into Interview.

'You had me picked up. You had me picked up and dragged in here like a criminal.'

'That's right, Vernon.' She shoved him, hard, and knocked him into the chair.

'I want a goddamn lawyer.'

This time she grabbed him one-handed by the collar and shoved him against the wall while Feeney, McNab, and Peabody stood aside and watched with varying degrees of interest.

'I'll get you a goddamn lawyer. You're going to need one. But you know what, Vernon, we're not on record yet. You notice that? And you notice how my pals here aren't making any move to stop me from pounding your ugly face in. I'm just going to kick you around the room a few times before we call for that goddamn lawyer.'

He tried to shove her, found her elbow hard in his gut. 'Get your hands off me.'

He took a swing at her that went wide as she sidestepped. Then he was doubled over, retching from the agony of her knee slamming into his crotch.

'I've got three witnesses here that're going to testify that you assaulted me. That's going to put you in lockup, where all the big, bad guys will be drawing straws to see who gets to be your date for Friday night. I bet you know what those big, bad guys do to cops in lockup, don't you, Vernon? They can do a lot of it in the couple of hours it's going to take me, given my physical distress as a result of said assault, to contact your representative.'

Every breath he drew cut into his throat like glass.

'Now, I came in here in the mood to dance with you, but I'm losing the urge. You don't want to talk to me and my pals, we'll just book you on the assault, then finish up by slamming you with corruption, misuse of authority, accepting bribes, collusion with suspected members of organized crime, and top it all off with conspiracy to murder.'

'That's bullshit.' He had most of his breath back, though his face was still white and sheened with sweat.

'I don't think so. Ricker's not going to think so, either, when it leaks you're in here squealing like a pig. And it will leak, because I've got a warrant out on Canarde.'

Not yet, she didn't, but she would.

'If we let you out, you're going to wish you were in a cage playing house with some guy named Bruno.'

'I came in to make a deal.'

'Yeah, but then you didn't show up on time.'

'I got sidetracked.'

'And I don't like your attitude. Fact is, Vernon, I don't need you anymore. I'll have the case wrapped by end of day, and I'm going to take Ricker down, just for my own amusement. You're what they call superfluous.'

'You're bluffing. You think I don't know how this works? I'm a fucking cop.'

'You're a fucking disgrace, and don't you call yourself a cop again in my presence, or I will kick your ass.'

If she had Canarde, he thought, if she was that close to Ricker, he was done. And he'd better save himself, quick and fast. 'You want to make your case, you're going to want what I know. I know plenty. You haven't scraped the surface at the One twenty-eight.'

'I've scraped it, and I'm busy mucking out the slime on the bottom. That's where I found you.'

'I can give you more.' Desperation had him trying out a shaky smile. 'I can give you a promotion. Names, Dallas, not just in the One twenty-eight. Names in the mayor's office, in the media, and right on through to East Washington. I want immunity, a new ID, and the seed money to relocate.'

She yawned, hugely. 'Jesus, Vernon, you're boring me.'

'That's the deal.'

'Here's mine. Peabody, dump this piece of garbage in lockup. And see if Bruno's back in town.'

'I believe he is, and he's lonely.'

'Wait, Jesus. What'd you bring me in for if you didn't want to deal? I gotta have immunity. You put me in, I don't come out. We both know it. What's the point in my talking if I'm going to get stuck in the heart?'

'Gee, Vernon, now you're breaking mine. Immunity, for everything up to conspiracy to murder. You get hooked to that, you go down. As for the new name, face, location, that's your problem.'

'That's not enough.'

'That's it; that's all. And even that leaves a taste in my mouth it's going to take weeks to get out again.'

'I didn't have anything to do with killing cops.'

'Then you don't have to worry, do you?'

'I got a right to my union rep.' He whined now, in a voice that reminded her of her father's in the flashback.

'Sure you do,' was all she said and turned to the door.

'Wait. Okay, wait. Reps just complicate things, right? We'll do it straight. You put the immunity on the record, and we do it straight.'

She turned back to the table. Sat. 'Interview with Vernon,

Detective Jeremy, conducted by Dallas, Lieutenant Eve. Also present are Feeney, Captain Ryan; McNab, Detective Ian; and Peabody, Officer Deliah. Subject Vernon has agreed to give statements and answer questions in return for immunity on any related charges of corruption and misuse of authority. Do you give these statements and agree to answer these questions of your own volition?'

'That's right. I want to cooperate. I want to make things right. I feel—'

'That's enough, Vernon. You are a ranked detective in the NYPSD, correct?'

'I've been a cop for sixteen years. Been a detective in Illegals at the One twenty-eight for the last six.'

'And at this time you are prepared to admit that you have accepted financial bribes and other favors in exchange for passing information to, aiding in the illegal practices of, and generally following the orders of Max Ricker.'

'I took money. Fact was, I was afraid not to. I'm ashamed of it, but I feared for my life and well-being. I'm not the only one.'

Once he got started, Eve thought, you couldn't shut him up. In the first hour, he reeled off streams of names, activities, connections.

He brought down the One twenty-eight, even as he doggedly treaded water to keep his own neck above the swamp.

'Captain Roth?'

'Her?' Vernon, feeling perkier, sneered. 'She didn't see. Didn't want to, you ask me. Has her own agenda. Wants to make commander. Plays a good game of politics, but she's got this problem. She don't have a dick and wishes she did. Always going off about how some of the men didn't like taking orders from her 'cause she's a woman. Then she's got that useless husband screwing around on her. She drinks. She got so hot on this op to take Ricker down, she didn't watch her back or look down at her feet neither. Made it easy to pull the rug out, you know. We just passed the data along, lost some key evidence, skewed a couple of reports, and that was that.'

'Yeah, that was that.'

'Listen.' Vernon leaned forward. 'Ricker's smart. He knows he doesn't need the whole squad. He gets key men, and they keep a look out for him, and for other recruits. You know who's up for a take and who's not.'

'Kohli wasn't.'

'Straight as a damn arrow, Kohli. One of the guys in the One two-eight, see, he'd heard something on an op from say, the Six-four. Easy to poke around, talking shop. Then you got a guy knows how to hack data, and you get the deets. Pass that to Ricker, and you get a nice fee.'

He lifted his hands, actually smiling. 'Smooth. Simple. If the op was after one of Ricker's connections, he had time to change locations, pull out, whatever, so the op's a bust. If it's one of his competitors, he can sit back, wait for the shit to fly, then pick up the clients, maybe even the merchandise, after. He's got key men in Evidence when he needs them. Then the media guys to spin stories his way, the politicians to keep the heat off. Thing is, I've been noticing, last couple years the guy's getting erratic.'

'Ricker?'

'Yeah. He's starting to dip into his own stock a little too heavy. Slurping that drink of his, laced with illegals, every time you turn around. He's a damn addict now, half gone to a funky-junky. I mean he's slipping and sliding in a big way, making some bad moves. Then offing a cop. I mean, Jesus.'

Eve's hand shot out, gripped his wrist. 'Do you have knowledge that Max Ricker arranged for the murder of Taj Kohli?'

He wanted to say yes. Somehow, it had all taken on the shining sheen of bragging. But if he didn't play it straight, she'd catch him up and find a way to hang him. 'I can't say as he ordered it, but I heard some talk.'

'Give me the talk, Vernon.'

'Now and again I'd maybe have a drink or share an LC with one of Ricker's guys. Lemme tell you, I wasn't the only one noticing he was losing his touch here and there. So this guy, Jake Evans, he was telling me about a month ago that Ricker was playing games with IAB, getting his jollies turning cops on cops. He knew IAB put a man into that club, looking for cops doing deals. Only there weren't cops doing deals. Get me?'

'Yeah, I get you.'

'Right. Ricker'd put that out, playing his games. Ricker, Evans tells me, has this bug up his ass to cause trouble there, in that club, and that's why he's having some of his men channeling illegals through it. But seems he got a better idea, and he thinks he's found a way to put a cop on a cop, all the way. Some psychological shit, Evans said. Ricker, he's big on mind games. He's feeding skewed data to this other cop on the first cop. The second cop . . . You following this?'

'Yes. Keep going.'

'Okay, the second cop's got some problems. Personal problems or something, and Ricker's chewing away on them, making them raw, giving this cop lots of little nudges so he'll think the first cop, that's Kohli, did something dirty. But it was more than that, like whatever the dirty was went back on the first cop. Evans said it was complicated and risky, and Ricker wasn't saying much, but he, Evans, didn't like it. Then Ricker's man in IAB . . . he's got one there, too. His man there was supposed to make sure all this shaded data sort of fell in the second cop's lap. I guess it worked.'

Vernon had the good sense to take the excitement off his face. 'I figured when Kohli got hit, and it came around he got hit by another cop, I figured Ricker's worked it.'

'What's the name in IAB?'

'I don't know. Swear to God,' he said when her eyes narrowed. 'We don't all know each other. Mostly we found out, but not every one, every time. Probably Bayliss, right? Bayliss is dead. Come on, Dallas. I've given you close to twenty names. You put a fire under some of them, you'll get more.'

'Yeah, I'll get more.' She got to her feet. 'But I can't stomach any more from you. McNab, get this thing into a safe house. Two guards at all times, on eight-hour shifts. Feeney, can you hand-pick them.'

'Can do.'

'I gave you a hell of a lot, Dallas. You could go to bat for me on the new ID.'

She didn't so much as look at him. 'Peabody, with me.'

'Dallas, hey!'

'Count your blessings, jerk,' Feeney muttered as Eve walked out. 'You only got your balls bruised. Another little while in here with you, if she didn't cut them off, I would have.'

'I can't even get mad.' Peabody stood in the hallway, turned away from Interview. 'I'm too sick to my stomach to get mad. I love being a cop, and he's made me ashamed of it.'

'That's the wrong take. He's beyond shame. You just do the job, day after day, and you've got nothing to be ashamed of. I need you to make a copy of that record and get it to Tibble. That's going to be his problem, thank Christ. I've got another meet at noon. I'll fill you in on it when I get back.'

'Yes, sir. What about Canarde?'

'We hold there. I'm saving him for later.'

'Do you want the results of the search and scan and probability you had me run?'

'Is it enough to pick him up?'

'Probability's under seventy-six percent with known data. But—'

'But,' Eve repeated, 'the computer doesn't count grief or

mind games. Or Ricker playing cop against cop. We'll bring him in. We'll do it quiet, when I get back.'

'He may try another hit.'

'No, he gave his word. He won't break it.'

Chapter Twenty

Eve marched into the house, emitted a low, rumbling growl at a hovering Summerset, and headed straight up the stairs. She had a great deal to say and intended to get started immediately.

The growl came again, a quiet threat, when she noted her office was empty. But the door leading to Roarke's was open. Rolling her shoulders, she started toward it, and heard the impatience in his voice as she approached the door.

'It's neither possible nor is it convenient for me to make the trip at this time.'

'But, sir, the situation requires your personal attention. With Tonaka dragging their feet over this acquisition, and the delays in the environmental clearance on the tropical sector, we can't hope to meet deadline without your immediate intervention. Cost overruns and penalties will—'

'You're authorized to deal with it. I pay you to deal with it. I'm unable to make the trip to Olympus for the next several days, perhaps longer. If Tonaka is dragging feet, cut them off at the knees. Understood?'

'Yes, sir. If I could have any sort of estimate as to when you might clear the time to survey on site, it would—'

'I'll let you know when I know.'

Roarke cut transmission, sat back, closed his eyes.

And two things occurred to Eve: First, that he had a complicated, vital, and demanding life apart from hers, one she too often took for granted.

Second, and more important, he looked tired.

He never looked tired.

The temper she'd hoarded like gold slipped away, unneeded. Unwanted. Still, instinct moved her into the room and kept a scowl on her face.

He sensed her instantly, his eyes opening. 'Lieutenant.'

'Roarke,' she said in exactly the same cool and measured tone. 'I have a number of things to say to you.'

'I'm sure you do. Would you prefer your office?'

'We can start right here. First, in my own fumbling way, I've managed to narrow my investigation – my *homicide* investigation – to one suspect. This suspect will be brought in, detained, and questioned before end of day.'

'Congratulations.'

'Premature. Questioning is not an arrest. At the same time, through another source and through police procedure, I've tied Ricker – loosely, but tied him – to those homicides and hope to charge him with conspiracy. It's a stretch, but it could work and will certainly be enough for me to pull him in and interrogate him. I did those things without you going behind my back and over my head to formulate an operation with my superiors. An operation that puts you at considerable risk, not only physically but in ways we both understand. If the operation goes through, what's said between you and Ricker will be admissible in court.'

'I'm perfectly aware of that.'

'Your immunity deal will keep you out of a cage, but could – and you know it – potentially damage your reputation and your business.'

Even through the fatigue in his eyes, she caught the glint of arrogance. 'Lieutenant, my reputation and my business was forged in the same unsavory fire.'

'That may be, but things are different now. For you.'

'Do you honestly think I can't weather this?'

'No, Roarke, I think you can and will weather anything,

everything. I think there's nothing beyond your capabilities when your mind is set. It's almost scary. You pissed me off,' she added.

'I'm perfectly aware of that.'

'You knew you would. If you'd come to me with the idea first—'

'Time was short, and we were both busy. This involves me, Eve, whether you like it or not.'

'I don't like it, but maybe not for the reasons you think.'

'Regardless, I did what makes sense, what's most direct. I'm not sorry for it.'

'No apologies? I could make you apologize, pal.'

'Is that so?'

'Yeah, that's so. Because you're soft on me. Ask anybody.' She moved to the desk now, watching him as he rose. 'I'm soft on you, too. Don't you know that's why, or part of why I was pissed off? I don't want him close to you. I don't want what he is to touch you. Is that supposed to be your exclusive property? Not wanting someone who means you harm to lay hands on you?'

'No.' He sighed, ran a hand through his hair in a rare show of frustration. 'No, it's not.'

'The other part was pride, and I don't have an easy time swallowing it. Neither do you. The thing you said, about me going along with you poking in when it works for me? You were right. I'm not saying that's going to change, but you were right. I'm not real happy about that, either. And this other thing I know. You only walk away like you did when you'd like to punch me.'

'I must do a great deal of walking away.'

She didn't laugh, as he meant her to. 'No, that's the thing. You don't.' She came around the counter, the console, then took his face in her hands. 'You just don't.'

'Eve.' He ran his hands up her arms, to her shoulders.

'I'm not finished yet. It's a good plan. Not a great one, but

299

we can fine-tune it. I'd rather another way. I'd rather you'd use that 'link to contact whoever it was you were just talking to and agree to go off planet and do whatever the hell it is you do nobody else seems to be able to pull off. I'd rather that, Roarke, because you mean more to me than anything ever has or ever could. But it's not going to happen. And if anything happens to you Friday night—'

'It won't.'

'If anything happens to you,' she repeated, 'I'm going to dedicate my life to making yours a living hell.'

'Fair enough,' he murmured as her mouth came up to his.

'An hour.' She wrapped herself around him. 'Let's go away from this for one hour. I need to be with you. I need to be who I am when I'm with you.'

'I know the perfect place.'

She had a fondness for the beach – the heat, the water, the sand. She could relax there in a manner she allowed herself so rarely.

He could give her the beach for an hour, take it for himself in the holo-room, where illusions were only a program away.

The island he chose, with its long sickle curve of white-sugar sand, its lazily waving palms, and fat, fragrant flowers, was a setting that suited both of them. The baking heat from the gold ball of sun was offset by the breeze that flowed in from the sea like the tide and brought the scent of it to the air.

'This is good.' She breathed deeply, felt the tension in her neck and shoulders melt away. She wanted the same for him. 'This is really good.' She started to ask if he'd set the timer, then decided not to spoil the moment or the mood.

Instead, she stripped off her jacket, yanked off her boots.

The water was a clear and dreaming blue, frothed with white at the shore, like lace on a hem. Why resist?

Her weapon harness came next, then her trousers. She angled her head, looked at him. 'Don't you want to swim?'

300

'Eventually. I like watching you strip. It's so . . . efficient.'

She laughed. 'Yeah, well enjoy yourself.' She tugged off her shirt, then the little scoop-necked tank beneath. Naked as a newborn, she raced to the sea and dived under the waves.

'I intend to,' he murmured, and watched her strike out, always just a little too far for safety, before he undressed.

She swam like an eel, fast and fearless. For a time he paced himself to her, a companionable competition. Then he simply heeled over on his back to float in the current, to let the water, the sun, the moment, wash away the fatigue that had nagged at him.

And to wait for her.

She swam up beside him, treaded water. 'Feel better?'

'Considerably.'

'You looked tired before.' And she wanted to stroke that fatigue away. 'You hardly ever do.'

'I was tired before.'

She let her fingers tangle in his hair. 'You get your second wind, I'll race you back to shore.'

He had his eyes closed and kept them that way. 'Who says I don't have a second wind?'

'Well, you're just floating there like flotsam. Or maybe it's jetsam. I never know which is which.'

'I've heard, in some circles, this is called relaxing. But . . .' His arm sneaked under the water, then around her. 'Since you have all this energy to spare.'

'Hey.' She laughed a little as their legs tangled. 'We're way over our heads here.'

'Just the way I like it.' His mouth came to hers, wet and teasing. His arm drew her close against him.

And they went under.

Warm, clear water, with the sun dancing on the surface. His mouth soft on hers, his body firm. For both of them, she let herself go, sliding deeper into the liquid blue. Sliding

301

deeper into the kiss. When they surfaced, she filled her lungs and pressed her cheek against his.

They let the water rock them, a steady, undulating rhythm that reflected the mood. Here, with light strokes over wet skin, was the tenderness they'd both needed. The brush of his lips on her shoulder made her smile and let her float on sensation as easily as she floated in the sea.

She turned her face to his, found his mouth again, and drugged herself on the taste of him.

They drifted lazily toward shore, rising up on the waves, sinking again, clinging together, drawing apart only far enough to touch.

When she felt sand beneath her feet, she stood in the waist-high water and watched his face as he traced his fingertips over her.

'I love the look of you, darling Eve. The way you look under my hands.'

Her breasts, small and firm, cupped neatly in his palms, seemed to heat as he captured them. Water sparkled over her skin, tiny diamonds that turned to tears and melted back into the blue.

'Give yourself to me.' His fingers trailed down her torso, over her hips. 'Go under for me.' And slid into her.

She let out her breath on a sigh, caught it again on a moan. Pleasure, languid, liquid, lapped at her senses. The sun dazzled her eyes until all she could see was blue. He dazzled her body until all she could feel was bliss.

Even as that pleasure swamped her, as her knees buckled from the thrill of it, the wave crashed over them, stealing her breath and sweeping them closer to shore.

He rolled in it with her, felt her release crest, her body tremble while the water sucked them down, tossed them free again. She was locked around him – trust, need, invitation – everything he wanted as they lay tangled together in the surf.

302

He took her mouth again, still patient, though the need had begun to throb through him like a restless heart. He skimmed his lips down her throat, her shoulders, her breasts, while her hands stroked, aroused, urged.

The water streamed over them, receded, and to its constant, endless beat, he filled her, moved with her. Dreamily, with that pulse matching his own, he watched her head arch back as the crest took her again.

'Roarke.' Her voice was husky with passion, her breath already quickening again. 'Give yourself to me. Go under for me.'

Love swamped him; more than need, it gushed through him, took his air, his heart, his thoughts. And with his eyes on hers, still and always on hers, he let himself drown.

The hour had to end. But she wouldn't feel guilty for taking it. Dry, dressed, standing in her office, she fully intended to brief Roarke and scan his readout of the security system at Purgatory.

Feeney would take a closer look at it, she thought, and coordinate with Roarke on that end. She'd station herself in Control, where she could oversee the club, monitor the moves, supervise all members of the team.

And be ready for any move Ricker might make.

'He knew my father.'

She blurted it out without realizing it was there, weighing on the center of her mind.

Roarke, about to explain the readout on-screen, turned, stared at her. She didn't have to say a name, didn't have to say anything. He knew by her face.

'You're sure of it?'

'I had a flashback last night . . . this morning,' she corrected, feeling ridiculously unsteady. 'Something tripped it, I guess, in the data I was studying, and I was back, just back.'

'Sit down and tell me.'

'I can't sit.'

'All right. Just tell me.'

'I was in bed. In my room. I had a room. I don't think I always had one – I *know* I didn't always. But I think there was some money to spare. I think it was Ricker's money. It was dark, and I was listening because he was drinking in the next room, and I was praying he would keep drinking. He was talking to somebody about a deal. I didn't understand. I didn't care. Because as long as he kept talking, kept drinking, he wouldn't come in. It was Ricker. He called him by name.'

It was hard. She hadn't expected it to be so hard to say it all, when the image of it was still so brutally clear in her mind. 'Ricker was telling him what would happen if he screwed up the deal. Illegals, I think. It doesn't matter. I recognized his voice. I mean, having the flashback, I remembered. I don't know if I'd ever heard it before that night. I don't remember.'

'Did you see him? Did he see you?'

'No, but he knew about me. My father said something about me when he was trying to get more money for the deal. So, he knew, and after he left, my father came in. He was mad. Scared and mad. He knocked me around a little, then he told me to pack. We were going to head south, he said. He had money, and I think the illegals, or some of them. I don't remember any more, except it was in New York. I'm sure we were in New York. And I think, I think we ended up in Dallas. After the money ran out, we were in Dallas. There wasn't any more money because we just had that horrible room, and hardly any food, and he didn't have enough to get drunk enough in Dallas. God.'

'Eve.' He was beside her now, his hands running up and down her arms. 'Stay here. Stay with me.'

'I am. I will. It spooked me, that's all.'

'I know.' He gathered her in for a moment. And realized on the heels of the flashback she'd been called to The Tower.

Ambushed.

'I'm sorry.' He turned her lips into her hair.

'It's a circle, a circle. Link to link. Ricker to my father, my father to me. Ricker to you. You to me. I don't believe in stuff like that. But here I am.'

'They won't touch you through me.' He tipped her head back. 'They'll never get through me to hurt you.'

'That's not what I meant.'

'I know, but it's a fact all the same. We'll break the circle. We'll do that together. I'm more inclined to believe in such things as fate.'

'Only when your Irish comes out.' She managed a smile but moved away. 'Could he know about me? Could he have connected me from all those years ago?'

'I can't tell you.'

'If he'd tried to track my father, could he have found out who I am? Is it possible to dig up the data on me from before?'

'Eve, you're asking me to speculate—'

'Could you?' she interrupted, facing him again. 'If you wanted the information, could you find it?'

She didn't want comfort, he knew, but facts. 'Given the time, yes. But I have considerably more to work with than he would.'

'But he could? He has the capabilities? Particularly if he'd begun to track my father when he was double-crossed.'

'It's possible. I don't believe he'd have wasted his time keeping track of an eight-year-old girl who was sucked into the system.'

'But he knew, when I went to see him, that I had been in the system. He knew where I'd been found, and in what condition.'

'Because he researched Lieutenant Eve Dallas. Not because he'd been keeping tabs on a young, abused girl.'

'Yes, you're probably right. It hardly matters, anyway.' She paused by her desk, lifted a small carved box he'd given her for odds and ends. 'You could find the data?'

'Yes, I could find it, if that's what you want.'

'No.' She set the box down again. 'It's not what I want. What I want is here. There's nothing back there I need to know. I shouldn't have let it get to me the way it did. I didn't realize it had.'

She sighed, and this time she did smile when she turned. 'I was too mad at you to think about it. We've got a hell of a lot of work to do in a short amount of time. You might as well come with me for now.'

'I thought you wanted to go over the security.'

'I do, but back at Central. I only set up this meet here so I could yell at you in private.'

'Isn't that odd? I agreed to the meet here so I could yell at you in private.'

'Shows how screwed up we are.'

'On the contrary.' He held out a hand for hers. 'I'd say it shows we're incredibly well suited for each other.'

As trying to squeeze more than two people into Eve's cramped office violated several laws of physics, she held the briefing in the conference room.

'Time's short,' she began when her team was seated. 'As the homicide cases and the matter of Max Ricker have dovetailed, we'll be pursuing them both on parallel lines. Lab results, data searches, and probability scans regarding the homicides are in your reports. I haven't requested a warrant but will do so, with an obligatory DNA test, if the suspect refuses to come in on his own volition. Peabody and I will pick him up, quietly, after the briefing.'

'Probability's low,' Feeney pointed out, frowning at the printout in his file.

'It'll get higher, and his DNA will match that of the fingernail found on the Bayliss crime scene. Due to Sergeant

Clooney's years of service to the department, his exemplary record, his emotional state, and the circumstances that built and were built around him, I prefer to bring him in personally, and hope to persuade him to make a full statement. Dr Mira is on call to counsel him and offer testing.'

'The media's going to rock and roll over this.'

Eve gave McNab a nod of acknowledgment. 'We can and we will spin the media.' She'd already decided to contact Nadine Furst. 'A veteran officer with a perfect service record whose son – only son – follows in his footsteps. A father's pride. A son's dedication. Because of that dedication, because of that honor to the badge in a squad where a few cops – and let's keep it at a few for public record – are corrupt, the son is targeted.'

'Proving that—' Feeney began.

'We don't have to prove it,' she interrupted. 'It just has to be said to be believed. Ricker,' she continued. 'He was behind it. I don't question that. Moreover, Clooney didn't. His son was clean, intended to stay clean. He moved up the ranks to detective. He couldn't be bought. He was assigned in the early stages of the Ricker op, I have that from Martinez's notes. Just a peg in the board, but a good cop. A hereditary cop. Put this together,' she suggested and rested a hip on the conference table.

'He's straight, he's young, and he's smart. He's ambitious. The Ricker task force is a good break for him, and he's going to make the most of it. He pushes, he digs. Ricker's sources in the squad relay that information. They're nervous. Ricker decides to make an example. One night, the good cop stops off in his neighborhood 24/7. He habitually swung by there on his way home after his shift. A robbery's in progress. Look at the report: That location hasn't been hit before or since, but it was being hit that night, at just the right time. The good cop goes in and is killed. The proprietor makes a frantic emergency call, but it takes a squad car ten full minutes to arrive on-scene.

And the med-techs, due to what's reported to be a technical delay, don't arrive for ten more. The kid bleeds to death on the floor. Sacrificed.'

She waited a beat, knowing any cop in the room would see it as clearly as she did. 'The squad car was manned by two men, and their names were on the list Vernon gave me this morning. Ricker's men. They let him die, one of their own. And the signal was sent: This is what happens if you cross me.'

'Okay, it plays,' Feeney agreed. 'But if Clooney's following the same dots, why didn't he hit the cops in the squad car?'

'He did. One of them transferred to Philadelphia three months ago. He was hanged in his bedroom. Ruling was self-termination, but I think the PPSD will reopen that case. Thirty credits were scattered on the bed. The other drowned, slipped in a bathtub while on vacation in Florida. Ruled accidental. The coins were found there, too.'

'He's been eliminating them for months.' Peabody blew out a breath. 'Just ticking them off, and going on with business.'

'Until Kohli. Kohli snapped him. He liked Kohli, knew his family, felt close to him. More, his son and Kohli were friends, and when Ricker, through IAB, planted Kohli, spread rumors that he was on the take, it was like losing his son all over again. The eliminations became more violent, more personal, and more symbolic. Blood on the badge. He can't stop. What he does now he does in his son's memory. In his son's honor. But knowing he killed an innocent man, a good cop, is breaking him down. That's Ricker's angle. He can sit back and watch us destroy each other from within.'

'He's not that clever, not anymore.' Roarke spoke up. 'He wouldn't understand a man like Clooney, or that kind of love and grief. Luck,' he said. 'He put the pieces on the tray, and luck, or if you prefer, love, linked them.'

'That may be, but putting the pieces on the tray is enough

308

to fry him. Which brings us to the second avenue of this investigation. As you are now aware, Roarke has been enlisted as temporary civilian liaison on the matter of Max Ricker. Peabody, are you familiar with the street name for civilian liaison?'

Peabody squirmed. 'Yes, sir.' When Eve merely waited, Peabody winced. 'Um . . . *weasel*, Lieutenant. The street name's *weasel*.'

'I imagine,' Roarke said, 'that weasels are adept at catching rats.'

'Good one.' Feeney leaned over and slapped Roarke on the back. 'Damn good one.'

'We have a very big rat for you.' She straightened, jammed her hands in her pockets, and outlined the plan for the rest of the team. -

There was no doubt who was in command here, Roarke thought as he watched her. Who was in control. She left no angle unexplored, no corner unswept. She prowled the room, thinking on her feet, and her voice was clipped.

In some past life she'd have been wearing a general's braiding. Or armor.

And this woman, this warrior, had trembled in his arms. That was the power between them. The miracle of it.

'Roarke?'

'Yes, Lieutenant.'

Something in his eyes had her heart stuttering a bit. She clamped down on it, frowned at him. 'I'll leave you to go over the security with Feeney and McNab. I don't want any holes in it. Not a single pinprick.'

'There won't be any.'

'Make sure of it. I'm calling Martinez in on this for the bust. And she'll get the collar when it goes down. Any objections?' She waited, got none. 'Peabody, you're with me.'

She started out, glanced back. Roarke was still watching

her, the faintest of smiles on that killer mouth, the faintest glint in those wild blue eyes.

'Jesus, he makes your mouth water.'

'Sir?'

'Nothing.' Mortified, she strode out. 'Nothing. Has my unit been repaired or replaced?'

'Dallas, that's so sweet. I didn't know you believed in fairy tales.'

'Damn it. We'll steal one from somewhere.' Then she began to grin. 'I'll just take Roarke's.'

'Oh, tell me it's the XX. The 6000. It's my favorite.'

'How the hell are we going to bring in a suspect in a two-seater? It's some snazzy sedan type today. I've got the code. Won't he be surprised when he goes down and finds it gone. I think—'

Distracted, she nearly walked into Webster. 'Lieutenant, a minute of your time.'

'I'm low on minutes, walk and talk.'

'You're going for Clooney.'

'Goddamn it.' Though he'd kept his voice low, she whipped her head around to be sure no one had heard, 'What makes you think that?'

'I still have my sources.' His face was grave, and his voice remained quiet. 'You left the breadcrumbs. I can still follow the trail.'

'Have you been in my files?'

'Dallas.' He laid a hand on her arm, felt the tremor of temper. 'I'm deep in this. Part of what I did, following orders, may have sparked what's gone down. I did the internal run on Clooney's son. I feel responsible. Let me go with you to pick him up.'

She angled her head. 'Someone in IAB's dirty, in Ricker's pocket. How do I know it's not you?'

His hand dropped away. 'You don't.' He let out a breath. 'You can't. Okay.' He stepped back, started to turn.

'Hold on. Peabody.' She gestured, moved a few steps away. 'Do you have a problem on staying with the briefing, finishing the paperwork?'

Peabody glanced back at Webster, who was standing with his hands in his pockets and a miserable look on his face. 'No, sir.'

'All right. Set up an interview room, block observation. I don't want anybody nosing in while I'm talking to Clooney. Let's give him what dignity we can.'

'I'll take care of it. Good luck.'

'Yeah.' She walked back to Webster. 'Let's go.'

He blinked, then took in a breath. 'Thanks.'

'Don't thank me. You're along for ballast.'

Chapter Twenty-One

Peabody dawdled. She procrastinated. She fiddled. Then when she couldn't avoid it any longer, she went back into the conference room.

Some complex schematic was on the wall screen, and Feeney was whistling at it as though it were the image of a naked and nubile woman.

'Hey, She-Body. What's up?' McNab asked.

'Just a change of plans. I'm going to sit in on the security briefing.'

'Dallas isn't going for Clooney?' Feeney asked.

'Yeah, yeah, she's going.' As if it was vitally important, she selected a chair, brushed off the seat, settled into it.

'Alone?' Roarke's voice made her want to cringe, but she looked up over his shoulder, shrugged her own. 'No, no, she's got somebody. Um, you'll have to explain the system to me in English. I only speak pidgin tech-speak.'

'Who's with her?' Roarke asked, though he already knew. It was just like her.

'With her? Oh, ah, hmmm. Webster.'

Silence fell, a clatter of broken bricks. Peabody folded her hands in her pockets and prepared for the explosion to follow.

'I see.' When Roarke simply turned back to the screen and continued, she didn't know whether to be relieved or scared to death.

*

Webster resisted, barely, making some smart comment about the sleek luxury car and instead settled in to enjoy the ride.

Or tried to, but his nerves were jumping.

'Okay, let's just get this out of the way. I'm not Ricker's man in IAB. I guess I figured there had to be one, but I don't have a line on it. I will have. I'm going to make a point of it.'

'Webster, if I thought you were hooked to Ricker, you'd still be back at Central, crawling over the floor trying to find what was left of your teeth.'

It made him smile. 'That means a lot to me.'

'Yeah, yeah, save it.'

'So . . . I went into your files. You can kick me about that later if you want. I had your code and password. Bayliss dug it out. I didn't have any right to and blah, blah, but I did it. I followed your line on Clooney. It was good work.'

'You expect me to blush and say aw, shucks? You try that crap again, and I'll have you up, toothless, before the review board.'

'Fair enough. You didn't get a warrant.'

'That's right.'

'What you got's thin, but it spreads enough that a judge would've issued.'

'I don't want a warrant. He's entitled to a little consideration.'

'Bayliss hated cops like you.' Webster looked out at New York, the jam of it, crowded, colorful, arrogant. 'I'd forgotten what it was like to work this way. It's not something I'm going to forget again.'

'Then listen up, here's how we do it. Clooney's living on the West Side. It's an apartment. He moved out of his house in the burbs a couple months after his son died. Hang a busted marriage on Ricker while you're at it.'

'It's the middle of shift. He's not going to be home.'

'You didn't finish his file. It's his day off. If he's not there, we knock on doors until somebody tells us where he might be. And we go find him, or we wait. I do the talking. He's going to come in voluntarily. That's the way we're going to make it happen.'

'Dallas, he's killed three cops.'

'Five. You didn't finish my notes, either. You're slipping, Webster. A thorough cop is a happy cop.'

She found the address, started to double-park, then remembered she not only had Roarke's snappy sedan, but didn't have her On Duty light.

Cursing under her breath, she cruised until she found a parking slot. Two blocks down and one level up.

'It's a secured building,' she noted, nodding toward the security cam and code box. 'We bypass it. I don't want him to have time to get ready for us.'

Webster opened his mouth to remind her of the lack of warrant. Then closed it again. It was her show, after all.

She used her master, keyed in her badge number. A more sophisticated system would have requested her to state her police emergency, but this one simply unlocked the outer doors.

'Fourth floor,' she told him, heading inside and to the single elevator. 'You carrying?'

'Yeah.'

'I wasn't sure you guys in IAB carried anything but a data book. Keep your weapon harnessed.'

'Well hell, I was looking forward to going through the door blasting. I'm not a moron, Dallas.'

'IAB, moron. IAB, moron. I can never tell the difference. But enough of this frivolity. Stand back,' she ordered when they reached the fourth level. 'I don't want him seeing you through the peep.'

'He may not open the door for you.'

'Sure, he will. He wonders about me.' She pressed the

314

buzzer on the side of the door. Waited. She felt herself being observed, kept her face blank.

Moments later, Clooney opened the door. 'Lieutenant, I wasn't—' He broke off when Webster shifted into the doorway. 'I wasn't expecting company.'

'Can we come in, Sergeant, and speak to you?'

'Sure, sure. Don't mind the mess. I was just making a sandwich the old-fashioned way.'

He stepped back, casual, easy. A good, smart cop, she thought later. That's why she missed it.

He brought up the knife fast, a smooth, quick motion, aimed at her throat. She was a good, smart cop, too. She might have dodged it. It was something she'd never know for certain.

Webster shoved her, hard enough to knock her off her feet, and the movement, the twist of his body put him in the path of the knife.

She shouted something as the blood spurted. Something as Webster went down. And was already scrambling to her knees, already reaching for her weapon as Clooney sprinted across the room. If she'd fired without warning, fired into his back, she would have had him. The instinctive hesitation, the ingrained loyalty, cost her an instant.

And he was out the window and clambering down the fire escape.

She rushed to Webster. His breathing was short, shallow, and the blood was coming fast from the long slice that ran from his shoulder down across his chest.

'Jesus, Jesus.'

'I'm okay. Go.'

'Shut up. Just shut up.' She ripped out her communicator as she leaped to her feet and ran to the window. 'Officer down. Officer down.' She rattled off the address, scanning for Clooney. 'Immediate medical assistance required this location. Officer down. Suspect fleeting on foot, heading west. Suspect is armed and dangerous. White male, sixty years.'

Even as she spoke, she was shrugging out of her jacket, tearing through the apartment for towels. 'Five feet, ten inches, one hundred and eighty. Gray and blue. Subject is suspect on multiple homicides. Hold on, Webster, you stupid son of a bitch. You die on me, I'm going to be supremely pissed.'

'Sorry.' He sucked in his breath as she ripped his shirt, pressed the folded towels over the wound. 'Christ, it really hurts. What the hell kind of . . .' He bore down, fighting to stay conscious. 'What the hell kind of knife was that?'

'How the hell should I know? A big, sharp one.'

Too much blood, was all she could think. Too much blood, already soaking through the towels. It was bad. It was really bad.

'They sew you up. You'll get a goddamn commendation out of this scratch. Then you'll be able to show it off to all your women and make them giddy.'

'Bullshit.' He tried to smile, but he couldn't see her. The light was going gray. 'He opened me up like a trout.'

'Shut up. I told you to shut up.'

He made a little sighing sound, then obliged her by passing out. She cradled him, sopping at blood, and listened for the sirens.

She met Whitney in the surgical waiting room. Her shirt and trousers were soaked with Webster's blood, her face pale as death.

'I screwed up. I was sure I could reason with him, that I could reach him and bring him in. Instead, he's at large and another good cop's dying.'

'Webster's getting the best care available. Every one of us is responsible for himself, Dallas.'

'I took him along.' *It could be Peabody on the operating table*, she thought. *Oh God, no way to win.*

'He took himself along. Regardless, you've identified the suspect, and have done so through skilled investigative work.

316

Sergeant Clooney won't be at large for long. We have an all-points. He's known. He fled with the clothes on his back. He has no funds, no resources.'

'A smart cop knows how to go under. I let him go, Commander. I did not take the opportunity to take him down nor did I pursue.'

'If you were again faced with making the choice of pursuing a suspect or saving a fellow officer's life, which way would you go?'

'I'd do the same thing.' She looked toward the operating room. 'For what it's worth.'

'So would I. Lieutenant, go home. Get some sleep. You'll need all the resources of your own to finish this.'

'Sir, I'd like to wait until they can tell us something on Webster.'

'All right. Let's get some coffee. Can't be any worse here than it is at Central.'

When she dragged herself home, her system was begging to shut down, but her mind refused. She replayed the moment in Clooney's doorway a hundred times. Had there been a flicker in his eyes, one she should have seen, responded to, an instant before the knife came up?

If Webster hadn't moved in, could she have dodged and deflected?

What was the point? she asked herself as she stepped into the house. Nothing changed.

'Eve.'

Roarke came out of the parlor where he'd waited for her. She'd come home bloody before, exhausted before, and carrying a cloak of despair. Now she stood with all three hovering around her and just stared at him.

'Oh, Roarke.'

'I'm sorry.' He moved to her, wrapped his arms around her. 'I'm so sorry.'

'They don't think he's going to make it. That's not what they say, exactly, but you can read it on their faces. Massive blood loss, extreme internal damage. The knife nicked his heart, his lung, and God knows. They've called his family in, advised them to hurry.'

However selfish it was didn't matter to him. All he could think was, *It could have been you. It could have been you, and I would be the one advised to hurry.*

'Come upstairs. You need to clean up and get some sleep.'

'Yeah, nothing more to do but get some sleep.' She started toward the steps with him, then just sank down on them, buried her face in her hands. 'What the hell was I thinking? Who the hell do I think I am? Mira's the shrink, not me. What made me think I could get inside this man's head and understand what was going on in it?'

'Because you can, and you do. You can't always be right.' He rubbed her back. 'Tell me what he's thinking now.'

She shook her head, got to her feet. 'I'm too tired. I'm too tired for this.'

She walked upstairs, stripping on her way across the bedroom. Before she could step into the shower, Roarke took her hand. 'No, into the tub. You'll sleep better for it.'

He ran the water himself. Hot, because she liked it hot, added scent to soothe, programmed the jets to comfort. He undressed, got in with her, and drew her back against him.

'He did it for me. Clooney was going for me, and Webster knocked me down and stepped into the knife.'

Roarke pressed his lips to the top of her head. 'Then I owe him a debt I can never repay. But you can. By finishing it. And that's what you'll do.'

'Yeah, I'll finish it.'

'For now, rest.'

Fatigue was a weight bearing down on her. She stopped resisting and fell under it.

*

318

She woke to sunlight and the scent of coffee. The first thing she saw was Roarke, with a mug of coffee in his hand.

'How much would you pay for this?'

'Name your price.' She sat up, took it from him, drank gratefully. 'This is one of my favorite parts of the marriage deal.' She let the caffeine flow through her system. 'I mean, the sex is pretty good, but the coffee . . . The coffee is amazing. And you're all-around handy yourself most of the time. Thanks.'

'Don't mention it.'

She took his hand before he could rise. 'I wouldn't have slept easy last night without you being here.' She gave his hand a squeeze, then shifted toward the bedside 'link. 'I want to call and check on Webster.'

'I've already called.' She wouldn't want it cushioned, so he told her exactly what he knew. 'He made it through the night. They nearly lost him twice and took him back in for more surgery. He remains critical.'

'Okay.' She set the coffee down to scrub her hands over her face. 'Okay. He felt like he needed vindication. Let's give it to him.'

Purgatory had taken on an edge. Glamour with a bright smear of sin.

'Fast repair work,' Eve muttered as she wandered through, scanning the trio of winding, open stairs with their treads edged with hot red lights. On closer study, she noted the banisters that curved down them were sleek and sinuous snakes, and every few feet, one was swallowing its brother's tail.

'Interesting.'

'Yes.' Roarke ran one of his elegant hands over a reptilian head. 'I thought so. And practical. Start up.'

'Why?'

'Humor me.'

With a shrug, she climbed the first three. 'So?'

'Feeney? Do we register on weapon check?'

'You bet. Scanner shows police-issue laser on staircase one, and secondary weapon in ankle harness.'

Eve glanced up toward Control, and the hidden speakers where Feeney's voice boomed. With a thin smile, she looked back at Roarke. 'Why don't you come on up for a weapon scan, ace?'

'I think not. Similar scanners are set in all entrances and exits, in the bathrooms, and privacy rooms. We'll know what we're up against in that area.'

'Boomers,' she said, coming down again. 'Knives?'

'We can scan for explosives. Knives are trickier, though the metal detectors will take care of any fashioned from that material. An hour before opening, the entire building will be swept a final time, just as a precaution.'

'Where do you plan to hold the meet?'

'We've divided the area into twenty-two sectors. Each will have individual security, and all will line to the main control. I'll have a privacy booth in sector twelve, there.'

He gestured to a table on the edge of the entertainment platform. She ran her gaze up over the gold and red poles that lanced up from the stage, the pie plate – topped columns, the human-sized gilded cages.

'Close to the action.'

'Well now, the show must go on. The booth's been rigged specifically for our purposes. Audio and video will be transmitted directly to the control.'

'He'll insist on a scan, probably a jammer.'

'Yes, he will, but the system design will override anything he has.'

'You're awfully cocky.'

'Confident, Lieutenant. I designed the system myself and have already tested it. Two of my hand-picked security will be onstage, performing, during the meet.'

'You've got security strippers?'

'Don't hate them because they're beautiful. If it's necessary to deal with any of Ricker's men, they'll do so.'

'The deal didn't include civilian hammers. We'll have cops in every sector.'

He nodded pleasantly. 'I could, of course, simply set up my personal security team without informing you of it. But as a temporary civilian attaché, I feel obliged to relay all pertinent information to the team commander.'

'Smart-ass.'

'I love you, too.'

'The bathroom's are mag,' Peabody reported as she strode up. 'Wait till you see, Dallas. The sinks are like little lakes, and there are like a million miles of counter. All this sexy art painted on the walls. And even sofas.'

She caught herself before Eve could reply, cleared her throat. 'McNab and I completed our run-through, sir, and all security – audio, visual, and scans – are operational.'

'Your uniform jacket is improperly secured, Officer Peabody.'

'My . . .' She looked down, turned bright pink to the roots of her bowl-cut hair, and hastily began to secure the brass buttons McNab had so hastily undone.

'Oh, for Christ's sake, Peabody, are you a damn rabbit? Go fix yourself up somewhere and put your hormones on hold for awhile.'

'Yes, sir. Sorry, sir.'

Peabody slunk away and left Eve scowling at Roarke. 'Don't think I don't know what a big, fat kick you're getting out of this. I *told* you this thing with McNab was going to screw up my aide.'

'As a recent liaison to the NYPSD, I found the conduct disgraceful.' He turned back, leading with the grin that made his face impossibly young, ridiculously beautiful. 'Absolutely disgraceful. I think we should go do a run-through of the lounges personally. Right now.'

'Pervert.' She jammed her hands in her pockets and was

about to walk away from him and up to Control when the main door opened. Rue MacLean stepped in.

She hesitated when Eve's cold stare blasted her, then straightened her shoulders and crossed the room. They met in front of the bar where Kohli had served his last drink.

'Ms MacLean.'

'Lieutenant. I'm perfectly aware of what you think of me, and you're entitled to say it to my face.'

'Why waste my breath? I walked through a cop's blood on this floor. That says enough.'

'Eve.' Roarke touched her shoulder. He turned to Rue. 'You've seen Ricker?'

'Yes. He's—'

'Not here.' He gestured to the side wall. The control panel, as the elevator it operated, was hidden in the mural depicting the fall of Adam. The door slid open to a small private car. They rode silently to the owner's office.

Roarke moved to a friggie behind a smoked mirror, took out chilled bottles of spring water, poured. 'Why don't you sit down, Rue? Conversations with Ricker have a tendency to shake the spirit.'

'Yes, thanks.'

'Aren't we polite?' Furious, Eve gestured away Roarke's offer of water. 'Aren't we just delightful and civilized. You want to trust her, pal, that's your privilege. Don't expect the same consideration from me. She set you up.'

'That's right.' Roarke put the glass in Rue's unsteady hand. 'And now she's returning the favor. And not without risk.'

Roarke took Rue's hand, and though she tried to jerk free, he calmly unbuttoned her cuff and rolled the sleeve up on the arm he'd noticed her favoring.

Dark, ugly bruises ran from wrist to elbow.

'He hurt you. I'm sorry.'

'He likes hurting people. Bruises fade. I'm sure your wife will agree, I deserve a great deal worse.'

'He has fingers like spikes,' was all Eve said, but she felt herself shift inside. 'Why did he use them on you?'

'Because he could, for the most part. If he hadn't believed me, I'd have gotten that and worse. Passing on the information from you put him in a good mood.'

She took a drink, set the glass aside. 'It ran almost exactly as you thought it would. I went to him, asked for money for information. That pissed him off, so I let him push me around a little until I gave it for free. That also cheered him up.'

Absently, she rebuttoned her cuff. 'I told him you were distracted, bad-tempered, how you were cracking the whip to get the place open because it was costing you money to keep the doors closed. That, and your feathers were ruffled because the cops were breathing down your neck. I topped it off by saying I overheard you arguing with your wife.'

'Good.' Roarke sat on the arm of a chair.

'You were going around about the investigation, how it was looking for you, and more, about the position she was putting herself in. You're frantic about that, and pushing her to resign from the force. You two had a real blowup about that.

'I told him there were some hard words about being on opposite sides of the line, and you just lost it. I hope you don't mind that I painted a very clear picture of a man on the edge. You were getting damn tired of walking on eggshells, tired of losing money by keeping your business on her side. A lot of threats and recriminations. You cried,' she said to Eve, not without some satisfaction.

'Well, thanks.'

'He liked that part. Anyway, after you stormed out, I went in, offered Roarke a sympathetic ear. He was prime for it, so we had a couple drinks. That's when you told me you'd had enough of the straight life. You were bored, restless, and your marriage was shaky. Not that you didn't love your wife, but you needed an outlet. She didn't have to know you were dipping back into the pool, did she? You needed something to distract you from worrying about her. And you figured you might kill two birds by going to Ricker and making a deal. A nice quiet business association, the high side of profit for him, and he leaves your wife alone. You're going to get her off the force, but you want her in one piece while you work on that. You're stupid in love with her, but damned if she's going to castrate you and keep you on a leash. I agreed with you, then offered to talk to Ricker for you. That was the part that took him awhile to buy.'

She touched her fingers to her sore arm. 'I convinced him you agreed to it because you haven't been yourself. You'd gone soft and careless in certain areas. I think he swallowed it because it's what he wanted and because he doesn't believe I'd have the guts to lie to him.'

She picked up her glass again, wet her throat. 'It wasn't as bad as I thought it would be,' she decided. 'He was biting at the bait before I'd finished hanging it. The lawyer, Canarde, he doesn't like it, but Ricker told him to shut up. When he didn't, Ricker threw a paperweight at him. Missed, but it left a hell of a dent in the wall.'

'Ah, to be a fly,' Eve murmured.

'It was a moment,' Rue agreed. 'In any case, Canarde shut up then, and Ricker will be here. He won't miss the chance to humiliate you, to grind you under his heel a bit. And if he sniffs out that he should've listened to the lawyer, to take you out where you stand. If he can't have you ruined, he'll have you dead. Those were his words, exactly.'

'Then it's perfect,' Roarke decided, and he felt the thrill of the hunt heat his blood.

'Not quite.' Eve hooked her thumbs in her front pockets, and turned toward Rue. 'Why didn't you have Roarke cry?'

Rue shot her a look of such profound gratitude Eve had hope it was all going to work.

Chapter Twenty-Two

Time was running short. Running two critical operations meant every hour was crammed with two hours' work and worry. She left Purgatory in Roarke's perhaps too-competent hands and, switching gears, drove out to Clooney's suburban house.

'Whitney already had Baxter question the wife,' Peabody said and earned a steel-tipped stare from Eve.

'I'm following up. Do you have a problem with that, Officer?'

'No, sir. No problem at all.'

Time might have been rushing by for Eve, but for Peabody it seemed the next thirty hours were going to crawl like a slug. She decided it best not to mention the surveillance car parked in full view of the single-story ranch house on the postage-stamp lot.

Clooney would spot it, too, if he attempted to get to the house. Maybe that was the point.

Keeping her silence, she followed Eve up the walk, waited at the door.

The woman who opened it might have been pretty in a round, homey way. But at the moment she merely looked exhausted, unhappy, and afraid. Eve identified herself and held up her badge.

'You found him. He's dead.'

'No. No, Mrs Clooney, your husband hasn't been located. May we come in?'

'There's nothing I can tell you that hasn't already been said.' But she turned away, shoulders slumped as if they carried a fierce burden, and walked across the tidy little living area.

Chintz and lace. Faded rugs, old, comfortable chairs. An entertainment screen that had seen better days. And, she noted, a statue of The Virgin – mother of Christ – on a table with her serene, compassionate face looking out over the room.

'Mrs Clooney, I have to ask if your husband's contacted you.'

'He hasn't. He wouldn't. It's just as I told the other detective. I think, somehow, there's been a terrible mistake.' Absently, she pushed a lock of brown hair, as faded as the rugs, away from her face. 'Art hasn't been well, hasn't been himself for a long time. But he wouldn't do the things you're saying he did.'

'Why wouldn't he contact you, Mrs Clooney? You're his wife. This is his home.'

'Yes.' She sat, as if her legs just couldn't hold her up any longer. 'It is. But he stopped seeing that, stopped believing that. He's lost. Lost his way, his hope, his faith. Nothing's been the same to us since Thad died.'

'Mrs Clooney.' Eve sat, leaning forward in an attitude that invited trust and confidence. 'I want to help him. I want to get him the kind of help he needs. Where would he go?'

'I just don't know. I would have once.' She took a tattered tissue from her pocket. 'He stopped talking to me, stopped letting me in. At first, when Thad was killed, we clung together, we grieved together. He was the most wonderful young man, our Thad.'

She looked toward a photograph, in a frame of polished silver, of a young man in full dress uniform. 'We were so proud of him. When we lost him, we held on tight, to each other, to that love and pride. We shared that love and pride with his wife and sweet baby. It helped, having our grandchild close by.'

She rose, picked up another photograph. This time Thad posed with a smiling young woman and a round-cheeked infant. 'What a lovely family they made.'

Her fingers brushed lovingly over the faces before she set the photograph down again, sat.

'Then, a few weeks after we lost Thad, Art began to change, to brood and snap. He wouldn't share with me. He wouldn't go to Mass. We argued, then we stopped even that. Existing in this house,' she said, looking around at the familiar, the comforting, as if it all belonged to strangers, 'instead of living in it.'

'Do you remember, Mrs Clooney, when that change in your husband began?'

'Oh, nearly four months ago. Doesn't seem like a long time, I suppose, when you think of more than thirty years together. But it felt like forever.'

The timing worked, Eve calculated, slid the puzzle piece of the first murder into place.

'Some nights he wouldn't come home at all. And when he did, he slept in Thad's old room. Then he moved out. He told me he was sorry. That he had to set things right before he could be a husband to me again. Nothing I could say could change his mind. And God forgive me, at that point I was so tired, so angry, so empty inside, I didn't care that he was going.'

She pressed her lips together, blinked away the tears. 'I don't know where he is or what he's done. But I want my husband back. If I knew anything that would make that happen, I'd tell you.'

Eve left, canvassed the neighborhood, talked to neighbors, and was given nothing but a picture of puzzled disbelief. Clooney had been a good friend, a loving husband and father, a trusted member of the community.

No one had heard from him – or would admit to it.

'Do you believe them?' Peabody asked as they headed back to the city.

'I believe his wife. She's too afraid and confused to lie.

327

He knows we'd cover the house. Friends and relatives. He's not stupid enough to go to any knowns, but I had to check. We'll go back to Central, run through his data again. Maybe something will click.'

But two hours through, and nothing had. She pressed her fingers to her eyes, thought about more coffee, then opened them and saw Mira in the doorway.

'You're overdoing it, Eve.'

'My back's to the wall. I'm sorry, did we have a meeting?'

'No, but I thought you could use my professional opinion on Clooney at this point.'

'Yeah, I could.' She glanced around, sighed. 'This place is a dump. I wouldn't let the cleaning crew in the last few days. Security clearances aren't enough right now.'

'Don't worry about it.' Mira made herself comfortable with a hip on the side of Eve's desk. 'I don't believe he has, or can, change his agenda. He'll still be focused on you, which means he'll stay close.'

'He said he wouldn't kill another cop, too. But he sure didn't hesitate to slice that knife into Webster.'

'That was impulse rather than calculated. He wanted you, and even then he would have considered it self-defense. You were coming for him. You and a member of Internal Affairs. I believe he's still in the city, still using whatever considerable skill he has to observe and regroup. Wouldn't you?'

'Yeah, that's exactly what I'd do if I'd decided I had to end something, would die trying.' She'd thought it over carefully, in one of her journeys into Clooney's head. 'He means to die, doesn't he, Doctor?'

'Yes, I think so. He'll give you until the stated deadline, and if you don't prove yourself to his satisfaction, he'll try to kill you. He may finish this by an attempted assassination of Ricker, then he will, almost certainly, self-terminate. He will not be able to face his wife, his colleagues, his priest. But he will face his son.'

'I'm not going to let that happen.'

She intended to go straight home. She'd called the hospital to check on Webster and was told there was no change. But, as with Clooney's wife, she had to check for herself.

She strode down the corridor toward ICU, dreading every step. Hating the scent, the sound, the *feel* of the hospital. When the nurse on duty demanded if she was family, she didn't hesitate. She lied.

And moments later found herself in the narrow cubicle, made smaller by the bed and machines, looking down on Webster's white face.

'Well, this is just dandy, isn't it? Didn't I tell you this was going to piss me off? You know how bad it makes me look for you to be lying here, taking the easy way? Damn it, Webster.'

She broke down and laid a hand over his. Cold, she thought. His was too cold. 'You think I have time for this? I'm up to my ears in work, and instead of lending a hand, you're just stretched out hiding in a coma. You'd better get up off your ass.'

She leaned down, spoke clear and strong into his face. 'You hear me, you bastard? You'd better get up off your ass, because I've had too many cops die on my watch just lately. I'm not letting you add to the number. And if you think I'll put a posy on your grave and shed a tear, you are wrong, pal. I'll spit on it.'

She squeezed his hand, waited for a response that didn't come. 'Jerk,' she muttered, with more affection than she'd realized she had for him.

She turned away, came to a skidding halt when she saw Roarke at the door. A thousand thoughts jumbled into her head, and not a single one of them came through clearly.

'I thought you might drop by here.'

'I was just . . .' Her hands found her pockets on the end of a shrug.

'Trying to help a friend,' he finished and crossed to her. He laid his hands on her shoulders, touched his lips to her forehead. The gesture was very gentle, very supportive, and very married. 'Do you think I begrudge that?'

'I guess not. It's a . . . the situation is a little weird, that's all.'

'Do you want to stay with him awhile longer?'

'No. I said what I came to say.' But she glanced back. 'When he comes out of this, I'm going to kick his ass just for the hell of it.'

'I'll hold your coat.' Roarke slipped an arm around her. 'Let's go home, Lieutenant. We have a busy day tomorrow.'

It was busy and went by too quickly. From her station in Security Control, she was able to watch any and every section of the club on-screen.

She argued about the lights – too dim – but he hadn't changed them. She sniped about the music – too loud – but he'd gone his own way there, as well. Now she saw she'd missed one more angle to hassle him over.

The crowd.

She hadn't anticipated the number of people who'd pour in, jam in, elbow in for the club's reopening. She went on slow burn, realizing that Roarke would have anticipated it.

'We don't have enough cops,' she said to Feeney. 'He hasn't been open an hour, and they're packed in like he's offering free drinks and group sex to every second customer.'

'Might be he is. He's got a way with drumming up business. We're okay, Dallas. This security setup'll handle it. Look there, we got a joker in sector two, table six, spiking his lady's drink. A little Exotica'd be my guess.'

'Let Roarke's security handle that kind of thing.' She rested a hand on Feeney's shoulder as they both watched the screen. 'I don't want police interference in the routine.' And she wanted to see just how good his security was.

Damn good, she decided, when within thirty seconds a large man in a black suit strolled up to the table in question, confiscated the drink, and lifted the offender out of his chair in one smooth move.

'Slick and quiet,' Feeney commented. 'That's the way to keep things steady.'

'I don't like it. I don't like the whole deal. Too much can go wrong.'

'Nothing's going to go wrong. You just got the heebie-jeebies.'

'The what?'

'Ants in your pants, nervous twitters.'

'Damn it, Feeney, I've never twittered in my life.'

'Doing it now,' he said solemnly. But there was a chuckle in his tone. 'The man can handle himself, Dallas. Nobody better.'

'Yeah, maybe that's what worries me.' On-screen, she picked Roarke out easily, watched him move through the crowd as if his biggest concern was the cut of his suit.

And she was two floors up, and breaking a sweat.

Because she was two floors up, she admitted. She'd have felt better, been cooler, if she'd been down in the action. Like Peabody, she thought, idling at the bar in plain clothes.

'Peabody, you read?'

At the bar, Peabody gave a barely perceptible nod as Eve's voice hummed in her ear.

'That better be a soft drink you're guzzling.'

Then came the smirk.

For some reason, it made Eve feel better.

The buzzer sounded at the door. With one hand on her weapon, she stepped over, checked the security screen. Disengaging locks, she opened it.

'Martinez, you're away from your station.'

'There's time. Can I have a minute? I didn't have the chance to say it before,' she continued, lowering her voice. 'And if things go the way we want, there won't be time after. I want to thank you for bringing me in on this.'

'You earned it.'

'You better believe it. But you didn't have to bring me in. You ever need a favor from me or my squad, you'll have it.'

'Acknowledged and appreciated.'

'Thought you'd like to know the word on Roth, too. She's getting slapped on record. They're sending in an evaluator, and she's going to be required to submit to counseling. She gets a six-month probationary period before they decide if she keeps her command.'

It was a hard knock for a woman like Roth, Eve mused. But . . . 'Could've been a lot worse for her.'

'Yeah, Some were betting she'd just toss in and resign. But no way. She'll tough it out.'

'Yeah, I think she will. Now, if we've finished our gossip session, get back to your station.'

Martinez flashed a grin. 'Yes, sir.'

Eve secured the door again and returned to the screens. She started to sit, to settle, then tensed. 'God. Why didn't I think of it? That's Mavis. Mavis and Leonardo.' Going with the gut, or the heart, she switched to Roarke's channel.

'Mavis just walked in. She and Leonardo are moving through section five. Get rid of them. Make them go home.'

'I'll take care of them,' was his murmured response, and all she could do was stand by helplessly.

'Roarke!' Mavis gave a squeal of delight, and launched herself, decked out in swirl of blue feathers over a gold body paint job, into his arms. 'The place is mag! Even more mag than before! Where's Dallas? Isn't she here for the big night?'

332

'She's working.'

'Oh, bum-time. Well, we'll keep you company. Listen to that band! They're incendiary. Can't wait to dance.'

'You'll have a better view from the second level.'

'Lots of action down here.'

'There, too.' He'd never get them out, not without an explanation. But he could calm Eve's nerves by moving them as far away as possible. 'Rue?' He signaled his manager. 'These are friends of mine. Get them the best table on the second level. Their tab's on the house.'

'That's gracious of you.' Leonardo clasped hands with Mavis. 'And unnecessary.'

'It's my pleasure. I've got some business to see to shortly. When it's done, I'll come up and join you for a drink.'

'Aw, you're so sweet. We'll see you upstairs later.'

When he was sure they were on their way, Roarke strolled over to McNab. 'Keep an eye on them. Make certain they're tucked up until this is played out.'

'Don't worry,' he replied.

Onstage, the dancers stripped and shimmied and managed to look as though they were enjoying the exercise. While the band pounded out a brutal drum beat, a thin and atmospheric blue mist crawled over the floor.

Prowling around the dancers was a hologram of a snarling black panther wearing a collar of silver spikes. Each time he threw back his head and called, the crowd roared back at him.

Roarke turned his back on gleaming skin and hunting cats and watched Ricker walk into Purgatory.

He hadn't come alone, nor had Roarke expected him to. A dozen men fanned out, scoping the room with hard eyes. Half of them began to move through the crowd.

They would be the front sweep, he concluded, and would be carrying miniscanners, high-powered, to locate and record the security cams, the alarms, the scopes.

They would find only what he'd elected to have them find.

Ignoring them, he cut through the bright glitter of people to face Ricker.

'Okay,' Eve said from her station. 'Run through the marks. I want everyone to acknowledge, everyone to move into first position. Let's do this right.'

And where before she'd sweat out the wait, she was now coldly in command. 'Feeney, give me a weapons check. I want to know who's carrying and how many.'

'Already coming through.'

And so, she thought as she kept her eyes on the screen, was Roarke.

'It's been awhile,' Roarke said.

Ricker's lips curved, just at the corners. 'Quite a long while.' He looked away from Roarke just long enough to sweep his gaze over the club. 'Impressive,' he said with the slightest hint of boredom. 'But a strip club is still a strip club, however it's trimmed.'

'And business is still business.'

'I'd heard you've had a little trouble with yours.'

'Nothing that hasn't been dealt with.'

'Really? You lost a few of your clients last year.'

'I did some . . . restructuring.'

'Ah yes. A wedding present perhaps, to your most charming wife.'

'Leave my wife out of it.'

'Difficult, if not impossible.' It was satisfying, extremely satisfying, to hear that hint of tension in Roarke's voice. There'd been a time, Ricker thought, it wouldn't have shown. 'But we can discuss just what you're willing to trade for that kind of consideration.'

As with an effort, Roarke took a breath, appeared to calm himself. 'We'll use my booth. I'll buy you a drink.'

As he started to turn, one of Ricker's guards laid a hand on his arm, stepped in to check him for weapons. Roarke simply shifted, gripped the man's thumb, and jerked it backward.

Too much weakness too quickly would, after all, be suspect.

'Do that again, and I'll rip it off at the knuckle and feed it to you.' His eyes went back to Ricker's. 'And you know it.'

'I'm glad to see at least that much hasn't changed.' Ricker gestured his man back. 'But you can hardly expect me to have a drink without some basic precautions.'

'Have one of the sweepers scan me and the booth. If that doesn't satisfy, fuck yourself. It's my place now.'

A muscle in Ricker's cheek jumped, and he felt the rush of heat through his gut. But he nodded. 'I never cared for that Irish temper of yours, however colorful. But as you say, it's your place. For the moment.'

'All right,' Eve said. 'They're moving to the booth. Feeney, tell me his system's going to override their scan.'

'It overrode mine. I asked him to show me the design, but he just smiled.' He swiveled toward a secondary monitor. 'Look, see, their sweep's coming up clean, getting just what Roarke said it would get and nothing else. Now we'll settle us down for a little alcoholic refreshment and conversation.'

'Peabody,' Eve said, reading off the weapons scan. 'Your man is left end of the bar, mixed race, black suit. Five-ten, a hundred fifty, shoulder-length black hair. He's armed with a police-issue laser, waist holster. Got him?'

At Peabody's nod, she continued. 'Everyone keep individual targets in close visual range, but do not move in, do *not* move in to apprehend or disarm until ordered. Martinez, your man is . . .'

'Your droid squad stays out of the booth,' Roarke said as he stepped into the tube. 'I don't talk business with an audience.'

'My thoughts exactly.' Ricker moved into the privacy dome, sat as the opening whisked shut behind him.

He had what he wanted now, what he'd planned for over the years. Roarke would beg. Roarke would fall. And if he struggled too hard, too long, the laser scalpel up Ricker's left sleeve would carve considerable regret in that young and handsome face.

'Hell of a view,' he commented as the dancers spun onstage. 'You always did have a taste for women. A weakness for them.'

'True enough. As I recall, you just like to knock them around. You put bruises on my wife.'

'Did I?' Ricker asked innocently. Oh, this is what he craved, what he'd been itching for. So very long. 'How careless of me. Does she know we're having this conversation, or does she let you keep your balls now and then?'

Roarke took out his cigarettes, tapping one on the table as he met Ricker's sneer. An inner struggle showed on his face and made Ricker laugh. Then Roarke turned to the menu. 'Whiskey,' he ordered, lifted a brow.

'The same, for old times' sake.'

'Two whiskeys. Jameson's. Doubles, and straight up.' Then he sat back, lighted the cigarette. 'And I'll say this straight up, and that's for old times' sake as well. My marriage stays out of your reach.'

Roarke's voice took on an edge; then he paused as if to control it. 'You've tried for my wife, and she's tossed what you've sent at her back at you.'

'She's been lucky.' But Ricker's mouth was tight as he reached for one of the glasses of amber liquid that came through the serving slot. 'Luck eventually breaks.'

Roarke's hand shot out. As if he caught himself at the last moment, he drew it back, glancing out toward the guard who had moved closer, whose own hand had drifted under his coat.

'What do you want in trade for a guarantee of her safety?'

'Ah.' Pleased, Ricker sat back again. 'That's a reasonable question. But why, I wonder, should you think I'd offer a reasonable answer to it?'

'I'll make it worth your while,' Roarke said quickly. Too quickly for pride or business sense.

'That will take some doing.' Thrilled, already desperate to push, he leaned forward. 'You see, I find I enjoy hurting your wife.'

'Listen—'

'No, you'll listen. You'll shut that arrogant mouth of yours as I should have shut it for you years ago, and you'll listen. Do you understand?'

'The man must have a death wish.'

Roarke heard Feeney's voice clearly enough, appreciated the truth of his observation. He fisted both hands on the table, let his breath in and out audibly. 'Yes, I understand. Just give me some terms, damn it. We're businessmen. Tell me what you want.'

'Please.'

Christ, you miserable prick, Roarke thought. Carefully, he cleared his throat, picked up his whiskey. Drank. 'Please. Tell me what you want.'

'Better. Much better. A number of years ago, you rashly severed our association, and did so in a manner that cost me one point two million in cash and merchandise and twice that in reputation and goodwill. So, to start, I'll take ten million, in U.S. dollars.'

'And what, precisely, will that ten million buy me?'

'Precisely, Roarke? Your wife's life. Transfer that amount to an account I'll give you by midnight tonight, or I will initiate the contract on her that I have pending.'

'You need to give me a little time to—'

'Midnight, or I terminate her.'

'Even you should hesitate before contracting on a cop, and such a high-profile one.'

337

'I owe you a great deal more than one cop. Your choice. Keep the money, lose the woman.' He ran the saber points of his nails over the side of the glass in a nasty, shrieking sound. 'It's not negotiable.'

'That's enough right there,' Eve murmured. 'It's enough to put him away.'

'He'll get more.' Feeney shifted in his seat. 'He's just warming up.'

'She's worth ten million to me, but . . .' Roarke lifted his glass, sipped slowly now, as if calculating. 'I believe we forge a truer trust in this matter by adding to the arrangement. I'm interested in more than a single deal. I have some funds I'd prefer to invest in a manner that doesn't require government scrutiny.'

'Tired of being an upstanding citizen?'

'In a word? Yes.' He shrugged, glanced around, and let his gaze linger just a moment too long on the dancer grinding out her routine on the other side of the dome.

And in doing so, he felt Ricker's amusement.

'I'm considering changing my home base, doing some traveling. I'm looking for some new business ventures. Something with some juice.'

'And you're coming to me? You would dare to come to me, as if we're equals? You'll have to crawl before I throw you a scrap.'

'Then this conversation is pointless.' Roarke shrugged again, but made it jerky, drained his glass.

'You used to be so cocky, so cold. Now look at you. She's sucked you dry. Gone soft, haven't you? Forgotten what it's like to give orders that change lives. That end them. I could end yours now with a snap of my finger.' Ricker's eyes gleamed as he leaned close, whispered. 'Maybe I will, for old times' sake.'

It was brutally hard not to smash that leering face with his fist and take out the guard with his hand under his coat.

'Then you won't get your ten million or anything else from me. Maybe you have a right to be angry with the way I backed out on you before.'

'Backed out? Backed out?' He pounded his fist on the table, shouting so that at the control station, Feeney's ears rang. 'You betrayed me, stole from me. You threw my generosity back in my face. I should have killed you for it. Perhaps I still will.'

'You want payback, Ricker, for what I did, or didn't do, I'm willing to pay. I'm willing. I know what you're capable of. I respect that.'

For effect, Roarke added a slight tremor to his hand as he ordered a second round. 'I've still got sources and resources. We can be an asset to each other. My connection to the NYPSD is valuable in itself.'

Ricker let out a short laugh. His chest was hurting from the pounding of his heart. He didn't want another whiskey. He wanted his beautiful pink drink. But he would finish first. Finish Roarke first. 'I don't need your cop, you pathetic fool. I've got a whole damn squad in my pocket.'

'Not like her.' Roarke edged forward, eager to deal. 'I want her out, but until I convince her, she can be useful. Very useful to you.'

'She's barely useful to you. Rumor is you and she are having some marital difficulties.'

'Just some bumps. They'll pass. The ten million will help that,' Roarke said as he took the second round of drinks. 'It takes the pressure off. And I'll get her to resign before much longer. I'm working on it.'

'Why? As you said, a police connection's useful.'

'I want a wife, not a bloody cop. I prefer having my woman available at my convenience, not running around all hours of the day and night investigating cases.' Scowling now, he drank deeply. 'A man's entitled to that, isn't he? If I want a cop, I'll buy one. I don't have to marry one.'

339

It was better, Ricker calculated. Even better than he'd expected. He'd have Roarke's money, his humiliation, and his obligation. And he could hold all of them until he killed him. 'I can arrange it for you.'

'Arrange what?'

'Her resignation. I'll have her out in a month's time.'

'In return for?'

'This place. I want it back. And there's a little matter of a shipment I'm expecting. The client I anticipated for it hasn't proved financially solvent. Take it off my hands for, we'll say, another ten million, turn the deed to this club over to one of my subsidiaries, and we'll have a deal.'

'What's the merchandise?'

'Pharmaceuticals.'

'You know I don't have the contacts to deal in illegals.'

'Don't tell me what you do or don't have.' Ricker's voice spiked, all but cracked. 'Who do you think you are to turn your nose up at me.' He lunged over the table, grabbed Roarke by the collar. 'I want what I want!'

'He's unstable. We need to move in.' She was already striding out of the room when Feeney called out.

'Hold on! Let it play out.'

'I can't stay up here.'

'I'm not turning up my nose,' Roarke said quickly, nervously. 'I haven't developed the sources for illegals distribution.'

'That's your problem. *Your* problem. You'll do what I say, all that I say, or get nothing. Take the deal or the consequences.'

'Let me think, for God's sake. Pull your men back. Let's not have any trouble in here.'

'Fine, that's fine. No trouble.'

Well, he's mad, Roarke thought. *Stark and raving.* The rumors of Ricker's instability hadn't touched on the reality.

'Twenty million's a lot of money. But I'm willing to risk

it to get what I want. And to . . . pay the debt I owe you. But I need to know how you'd work her out of the department without it coming back on me.'

It was Ricker's breathing that was audible now, but he didn't hear it. He picked up his whiskey, and his hand trembled, but he didn't see it. All he saw was the fulfillment of a long-cherished wish.

'I can ruin her career inside of a week. Yes, in no time at all. Strings to be pulled. The case she's working on now . . . she annoys me. She insulted me. Laughed at me.'

'She'll apologize.' Roarke all but crooned it. 'I'll see to it.'

'Yes, she'll have to do that. Have to apologize. I won't tolerate anyone laughing at me. Especially a woman.'

He had to be pushed, Roarke thought. Gently and quickly. 'She will. You have the controls. You have the power.'

'That's right. Of course. I do. If I let her live, as a favor to you, I'll take a fee for moving her off the case and out of the department. Misinformation, skewed data in the right computer. It works.'

Roarke rubbed the back of his hand over his mouth. 'The cops who've been killed. For Christ's sake, Ricker, you're behind that?'

'And there'll be more before it's done. It amuses me.'

'I don't want any part in cop killing. They'll bury you.'

'Don't be ridiculous. They'll never touch me. I didn't kill anyone. I simply put the idea in the right head, the weapon in the most vulnerable hand. Just a game. You remember how fond I am of games? And how I enjoy winning them.'

'Yes, I remember. No one did it better. How did you pull this off?'

'Arrangements, Roarke. I enjoy arrangements and watching how the pieces fall into place.'

'I sleep with a woman in the department, and I can't

get that close.' Roarke's voice filled with admiration. 'I underestimated you. It must have taken years to set up.'

'Months. Only a few months. It's simply a matter of selecting the right target. A young cop, too stiff-necked to play the game. Eliminating him is simple enough, but the beauty is how it can be connected, how it can be *expanded* upon by planting the seeds in the heart of the grieving father. Then I simply sit back and watch a once-dedicated cop kill. Again and again. And it costs me nothing.'

'Brilliant,' Roarke murmured.

'Yes, and satisfying. Best, I can do it again, any time I like. Murder by proxy. No one's safe, certainly not you. Transfer the money, and until the wind changes, I'll protect you. And your wife.'

'That was twenty million?'

'For the moment.'

'A bargain,' Roarke said quietly, brought the hand he'd slipped under the table, under his jacket back into view. And the gun with it. 'But I find the idea of doing business with you turns my stomach. Oh, tell your man to hold, or it'll give me great pleasure to use this. Recognize it, Ricker? It's one of the banned weapons you trafficked in, years back. I have quite a collection of twentieth-century handguns – and a collector's license. They leave a horrible nasty hole in a man. This one's a nine-millimeter Glock and will blow your face right off the skull.'

The shock of having a weapon aimed at him robbed Ricker of speech. It had been years, a lifetime, since anyone had dared. 'You've lost your mind.'

'No, indeed. Mine's sound enough.' He slapped a hand on Ricker's wrist, twisted viciously until the laser scalpel fit into his own palm. 'You always had a weakness for sharp things.'

'You'll die painfully for this. Painfully. Do you think you'll walk out of this place breathing?'

'Certainly. Ah, there's my wife now. Lovely, isn't she? And by the sound of things through the scanner your inferior sweepers missed, it appears your team of fools is even now being rounded up and moved along.'

He waited while Ricker focused beyond him, through the dome, and saw for himself.

'One of us has lost his touch, Ricker, and it appears to be you. I set you up, and it was child's play.'

'For a cop.' Eyes wild, Ricker leaped to his feet. 'You rolled on me for a cop.'

'I'd have done it for a mongrel dog, given half the chance. Ah, please, try for it,' Roarke murmured. 'And make my life worth living.'

'Enough. Roarke, back off.' Eve opened the door to the booth, slide her police issue into Ricker's ribs.

'You're dead. You're both dead.' He whirled, backhanded Eve as he leaped. She took the blow and dropped him.

'Tell me you had it on full.'

'He's stunned, that's all.' She wiped the blood from her mouth with her sleeve and ignored the scramble of people who rushed away from the trouble. Onstage, the strippers continued to dance.

Roarke handed her a handkerchief, then reached down, lifting Ricker's head off the floor by his throat.

'Don't—'

'Keep back,' he snapped as Eve crouched to hold him off. 'You'll bloody well keep back till I've finished this.'

'If you kill him, it's been for nothing.'

He stared at her face, and all the strength, the purpose, all the danger he hadn't shown to Ricker leaped out of them. 'It would be for everything, but I don't mean to kill him.' To prove it, he handed her the Glock.

But he kept the scalpel and, holding its keen point to the pulse in Ricker's throat, imagined. 'You can hear me, can't you, Ricker? You can hear me well enough. I'm the one who took you down, and you'll remember it while you're pacing the box they'll put you in. You'll think of it every day with what's left of your mind.'

'Kill you,' Ricker choked out, but he couldn't so much as lift his hand.

'Well, you haven't managed that as yet, have you? But you're welcome to try again. Listen to me now, and carefully. Touch her, put your hand on what's mine again, and I'll follow you to hell and peel the skin from your bones. I'll feed you your own eyes. I take an oath on it. Remember what I was, and you'll know I'll do it. And worse.'

He straightened again, his body rigid. 'Get someone to drag him out of here. This is my place.'

Chapter Twenty-Three

She didn't sleep long, but she slept deeply, knowing Ricker was in a cage. He'd screamed for his lawyer, quite literally, once the effects of the stun had worn off.

Since she'd whipped right around and dumped Canarde in a cage as well, Ricker's lawyer was going to be a very busy boy for awhile.

She'd made two copies of every record disc of the operation in Purgatory. She sealed all of them, and secured one copy in her home office.

There would be no lost evidence, no missing data, no damaged files this time around.

And they had him cold.

She told herself it was enough, would have to be enough, then had tumbled into bed. She switched off like a frayed circuit, then came awake with a jolt when Roarke put a hand on her shoulder and said her name.

'What.' Instinctively, she reached down where her weapon would have been had she not been naked.

'Easy, Lieutenant. I'm unarmed. And so are you.'

'I was . . . whoa.' She shook her head to clear it. 'Out.'

'I noticed. I'm sorry to wake you.'

'Why are you up? Why are you dressed? What time is it?'

'A bit past seven. I had some early calls to take. And while I was at it, one came in. From the hospital.'

'Webster,' she whispered. She hadn't checked on him the night before after the operation was complete. *and now . . .* too late, she thought.

'He's awake,' Roarke continued, 'and it seems he'd like to see you.'

'Awake? Alive and awake?'

'Apparently both. He improved last night. He's still in serious condition, but stable. They're cautiously hopeful. I'll take you.'

'You don't need to do that.'

'I'd like to. Besides, if he thinks I'm guarding my territory . . .' He lifted her hand, nipped the knuckle. 'It might cheer him up.'

'Territory, my ass.'

'Your ass is, I'll point out, my exclusive territory.'

She tossed the cover aside, and gave him a good view of that territory as she dashed toward the shower. 'I'll be ready in ten minutes.'

'Take your time. I don't believe he's going anywhere.'

She took twenty, because he bribed her with coffee. And she indulged in a second cup as he got behind the wheel. 'Do we take him flowers or something?'

'I think not. If you did that, the shock would likely put him back in a coma.'

'You're such a funny guy, and so early in the morning, too.' She sipped her coffee, bided her time. 'That, um, phrase – feed you your own eyes? Is that some kind of Irish curse?'

'Not that I'm aware of.'

'So you just made it up on the spot last night? I've said it before, and I'll say it again: You're scary.'

'I'd have killed him for striking you if you hadn't been in the way.'

'I know it.' So she'd made certain she'd stayed in the way. 'You had no business bringing that handgun. Carrying a banned weapon into a public place. You know how much dancing I'm going to have to do on that one?'

'Who says it was loaded?'

'Was it?'

'Of course, but who's to say? Relax, Lieutenant. You brought him down.'

'No, I didn't. You did.'

'Compromise,' he decided. 'Which we've neglected to do just lately. *We* brought him down.'

'I'll take that. One more thing. All that business about a man having this right and that right, and wanting your woman when you want her. That was just show, right?'

'Are you going to share that coffee?'

She moved it just a little farther out of reach. 'No. It was just show. Right?'

'Well, now, let me think. It might be nice to have the little woman puttering about the house and meeting me at the door of an evening, after a hard day's business, with a smile and a drink. That's a lovely image, isn't it?'

He turned to see her snarling at him and laughed. 'How long before we'd be bored brainless with it, do you figure?'

'It's a good thing you said that before I wasted this very nice coffee by pouring it into your lap. But I'm still not sharing it.'

When they turned into hospital parking, she shifted on her seat to face him. 'It's going to take several days to close this Ricker business and hand it over to the PA. His psych evaluation is going to be one big mess, seeing as he's loon crazy.'

'He'll end up in a mental defective prison unit.'

'Oh yeah, and believe me, they're no picnic. Anyway, we've got a lot of people to interview, and I can't calculate how many of his businesses and properties to search and seize. I'm letting Martinez take the bulk of it, but I'm still going to be tied up for awhile. If you can put off the trip you need to take to Olympus, I'd like to go with you.'

He pulled into a slot, stopped the car. 'You'd voluntarily take off several days? Not only that, but go off planet without me having to drug you?'

'I said I'd like to go with you. If you're going to make a big deal out of it, we can just—'

'Quiet down.' He leaned over, kissed her sulky mouth. 'I'll put it off until we can go together.'

'Okay. Good.' She climbed out of the car. Stretched. 'Look, there's some whattayacallems.'

'Daffodils,' he said and caught her hand in his. 'Daffodils, Eve. It's spring.'

'Finally feels like it, too.'

She kept her hand in his as they walked into the hospital, and all the way to Webster's tiny room.

His face wasn't gray as it had been the last time she'd been there, but it wasn't pink with health, either. Instead, it was as white as the bandages stretched across his chest.

She felt a trip of alarm cut into her cheerful mood as he lay, silent and still.

'I thought they said he was awake.'

Even as she said it, in a sickroom whisper, Webster's eyes fluttered open. They stayed dazed for a moment with the baffled, vulnerable look of the very ill. Then, as they focused the faintest glint of humor shot into them. 'Hey.'

She had to step closer; his voice was pitifully thin.

'You didn't have to bring the guard dog. I'm too weak to make a half-decent pass at you.'

'You never worried me in that area, Webster.'

'I know. Damn it. Thanks for coming.'

'It's okay. It's not much out of my way.'

He started to laugh, lost his breath, then just lay there concentrating on finding it again.

'You stupid bastard.' She said it with enough passion to bring that baffled look back on his face.

'Huh?'

'You think I can't handle myself? That I need some idiot IAB moron half-ass to knock me down and stick out his chest for a knife?'

'No.' The humor was coming back. 'I don't know what got into me.'

'If you'd stuck with the streets instead of getting fat and happy behind a stupid desk, you wouldn't be lying here. And when you're on your feet, I'm going to put you right back in the hospital.'

'That'll be fun. Give me something to look forward to. Did you get him? They won't tell me a damn thing in here.'

'No. No, I didn't get him.'

'Shit.' He closed his eyes again. 'That's on me.'

'Oh, shut up.' She stalked to the tiny window, fisted her hands on her hips, while she tried to calm down.

In her place, Roarke moved to the side of the bed. 'Thank you.'

'You're welcome.'

And that was all they needed to say on the subject.

'We got Ricker,' Eve continued, as her anger abated. 'Took him down last night.'

'What? How?' Webster tried to sit up, couldn't even lift his head. And swore with as much energy as he could muster.

'It's a long story. I'll fill you in some other time. But we got him, solid, and have his lawyer on the hot seat for good measure, and a dozen of his men.'

She turned back, walked to the bed. 'He's going to stay in MD status by the looks of things, and we're going to take his organization apart, piece by piece.'

'I can help. Do some of the data searches, run scans. Let me in on this. I'll go crazy in here with nothing to do.'

'Stop, you're breaking my heart.' Then she shrugged. 'I'll think about it.'

'Come on, you know you'll cave on it. You feel sorry for me.' He managed a grin. 'And I should tell you, both of you,

349

so there's no baggage, I'm pretty much on the way to getting over you.'

'That really adds to my peace of mind, Webster.'

'It does a lot for mine. Only took getting sliced in half, more or less. Nothing like a good coma to give a guy the opportunity to put things in perspective.'

His eyes drooped, nearly shut before he fought them open again. 'Man, the meds just knock you out.'

'So, get some sleep. Word gets out you're coming around, you'll have plenty of company. You'll need all the rest you can manage.'

'Yeah, but wait.' He was losing it, struggling to hold out another minute. 'I gotta ask you a question. Did you come in before?'

'Before what?'

'Come on, Dallas. Before now. Did you come in and talk to me?'

'Maybe I dropped in to see what an idiot looked like. Why?'

''Cause I had this dream. Maybe a dream. You were standing over me. I was just floating and you were standing there, ragging my ass. Ever tell you how sexy you look when you're ragging ass?'

'Jesus.'

'Sorry, a little re . . . residual lust. D'ya say you'd spit on my grave?'

'Yeah. I will, too, if you try to cash out again.'

He gave a weak chuckle. 'Who's the idiot? Not gonna have a grave. You gotta be rich or religious these days for that. Recycle and cremation, thatsa way to go. Return and burn. Sure nice to hear your voice though. Made me think I'd prob'ly get bored floating. Gotta go. Tired.'

'Yeah, you go on.' And because he was asleep, and Roarke would understand, she gave his hand a little pat. 'He'll be okay.'

'Yes, he'll be okay.'

'I think he was glad you came along.' She pushed a hand through her hair. 'Return and burn. What a jerk. But I guess he's right. Graves are out of style, mostly. Except . . . Oh no.' She whirled to Roarke. 'I *am* such an idiot. Rich or religious. I know where he'll go, where he'll go to end it. You drive.'

She was already out of the room, running down the hall.

'His son's grave.'

'Yeah, yeah.' She yanked out her PPC. 'Where the hell is it? They'd have one. People who have religious statues in the living room want to bury their dead and put crosses up.'

'I'll find it faster.' He had his own unit out as they hit the elevator. 'Call your backup.'

'No, no backup, not yet. I have to find him first, to be sure. Son's name was Thad. Thadeus Clooney.'

'I've got it. Three plots, Sunlight Memorial. New Rochelle.'

'Near the house. Makes sense.' She exchanged her PPC for her communicator as she strode across the lobby and out to the lot. 'Peabody. Listen up.'

'Sir? Dallas?'

'Wake up, get dressed. You're on call.' She climbed into the car. 'I want you to get a squad car, have it and an officer ready to transport you. I'm following a lead on Clooney. If it pans out, I'll contact you. I want you to move fast.'

'Where? Where are you going?'

'Back to the dead,' Eve said. 'Push this thing,' she added as Roarke headed out of the lot. 'He could have heard about Ricker by now.'

'Strap in,' Roarke advised, and he punched the accelerator.

The dead rested in sunlight and dappled shade, in gentle green hills, with markers of soft white, soft gray. The rows of them, the crosses and curves, made Eve wonder how the living could find comfort there, faced with the unassailable proof of their own mortality.

But some must. For even in these days when few chose to go into the ground or could afford the real estate, many of the graves were splashed with flowers. That symbol of life given to the dead.

'Which way?'

Roarke had a diagram of the cemetery on his pocket screen. 'To the left, over that rise.'

They walked around the markers together. 'The first time I spoke to you,' she remembered, 'we were in a graveyard. Kind of creepy, I guess.'

'Apt.' He laid a hand on her shoulder. 'There he is. Your instincts are excellent.'

She paused, taking a moment to study the man sitting on the tended grass beside a flower-strewn grave. And the marker was indeed a cross, pure and white.

'I need you to hang back.'

'No.'

Saying nothing, she crouched, pulled out her clinch piece. 'I'm trusting you not to use this unless you have no choice.' She handed it to him. 'Trust me to do my job. I need to try to talk him in. I'm asking you to let me give him that chance. Compromise.'

'All right.'

'Thanks. Call Peabody. Tell her where to come. I need her here.'

Alone, she walked down the gentle slope and through the graves. He knew she was coming. He was cop enough to hold his ground, to bide his time, but she saw from the slightest shift in his body, he knew.

Better that way, she thought. She preferred not to surprise him.

'Sergeant.'

'Lieutenant.' He still didn't look at her, didn't take his

attention from the name carved in that perfect white cross. 'I want you to know I'm carrying. I don't want to harm you.'

'I appreciate that. You should know I'm carrying, and I don't want to harm you, either. I need to talk to you, Sergeant. Can I sit down here?'

He looked at her then. His eyes were dry, but she could see he'd been weeping. There were still tracks of the tears on his cheeks. And she saw, too, that his weapon, the same make and model as her own, was in the hand resting in his lap.

'You've come to take me in. I don't intend to go.'

'Can I sit down?'

'Sure. Sit. It's a good spot for it. That's why we picked it. But I always thought that Thad would be the one to sit here, to sit and talk to me and his mother. Not that I would be the one to sit. He was the light of my life.'

'I read his service record.' She sat on the opposite side of the grave. 'He was a good cop.'

'Yeah, he was. Oh, I was proud of him. The way he carried himself, the way he took to the job like he was born to it. Maybe he was. I was always proud of him, though, from the first instant they put him in my arms and he was squalling and wriggling. All that life in one little package.'

With his free hand, he brushed at the grass that grew over his son. 'You don't have children as yet, do you, Lieutenant?'

'No.'

'I'll tell you that whatever you feel for anyone, however much love's inside you, there's more of it when you have a child. You can't understand it until you've experienced it. And it doesn't change as they grow into men, into women. It just grows with them. It should be me in there, and not my boy. Not my Thad.'

'We took Ricker.' She said it quickly, because she'd seen his hand tighten on his weapon.

'I know it.' And relax again. 'I heard it on-screen in the

little room where I've been staying. My hidey-hole. We all need our hidey-holes, don't we?'

'He's going down for your son, Sergeant.'

She used his rank, and would use it, again and again, to remind him what he was.

'I want you to know that. Conspiracy to commit murder. The murder of a police officer. And he'll go down for the others, the same way. With everything else we'll nail on, he'll never get out of a cage. He'll die there.'

'It's some comfort. I never thought you were part of it. Not in my gut. I can't say I've been clear in my mind for the last bit of time. After Taj . . .'

'Sergeant—'

'I took that boy's life, a life as innocent as my son's. Made a widow of his sweet wife, and took away a good father from those babies. I'll carry that regret, that shame, that horror to my own grave.'

'Don't.' She said it quietly, urgently, as he lifted his weapon and placed it to the pulse at his throat. It would be lethal there. And on maximum setting would end it instantly. 'Wait. Is that the way you honor your son, by taking another life on his grave? Is that what Thad would want? Is that what he'd expect from his father?'

He was so tired. It showed in his face now, in his voice. 'What else is there?'

'I'm asking you to listen to me. If you're set on this, I can't stop you. But you owe me some time.'

'Maybe I do. The boy who was with you when you came to my door, when I knew you knew. I panicked. Panicked,' he said again like an oath. 'I don't even know who he was.'

'His name's Webster. Lieutenant Don Webster. He's alive, Sergeant. He's going to be okay.'

'I'm glad of that. One less stone to carry.'

'Sergeant . . .' She fumbled for the words. 'I'm a murder

354

cop,' she began. 'You ever work Homicide?' She knew he
hadn't. She knew it all.

'No, not as such. But you deal with it wherever you are if
you're a cop. And you deal with it too much if you've been
one as long as me.'

'I work for the dead. I can't count the number of them I've
stood over. I don't think I could stand to try. But I dream of
them. All those lost faces, those stolen lives. It's hard.'

She was surprised she was telling him this, surprised it
seemed the way. 'Sometimes it's so hard to see those faces
in your sleep, you wake up hurting. But I can't do anything
else. I've wanted to be a cop as long as I can remember. It
was my one clear vision, and it's all I can do.'

'Are you a good cop?' The tears were overflowing again.
In sympathy or despair, she couldn't tell. 'Eve. Your name's
Eve, isn't it? Are you a good cop, Eve?'

'Yeah. I'm a damn good cop.'

Now he wept, and she felt her eyes tear up in concert.
'Thad, he wanted the same as you. The one clear vision. I
like that. Yeah, his one clear vision. They let him bleed to
death. They let him die. And for what? For what? Money. It
rips my heart.'

'They've paid, Sergeant. I can't tell you what you did was
right, or what the judgement on you will be in the end of
things. But they've paid for what they did to your boy, for
what they did to their badge. Ricker's going to pay, too, I
swear it to you, here on the grave of this good cop. He'll pay
for playing them all like puppets. He played you, too. Played
on your love for your son. Your grief. Your pride. Will you
let him keep pulling your strings? Will you dishonor yourself
and your son by letting him win?'

'What can I do?' Tears streamed down his cheeks. 'I've
lost. I'm lost.'

'You can do what Thad would expect of you. You can
face it.'

'I'm shamed,' he whispered. 'I thought when it was over, I'd be glad. I'd be free. But I'm shamed.'

'You can make up for it, best you can. You can erase some of the shame. You can come with me, Sergeant. You can be a cop now and come with me.'

'Prison or death.' He looked at her again. 'Those are hard choices.'

'Yes, very hard. Harder to live, Sergeant, and balance the scales. Let the system make its judgement on you. That's what we believe in, people like us, what we work for when we pick up the badge. I'm asking you to do that, Sergeant. I'm asking you not to be one of the faces I see in my sleep.'

He bowed his head, rocked, so his tears fell on the flowers he'd laid on the grass. He reached out a hand across the grave, clasped Eve's. Clung. She sat like that while he sobbed.

Then he leaned forward, pressed his lips to the white cross. 'I miss him. Every day.' With a sigh, he held out his weapon to Eve. 'You'll want this.'

'Thank you.' She got to her feet, waiting for him to get laboriously to his.

He wiped his face with his sleeve, drew in a breath. 'I'd like to call my wife.'

'She'll be glad to hear from you. I don't want to put restraints on you, Sergeant Clooney. I'd like you to give me your word you'll go with my aide and walk into Central of your own volition.'

'You have my word on it. Eve. It's a good name. I'm glad it was you who came today. I won't forget it was you. It's spring,' he said as they walked up the rise. 'I hope you'll take time to enjoy it. Winter comes too soon, and always lasts too long.'

He paused at the top where Peabody waited with Roarke. 'Those faces in your dreams? Have you thought they might be coming to thank you?'

'No. I guess I never thought of that. Officer Peabody will

accompany you in the black and white, Sergeant. I'll follow you in. Officer, Sergeant Clooney is turning himself in.'

'Yes, sir. Will you come with me, Sergeant?'

As they moved off, Eve slipped Clooney's weapon into her pocket. 'I thought I was going to lose him.'

'No, you had him the minute you sat down.'

'Maybe.' She blew out a breath. 'It's a hell of a lot easier just to put a boot to their throats. He got to me.'

'Yes. And you to him.' He crouched down, and to her amusement, tugged up her trouser leg and slipped her weapon back into the ankle harness. 'Our own variation on Cinderella.'

The laugh went a long way to easing the rawness around her heart. 'Well, Prince Charming, I'd ask for a lift to the ball, but how about giving me one in to work?'

'My pleasure.'

They linked hands, skirted around a young tree with leaves unfurling tender green. And walked away from the dead.

If you enjoyed *Judgement in Death*, you won't want to
miss J.D. Robb's next thrilling novel . . .

BETRAYAL

IN

DEATH

Chapter One

In death there were many layers. Violent death added more. It was her job to sift through those layers and find cause. In cause, to meet justice.

However the act of murder was committed, in cold blood or hot, she was sworn to pursue it to its root. And serve the dead.

For tonight, Lieutenant Eve Dallas of the New York City Police and Security Department wore no badge. It, along with her service weapon and communicator, was currently tucked in an elegant, palm-sized silk purse she considered embarrassingly frivolous.

She wasn't dressed like a cop, but wore a shimmering apricot-hued gown that skimmed down her long, slim body and was sliced in a dramatic V in the back. A slender chain of diamonds hung glittering around her neck. More sparkled at ears she recently, and in a weak moment, had been persuaded to have pierced.

Still more were scattered like raindrops through her short chop of brown hair and made her feel faintly ridiculous.

However glamorous the silk and diamonds made her appear, her eyes were all cop. Tawny brown and cool, they scanned the sumptuous ballroom, skimmed over faces, bodies, and considered security.

Cameras worked into the fancy plasterwork overhead were unobtrusive, powerful, and would provide full scope. Scanners would flag any guests or staff who happened to be carrying concealeds. And among the staff, weaving their way through the chatter to offer drinks, were a half-dozen trained security personnel.

The affair was invitation only, and those invitations carried a holographic seal that was scanned at the door.

The reason for these precautions, and others, was an estimated five hundred and seventy-eight million dollars' worth of jewelry, art, and memorabilia currently on dazzling display throughout the ballroom.

Each display was craftily arranged for impact and guarded by individual sensor fields that measured motion, heat, light, and weight. If any of the guests or staff had sticky fingers and attempted to remove so much as an earring from its proper place, all exits would close and lock, alarms would sound, and a second team of guards hand-selected from an elite NYPSD task force would be ordered to the scene to join the private security.

To her cynical frame of mind, the entire deal was a foolishly elaborate temptation for too many, in too large an area, in too public a venue. But it was tough to argue with the slick setup.

Then again, slick was just what she expected from Roarke.

'Well, Lieutenant?' The question, delivered with a whiff of amusement in a voice that carried the misty air of Ireland, drew her attention to the man.

Then again, everything about Roarke drew a woman's attention.

His eyes, sinfully blue, set off a face that had been sculpted on one of God's best days. As he watched her, his poet's mouth, one that often made her want to lean in for just one quick bite, curved, one dark brow lifted, and his long fingers skimmed possessively down her bare arm.

They'd been married nearly a year, and that sort of casually intimate stroke could still trip her pulse.

'Some party,' she said and turned his smile into a fast, devastating grin.

'Yes, isn't it?' With his hand still lightly on her arm, he scanned the room.

His hair was black as midnight and fell nearly to his shoulders into what she thought of as his wild Irish warrior look. Add to that the tall, tautly muscled build in elegant black-tie, and you had a hell of a package. Obviously a number of other women in the room agreed. If Eve had been the jealous type, she'd have been forced to kick some major ass just for the hot and avaricious looks aimed in her husband's direction.

'Satisfied with the security?' he asked her.

'I still think holding this business in a hotel ballroom, even your hotel ballroom, is risky. You've got hundreds of millions of dollars' worth of junk sitting around in here.'

He winced a little. 'Junk is not quite the descriptive phrase we hope for in our publicity efforts. Magda Lane's collection of art, jewelry, and entertainment memorabilia is arguably one of the finest to ever go to auction.'

'Yeah, and she'll rake in a mint for it.'

'I certainly hope so, as for handling the arrangements for security, display, and auction Roarke Industries gets a nice piece of the pie.'

He was scanning the room himself, and though he was anything but a cop, he studied, measured, and watched even as his wife had.

'Her name's enough to push the bidding far above actual value. I think we're safe in predicting that twice the actual value will make up that pie by the end of things.'

Boggling, Eve thought. *Boggling*. 'You're figuring people will choke out half a billion for somebody else's things?'

'Conservatively and before the sentiment factors in.'

'Jesus Christ.' She could only shake her head. 'It's just stuff. Wait.' She held up a hand. 'I forgot who I was talking to. The king of stuff.'

'Thank you, darling.' He decided not to mention he had his eye on a few bits of that stuff for himself, and his wife.

He lifted a finger. Instantly a server bearing a tray of champagne in crystal flutes was at his side. Roarke removed two, handed one to Eve. 'Now, if you've finished eyeballing my security arrangements, perhaps you could enjoy yourself.'

'Who says I wasn't?' But she knew she was here not as a cop, but as the wife of Roarke. That meant mingling, rubbing shoulders. And the worst of human tortures in her estimation: small talk.

Because he knew her mind as thoroughly as he knew his own, he lifted her hand, kissed it. 'You're so good to me.'

'And don't you forget it. Okay.' She took a bracing sip of champagne. 'Who do I have to talk to?'

'I think we should start with the woman of the hour. Let me introduce you to Magda. You'll like her.'

'Actors,' Eve muttered.

'Biases are so unattractive. In any case,' he began as he led her across the room, 'Magda Lane is far more than an actor. She's a legend. This marks her fiftieth year in the business, one which often chews up and spits out those who dream of it. She's outlasted every trend, every style, every change in the movie industry. It takes more than talent to do that. It takes spine.'

It was as close as Eve had ever seen him to having stars in his eyes. And that made her smile. 'Stuck on her, are you?'

'Absolutely. When I was a boy in Dublin, there was a particular evening where I needed a bit of a dodge off the streets. Seeing as I had several lifted wallets and other pocket paraphernalia on my person and the garda on my heels.'

The wide mouth she'd forgotten to dye for the evening sneered. 'Boys will be boys.'

'Well, be that as it may, I happened to duck into a theater. I was eight or thereabouts and resigned myself to sitting through some costume drama I imagined would bore me senseless. And there sitting in the dark, I had my first look at Magda Lane as Pamela in *Pride's Fall*.'

He gestured toward the display of a sweeping white ball-gown that shimmered under a firestorm of icy stones. The droid replica of the actor turned in graceful circles, dipped into delicate curtsies, fluttered a sparkling white fan.

'How the hell did she walk around in that?' Eve wondered. 'Looks like it weighs a ton.'

He had to laugh. It was so Eve to see the inconvenience rather than the glamour. 'Nearly thirty pounds of costume, I'm told. I said she had spine. In any case, she was wearing that the first time I saw her on screen. And for an hour I forgot where I was, who I was, that I was hungry or that I'd likely get a fist in the face when I got home if the wallets weren't plump enough. She drew me out of myself. That's a powerful thing.'

He avoided interruption by simply aiming a smile or wave in the direction of those who called him. 'I went back and saw *Pride's Fall* four times that summer, and paid for it. Well, paid the fee once anyway. After, whenever I needed to be drawn out of myself, I went to the movies.'

She was holding his hand now, well able to visualize the boy he'd been, sitting in the dark, transported away by the images flickering on screen.

At the age of eight he'd discovered another world outside the misery and violence of the one he lived in.

And at eight, she thought, *Eve Dallas had been born to a young girl too broken to remember anything that had come before.*

Wasn't it almost the same thing?

Eve recognized the actor. Roarke didn't really go to the movies these days – unless you counted his private theaters – but he had copies on disc of thousands of them. She'd watched more screen in the past year with him than she had in the previous thirty.

Magda Lane wore red. Screaming siren red that painted a stunning and voluptuous body like a work of art. At sixty-three she was just dipping into middle age. From what Eve could see, she was approaching it with a snarl. This was nobody's matron.

Her hair was the color of ripening wheat and tumbled to her bare shoulders in snaking spirals. Her lips, full and lush as her body, were painted the same bold red as her gown. Skin, pale as milk, was unlined and highlighted by a beauty mark just at the outer point of one slashing eyebrow.

Beneath those contrastingly dark brows were eyes of fierce and brilliant green. They landed on Eve coolly, a female to female measuring, then shifted to Roarke and warmed like suns.

She was surrounded by people, and simply shot them a careless smile, then stepped out of the circle, hands outstretched.

'My God, but you're gorgeous.'

Roarke took her hands, kissed both. 'I was about to say the same. You're stunning, Magda. As ever.'

'Yes, but that's my job. You were just born that way. Lucky bastard. And this must be your wife.'

'Yes. Eve, Magda Lane.'

'Lieutenant Eve Dallas.' Magda's voice was like fog, low and full of secrets. 'I've been looking forward to meeting you. I was devastated I couldn't make the wedding last year.'

'It seems to have stuck anyway.'

Magda's brows rose, then the eyes beneath them began to glitter with appreciation. 'Yes, it has. Go away, Roarke. I want to acquaint myself with your lovely and fascinating wife. And you're too much of a distraction.'

Magda waved him away with one slim hand. Light shot off the diamond on her ring finger like the tail of a comet before she tucked her arm companionably through Eve's.

'Now, let's find someplace where a dozen people won't

insist on speaking to us. Nothing more tedious than idle conversation, is there? Of course, you're thinking that's just what you're about to be trapped into with me, but I'll assure you I don't intend to make our conversation idle. Shall I start off by telling you one of my own regrets is that your ridiculously attractive husband is young enough to be my son?'

Eve found herself sitting at a table in the back corner of the ballroom. 'I don't see why that would have stopped either of you.'

Laughing delightedly Magda snagged fresh flutes of champagne, then shooed the server away. 'My own fault. I made a rule never to take a lover more than twenty years older or younger. Stuck with it, too. More's the pity. But . . .' She paused to sip, studying Eve. 'It isn't Roarke I want to talk about, but you. You're exactly what I thought he'd fall for when his time came around.'

Eve choked on her wine, blinked. 'You're the first person who's ever said *that*.' She struggled with herself a moment, then gave up. 'Why do you say it?'

'You're quite attractive, but he wouldn't have been blinded by your looks. You find that amusing,' Magda noted, nodding in approval. 'Good. A nice sense of humor's essential when dealing with any man, but particularly one of Roarke's nature.'

They were solid looks though, Magda mused. Neither glamorous nor staggering, but solid with good bones, clear eyes, and an interesting dent in the center of a strong chin.

'Your looks might have attracted him, but they didn't snare him. I wondered about that as Roarke has an interest, and an affection, for beauty. So I, having some interest and affection of my own in the man, followed the media on you.'

Eve angled her head, a kind of challenge. 'Do I pass?'

Amused, Magda ran one scarlet-tipped finger around the rim of her flute, then lifted it to equally bold lips, and sipped.

'You're a smart, determined woman who doesn't merely stand on her own feet but uses them to boot whatever asses need booting. You're a physical woman with brains, and a look in your eyes when you glance around an event like this that says: 'What a bunch of nonsense. Haven't we all got something better to do?''

Intrigued, Eve studied Magda in turn. More here, she realized, than some fluff piece who liked to play make-believe. 'Are you a shrink or an actor?'

'Either profession requires solid elements of both.' She paused again, sipped again. 'My guess is you didn't – don't – give a hang about his money. That would have intrigued him. I can't see you falling at his feet either. If you had, he'd likely have scooped you up and played with you awhile. But he wouldn't have kept you.'

'I'm not one of his damn toys.'

'No, you're not.' This time Magda lifted her glass in a toast. 'He's madly in love with you, and it's lovely to see. Now, tell me about being a policewoman. I've never played one. I have played women who go outside the law to protect what's theirs, but never one who works within it to protect others. Is it exciting?'

'It's a job. It has its ups and downs like any.'

'I doubt like any. You solve murders. We . . . civilians, I suppose you'd say, can't help but find the process, including the murder, fascinating.'

'That's because you're not the one who's dead.'

'Exactly.' Magda threw back her magnificent head and roared with laughter. 'Oh, I like you! I'm so glad. You don't want to talk about your work, I understand. People from outside think mine is exciting, glamorous. When what it is . . . is a job, with its ups and downs like any.'

'I've seen a lot of your work. I think Roarke has everything you've done on disc. I like the one where you're a scheming conwoman who falls for her mark. It's fun.'

'*Bait and Switch*. Yes, it was. Chase Conner was my leading man in that, and I fell for him, too. It was also fun, while it lasted. I'm auctioning off the costume I wore in the cocktail party scene.'

She glanced around the ballroom, scanning her things, things that had once been vital to her, with amusement. 'It should bring a good price, and help get The Magda Lane Foundation for the Performing Arts off the ground. So many bits and pieces of a career, of a life, going on the block before much longer.'

She turned, studying a display arranged like a lady's boudoir, with a shimmering nightgown, an open jewelry case where chains and stones spilled gloriously onto a gleaming dressing table. 'That's a lovely bit of female business, isn't it?'

'Yeah, if you're into that.'

Magda swiveled back, smiling. 'At one time I was desperately into that. But, a smart woman doesn't survive a fickle career like acting without regularly reinventing herself.'

'What are you now?'

'Yes, yes,' Magda murmured. 'I like you very much. People ask me why I'm doing this, why I'm giving so much of it up. Do you know what I say?'

'No, what?'

'That I intend to live and to work for a great deal longer. Time enough to collect more.' She gave that lusty laugh again, turned back to Eve. 'That's true enough, but there's more. The Foundation's a dream of mine, a cherished one. Acting's been good to me. I want to pass it on, while I'm still around and young enough to enjoy it all. Grants, scholarships, facilities for all that new blood to swim in. It pleases me that a young actor or director might get his or her start from a break given in my name. That's vanity.'

'I don't think so. I think it's wisdom.'

'Oh. Now I like you even more. Ah, there's Vince, giving me the eye. My son,' Magda explained. 'He's handling the media and assisting in the security for this extravaganza. Such a demanding young man,' she added, signaling across the room. 'God knows where he got that particular trait. So that's my cue to get back to work.' She rose. 'I'm going to be in New York for the next several weeks. I hope we'll see each other again.'

'That would be nice.'

'Ah, Roarke, perfect timing.' Magda turned to beam at him as he walked to the table. 'I have to abandon your delightful wife as duty calls. I expect an invitation to dinner, very soon, so I can spend more time with both of you, and indulge in one of those spectacular meals your man arranges. What is his name?'

'Summerset,' Eve said, lip curling.

'Yes, of course. Summerset. Soon,' she said, and kissed both Roarke's cheeks before gliding off.

'You were right. I did like her.'

'I was sure you would.' As he spoke, he began to guide her smoothly toward the exit. 'I'm sorry to interrupt your evening off, but we have some trouble.'

'A problem with security? Somebody try to duck out with a pocketful of baubles?'

'No. It's nothing to do with theft, and everything to do with murder.'

Her eyes changed. Woman to cop. 'Who's dead?'

'One of the housekeeping staff, from what I'm told.' He kept her arm, steered her toward a bank of elevators. 'She's in the south tower, forty-sixth floor. I don't know the details,' he said shortly before she could interrupt. 'My head of hotel security just informed me.'

'Have the police been contacted?'

'I've contacted you, haven't I?' Eyes grim, he waited while the elevator shot up to the south tower. 'Security knew I was on site, and that you were with me. It was decided to inform me – and you – first.'

'Okay, don't get testy. We don't even know if it's a homicide yet. People are always yelling murder at unattended deaths. Mostly they're accidents or natural causes.'

The minute she stepped off the elevator, her eyes narrowed to slits. Too many people in the hallway, including one hysterical female in a housekeeper's uniform, lots of guys in suits, and several people who were obviously guests who'd popped out of their rooms to see what the commotion was.

She reached into her foolish little purse, pulled out her badge, and held it up as she strode forward.

'NYPSD, clear this area. You people go back in your rooms, anyone with hotel security stand by. And somebody deal with this woman here. Who's security chief?'

'That would be me.' A tall lean man with a coffee-colored complexion and mirror-sheened bald head stepped forward. 'John Brigham.'

'Brigham, you're with me.' Since she didn't have her master code, she gestured to the door.

When he opened it, she stepped through, scanned the parlor area.

Sumptuous, chock-full of fancy furniture, including a full bar setup. And tidy as a church. The privacy screens on the generous windows were engaged, and the lights on full.

'Where is she?' Eve asked Brigham.

'Bedroom, to the left.'

'Was the door open or closed as it is now when you arrived on scene?'

'It was closed when I got here. But I can't say it was that way before. Ms Hilo from Housekeeping found her.'

'That's the woman in the hall?'

'That's right.'

'All right, let's see what we've got.' She moved to the door, opened it.

Music poured out. The lights were on full here as well, and

371

shone harshly on the body lying on the bed like a broken doll that had been tossed there by a spoiled child.

One arm was cocked at an impossible angle, her face was raw and blackened from a vicious beating, and her uniform skirt was hiked up to her waist. The thin silver wire used to strangle her cut deep into her throat like a slender and deadly necklace.

'I think you can rule out natural causes,' Roarke murmured.

'Yeah. Brigham, who's been in this suite besides you and the housekeeper since the body was found?'

'No one.'

'Did you approach the body, touch it or anything other than the doors in any way?'

'I know the drill, Lieutenant. I was on the job – Chicago PSD, Anti-Crime Division. Twelve years. Hilo alerted me. She was screaming into her communicator. I got here within two minutes. She'd run back to her base on the fortieth floor. I entered the suite, came to the doorway here, determined by visual that the victim was deceased. Aware that Roarke was on site, and accompanied by you, I contacted him immediately, then secured the suite, sent for Hilo, and waited for your arrival.'

'I appreciate it, Brigham. Since you were on the job, you know how many times a crime scene's corrupted by helping hands. Did you know the victim?'

'No. Hilo called her Darlene. Little Darlene. That's all I could get out of her.'

Eve was scanning the scene, keeping herself back from it, and calculating the steps that had led to murder. 'You could do me a big favor and get Hilo somewhere quiet and private where she can't talk to anyone but you until I send for her. I'm going to call this in. I don't want to go into the room until I can seal up.'

Brigham reached in his pocket, pulled out a minican of

Seal-It. 'I had one of my men bring this up. And a recorder,' he added, handing her a collar clip. 'Didn't figure you'd have a field kit with you.'

'Good thinking. Do you mind sticking with Hilo for a while?'

'I'll take care of it. You can tag me when you want to talk to her. Meanwhile, I'll leave a couple of men at the door until your crime scene unit gets here.'

'Thanks.' Idly she shook the can. 'Why'd you go off the job?'

For the first time Brigham smiled. 'My current employer made me a hell of an offer.'

'I bet you did,' Eve said to Roarke when Brigham stepped out. 'He's got a cool head, good eyes.' She started to spray her shoes, then decided she'd do a hell of a lot better without them. After stepping out of them, she sprayed her feet, her hands, passed off the can, then the clip, to Roarke.

'I'll need you to record the scene.' She pulled out her communicator and called it in.

'Her name's Darlene French.' Roarke read off the data he'd called up from his PPC. 'She's worked here for just over a year. She was twenty-two.'

'I'm sorry.' She touched his arm, waited until he shifted those hot, angry eyes to hers. 'I'm going to take care of her now. Record on, okay?'

'Yes, all right.' He slipped the PPC back in his pocket, engaged the clip recorder.

'The victim is identified as Darlene French, female, age twenty-two, employed as housekeeper, The Roarke Palace Hotel. Apparent homicide, this location, Suite 4602. Present and acting as primary, Dallas, Lieutenant Eve. Also present and acting as temporary aide in recording this log, Roarke. Dispatch has been notified.'

Now Eve approached the body. 'The scene shows little sign of struggle, but the body shows bruising and lacerations consistent with a violent beating, particularly around the face. Blood spatter pattern indicates that beating was administered while the victim was on the bed.'

She glanced around the room again, noted the beeper on the floor just outside the bath.

'The right arm is broken,' she continued. 'Other bruising on the victim's thighs and vaginal area indicates premortem rape.'

Gently, Eve lifted one of the limp hands. Wishing for microgoggles, she examined it carefully. 'Got a little skin here,' she murmured. 'Managed to get a swipe in, didn't you, Darlene? Good for you. We have skin, possibly hair and fiber under victim's fingernails.'

Meticulous, she moved up the body. The uniform was still buttoned over the breasts. 'He didn't bother with much foreplay. Didn't rip at her clothes or bother to take them off her. Just beat her, broke her, raped her. A thin wire, silver in appearance, has been used, garrote-style, to strangle the victim. The ends of the wire were crossed in front, then twisted into small loops, indicate the killer strangled her face-to-face, while he was ranged over her, and she was down. Have you got this from all angles?' she asked Roarke.

'Yes.'

With a nod, she lifted the victim's head, tilting her own so that she could see the back of the wire. 'Get this,' she ordered. 'It might shift a little when we turn her. The wire's unbroken in the back, and the bleeding's minimal. He didn't use it until he'd finished the beating, until he'd finished the rape. Straddling her,' she said, narrowing her eyes to bring it into focus. 'One knee on either side. She's not putting up much of a fight, if any, by this point. He just slips the wire over her head, crosses the ends in front, then pulls, opposite directions. It wouldn't have taken long.'

But she'd have bucked, her body instinctively struggling to throw off the weight, her throat burning from the wire and the trapped screams of pain and terror. Her heart would have pounded, and that storm-at-sea sound would have exploded in her ears at the lack of oxygen.

Heels drumming, hands clawing for air. Until the blood begins to burst in the head, behind the eyes, and that frantic heart surrenders.

Eve stepped back. There was little more she could do without a field kit. 'I need to know who this room is registered to. What the housekeeping routine is. I'll need to talk to Hilo,' she added as she walked to the closet, glanced in. 'And it would help for me to be able to interview anyone on staff who knew her well.' She checked the dresser.

'No clothes. Not even a lint ball. A couple of used towels she might have dropped or simply set down on her way out of the bathroom. *Was* anyone registered to this room?'

'I'll find out. You'll want her next of kin.'

'Yeah.' Eve sighed. 'Husband, if she had one. Boyfriends, lovers, exes. Nine times out of ten that's what you find in a sexual homicide. But I think this is number ten. Nothing personal about this, nothing intimate or passionate. He wasn't mad, wasn't particularly involved.'

'There's nothing intimate about rape.'

'There can be,' Eve corrected. And she knew that, better than most. 'When there's knowledge between the assailant and the victim, any sort of history – even just a fantasy on the part of the assailant, it lends intimacy. This was cold. Just ram it in and get off. I bet he spent more time beating her than he did with the rape. Some men enjoy the first more. It's their foreplay.'

Roarke switched off the recorder. 'Eve. Turn the case over to someone else.'

'What?' She blinked herself back to the moment. 'Why would I do that?'

'Don't put yourself through this.' He touched her cheek. 'It hurts you.'

375

He was being careful, she noted, not to mention her father. The beatings, the rapes, the terror she'd lived with until she was eight.

'They all hurt if you let them,' she said simply, and turned back to look at Darlene French. 'I won't turn her over to someone else, Roarke. I can't. She's already mine.'